Remember Me

Remember Me

MARGARET THORNTON

Allison & Busby Limited
13 Charlotte Mews
London W1T 4EJ
www.allisonandbusby.com

Hardcover published in Great Britain in 2008.
This paperback edition published in 2009.

A CIP catalogue record for this book is available from
the British Library.

10 9 8 7 6 5 4 3 2

ISBN 978-0-7490-7904-8

Typeset in 10.5/14 Sabon by
Terry Shannon

The paper used for this Allison & Busby publication
has been produced from trees that have been legally sourced
from well-managed and credibly certified forests.

Printed and bound in the UK by
CPI Bookmarque, Croydon, CR0 4TD

MARGARET THORNTON was born in Blackpool and has lived there all her life. She was a teacher for many years but retired early in order to concentrate on writing. She has had seventeen novels published.

Available from
ALLISON & BUSBY

Above the Bright Blue Sky
Down an English Lane
A True Love of Mine
Remember Me
Until We Meet Again

Dedication

For my friends at Bispham Townswomen's Guild, especially the choir members who will recognise the songs.

And with love to my husband, John, as always, with happy memories of our holidays in Scarborough. It is very much 'our place'.

Chapter One

'And now, for your delight and delectation we have a dainty, adorable and – oh so demure! – young damsel… Ladies and gentlemen, please give a big welcome to… Miss Madeleine Moon…'

Maddy grinned at Percy, the master of ceremonies. She still couldn't help but feel a giggle inside her at the effusive introduction afforded not only to her, but to all the members of the troupe. To a ripple of applause she stepped onto the stage, then stood in the spotlight, looking out at the darkness in the auditorium and the sea of faces, only those in the first couple of rows being distinguishable. Samuel would be there somewhere, much further back she guessed, so there was no point in trying to look for him.

She gave a nod to the pianist, Letty, in the orchestra pit below her, and after a single note on the piano she began to sing…

'Dear thoughts are in my mind
And my soul soars enchanted
As I hear the sweet lark sing
In the clear air of the day…'

She sang this first song unaccompanied, in the way that traditional folk music, like this lovely Irish air, was supposed to be sung. It was what she had always done when singing with the Pierrots on the beach at Scarborough. Percy Morgan, the leader of the troupe, had wondered at first whether this type of singing would go down as well with the music hall audiences, who tended to be more worldly and certainly more critical. But he had soon realised that his fears were unfounded. The audiences in the Yorkshire and Lancashire towns that they visited during the autumn and winter of each year, when the summer Pierrot season finished, had taken Maddy to their hearts, accepting her simplicity and sincerity at face value. She was an unaffected young girl with no airs and graces; a pleasant change, indeed, from some of the more raucous acts that they saw from time to time. Though never, it had to be said, when Morgan's Melody Makers were performing.

All eyes were drawn to Maddy as she stood perfectly still in the centre of the stage, her lilting silver-toned voice ringing out clearly across the rows and rows of seats. She was a picture of innocence and purity in her simple dress of cream-coloured silk and lace, with a sweetheart neckline and large puffed sleeves. Her golden hair was loose, waving gently around the nape of her neck and her forehead. A sweet and pretty girl whom the audience guessed could not be more than sixteen or so, standing in front of an idyllic painted landscape of hills, trees and flowers.

Their guess was correct. Maddy would be seventeen years old in the June of 1907, that would be in three months' time. And she already believed herself to be deeply in love. Her thoughts strayed to the young man who was the object of her affections as she sang the last verse of her song.

> *'I shall tell him all my love,*
> *All my soul's adoration,*
> *And I think he will hear*
> *And will not say me nay.*
> *It is this that gives my soul*
> *All its joyous elation,*
> *As I hear the sweet lark sing*
> *In the clear air of the day.'*

The applause that followed was spontaneous and sustained. She could feel the warmth of feeling reaching out to her from the members of the audience. You could always tell when you had a receptive audience and she knew that they certainly had one tonight. She smiled and bobbed a curtsy before continuing with her second song.

Percy Morgan had decided that enough was enough with regard to the soulful, often plaintive, folk music that Maddy sang unaccompanied, and that her second song should be more in keeping with the mood of a music hall audience. Letty, who was the pianist for the troupe as well as being Percy's wife, always played for her second number, which was usually a popular song of the day. 'Just like the Ivy', Maddy sang, with friendliness now rather than with longing in her voice. She raised her hands, beckoning to the audience to join in the last chorus.

> '...As you grow older
> I'll be constant and true;
> Just like the ivy
> I'll cling to you.'

Once again she curtsied to the audience, gave a cheery wave of her hand and tripped off into the wings. Barney and Benjy, the tap-dancing duo who were the next act, were waiting there. She gave them a thumbs-up sign as Percy Morgan stepped onto the stage again. 'And now, ladies and gentlemen, we have the dashing, debonair dancing duo, Mr Barnaby Dewhurst and Mr Benjamin Carstairs. Please give a big hand to... Barney and Benjy.'

The strains of 'Lily of Laguna' followed Maddy as she went backstage to the dressing room she shared with the other women in the troupe. An odd couple, Barney and Benjy, she mused as she went up the flight of stone steps to the rather shabby, but clean, room that the ladies had been allotted for their week in Leeds. This was not the famous Leeds

City Varieties Theatre, where such renowned stars as Marie Lloyd and Vesta Tilley had performed, but a much smaller theatre tucked away in a narrow street off the Headrow.

There were five women in the troupe. Their room was quite large enough, though basic, and fortunately they all got along quite well together. Susannah Brown, who was known as the 'soubrette' of the group – a comedienne who sang light-hearted songs and joked with the audience in a friendly and somewhat cheeky manner – was putting the finishing touches to her hair and make-up. Hers would be the last act before the interval. As a new innovation this season, however, she would be joined in her act by Frank Morrison, the 'Music Man'. He could play a variety of instruments as well as being a passable singer and quite a comic. As the two of them had recently become a couple in their private life, they had decided, with Percy's permission, to join forces on the stage as well, now and again.

'Barney and Benjy seem to have sorted out their difference of opinion,' Maddy remarked as she sat down on one of the bentwood chairs. The only armchair, of worn plush and with sagging springs, was occupied by Queenie Colman, the eldest lady of the troupe, who considered it her right. She always had trouble getting up from it, though, as she was certainly no lightweight. 'They were smiling at one another while they were waiting to go on. A strange pair, Barney and Benjy, aren't they?' Maddy continued. 'I'm not saying anything wrong about them, 'cause I like them, I really do. They've been ever so nice to me since I joined the troupe. But they do seem to fall out a lot... I wonder why they've not got married, either of them. They're both handsome, aren't they? And the ladies in the audiences seem to like them a lot.'

Susannah laughed and shook her head and Maddy saw her exchange an amused glance with Queenie. 'Get married? Barney and Benjy? Good gracious me, no! You're barking up the wrong tree there, luv. They're wedded to...their art, shall we say? And falling out and making up again is part of their...friendship. Don't you worry your head about them. And you can be sure that their quarrels don't make any difference to their performance on stage. They're true pros, both of them. Now, I'd best love you and leave you...' Susannah blew them a kiss and hurried out of the room, a bright pink confection of frilly satin and lace, finished off with a large-brimmed hat covered in pink roses, like the icing on the cake.

Queenie was engrossed in a copy of the *Stage* magazine so Maddy, who found the older woman rather difficult to talk to anyway, busied herself by filling the kettle and putting it on the single gas ring. They would all be glad of a cup of tea during the interval and it was Maddy's job, as the youngest member, to make it.

Maddy was still the same innocent young girl that she had been eighteen months ago when she had persuaded her father to let her join Morgan's Melody Makers on their autumn and winter tour. And as she had turned fifteen and had left school two years previously, William Moon had agreed. She had been singing with the Pierrot troupe – Uncle Percy's Pierrots, as they were known when they performed each summer in Scarborough – quite frequently, ever since she had won their talent contest at the age of eleven. Since leaving school at thirteen she had worked in the gown shop of Louisa Montague, an old family friend, where she had learnt some basic dressmaking skills. But singing was what she had set her heart and mind upon, and despite a little homesickness at first, she was happy and proud to be a member of Percy Morgan's fine troupe. Percy was a good man, trustworthy, hard-working and fair-minded, who set a high standard of behaviour for the troupe, as did his wife, Letty. If it had been otherwise Maddy's father would never have allowed her to join them.

It was a busy, and at times a hectic life, but Maddy, being young, strong and enthusiastic, had adapted to it very well. They usually gave ten performances in all throughout the week, varying slightly in whichever town they happened to be in. Here, in Leeds, they gave two performances each night, except on Wednesday and Saturday when there was a matinée followed by only one house in the evening. Monday night's first house in all the towns consisted largely of free seats handed out to shopkeepers and others who had displayed posters in their windows, or to landladies at the various digs, or anyone, in fact, who was connected in any way with the players or the theatre. It was regarded as a 'warming up' session by the artistes, when they could become acquainted with the stage and lighting and the positioning of the props and backcloths.

They were free during the daytime to do as they wished. Many experienced pros, who had seen it all before many times, spent the mornings in bed catching up on lost sleep. But for Maddy, especially during her first year, it had been an opportunity to explore the different towns of Yorkshire and Lancashire, most of which she had never visited before. This was her second visit to Leeds; she had also become acclimatised with York, Bradford, Halifax, Sheffield and Doncaster, and across the other side of the Pennines, the cotton towns of Rochdale and Oldham, Blackburn, Bury and Bolton, and the largest of them all, Manchester.

Percy had insisted at first that she should have another member of the troupe with her on her explorations, especially when she was making her way back to her digs late at night. And so she had come to know Susannah Brown quite well, also Nancy Pritchard, who had an act with performing dogs, and Letty Morgan. Letty was a very motherly person who had no children of her own and she had developed a fondness for the teenage girl. A feeling that was reciprocated. Maddy had become very fond of Letty, and having lost her own mother a few years previously she had been glad of the comforting presence and the help and advice of this warm and sympathetic person. She had been very close to her step-mother, however, back in Scarborough, the woman whom she still referred to as Aunty Faith. But Faith was miles away with Maddy's father, William; her brother, Patrick; and three of Faith's own children, Maddy's stepsisters and stepbrother. The worst thing about all this travelling around was that she saw her family only infrequently, not nearly so much as she would have liked to have done. During the summer, though, she lived at home again, becoming a Pierrot in a white costume and pointed hat, like the rest of the troupe.

Sunday was their travelling day when they boarded the train with all their bags and baggages, their props and portable items of scenery, and moved on to their next port of call. They had travelled from Bradford last Sunday, only a short distance away, and next week they had a booking in Wakefield, which would involve a rather longer journey.

Another thing that artistes had to get used to was the unpredictable meal times. Some landladies might provide a midday cooked meal, with others it might be in the early evening, or not at all. Maddy had been used to regular meal times; dinner at six o'clock on the dot every evening, which was the time best suited to the working hours of her father and grandfather. First house in most towns started at six o' clock, followed by the second house at eight-thirty. She could not sing after a large meal and there was often very little time left for food. So Maddy would snatch a sandwich when she could or sometimes ate a meal very late at night, a habit which did not seem at all unusual to the rest of the company.

But tonight she was looking forward to a leisurely meal in the company of her stepbrother, Samuel. He was the eldest of Faith's four children, aged twenty-one, and was in his final year at Leeds University. When he had heard that the troupe was performing in Leeds he had contacted Maddy. They had arranged that he would meet her after the Wednesday evening performance at nine-thirty or so. He would take her out for supper and then see her back safely to her lodgings, not far from City Square.

When she had finished her next appearance in the second half of the show she changed out of her cream-coloured dress into her smart costume, the one that she wore for best or if she was going anywhere special. She felt that it made her look much older, much more a woman of the world, than the simple girlish dresses she wore for her stage appearances. It was made of a royal blue light woollen material and had an ankle-length pleated skirt and a double-breasted jacket edged with red braid, and sported shiny golden buttons. With it she wore a small brimless hat with a red ribbon bow and pom-pom. It had been featured in the shop as a 'sailing costume', but she guessed that many of the women who wore a similar costume would, like Maddy herself, not be going anywhere near a boat. She had worn it only twice since she had bought it in January, but tonight was a very special occasion. She wondered if the lightweight wool would be warm enough; the March weather could be unpredictable and there had been a chilly wind when she had walked to the theatre earlier that evening. On the other hand, she doubted that she would notice the weather when she was in the company of Samuel.

'You look very nice and smart,' said Susannah. 'All dressed up in your glad rags. Are you going out after the show?'

'Yes, as a matter of fact I am,' replied Maddy, unable to suppress a satisfied smile. 'I'm meeting a young man – a friend of mine from home – and he's taking me out for supper.'

'Oh! Not one of those stage door Johnnies, is he?' asked Susannah, looking rather anxious. 'I promised Letty I would keep an eye on you and see you back safely to our digs. You can't be too careful, you know.'

'No!' said Maddy, a trifle impatiently. 'I've just

told you, he's a friend from home. I've known him for ages. Actually...' she sighed, 'he's my stepbrother; you know, my Aunty Faith's son. He's at university in Leeds.' She hadn't wanted to admit that it was her stepbrother she was meeting. It sounded much more grown-up to say she was meeting a 'friend'. But it didn't really matter so long as it would stop Susannah from worrying about her.

'Oh, I see. That's all right then,' said Susannah. 'And he'll see you home afterwards, will he?'

'Of course he will,' said Maddy. She got a little tired sometimes of the older women's fussiness, although she knew that they had her best interests at heart, and that their solicitude made her father and Faith feel less anxious about her being away from home.

Susannah might not have been too happy, however, about Maddy meeting her stepbrother had she known that the girl's feelings towards him were not the least bit sisterly. And Maddy felt, deep down, that his feelings towards her were just the same. She had not, of course, divulged this secret to anyone, not even to Jessie, who was Samuel's sister and Maddy's best friend. Maddy had felt an attraction to Samuel when she had first met him, seven years ago, when she and Jessie were both ten years old, and Samuel and her own brother, Patrick, were fourteen. She had admired his handsome looks: his dark eyes and dark hair and his serious-looking face that reminded her of a picture of a knight of old in a history book. And how different he had seemed from her brother, Patrick, who was forever laughing and joking and teasing her.

She knew that Jessie, likewise, had at first developed fond feelings for Patrick; but she also knew that those feelings had passed and that Jessie did not mind at all that Patrick was now engaged to be married to Katy, the girl he had been courting for several years. Their relationship – that of Jessie and Patrick – had become very much a sisterly, brotherly friendship.

When they had all met in the summer of 1900, Maddy's mother, Clara, had still been living. Indeed, who could possibly have imagined that within a few months, in the February of 1901, she would have died following an attack of pneumonia? Maddy and Jessie had met on the beach at Scarborough whilst they were both watching a performance by 'Uncle Percy's Pierrots', the troupe to which Maddy now belonged. The Moon family and the Barraclough family had become friendly, although Faith and her husband, Edward, had already been living more or less separate lives. William Moon would never have become enamoured with another woman so long as his beloved wife, Clara, was living. Maddy, with a wisdom beyond her years, had known that. She had not objected, therefore – and neither had Jessie – when their respective father and mother had fallen in love and been married a few years later.

The only member of either family who had shown any animosity was Samuel Barraclough. He had always been much closer to his father than Jessie and the twins, Tommy and Tilly, who were several years younger. Maddy thought she could understand how Samuel felt. Divorce was a rare occurrence, something that was still spoken of in hushed tones; and he had always seemed to Maddy to be a very upright and serious-minded young man. She guessed that he did not approve of his mother's re-marriage. On the other hand, she knew that he still visited his father from time to time. Edward Barraclough was now living in York with his new wife, who had formerly been his mistress, and the young man did not seem to object to that.

Samuel had been about to leave home anyway at the time of his mother's marriage to William Moon, to start his training at Leeds University. He occasionally visited the family home in Scarborough when his college was on vacation. He spent a good deal of his time, though, in the homes of various friends he had made.

He had scarcely seemed to notice Maddy at first. He had always been polite enough to her and chatted to her on occasions, although Samuel was not what you might call a garrulous person. And he had been oblivious, seemingly, to the amorous thoughts building up inside his stepsister as the years passed and she became more and more aware of him.

Until last Christmas, that was, when he had begun to regard her in a different light. She had been conscious of his eyes on her, when they were dining, for instance, or sitting at leisure in the drawing room. His visit, that time, had lasted rather longer than the three or four days that he usually spared for his family. They had had a party on Boxing Day, to which a few family friends had been invited. After a few grown-up games they had played a form of hide-and-seek, to please the ten-year-old Tommy and Tilly.

Maddy had found Samuel hiding behind the long velvet curtains in the dining room. As soon as he saw her he had pulled her close to him, putting his finger to his lips, warning her not to let on where they were. And then he had put his arms around her, lowered his face to hers and kissed her lovingly and tenderly.

'I've been wanting to do that all week,' he whispered. 'Little sister...' he added teasingly, touching the tip of her nose. 'But you're not anymore, are you? You're a beautiful young woman.' She had been unable to speak for the pounding of her heart and the feeling of wonderment that was spreading through her. Then he had kissed her again on her half-open lips, more fervently this time, and she had felt herself responding to him in a way she had never dreamt of. When they heard someone entering the room they drew apart. It was Tilly who had found them and she came to hide alongside them. She was unaware, though, of Samuel stroking Maddy's thigh and then, tentatively, her breasts behind the concealment of the curtain.

There had been little chance after that for them to be alone together. There always seemed to be one or another of the family around. But Maddy knew that their relationship had moved onwards, on to a new footing. He had said, hadn't he, that she was no longer his little sister? Maddy knew, also, that she had fallen in love with him. When he had contacted her and said that he would meet her after tonight's performance she had hardly been able to contain her delight. She had played it down to Susannah, pretending that it was just her brother. But Samuel was much, much more than that...

Chapter Two

He was waiting outside the stage door and her heart gave a leap on seeing him there. He was dressed more as a stylish young man about town than as a university student. The students were often to be seen in the streets of Leeds, casually, some of them scruffily, dressed and nearly all with their college scarves slung around their necks. Samuel, however, was wearing a smart three-piece suit of charcoal grey with a faint white pinstripe and he sported a rather showy necktie of red and grey stripes.

'Hello there, Maddy. Good to see you again.' He stepped forward to greet her, kissing her chastely on the cheek, then he held out his arm for her to link.

'Good to see you too, Samuel,' she said with a casual air. It would not do to let him be conscious of her beating heart. 'I hope you enjoyed the show?'

'Yes...I must admit that I did,' he replied, sounding almost as though he hadn't expected to enjoy it, she thought. But that was typical of Samuel; he liked everything to be just so and could be very critical. 'A good variety of acts,' he conceded, 'and rather more polished, if I may say so, than the old Pierrot shows. City audiences are much more demanding, of course, and expect good value for their money. Haven't you found it so?'

'Possibly,' Maddy replied, not wanting to disagree with him outright. 'They're usually very receptive, though, and seem to enjoy the shows. At least we haven't had any catcalls or any eggs and rotten tomatoes thrown at us. No; the audiences have been just fine.'

'That's good then,' he said, squeezing her arm and smiling down at her. 'They couldn't help but fall for you, could they? You stole the show, Madeleine. That sweet and innocent act would get all the fellows going, and I should know.'

'It's not an act, Samuel,' she retorted. 'I am sweet and innocent...aren't I?' He grinned at her.

'We'll see,' he said darkly. 'That Susannah now; she went down well with the audience, especially the men. I should imagine she's rather...naughty, isn't she?'

'I wouldn't say so,' replied Maddy. 'That really is part of her act. She's very nice and friendly and she's been real kind to me. I believe she's had quite a few gentlemen admirers, but she's settling down with Frank now. You know – the one who plays all the musical instruments. I think they're going to get married.'

'Oh well, that's nice for them, isn't it?' replied Samuel, sounding not terribly interested. 'Anyway, never mind them, eh? Here we are, see... This is where we are going to have our supper.'

They had turned off the Headrow onto Briggate, and Samuel had stopped outside a small restaurant which Maddy realised at a glance was select and...expensive! She had never dined in such a place before. Even though her father, and her stepmother, too, might be considered 'well off', William Moon did not believe in throwing his hard-earned brass around in fancy restaurants, especially when you could dine in the comfort of your own home with meals prepared by your own excellent cook-housekeeper.

Maddy followed Samuel into the dimly lit interior, her feet sinking into the deep-piled red and gold carpet. The head waiter – at least that was who she guessed him to be – stepped forward to greet them. 'Good evening, Mr Barraclough. And good evening to you, too...miss. Your table is ready for you.'

All the tables were discreetly illuminated by red candles in glass holders, and the red-shaded wall-lights above each table cast a rosy glow on the snowy-white tablecloths and napkins, the gleaming silver cutlery and the single red rose in a crystal vase. The tables at the side of the restaurant were in separate booths with high-backed settles of dark oak cushioned in red plush.

Maddy slid into the booth and sat down on the cushioned seat with Samuel sitting opposite her. The waiter, bowing a little, handed them each a large menu card filled with what seemed to Maddy to be hundreds of different dishes: hors d'oeuvres, soups, meat and fish dishes, entrées and sweets. 'Would sir like some wine?' asked the waiter, a trifle obsequiously, and when Samuel inclined his head in an affirmative nod he produced another large card, with a long list of wines, beers and spirits.

'Mmm…an impressive wine list,' observed Samuel in a knowledgeable voice as the waiter left them alone for a little while to make their choice. 'I will choose the wine, Madeleine, if that is all right with you?' He smiled at her, a little patronisingly, Maddy thought, and she felt, momentarily, a stab of annoyance.

'Yes, of course,' she replied. Samuel knew that only on special occasions had she drunk wine; that was at family parties, notably at the Christmas dinner. At least, that was what he was assuming. For all he knew, though, she might have become an habitual wine drinker since joining the concert party. The fact that she hadn't – that she hardly ever touched alcohol at all – was immaterial. Samuel was treating her like a child, like his 'little sister', and that was something she did not want.

She lowered her head, studying the menu. Some of it was written in French although, fortunately, the English translation was there too. Her eyes wandered up and down as she tried to decide on her choice. She liked roast beef and Yorkshire pudding, and steak and kidney pie – and, rather surprisingly, they were both on the menu – but she knew that Samuel would expect her to choose something different, something more sophisticated. When she looked up, after several moments, it was to see Samuel watching her with his eyebrows raised and a quizzical look on his face.

'Spoilt for choice, aren't we?' He grinned at her amiably. 'Have you decided? Or would you like me to choose for you? I've been here before, so I know which are their specialities, you see.'

'Very well then,' she agreed as she was truly mesmerised by the array of dishes. 'What do you suggest?'

'Let me see...' Samuel pondered. 'Their Jerusalem artichoke soup is superb.'

'Sounds exotic,' observed Maddy. 'I don't know that I've ever had artichokes, at least not Jerusalem ones.'

'Just a fancy name for the soup, but I can assure you that it's delicious.'

She nodded. 'Yes...I'll try that.'

'And then...' Samuel frowned a little, running his finger down the menu. 'How about turbot with shrimp sauce, served with duchess potatoes and a selection of the chef's vegetables of the day? How does that sound to you?'

'That sounds...very nice. Turbot – that's a fish, isn't it?'

'Yes, of course.' He gave an amused smile.

'Well, I like fish, don't I?' said Maddy. 'I should

do, seeing that I come from Scarborough. But I've only ever had cod or haddock, or hake occasionally. Yes, I'll give it a try, the turbot.'

'It won't come covered in batter, with chips and mushy peas,' teased Samuel.

'Oh dear,' retorted Maddy. 'No salt and lashings of vinegar? Or what about tomato sauce?' She laughed to show him that she was joking. He had used to be such a sobersides, but recently she had noticed that he had a sardonic wit. You needed to be on the alert, though, because he had a tendency to poke fun at people, and not always in a kindly way. 'Don't worry, Samuel. I'm not going to show you up by asking for the bottle of HP.'

'I didn't think that for a moment,' he replied seriously. 'You will enjoy the turbot; it's a highly prized fish... Ah, here comes the waiter.' He ordered the same dishes for both of them for the first two courses. 'We will choose from the dessert menu later,' he added. 'And would you bring us a bottle of Riesling, please? A medium-sweet would be best. That might be more palatable for the young lady...'

'Yes, sir, thank you, sir, very good, sir...' The waiter bobbed up and down, like a penguin Maddy thought, suppressing a giggle; then he waddled back in the direction of the kitchen.

'A highly prized fish...' repeated Maddy. 'Did you catch any turbot then, when you used to go fishing off Scarborough pier?'

'Hardly,' replied Samuel. 'One would need to be in much deeper waters. Dabs and whiting, that was the extent of my catch. Mmm... It all seems a long time ago now.'

'Don't you go fishing anymore then?'

'Leeds is just about as far from the sea as one can get. Besides, I have very little time for fishing, always supposing that I wanted to do it – which I don't.'

'You used to enjoy it, though, when you were in Scarborough for the summer holiday.'

'So I did...' replied Samuel thoughtfully. 'I think I enjoyed the solitude though as much as the fishing; being completely on my own, away from the family. My mother was trying so hard to pretend that everything was normal. But we all knew – at least Jessica and I knew – that our parents were not getting on well together at all. Mother thought that going to Scarborough each summer would ease the situation. She seemed to enjoy the change, and the twins did, of course, and Jessica. But I always felt like a fish out of water.' He gave a wry smile. 'Yes, a suitable metaphor, isn't it? I believe I was the only one who missed my father. He used to come and see us occasionally at the weekends, but I knew it was only because he felt he ought to do so... And then we met up with your family, didn't we? Thanks to you and Jessie and the Pierrot shows.'

He sounded almost as though he regretted the

encounter, and Maddy felt annoyed. She knew, of course, that Samuel had not really become a member of their united family in the way that his siblings had done, following the marriage of his mother and her father. He had chosen to remain aloof, but she had hoped that their friendship – hers and Samuel's – would bring him closer to all of them.

'You sound as though you didn't enjoy our times together,' she remarked. 'But I seem to remember that you enjoyed the teas that my mother made for us all. And the sandcastle competition; we won that thanks to your ambitious plan. And you and Patrick got on quite well together; he even went fishing with you once or twice. What happened with my father and your mother, that was quite a while afterwards, you know. A long time after…after my mother died. There was nothing improper going on.'

'Hey, hey, calm down.' Samuel waved an admonitory hand at her. 'Come down off your high horse. I wasn't suggesting that there was any impropriety, of course not. I was really sorry when I heard that your mother had died; she was a lovely lady. And I did enjoy being with the Moon family…some of the time. Especially with you, Maddy.' He reached out and put his hand over hers, and she felt at one with him as their eyes met and held for several seconds.

'If there were any improper goings-on,' he

continued, 'it was my father who was the guilty party. We learnt afterwards that he had had a mistress for several years, and my mother had known about it for quite a while. But he has married her now so it's all above board. Gwendolen, she's called. She's not a bit like my mother. She's much more – what shall I say? – earthy, and always good for a laugh.' He chuckled as though he quite approved of that. 'But not nearly so beautiful...' he added musingly. 'My father seems very happy though, and that's the main thing.'

'So you visit them quite often?' asked Maddy, knowing full well that he did.

'Yes...I suppose I do. I was fond of my mother; I still am, I wouldn't want you to think otherwise. But she always seemed rather distant; with me at any rate. I was always much closer to my father. That's why it was such a trauma to me.'

Maddy nodded, unsure as to how to reply. It was the first time he had talked to her of family matters. 'They are happy, though, my father and your mother,' she ventured. 'And the rest of us have all settled down well together.'

'Yes, yes, I know,' he replied. 'Don't get me wrong; I like your father; he's a real good sort, is William.' That was how Samuel always addressed William Moon; not as 'Uncle Will' as did Jessie, Tommy and Tilly. But he always showed respect to the patriarch of the family by addressing him as Mr

Moon. 'And your grandfather as well. He's a real character is Mr Moon.' To the other children Isaac Moon had very quickly become 'Grandad'.

'Anyway, we are not going to fall out about them, are we, you and I?' He squeezed her hand briefly, then let it go as he saw the waiter returning. 'Ah, here comes our first course.'

Maddy agreed that the soup was delicious, savouring the subtle yet satisfying taste of the artichokes with celery, onion and a hint of garlic. She enjoyed the firm meaty texture of the turbot, too, attractively served with shrimp sauce and a side dish of butter-glazed carrots, florets of broccoli and minted garden peas.

They conversed very little at first as they concentrated on enjoying their meal. Maddy sipped tentatively at the wine, rolling it gently around her mouth. She found it very palatable; quite sweet but with an underlying richness of green grapes. She took a longer drink and then realised that Samuel was watching her with an amused glint in his eyes.

'Hey, steady on!' he laughed. 'It's not to be drunk like water. I don't want to get you tipsy, or else your father would have something to say.'

'He's not here, is he?' retorted Maddy, throwing caution to the winds and taking another gulp of wine. She realised what he had meant, though, when her glass was empty and Samuel, despite his warning, started to pour her some more. She was beginning to feel a bit light-headed. She put her hand over her glass. 'No more,' she said. 'I've had what you might call an...an elegant sufficiency.'

It was quite pleasant, though, this feeling of euphoria. It was as though she was in a dream, starting to lose touch with reality. Part of her mind was warning her, however, that it would not do for her to lose control. She managed to get a grip of herself before it was too late, realising that she had imbibed rather too much. She had seen men – and women, too – the worse for drink, and she realised how easy it would be to allow that to happen.

She focused on the food on her plate, taking a good drink of the water that the waiter had poured out at the same time as the wine. She was not aware, at that moment, of Samuel watching her carefully. He, too, knew that she had drunk quite enough to make her mellow. Any more might prove dangerous and he wanted to avoid, at all costs, an inebriated young woman on his hands. The way she was at the moment, though, she might be ready, later, for a spot of fun...

'How is Patrick?' he asked casually. 'You mentioned him earlier. Is he still working for your father's firm?'

'Yes, of course. It's a job for life,' she replied. Then she laughed, realising how odd that might sound. 'If you can call undertaking a job for life, but you know what I mean. Actually, it's still my grandfather's firm until...well, until such time as it passes to my father.' But she did not want to think about a time when her beloved grandfather would not be there. 'It's still called "Isaac Moon and Son".'

'A strange sort of career for a young man,' Samuel observed. 'Does Patrick really enjoy it, or is he just doing it because he feels he must?'

'It's what he has always done, what he always knew he would do when he left school,' replied Maddy. 'He never complains. Besides, it's an important job and somebody has to do it,' she added, somewhat indignantly. 'And our Patrick has the right temperament for it. He never lets it get him down. He's still as cheerful and carefree as ever.'

'They didn't expect you to go into the business, then, when you left school?' asked Samuel.

'No; my father knew it would not be what you might call my cup of tea.' She grinned. 'I remember how horrified Jessie was when she first found out what my parents did for a living. My mother used to help out as well, you know…with the laying-out; but I'm glad to say that Dad never expected me to do so.'

'And my mother is not involved either, thank goodness,' said Samuel.

'Not in the undertaking side of the business, no,' said Maddy. 'But Aunty Faith has taken over as manageress of the gown shop that my father owns. I still call her Aunty Faith,' she added. 'Old habits die hard. Perhaps you'll be going to see them soon, will you?' she asked cautiously. 'During your Easter holiday, maybe?'

'I don't know; I might,' he answered, sounding as though he was not very keen on the idea. 'Now, are you ready for a dessert? They do the most delicious Queen's Pudding. That's what I shall have. Shall I order the same for you?'

'No,' said Maddy decidedly. 'I'm going to have Yorkshire curd tart. My mother used to make it and it reminds me of home.'

Samuel nodded but made no comment. After the dessert they drank dark coffee from tiny cups. Maddy thought it had a bitter taste, but it helped to clear some of the wooziness from her head.

'Ready now?' asked Samuel when he had paid the bill. 'Is it to be my place or yours?'

'What do you mean?' she asked, feeling a gust of refreshingly cool air blow over her as they stepped outside. 'You're going to see me home, aren't you? I mean…back to my digs?'

'Eventually,' smiled Samuel. 'But I thought you might like to come and see where I hang out first. It's not very far; and of course I'll see you back safely, later on.'

'All right then,' she said, taking his arm again as they walked back along Briggate and the Headrow, and then into Woodhouse Lane.

'We'll catch a tram back later,' Samuel told her, 'to City Square. You're not far from there, are you?'

'No, very near. But I mustn't be too late getting back. The others might worry, especially Letty and Susannah.'

'You tell them you're a big girl now,' said Samuel, a trifle brusquely. 'Anyway, the night's still young.'

As Samuel had said, his lodgings were about ten minutes' walk away from the city centre, in a large three-storeyed house in a side street, near to the university buildings where he was studying. Maddy's first impression was that the house, from the outside at least, looked shabby and uncared-for, with peeling paintwork and grimy windows. He had told her as they walked from the restaurant how he and his friend, Mark, had lodged with a middle-aged woman for the first two years of their course. She had provided them with breakfast and an evening meal, which they had greatly appreciated. Obviously neither of them had been used to fending for themselves, thought Maddy. This year, however, for their final year, the two of them had decided to go it alone. They had found that lodging with the motherly, but over-fussy, Mrs Giles had not allowed them as much freedom as they might wish for. They were now sharing a flat with a third young man and, despite having to look after themselves, they were enjoying the independence this gave them.

Samuel opened the door with his key and led her into the dark hallway. She was surprised when he pressed a switch to turn on the electric light. The majority of houses and homes were still lit by gas. They must have a very enterprising landlord, or landlady, despite the shabbiness of the property.

They must also, she surmised, be paying a pretty high rent; the other two young men, no doubt, had fathers who were comfortably off, as was Samuel's father. The naked light bulb hanging from the ceiling was of a low wattage, illuminating only dimly the hallway and stairs. The woodwork was dark brown, the wallpaper an indiscriminate pattern of brown and beige and the carpet was threadbare in parts. A far cry from what Samuel had been accustomed to in his home in York, thought Maddy, or, indeed, in the house in Scarborough which he could now call home…if he wished to do so.

The flat shared by Samuel and his two friends, whom he referred to as Mark and Jeremy, was on the first floor. He opened the door with a second key and, again, switched on the electric light. This time the light bulb, protected by a glass globe, revealed a room that was, to Maddy's eyes, not at all bad; much better than she had been led to expect from the dingy and dismal exterior; and much better, she guessed, than the lodgings occupied by the vast majority of students. The room was spacious, furnished with a three-piece suite covered in dark brown moquette, enlivened with cushions of a brown, orange and yellow paisley design, which colours were repeated in the – somewhat worn – carpet square and the window curtains. There was a fold-down table and four sturdy dining chairs with leatherette seats, and an old-fashioned

Victorian sideboard with a mirror and a carved design of leaves and flowers. The top was covered with books, folders and piles of papers, and more books – appertaining to their respective studies, Maddy surmised – filled two sets of bookshelves.

Samuel strode across the room to draw the curtains. Then, 'Why don't you take off your jacket?' he said, opening another door, which led to the bedroom. Maddy caught a glimpse of a double bed covered with a folkweave counterpane and, a few feet away from it, a smaller bed that looked like a camp bed. She hesitated in the doorway; this was strange territory to her, to be standing on the threshold of a bedroom shared by three young men.

'Come along,' said Samuel, smiling at her discomfiture. She felt like a frightened rabbit and no doubt Samuel knew it. 'Slip your jacket off, or else you won't feel the benefit of it when you go out again... That's what my mother always used to say,' he added with a chuckle.

'She still does,' replied Maddy, taking off her jacket and handing it to him; she was wearing a white cotton blouse beneath it. She took off her little hat as well, pinning the hat-pin to it securely. Samuel placed them on the nearest bed and then closed the door again.

'That is where we sleep,' he said, 'obviously. The big bed is much more comfortable than the small one, so we take it in turns to sleep in it, week and week about. And this is the kitchen.' He opened another door which revealed a small room, not much bigger than a cubbyhole. Maddy could see a gas stove, an earthenware sink and a small glass-fronted cupboard. She guessed that there would not be room to swing the proverbial cat.

'And down the passage there's the bathroom, with all the usual requisites. Would you care to use the bathroom now?' he asked politely.

'Er…yes, please,' replied Maddy, a little self-consciously. What he was really asking was did she want to use the toilet, and that was embarrassing. She felt herself blushing, but the butterflies dancing away in her tummy told her it would be as well to avail herself of the opportunity.

'First door on the right,' he said. 'I hope it's been left nice and tidy. We share it with the occupants of the other flat, across the landing.'

The lavatory was as large as a throne, the white porcelain decorated with a design of blue flowers, and it had a mahogany seat and lid. The bath, also, was encased in mahogany and looked almost as though one would need a stepladder to climb into it. Maddy held her hands beneath the brass taps of the washbasin, noting that the soap was pink carbolic and the towels were all of a manly striped design.

'Come along and make yourself at home,' said Samuel when she re-entered the room. 'I'll just nip along to the bathroom and then I'll be with you in a jiffy.'

Maddy sat down on the settee, then thought better of it and moved across to an armchair. She didn't want it to look as though she was inviting Samuel to come and sit next to her. In fact, now that she was alone with him she was beginning to feel a little ill at ease. It was the first time she had been completely alone with him, apart from those few moments at Christmas time, and there was something that was puzzling her.

'Where are your friends?' she asked when he came back into the room. 'Mark and...Jeremy, did you say?'

'They're not here,' he grinned. 'Why? Were you expecting to meet them?'

'Well... Yes, I suppose so. I mean...I don't know,' faltered Maddy. 'They live here, don't they? And it's quite late.'

Samuel laughed. 'Oh, we respect one another's privacy. Anytime one of us wants to...to entertain a guest, then the others know to make themselves scarce. I told them I was taking a young lady out for supper, and bringing her back afterwards. I didn't say that you were my sister. But then...you're not really, are you?' He narrowed his eyes, looking at her in a quizzical, sort of teasing, manner. 'We made up our minds about that, didn't we?'

Maddy smiled, a little foolishly, not knowing how to reply.

'Shall I make us some coffee?' he asked, taking a step towards the kitchen. 'It's amazing what I've learnt to do since I've been looking after myself.'

'Er…I don't think so,' replied Maddy. 'We've just had some, haven't we? And I don't usually drink coffee at night in case it keeps me awake.'

'And that would never do, would it? You need your beauty sleep… Actually, I was hoping you would say no. I don't want any either.' He grinned at her, flopping himself down on the settee with his long legs sprawled out in front of him. 'Now, how about you coming to sit next to me?'

She hesitated, although she was not sure why. 'I'm…I'm all right here,' she said. 'I can see you better from here while we're talking. And I'm sure you want to know what's going on at home, don't you? With Jessie and Tommy and Tilly and…and your mother?'

'If you want to tell me,' he replied, 'and it sounds as though you do, then I'm all ears. But come and sit here, for goodness' sake Maddy. Why are you going all coy on me?'

She didn't answer, but feeling a little worried at the sharpness of his tone she did as she was bid. He put his arm casually around her shoulders.

'That's better. Now…tell me all the news from Scarborough.' She told him that his sister, Jessica, was coming to the end of her course at the clerical college and, come the summer, would be seeking a position as a shorthand typist. William Moon, with all his contacts, should be able to help her with that. And Tommy and Tilly seemed happy enough at their private school in the South Bay area. Maddy and Patrick Moon had attended the local board school, as had their parents before them, both leaving at the age of thirteen; but the Barraclough children had been used to private tuition in York, and so had continued with this in Scarborough when their mother had married William.

'Very good...' said Samuel, sounding mildly amused at Maddy's chatter. 'And how about you? You are enjoying being a – what are you called? – a Melody Maker? I was very proud of you, you know, when I saw you up there on the stage this evening.'

'Were you really?' said Maddy, smiling delightedly up at him and feeling his arm drawing her closer. 'Yes, I'm enjoying it ever so much. I've been to all sorts of places I'd never been to before: Manchester and Liverpool and Leeds; and at Easter we're going to Blackpool!'

'That sounds really too, too exciting,' said Samuel. Teasingly, he touched her nose with his fingertip then, holding her by her arms, he lowered his head to hers and their lips met in an exploratory kiss, gentle at first, his lips brushing softly against hers, then more lingeringly as he held her tightly against him. She felt herself responding, her mouth opening beneath his.

He drew away from her for a moment. 'That's quite enough talking for the moment... Madeleine,' he murmured. Then he kissed her again. She felt his teeth hard against her lips, and then, startlingly, his tongue pushing against hers, probing further into her mouth. She pulled back; this was strange to her, but then, as he continued to kiss her, not releasing his hold on her, she felt herself giving way to the ardour of his embrace. This was what she had been waiting for, for so long, she thought, as she felt the warmth and moistness of his lips and tongue, then his hand stroking her hair, her neck and then...her breasts. She gave an involuntary start, pulling away from him a little, but he did not stop nor draw back. His fingers were tugging at the buttons of her blouse, then she became aware of his other hand touching her thigh, fondling the soft skin above the top of her silk stocking. And she felt a tingling, a strange sensation in that region...

But...no! This was wrong. This should not be happening at all. This was not what she had expected or wanted. She struggled to free both her hands then she pushed him away. 'Samuel...no!' she cried. 'We can't... We mustn't... It's not right. I didn't know. I wanted you to kiss me, that's all. I don't understand...' Her voice petered out as she looked at him in puzzlement and fear.

His eyes were dark and brooding. She could see the disbelief there and the annoyance, verging on anger. 'Don't start that silly nonsense with me,' he began as she straightened her skirt and, fumblingly, tried to fasten the buttons on her blouse.

'I could tell you were dying for it; so why the play-acting now, eh?'

'I'm not… I wasn't…' she faltered. 'I don't know what you mean…'

'Of course you know what I mean. You've been making up to me for months, for years, really. It's a bit late now to tell me that you don't want to. You're nothing but a tease, Madeleine Moon. There's a name for girls like you… But I won't offend your delicate little ears by uttering it.' He was looking at her more dispassionately now, the fury in his eyes abating. But his face was still stern and unsmiling as he said, 'I really thought you had grown up. And I thought, well…' He gave a dismissive shrug. 'I thought with you being a pro – an artiste, if you like – that you would be only too willing, if you know what I mean.' He sighed. 'It really is time you knew what was going on in the world around you, Maddy.'

A myriad of thoughts were flashing through her mind as she listened to what he was saying. And she realised that it was true; that she knew very little at all about what went on between a man and a woman when they did what was called 'making love'. It was still a mystery to her, although she knew it must have a lot to do with kissing, the passionate sort of kissing that Samuel had wanted to do, and the other things: the feeling in her breasts and in that other more intimate part of her. And it was vaguely connected with having monthly periods as well; she knew that.

When her periods had started it had been soon after her father and Faith had got married. She had known a little about it from what some of the other girls at school had said. But it was not something that was supposed to be talked about. Aunty Faith had explained to her what was happening to her body; that she was growing up and it was nature's way of preparing her for when she got married and had babies. But Aunty Faith was far too ladylike to tell her anything other than that. Now, however, she was beginning to have an inkling as to what might be involved. She remembered something that a very rude boy had once said in the playground, but she and Evie, her best friend at that time, had been too shocked to even think about it or believe it might be true.

'I'm sorry, Samuel,' she said now. 'I didn't...I don't understand, honestly I don't. I wanted you to kiss me because...because I thought you loved me.'

He smiled at that, rather sadly. 'I'm fond of you, Maddy,' he replied. 'Of course I am. I've known you ever since you were a little girl. You were my sister's friend. And I couldn't help but notice that you liked me,' he added with a touch of superiority. 'You weren't exactly backward in coming forward, as one might say. You made your feelings very clear. That's why I thought...'

'I loved you, Samuel,' she replied, feeling puzzled. 'I do...love you. And I thought – well, you know, after what you said at Christmas...an' all that – I thought there was something special between us…'

'Oh, Maddy, Maddy,' he cried, shaking his head and giving an exasperated sigh. 'I've told you – I'm fond of you. And I'm sorry if I misread the signs. But let's forget all this nonsense about love, shall we? Believe me, Madeleine, you will fall in love many many times, or imagine you have done so, before you meet the man who is the one for you. And I know that I am certainly not the one,' he added, with a brusqueness that caused a stab of anguish right through her. But she managed to control herself.

'I'm sorry,' she said. 'I'm a silly fool and I've made such a mess of things. You won't say anything, will you – to Jessie? I haven't told anybody, not even Jessie about…about what I thought.'

'Give me credit for a bit of common sense, Madeleine,' scoffed Samuel. 'I'm not in the habit of having intimate conversations with my sister, or with any of my family for that matter. I seem to recall, though, that Jessica had a soft spot for your brother at one time, didn't she? But I'm pleased to say she seems to have got over it.'

'Patrick…yes,' agreed Maddy. 'I think she did rather…like him. But he's engaged to Katy now and Jessie's concentrating on her exams and getting a good job.'

'Good for her,' said Samuel, although he sounded

as though he were not particularly interested. 'Now, I think it's time that you should be going home. We don't want – what is she called…Susannah? – getting worried about you. Come along then. "Put on your ta-ta, little girlie…"' He laughed as he quoted the music hall song he had heard earlier that evening, helping Maddy to slip on her jacket and watching with a grin on his face as she fastened her saucy little hat on top of her golden curls.

Conversation did not flow easily as they walked to the tram stop, nor on the rattling noisy tramcar as it made its way down Woodhouse Lane and thence on to City Square, where they alighted. Maddy's lodgings were just off Wellington Street, a couple of minutes' walk away. It wasn't until they reached her door that he told her, with an air of nonchalance, that it was more than likely that she would not be seeing him at all in the near future, at least not for a while, and neither would the rest of his family.

'When I have been awarded my degree this summer,' he said, with the confidence of one who would never consider the possibility of failure, 'I am hoping to join an expedition to Peru.'

'Peru?' gasped Maddy. 'You mean… South America?'

'Of course,' smiled Samuel. 'I'm glad your geography is up to scratch. Yes; a silver mining expedition. The sort of thing I have always wanted to do.'

'Yes, so I remember,' said Maddy, recalling his interest in fossils and old rocks and such like from the very first time she had met him, which had led him eventually to go on to study for a degree in Geology. 'Well then, I hope it all works out for you, according to plan.'

'I'm sure it will,' he replied. 'I'll see you before I go, though, to say cheerio.' He leant forward to kiss her cheek. 'Goodnight, Maddy. Thank you for a very nice evening. I have enjoyed your company…in spite of everything. Now, promise me that you won't worry about anything? It's all water under the bridge, as they say.'

'No…no, I won't,' she replied, feeling a lump forming in her throat. 'And thank you too, Samuel.'

With a casual salute he was gone, leaving Maddy to find her key and let herself into the dark hallway. She was sharing a room on the first floor with Susannah and Nancy, the menfolk being across the corridor. There was only a vague stirring from the other two beds as she undressed in the dark and then crept between the sheets. She did not even consider whether or not they could hear her muffled sobs, sobs of misery and perplexity and humiliation, as she said goodbye to her foolish and naive girlhood dream.

Chapter Three

Maddy slept surprisingly well, despite the trauma of the evening. When she awoke it took a few moments for her to become acclimatised to yet another strange bedroom. Her eyes took in the dark brown, floral pattern of the wallpaper, the massive wardrobe looming like a giant in the corner, the two other beds in close proximity to her own, and the early morning sunlight stealing through the thin fabric of the curtains. Yes, of course; they were in Leeds this week.

And the remembrance of what had happened the previous night hit her then with the force of a thunderbolt. Samuel...his kisses, which had turned out to be not what she had expected; and then her own stupid, childish behaviour. She had ruined everything that there might have been between them. But Samuel had said that there wasn't anything; she had been mistaken. He didn't love her; he was fond of her, that was all. And neither should she imagine that she loved him, or so he had told her. But I do! I do! a part of her cried out; whilst the more rational side of her mind was conjuring up, almost against her will, the memory of the annoyance in his eyes when things had started to go wrong; and then the casual way in which he had told her of his plans for the future, and the lack of warmth in his goodbye to her.

It hurt; goodness, how it hurt! There was a pain in the region of her heart and an odd feeling of emptiness. But there was embarrassment, too, when she recalled how she had behaved like an idiot, like a foolish little girl who didn't know anything about…anything.

Susannah, in the bed nearest to her, was stirring, raising herself up on one elbow to look at Maddy. A Susannah that her public would never be allowed to see, with a pink sleeping net covering her blonde curls and her face devoid of make-up.

'Hello there, Maddy,' she called. 'Finding it hard to wake up this morning, are you?'

'Mmm…yes; I was rather late getting in,' replied Maddy.

'You dirty stop-out, you!' Susannah laughed. 'I didn't wait up for you, 'cause I knew you'd be all right with your brother. Did you have a good time? It would be nice to see him again, wouldn't it?'

'Yes, it was,' said Maddy. 'And, yes…we had a good time, a very nice meal.' She paused. 'Actually, he's my stepbrother, not my real brother.'

'I think you told me that.' Susannah nodded, looking at her keenly. 'Why? Is there something wrong? You look rather worried, love. You haven't had some bad news, have you; family news?'

'No, not at all; nothing like that,' replied Maddy. 'But I'm…well, yes, I am rather worried about something. D'you think I could have a chat with you, Susannah, sometime today? Perhaps this afternoon?'

'Yes, why not?' agreed Susannah. 'We're free until the first house starts, aren't we? Shall we find a nice little café and have lunch together? Just you and me, eh?'

'Yes, that sounds like a good idea,' said Maddy, but a little doubtfully. She didn't want people on the nearby tables eavesdropping; she wanted to ask her friend something very, very personal.

Susannah put her head on one side, watching her a trifle anxiously. 'I take it you want to have a heart-to-heart chat about something? Am I right?' Maddy nodded. 'Well, whatever it is, don't look so worried. I'm sure we'll be able to sort it out.'

'I'm sure we will,' said Maddy, smiling uncertainly.

Susannah grinned. 'That's right; you tell yer Aunty Susie what's worrying you. I daresay it'll all come out in the wash, as my mam used to say. I tell you what; I've got a better idea. It looks as though it's going to be a nice day. How about us getting a tramcar out to Roundhay Park and spending a couple of hours there? I've been told it's well worth a visit and we ought to find out what the city has to offer whilst we're here.'

'Yes, that's a much better idea,' agreed Maddy,

with more enthusiasm. 'Like you say, there's the promise of a fine day.' She glanced across to the third bed, which was empty. 'It looks as though the sunshine has got Nancy out of bed already.'

'Oh, Nancy's always an early bird,' said Susannah. 'She's probably taking her little doggies for a walk before breakfast.'

Maddy nodded. 'Yes, I expect so... There'll be just you and me going to the park, won't there?'

'Yes, of course; I said so, didn't I?'

'Yes, you did. It's just that...well, it's rather private. I don't want the rest of the troupe to know anything about it. Frank won't mind, will he, you going off on a jaunt without him?'

'No, why on earth should he?' Susannah laughed. 'We don't live in one another's pockets, you know. I must admit we've got rather friendly recently; well, a great deal more than friendly, as I'm sure everybody knows. But we'll have to see how it goes. We're both pretty independent people, Frank and me. It's strange; we'd known one another for years, always enjoyed a chat and a laugh together, and then, somehow, something just clicked between us and... Bob's yer uncle!

'Now then...' She pushed back the bedclothes, revealing her shapely legs as her feet felt around for her fur-trimmed slippers. 'Shall I use the bathroom first, or do you want to?'

'No, it's all right; you have first turn,' replied Maddy. 'I'll put my clothes away in the wardrobe. I left them all higgledy-piggledy when I came in last night.' Her garments of underwear were scattered on the floor with her hat on top of them, and her blouse and smart suit had been flung untidily over the back of a chair.

'Very well then; I won't be long,' said Susannah, slipping a pink velvet dressing gown over her pink silken nightdress. 'Toodle-oo...'

Maddy guessed that she would, in fact, be a good fifteen or twenty minutes, having a strip-wash in the small bathroom at the end of the corridor. Guests were not permitted to take baths in the morning or, indeed, at whatever time they wished. Hot water was in short supply and so each guest was allowed one bath per week, or per stay.

Maddy, along with the other members of the troupe, was learning to accept the rules and regulations of the various lodging houses in which they stayed. She knew that they were quite fortunate to have a bathroom at all, and an indoor toilet. At some of their digs there was a bowl and a large jug on a washstand in the corner of the bedroom, which the landlady would fill with hot water twice a day, if they were lucky. In those households they had to resort to a chamber pot beneath the bed, or the whitewashed lav at the end of the backyard.

Sleeping arrangements varied as well. Sometimes the married couples managed to get rooms on their own, and Maddy knew that sometimes Susannah and Frank shared a room as though they, too, were a couple. At other times the men shared one or two rooms and the ladies another, as they were doing this week. On the whole, their digs at Mrs Howard's establishment in Leeds were more than adequate. She provided a cooked breakfast and would rustle up a snack for them at other times if they required one. She even accommodated Nancy's two West Highland terriers in comfortable baskets in the kitchen. Daisy and Dolly were a very popular turn on the programme, wherever they were playing. Because they were performing dogs they were well-trained and obedient, though not meek or subservient. Nancy loved them as though they were her children, which, indeed, they were as she and Pete had no sons or daughters. Sometimes the dogs had to make do with a makeshift kennel or a garden shed in which to sleep, if the landlady was not fond of animals. It was not often that they were allowed in the bedroom, which was what Nancy would have liked.

Maddy tidied up her clothes, hanging her suit in the wardrobe, then she made her bed. She was feeling a little calmer now and she tried to push to the back of her mind the thoughts of what a silly fool she had made of herself last night. Well, at least she knew where she stood now with regard to Samuel. She would just have to put it behind her and get on with her life. Like a true 'pro', she thought wryly. She had heard many stories of how dedicated artistes carried on despite their heartbreak and misery. What was it they said? The show must go on...

She guessed that Susannah might well have suffered her share of heartache along the way. Maddy knew that she had had a succession of gentlemen friends and admirers, but had never been married. She had attracted a fair number of what she called 'stage door Johnnies' in the past, but since Maddy had joined the troupe Susannah seemed to have settled into a stable relationship with Frank Morrison. Audiences, seeing her up on the stage, singing and dancing and flirting with the menfolk in her own inimitable style, might take her to be nineteen or twenty years of age, but when you observed her more closely you realised she was older than that. Maddy was not sure how old, and no one else seemed to be sure either, but the consensus of opinion was that she was well past thirty.

Maddy admired her very much, and in spite of her being considerably – well, quite a few years – her senior, Susannah was still the nearest female to her in age, and the one who had treated her more as a friend than as a child who needed taking care of. She sat on the bed now, thinking about Susannah, who was, as usual, taking a good deal of time over her morning ablutions; and about the other members of the troupe. They had hardly changed at all since she had watched them on the sands with Jessie, when she was a little girl...

Frank Morrison, Susannah's friend, was still something of an enigma to Maddy. She liked him well enough, but she was a little in awe of him and dubious about his droll sense of humour. She could never tell whether he was being serious or having her on. He was a very talented performer who could turn his hand to almost anything. He played the piano accordion, the mouth organ and the banjo; he could sing quite passably and dance a little; and he was also a 'funny man' with a good selection of amusing – rather lengthy – stories, which he related in his own peculiar style. His lugubrious expression would convince the audience he was being serious until, at the last minute, there would come the punchline, and they would shriek with laughter as his solemn face broke into a beaming smile.

Frank was what might be called a jack of all trades, but far from being master of none he had a talent for most of the performing arts. This, indeed, was a requirement for anyone who joined Percy Morgan's troupe, either in the summer as a Pierrot or out of season as a Melody Maker. They all needed to be versatile enough to take part in sketches, to act as a stooge to a comedian, or to join in a chorus line, singing or dancing. Percy Morgan himself was a good baritone singer as well as being able to act and to take part in comedy duos. But his chief function was to act as leader and to make sure that all was running smoothly amongst the members of his little concert party. His wife, Letty, was a very able musician who could tackle the music for all kinds of songs and dance routines, and act in sketches as well, when required.

Nancy Pritchard's act was unique because she had the performing dogs, Daisy and Dolly, who danced, jumped through hoops and over obstacles, obeyed all her commands in a delightful manner, and endeared themselves to audiences with their friendly faces, wagging tails and immaculately white coats. It was obvious, too, that they were much loved. Nancy, it must be admitted, did little else but perform with her dogs and look after them, but her husband, Pete, was a good all-rounder. He sang a little, danced a little, was the chief comedian and played the male lead in the sketches; and during the summer at the Pierrot shows he acted as the 'bottler', collecting the money from the crowd. Pete and Nancy did not really need to earn money in this way; it was well known that they had 'independent means'. They lived in York in a leafy suburb where they owned a comfortable detached house, left to them by Pete's parents. So Nancy had told Maddy, but not in a boasting fashion; Nancy knew that they were very fortunate. Pete had been the only child of a successful solicitor. He had tried, but without a great deal of enthusiasm, to follow in his father's footsteps. But his heart was not in it and so, eventually, he had left the business in a partner's capable hands and concentrated on his first love, the stage. A decision with which Nancy had only been too pleased to concur.

Barney and Benjy – Barnaby Dewhurst and Benjamin Carstairs; now they were an unusual couple and no mistake! Maddy had been puzzled at Susannah's remarks about them and the reason why neither of them had married. Come to think of it, she hadn't stated a reason except that they were wedded to their art. They were certainly brilliant in their tap-dancing routines, their feet, clad in shiny patent leather, flashing to and fro like quicksilver; their equally flashing smiles which delighted the audiences revealing gleaming pearly white teeth. Benjy was blonde-haired and fresh-faced, a perfect complement to Barney, whose hair was dark and sleek and who had a leaner look about him. Admittedly they, too, did little else besides dance. They might, occasionally, be coerced into taking part in a sketch or a chorus line, and always, of course, in the final scene when all the troupe appeared on the stage; but it was their song and dance routines that were a favourite with the audiences, especially with the ladies.

Carlo – his real name was Charles – and Queenie Colman had joined the troupe somewhat later than the other members, when Charlie Wagstaff, the 'character man', had retired. Carlo had stepped partially into Charlie's shoes. He performed monologues such as 'Gunga Din' and 'The Wreck of the Hesperus', and acted in character as a tramp, a policeman or a Chelsea pensioner. But his chief asset was his superb tenor voice. He sang solos, and also duets with Queenie. She was – or had been at one time – a vibrant mezzo-soprano. Her voice was now a little wobbly, as was her magnificent bosom. Maddy remembered how she and Jessie had hardly been able to control their giggles the first time they had seen her perform on Scarborough sands.

There were eleven acting members, including Maddy, in Morgan's Melody Makers. But there was a twelfth non-performing member as well, too important to be overlooked, and that was Henry Morgan, Percy's father, who was now in his early seventies. It was Henry who, years and years ago, when Percy was a very young man, had started the troupe. It had begun on Scarborough sands as Morgan's Merry Minstrels; a group of black-faced performers, all men, which had been the custom back in the 1880s. Maddy had heard the story many times both from Henry Morgan himself and from her grandfather, Isaac Moon, who had always taken a keen interest in the troupe, of how the Negro minstrels, as they were called, had first appeared on the beaches of the English seaside resorts in the middle years of Queen Victoria's reign. They had originated in America where the players – the Negroes – really did have black faces. On the other side of the Atlantic Ocean, however, the faces of white men were blackened with burnt cork. They sang, danced, cracked jokes and played banjos and tambourines.

This form of entertainment was to be seen on the beaches of all the popular resorts until, in the 1890s, they were superseded by the first Pierrot troupes. These were the very antithesis of the Negro minstrels. Their faces, in the early days, were whitened with zinc oxide to heighten the contrast; they dressed in ruffled white suits with black or red pompoms and conical hats, and brought with them an air of romance and refinement.

Henry Morgan, eager to move with the times, had not been slow to change the image of his troupe of players. In the early 1890s Morgan's Merry Minstrels became Uncle Percy's Pierrots; Percy, at that time, took over the leadership of the concert party, although his father was still an active performer. The all-male tradition had very soon been altered, as Percy's young wife, Letitia – Letty – became involved, and in the years leading to the new century so did Nancy, Susannah, Queenie Colman and, of course, Madeleine Moon. The men, however, still outnumbered the women, as was the case in most troupes.

Henry Morgan had now taken over the administration of the group, dealing with the bookings and transport, the 'hiring and firing' – although there was not very much of the latter – and all the details which went to make a successful concert party. In 1903 they had taken to the road –

or to the railway, to be more accurate – and became a travelling company for the autumn and winter months, from September to April. Maddy, who had been a part-time Pierrot since she was twelve, had joined them in their travels in 1905 when she was fifteen.

'Daydreaming, are we?' said Susannah as she came back into the bedroom. 'Well, at least I'm pleased to see you've got a smile on your face now.'

'What?' said Maddy, coming suddenly out of her reverie. 'Yes...yes, I suppose I was. I was thinking about the Pierrot show, how the artistes haven't changed much at all since I joined.'

'That's true,' replied Susannah. 'It's because we're all very contented working for Percy and Henry. There was that conjuror fellow, of course, last winter, who thought he was too high and mighty for the likes of us. The Marvellous Malvolio, or some such name.'

'Yes; he wanted top billing, didn't he?'

'So he did, and when Henry told him he couldn't have it he took umbrage and left. We can't do with folks like that. We're all equal here, in Henry's eyes at least, and Percy's. Though I can think of one or two who might consider themselves superior.'

Susannah didn't enlarge upon her statement, and neither did Maddy enquire any further. She didn't like to tittle-tattle about other members of the troupe. Letty had told her it was a most unprofessional thing to do and something they did not encourage in their company.

Maddy assumed that Susannah was referring to the Colmans. Carlo was all right, very much under his wife's thumb though, and as for Queenie, she didn't half fancy herself...

Maddy was surprised to realise that she hadn't thought about Samuel for at least ten minutes.

'My turn for a wash now,' she said. 'Wait for me; I won't be long, then we can go down for breakfast together.'

Mrs Howard served them with porridge, followed by bacon, egg, sausage and fried bread. Nancy, who had already taken her dogs for a walk – they were now sitting obediently at her side – was halfway through her breakfast.

'Carlo and Queenie haven't put in an appearance yet,' she told them. 'I gather she is a habitually late riser.'

Mrs Howard overheard her. 'I serve breakfast until ten o'clock,' she said. 'I think that's late enough for anybody and I'm not prepared to extend it any further. They've just managed to scrape in so far, with five minutes to spare. Of course I know you professional people keep odd hours, but I do have to draw the line somewhere.'

'And quite right too,' agreed Nancy as the landlady took her plate away. 'Queenie and Carlo insisted on a double room,' she commented as Mrs Howard went into the kitchen. 'Pete and me, we'll always fit in where we can if we can't get a room together. Pete's sharing with Henry this week, and your Frank.' She nodded towards Susannah. 'And Barney and Benjy too. But Lady Muck doesn't like to mix with the "hoi polloi"; in other words, you and me.' She grinned suddenly. 'Forget I said that, will you, please?'

'Of course,' said Susannah with a knowing wink. And Maddy smiled. It seemed she was not alone in her summing-up of the Colman couple.

Maddy and Susannah boarded a tramcar later that morning, travelling north-east out of the city centre to the fringes of Roundhay Park. They soon decided that the park was, indeed, well worth a visit, as they strolled along the avenue of elm trees, their buds just beginning to show green, past beds of crocuses and early daffodils. They found an empty bench beside the lakeside and sat down. There were very few visitors to the park apart from themselves, it being a midweek morning. No doubt they would be there in their droves come Saturday and Sunday.

Maddy was glad she had put on her winter coat and a more serviceable felt hat than the one she had worn the night before. The sunshine was deceptive and there was a chilly wind on this mid-March day.

'You've gone a bit broody again,' said Susannah, looking at her keenly. They had not talked much on the journey out, both of them staring out of the tram window at the suburbs of Leeds – Sheepscar, Harehills, then on to Roundhay – that they had never visited before. Maddy, at that moment, was thinking how to broach the subject about which she wanted to question her friend. She was somewhat startled therefore when Susannah went on to say, 'Tell me, Maddy – please forgive me, but I've got to ask – you're not pregnant, are you?'

'What?' exclaimed Maddy. 'Of course I'm not!' She could feel herself turning bright pink. 'Why ever should you think that? I'm not...although I probably wouldn't know if I was...' she added, her voice fading away unsurely.

'Oh dear! I've gone and upset you now,' said Susannah, reaching out and placing her gloved hand on top of Maddy's. 'I'm sorry; I'm really and truly sorry. But you seemed so upset and bewildered.'

'So I am,' said Maddy, 'but that's not the reason. At least...well...it's got something to do with it, I suppose.'

'What do you mean?'

'Oh...I'll tell you in a minute. There's something I want to know...about being pregnant and babies an' all that.'

Susannah squeezed her hand then let go of it. 'Oh deary me! What an idiot I am; in with both feet, eh? I wouldn't be surprised if you never wanted to speak to me again. But when you said that – Samuel, is he called? – that Samuel wasn't your real brother, I started to smell a rat. I mean, he's no relation at all really, is he? No blood relation? And

I started to think that perhaps you'd been – well – too friendly, if you know what I mean, when you saw him at Christmas, and that when you saw him last night you told him. But I've jumped to the wrong conclusion, haven't I? Silly me! Please, please forgive me, Maddy.'

'Of course I do,' said Maddy. 'Actually, you've made it all a lot easier – what I wanted to ask you – because it is something to do with…with all that. You see…I'm not actually sure what you have to do – you know – to have a baby. Nobody's ever told me, not properly, and I'm really confused about it.'

'Oh dear, oh dear!' exclaimed Susannah. 'Yes, I think I understand now. I suppose girls can grow up in ignorance, especially nice quiet girls like you.' She chuckled. 'I reckon I was always a good deal more worldly-wise. So you have…no idea?'

'Well, yes, I suppose I have,' admitted Maddy. 'I've heard playground talk, but I dismissed it from my mind at the time and so did my friend. We were only about nine or ten, I think. It all sounded so silly and so…rude.'

Susannah laughed. 'Yes, to a schoolgirl I suppose it would. Children can be little horrors, can't they? Was it a boy who told you? A lad who knew it all, or thought he did?'

'Yes, I can see him now,' said Maddy, 'though I can't remember his name. A big rough lad with a big red face and black hair, the backside of his trousers always torn. His father was a fisherman from what I can remember; they lived near the harbour.'

'And I should imagine that what he told you was – basically – true,' said Susannah. She went on to describe the act of sex – or love, she explained, as it really ought to be – in quite a matter-of-fact manner. 'Yes, that is what happens, and the bald facts do sound rather...repellent. But you must remember that making love, or whatever you choose to call it is – or should be – accompanied by feelings of tenderness and trust and...passion as well.' She smiled as she saw Maddy looking at her somewhat quizzically.

'Yes, I think I can guess what's going through your mind,' she smiled. 'I'm an unmarried lady. How do I know about it? Some folk might think I have no business knowing about it...' Susannah's eyes grew misty and thoughtful as she stared unseeingly into the distance. 'There was a young man once; Simon, he was called. We were very much in love; childhood sweethearts, we were. He lived in the next street to us and we'd been courting for ages. But he went and joined the army – answered the call, you might say – against the wishes of his parents and against mine, of course. But he was hot-headed, was Simon, as well as being romantic, and I'm sure he believed he was indestructible. But he wasn't...' Maddy stared at her, wide-eyed with sympathy, guessing what was coming next.

'He went to fight in the Boer War. He was killed during the siege of Mafeking. I was doing my first season with the Pierrots, but there was only Percy and Letty knew about it; and I daresay Henry knows.'

'I'm so sorry,' said Maddy softly. 'I had no idea.'

'No, how could you have?' Susannah shrugged. 'I've had a few men friends since then, I must admit. I know some folk think I'm a flirt, but it hurt for a long time when Simon died. He was my first love, my true love…'

'But now you've got Frank?' Maddy ventured to ask.

'Yes, indeed I have. And we are very good for one another. We don't really care what people say. We know that what we have will last. We were close friends at first before anything else, and that's always a good start.'

'Are you going to get married?' asked Maddy boldly.

'All in good time,' laughed Susannah. 'He has a wife, you know, but he and Hilda – that's her name – have gone their separate ways for years. She has a thriving second-hand clothes business in York. And their daughter, their only child, has just left home to get married. Frank's a good ten years older than me, you know. Yes, we'll tie the knot eventually… Now, I hope I have set your mind at rest, regarding the other problem?'

'Yes…yes, thank you, you have.'

'Did it have something to do with that stepbrother of yours? You sounded a bit cagey about him. I guess you regarded him as something rather more than a brother, didn't you, Maddy?'

'Yes, yes, you're right. I did…'

'Do you want to tell me about it? Only if you would like to.'

'Oh, I would,' replied Maddy. 'It all went wrong last night…' She explained about her feelings of love for him and how she thought they were reciprocated by Samuel. 'But he just wanted to…you know. I realise now what it was he wanted to do; but I knew it was wrong, that I couldn't. And he didn't really love me at all… But I feel much better now, Susannah, really I do, after talking to you.'

'It sounds to me as though he is not a very nice sort of young man,' she replied. 'You will know to keep out of his way.'

'I may not have any choice. He said he's going on an expedition fairly soon, to Peru.'

'Good riddance then,' said Susannah. 'Don't be too ready to lose your heart, Maddy. You may meet quite a few young men before you find the one who's right for you. What you must do now is make up your mind to enjoy your time with the troupe. Don't forget we'll be in Blackpool in a few weeks' time.'

'Yes, I'm looking forward to that,' said Maddy. 'I've never been to Blackpool.'

'And then, before you know it, we'll be back in Scarborough for our summer season. You'll be back with your family for a while. I'm sure you must miss them all.'

'Yes, I do,' agreed Maddy.

'Now, how about a spot of lunch before we catch the tram back? There's a restaurant over there, see, beyond the trees. We won't need much though, after that mammoth breakfast.' They linked their arms in a friendly fashion as they made their way around the lake.

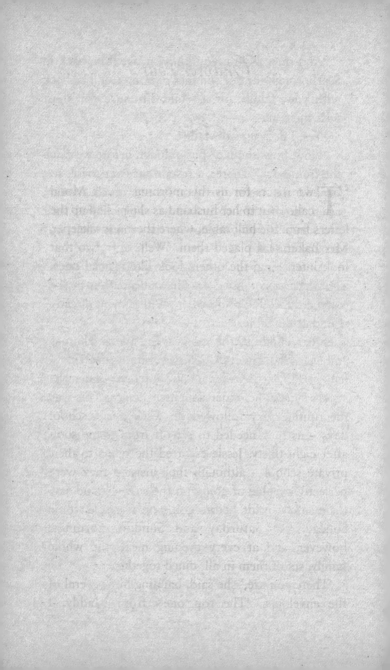

Chapter Four

'Two letters for us this morning,' Faith Moon called out to her husband as she picked up the letters from the hall table, where their housekeeper, Mrs Baker, had placed them. 'Well, only two that look interesting; the others look like official ones. Your department, my dear.' She smiled at him as she entered the dining room where William was already seated at the table.

Faith's children, the ten-year-old twins Thomas and Matilda – always known as Tommy and Tilly – had breakfasted earlier, in the kitchen, under the supervision of her elder daughter, Jessica. This was the routine they followed on weekdays – school days – as they needed to set off from home soon after eight-thirty. Jessie escorted the twins to their private school – although they insisted they were perfectly capable of going on their own – and saw them safely inside before going on to her daytime college. On Saturday and Sunday mornings, however, and at every evening meal, the whole family, six of them in all, dined together.

'There you are,' she said, handing him several of the envelopes. 'The top one's from Maddy; I recognise her handwriting. And this one's from Samuel. It's addressed to both of us, though,' she added.

'Well, that's a step in the right direction anyway,' replied William Moon with a grin. There had been a time when any letters that Samuel wrote would be addressed solely to Mrs Faith Moon, as though he were trying to ignore the fact that his mother now had a new husband. Even Samuel, however, would not have dared to address her in her former name of Barraclough. But Faith had pointed out to him that it was rather rude and churlish behaviour, very childish, in fact; and so he had eventually come round to doing as she said.

'He's addressed the letter to both of us as well,' said Faith, after slitting open the envelope with a knife and taking out the two pages. 'It says… Dear Mother and William… Oh, I'd better read it later,' she went on as Mrs Baker entered with the first part of their breakfast, two bowls of steaming hot porridge.

'Lovely! Thank you, Mrs Baker,' Faith said sincerely, as she did every morning. Their live-in cook and housekeeper, the aptly named Mrs Baker, was a veritable treasure. She had been with them ever since they had moved to their present home some three years before. Faith slid the letter beneath her side plate before adding brown sugar and cream to her porridge.

'Aye, first things first,' agreed her husband. 'I'll

read our Maddy's letter later, an' all. That's addressed to both of us, of course, as they always are.' He sneaked a look at the first page. 'Yes... Dear Dad and Aunty Faith...' He smiled fondly as he thought of his daughter. 'She's a grand lass is our Maddy. It seems ages since we saw her. Anyway, mustn't let this go cold, eh?'

He tucked into the porridge, remarking, between mouthfuls, 'I see Father hasn't joined us yet. I've known the time he'd've been first down and raring to go. I suppose his age is catching up with him; Anno Domini, as he likes to call it.'

'Yes,' Faith agreed. 'How old is your father now? Mid-seventies, isn't he? But I can never quite remember.'

'Aye, he's seventy-four, seventy-five next birthday; that's in September. He's just thirty years older than me. Happen we could have a special do when the time comes. It might even be a retirement do, of course...' he added thoughtfully.

'Why? Is Isaac thinking of giving up the business?' asked Faith, sounding surprised. 'Well, handing it over to you and Patrick, I mean. Not that I don't think it's time he did. But you know what he's always said. "You'll have to carry me out feet first...".'

'Aye..."In one of me own coffins,",' agreed William with a sad smile. 'Yes, I know he said he'd never retire, that he'd die on the job, but he's slowing down, there's no doubt about that. He's doing less and less at the workshop, although I don't think he realises that Patrick and I have noticed. Oh... I'd best shut up. He's here now,' he added in an undertone as his father came into the room.

'You've beat me to it again, the pair of you,' Isaac remarked. 'Reckon I must have overslept.' He shook his head in a befuddled manner. 'Anyroad, good morning to you both.'

'Good morning, Father,' said William, whilst Faith smiled welcomingly at him.

She was never sure what to call the father of her second husband. Her own father – and mother – were still alive, although somewhat estranged from her since her marriage to William. They had disapproved strongly of the divorce and subsequent remarriage of their daughter and that of her ex-husband. As had Edward's parents. It had seemed to them all an ideal match, the marriage of Edward and Faith, the son and daughter of families who had long been friends, and they had regarded their divorce as a shameful state of affairs. Faith had always addressed Edward's father as Mr Barraclough; she had been too much in awe of him for anything more familiar. William's father, however, had tried to persuade her to call him Isaac. Perhaps one of these days she might do so. Most people did, but somehow it seemed to her to be a mite disrespectful to address him in that familiar way.

'Good morning, Mr Moon,' said Mrs Baker, coming in with a third bowl of porridge. 'I've been keeping it warm for you, see, in t'pan. I've kept stirring it so as it wouldn't stick.'

'You're a woman in a million, Mrs Baker,' Isaac told her, as he very often did. She grinned at him with the familiarity of a servant who was on friendly terms with the family, but who still knew her place.

The porridge was followed by bacon, eggs, tomatoes and slices of black pudding, accompanied by toast and – for Isaac and William – the customary pot of strong tea, without which the menfolk would not be ready to start the day. Faith preferred coffee, which Mrs Baker ground freshly for her each day.

William cast a covert glance at his father. Isaac was, in effect, an older edition of his son. When William looked in a mirror he could see, more than ever now that he was approaching middle age, his father's face looking back at him. The same lean features, with the longish nose and wide mouth, characteristic of the males of the family. William sported a well-groomed moustache whereas his father had both a moustache and a beard, as did many older men, emulating – intentionally or otherwise – their monarch, King Edward the Seventh. The eyes that William saw looking back at him were the same shrewd greyish-blue eyes of his father. He noticed now, though, that Isaac's had lost a good deal of their brightness and that he blinked frequently. He did not like to admit to his failing sight, but he was forced to wear his spectacles all the time now when he was at the workshop. Another difference was that Isaac's hair, once dark brown like his son's, was now completely white, whereas William's was almost as dark as it had ever been. Just a sprinkling of silver at his temples, which his loving wife insisted made him look distinguished.

'I shall read my letter now,' said Faith, when Mrs Baker had cleared away their plates. She applied a small amount of butter and marmalade to a dainty sliver of toast, with which she always finished her breakfast.

'Oh, that's nice,' she remarked a minute or two later, looking up from the first page of her letter. 'Samuel says he's seen Maddy. Their concert party was performing in Leeds last week – she told us that, didn't she? – and he took her out for an evening meal. That was very thoughtful of him... He says they had a good time. Anyway, I'll let you read it when I've finished.'

'Good,' remarked William perfunctorily, his eyes scanning one of his letters. 'I'm saving Maddy's till I've looked at this other stuff. It all amounts to summat and nowt from what I can see.' He perused the circulars, adverts and a bank statement whilst his wife was deeply engrossed in Samuel's letter. After a moment or two he was aware that she had gone very quiet, no longer telling him snippets of news, and he saw her frown.

'Oh dear!' she exclaimed. 'I don't like the sound of that at all.' She slowly shook her head as her eyes took in the rest of the page.

'What's the matter, love?' he asked. 'Not bad news, is it? Samuel's not ill is he…or Maddy?' he added; she had just told him that Samuel had seen her.

'No, nothing like that. Neither of them is ill. Whether it's bad news or not depends on your point of view, I suppose. No doubt Samuel thinks it's good.' She looked across the table at her husband, her lovely blue eyes clouded with anxiety. 'Samuel says he's going to work abroad when he gets his degree. He's joining an expedition that will be involved in silver mining…in Peru! That's a very long way away, isn't it, William?'

'Well, yes, I reckon it is, love,' he replied. 'But it's only what we might have expected, isn't it?' He smiled encouragingly at her. 'He's taking a degree in Geology. That's the study of the earth and of…of all the stuff that comes out of it, isn't it? So it stands to reason it'll involve mining of some sort or another. Why? What did you think he might do when he had his degree?'

'I don't know,' replied Faith. 'I took it for granted he would stay in this country. Very silly of me, I daresay. I thought he might want to be…oh, the curator of a museum or something of the sort. He's spent a lot of time going round museums: the one here in Scarborough, and I know he's been to several others, much bigger ones, no doubt.'

'Those sorts of jobs, curatorships, are very hard to come by, I should imagine,' remarked William. 'It's often a case of stepping into dead men's shoes or waiting for somebody to retire. They hang on to them as long as they can. Anyway, I can't see Samuel wanting to stay in one place. Personally, I'm not at all surprised.

'Don't let it upset you, my dear,' he continued, looking at his wife's troubled face, although she was not crying. Faith was made of sterner stuff than that and didn't dissolve into tears at the slightest setback as he knew some women were wont to do. 'I'm sure Samuel will be perfectly all right; it will be a well-organised expedition. I should think it's quite an honour that he's been asked to join it, straight out of college.'

'Yes, I suppose so,' agreed Faith. 'He's always been studious and hard-working, so it's probably no more than he deserves. It was a shock though; he's never mentioned anything of the sort before.'

William nodded. He was aware – and no doubt his wife was too, although she didn't admit it – that Samuel told them only what he wanted them to know; and sometimes that amounted to very little. 'It isn't as if we see him all that much,' he remarked. 'I'm not saying anything wrong about him, mind, but his visits home are very few and far between.

He's no doubt got other interests and friends that are important to him. Is he coming home for Easter? They'll be finishing soon, won't they, for the holiday, or vacation, or whatever they call it?'

'He doesn't say,' replied Faith, sounding a mite dispirited. 'He's only one term left to do; that will be his exam term so I doubt if we will see much of him then. But he's sure to pay us a visit during the summer before he goes away.'

'Of course he will,' said William, smiling at her confidently. 'When is this expedition? Does he say?'

'Yes; they're setting out in September.'

'Well then, you can be sure he'll come back to Scarborough for a week or two at least. And Maddy will be home for the summer months, won't she, with the Pierrot show?'

'Yes, of course she will.' Faith's face lit up at the thought of seeing Maddy again. William knew that she had come to care for his daughter almost – or possibly just as much – as she cared for her own children. 'Have you read her letter, William? What does she say?'

'I'm just going to read it now,' he replied. 'I was sidetracked by your news about Samuel. Now, you mustn't worry anymore about him. Promise me you won't; he's a big boy now, you know!'

'Very well; I promise,' smiled Faith. 'It's hard, though, at times, to see your children growing up…and growing away from you.'

William read his letter, nodding from time to

time. 'Good… She still seems to be enjoying her travels.' He glanced across at his wife. 'You see, I worried about Maddy when she first went off with Percy Morgan's troupe, but she was perfectly all right. I expect she was a bit homesick at first; she never said, but I could tell; but she's fine now… Yes, she says she's seen Samuel. He went to see the show, then they went out for supper; that's all she says about it… Oh, they're off to Blackpool soon – the concert party, I mean – for Easter week, two weeks in fact. She'll enjoy that; our Maddy's never been to Blackpool.'

'Have you, William?'

'Yes, Clara and I went for a few days once. I didn't reckon much to it, to be honest. It's big and brash, not at all refined. Not a patch on Scarborough.'

Faith laughed. 'You couldn't be a little bit prejudiced, could you, William?'

'Aye, maybe I am, a little bit,' he smiled. 'And I suppose I have to admit that Scarborough's got its more seamy side an' all. I daresay folks that live in Lancashire think there's no place like Blackpool, just as we Yorkshire folk think there's no place like Scarborough.'

'Blackpool?' said Isaac, becoming aware of the conversation. 'Aye, I remember going there as a lad, only once, mind. One o' t'few times I managed to escape from me father's tyranny.' He chuckled. William had heard, many times, how his grandfather had ruled the young Isaac with a rod of iron. 'We had a jolly good time there. By heck! You should see all t'rows and rows of boarding houses. And the length o' t'promenade; seven miles of golden sand, that's what they boast. Aye, Blackpool's a grand place. But I know what you mean, lad. There's no place like home, is there?'

'Very true,' replied William. 'We're very fortunate to live in such a lovely place with such clean air. In Leeds, now, where our Maddy's just been, you sometimes can't see the sun for the clouds of smoke and grime. And it's the same in Bradford and Halifax an' all them mill towns. Aye, I reckon we're very lucky... Here you are, Faith, love.' He handed her Maddy's letter. 'Have a read of that and then we'd best get moving.'

'And here's Samuel's letter,' said Faith, 'if you'd like to see it.'

William had already risen from the table. He shoved the letter in his waistcoat pocket. 'I'll read it later; see what he has to say about this expedition.'

'Not a lot yet,' said Faith. 'I don't suppose he knows very much himself at the moment... I'll be with you in a few minutes, dear. Are you going to call a cab, or are you cycling to work?'

'No, not this morning,' replied William. 'We'll all travel in together. How about you, Father? Are you ready to be off?'

'Aye, I'll just pay a visit to the you-know-what, then I'll be with yer.'

William went outside and hailed a hansom cab for the three of them. It was a good half hour's walk from their home on Victoria Avenue in the South Bay area of the town, across to their place of work on North Marine Road in the North Bay. He walked there occasionally, but more often he rode there on his bicycle, a modern safety bicycle with Dunlop pneumatic tyres. Maddy and Jessie owned bicycles too, but more for means of recreation, and because it had become a popular pastime for both young men and young ladies, in fact for all ages and classes of society. The girls' cycles were not in use at the moment, tucked away in the garden shed; but come the early summer Jessie would be out and about with the cycling club she belonged to; and when Maddy came home for the summer season the two of them would enjoy exploring the countryside around Scarborough.

Motor cars were beginning to appear on the streets of the town, Fiats and Fords and Renaults, and, very occasionally, a Daimler. A Daimler motor had been made at the beginning of the century for Bertie, the Prince of Wales, who was now King Edward the Seventh. He had become a great patron of the motor car, and the fact that he used one had made a major impression on the public and was acting as a big boost for the industry, which was still in its infancy.

William had not been tempted to buy one as yet, although he knew the time would come when it would be deemed necessary for him, as a prosperous man of business, to own a motor car; just as he knew that, in time, their horse-drawn hearses would be replaced by motor transport. Not yet awhile, though; certainly not while his father was still alive.

Neither William nor Isaac had ever been wealthy enough to belong to the 'carriage class'. Indeed, it had not been necessary, even if they could have afforded it, as for many years they had lived on the premises, their undertaking business being conducted from an office and workshop at the rear of the property. Now there was a larger office and showroom at the front of the premises. The reduced living quarters at the back and upstairs were occupied by Patrick, William's 21-year-old son. He was engaged to Katy, his long-time girlfriend, and they hoped to marry in the spring of the following year.

Patrick had proved to be capable at fending for himself at home, and also at opening up at nine o'clock in the morning. He and their assistant, Joe Black, would start work on the coffin making until William and – sometimes a little later – Isaac arrived. The three generations of men worked well together; it had always been a close-knit family business. When William's first wife, Clara, had been alive, she had helped as well with some of the laying-out tasks and, later, in the adjoining shop which they had opened some twelve years ago.

They now employed, in addition to Joe Black, a part-time worker, Mrs Price – a lady who attended the same Methodist chapel as the Moon family – who assisted with the laying-out and arranging for burial of the women's bodies; something which William considered to be more seemly for a member of the same sex to do.

His second wife, Faith, had been more delicately bred than Clara, who had been brought up in a fisherman's cottage in the poorer part of the town. Faith had been accustomed to a more affluent lifestyle when she had lived in York as a girl, and this had continued when she had been married to her first husband. And so William had never even considered asking her to help him with the intimate tasks that Clara had performed. But the wealth and comfort had not been able to compensate for the unhappiness that Faith had experienced in her first marriage. He had wondered how she might adapt to a different way of life, but he need not have troubled himself. She had volunteered, of her own accord, to take over the supervision of the clothing shop, if William wished her to do so. He had been more than happy to concur with her suggestion. During her marriage to Edward Barraclough she had, of course, not worked outside of the home, and they had always had servants aplenty to see to their every need. But she had settled into her new life, both at home and in the shop, with not the slightest doubt or hesitation.

William was in a reflective mood later that morning as he worked with his plane on an elm wood coffin. It was work he always found soothing despite the sorrowful concepts associated with such a task. He was thinking of the conversation they had had earlier at the breakfast table, about how lucky they were to live in such a place as Scarborough. William knew that he was not just lucky; he was, indeed, blessed, and not only because he lived in such a fine seaside resort. He was singularly blessed in all aspects of his life: in his home and family and with his lovely wife, Faith, just as he had been with Clara.

He would never have imagined that he could experience such happiness in a second marriage. When Clara had died he had felt that the light had gone out of his life. She had died so suddenly and unexpectedly at an early age, after an attack of influenza which had turned to pneumonia. He had felt that Fate – or God, because he had always tried to believe in the words he heard at chapel – had been cruel to him. But he had had to carry on, trying to hide much of his sadness for the sake of his son and daughter.

His friendship with Faith had started some years previously, in the first year of the new century, when she had visited Scarborough during the summer season for an extended holiday. Maddy and Jessie, meeting on the beach, had become firm friends, and thus Faith had also become a friend to both William and Clara. He had been glad of her continuing friendship after his wife had died, although at that time he had not believed it would be possible for him ever to care for a woman in the way that he had cared for Clara. But gradually their friendship and affection, for both William and Faith, had developed into love. He would not – could not – forget Clara. Maddy, in particular, with her golden hair, brown eyes and finely drawn features, was a constant reminder of her mother. But his memories of Clara were now tinged with happiness, subduing the overwhelming sadness he had felt at first.

He was blessed in his family life too; not just with his own son and daughter, but with the new family he had acquired since his marriage to Faith. Jessica – Jessie – was a grand lass; he had always been fond of her ever since the early days when she and Maddy had discovered that they were kindred spirits. And Tommy and Tilly were delightful; high-spirited and naughty at times, but a constant source of joy and amusement.

The only fly in the ointment was Samuel. He was the only one who had seemed to resent his mother's remarriage; the only one of the brood to call him William and not Uncle William; although he would never have expected them to call him Dad or Father. He had tried hard to like Samuel, but he feared that the lad had inherited far more of his father's character traits – and looks, too – than those of his mother. He had not been sorry to hear the news that

Samuel would be working abroad for a while. He did not know for how long, but the longer the better in William's view. There was always an atmosphere, a certain tension in the air whenever he stayed with them. He had noticed, also, the signs of a developing attraction between Samuel and Maddy. He had seen the way the young man glanced at her, and he had noticed, too, that Maddy was always pleased to see him; her eyes sparkled more than ever when she was in his company. It was an attachment that he, William, would not wish to encourage. The news that they had met in Leeds did not please him. There was something about Samuel that made him distrustful. Yes, William was not at all sorry that his stepson was going to Peru.

And then there was Henrietta – Hetty – his elder daughter from a relationship he had formed with Bella Randall when he was a young man of eighteen. It was with a sense of guilt and self-dislike that he looked back on that period of his life. Bella had been one of the herring girls working at the harbour. He had given little heed to the consequences when he had become enamoured of her, and when she had told him that she was expecting his child he had refused, to his subsequent shame, to take responsibility. The young woman had disappeared, back to Northumberland, whence she had come and the child had been adopted.

When Bella had reappeared in Scarborough

several years later William was, by then, happily married to Clara. She had been a disturbing irritant in his life especially when she had come to work in their store alongside his wife. But, to her credit, Bella had never revealed their shameful secret to Clara. William had not told his first wife about his one and only dalliance, something which had preyed on his mind, but which he had never found the courage to divulge.

Bella had vanished from his life once again, just before his marriage to Faith; and he had believed that it was the end of the chapter. He had not wanted there to be any secrets between himself and his new wife, and so he had told Faith about Bella and about the child born out of wedlock, assuaging, to some extent, the guilt he had always felt at being less than honest with Clara.

It had not, however, been the end of the story. William had been astonished when, two years ago, his long-lost daughter, Hetty, had come to find him. Her adoptive parents had both died, and so had Bella, with whom the young woman had been reunited during the last two years of her real mother's life.

William had realised almost at once that he liked Hetty. He had recognised her immediately; with her black curly hair, deep brown eyes and bold features she was the image of Bella, as she had been when he first met her. But Hetty was of a kinder, more gentle disposition than her mother; and William's wife, children and stepchildren had gradually come to welcome her as a member of their family. The only one who had not met her was Samuel.

Hetty had been brought up, as Henrietta Collier, by her adoptive parents in the town of Ashington in Northumberland. She still lived there, working in the office of one of the many coal mines. Her visits to Scarborough to see her father and her newly discovered family were not very frequent, but were always happy and enjoyable occasions. William had grown very fond of her during the two years he had known her; she was now twenty-six years old. He had realised that good could come out of something which, at one time, he had regarded as a disaster.

The firm of Isaac Moon and Son was continuing to prosper, too, which was satisfying to William and his father, and also to Patrick, who, one day, when William took over, would become the 'son' of the establishment.

The business had been started in the mid-nineteenth century, in quite a small way at first, by Joshua Moon, Isaac's father. Over the years the firm had thrived and grown, earning them a good reputation in the town, due to their sympathetic dealings with their clients. In the early years much of the laying-out process had been done by a 'handywoman' of the neighbourhood, often the same woman who acted as midwife at the births. Nowadays the undertakers frequently performed this task themselves. For many years now they had owned their own hearse and two black horses. Jet and Ebony, however, the two original mares, had been put out to grass for a well-deserved retirement. They had been replaced by two different mares, Velvet, an all black horse, and Star, who was black with a white star shape on her forehead.

Some twelve years ago William and Clara, with Isaac's blessing, had opened an adjoining shop. This at first had been called Moon's Mourning Modes and had sold all manner of clothes, for both men and women, and artefacts concerned with the cult of mourning, at its height during the reign of Queen Victoria.

Now, however, in keeping with the times and the reign of a new monarch, the store had diversified. It was now known as Moon's Modes for all Seasons and stocked, in addition to a certain amount of mourning wear, clothing for all occasions: bridal gowns and wedding accessories as well as garments, both casual and more sophisticated, for afternoon and evening wear. Faith had now taken over as joint manageress, along with Miss Muriel Phipps, who had served them well for several years. It was typical of Faith that she had not wanted to rule the roost, even though she was the owner's wife. The two women worked well together and that business, too, was flourishing.

William Moon, in the March of 1907, was a contented man.

Chapter Five

Morgan's Melody Makers were to perform for two weeks in Blackpool at the Eastern Pavilion, at the landward end of the North Pier. It was a fairly new building, having been completed in 1903, its architecture consisting of a domed roof with pagoda-shaped turrets, and, inside the building, ornate marble pillars, brightly coloured paintwork and a multitude of chandeliers, each with a circle of electric light bulbs, suspended from the concave ceiling. The only drawback, to the audience if not to the performers, was the seating arrangement: rows and rows of wooden benches, with backs admittedly, but not nearly so comfortable as the plush seats to be found in the town's Grand Theatre or the Winter Gardens Pavilion. But the members of the audience would not care overmuch about the numbness in their rear quarters if the entertainment on the stage was worth watching. And word soon got round the town in the week leading up to Easter that the present show was worth a bob or two of anybody's money.

Maddy was very soon fascinated and overwhelmed

by Blackpool: the size of it, the noise, the brightness and the sheer exuberance of it all. She had been captivated the moment that she and her fellow artistes had emerged onto the forecourt of Central Station and she had seen the famous Tower, right there in front of her, its 518 feet of ironwork girders pointing up into the sky. You could not help but stare upwards at it, your eyes drawn to the topmost pinnacle where the Union Jack fluttered in the breeze. During the days that followed Maddy was to see countless visitors standing stock-still on the pavements of Bank Hey Street, which ran alongside the back of the Tower buildings, gazing into the heavens, pointing and exclaiming in wonderment.

'Eeh, Fred, I've nivver seen owt like that before…'

'Aye; ruddy marvellous, i'n't it?'

'Hey up; it looks as though it's movin'…'

'Don't talk so daft, woman; of course it's not. It's been there ten year or more, so I reckon it's pretty steady, like…'

It was, in fact, an optical illusion that the tower appeared to be swaying a little if you stared at it long enough. It was what visitors always did, gaze up at the Tower. The residents were more used to it by now. It had been there since 1894 and was no longer a novelty.

On that Sunday afternoon, the week before Easter, just a sprinkling of visitors were arriving in the resort for an early holiday, but that would increase a hundredfold by the height of the season, in July and August. On the forecourt of the station there were hansom cabs and landaus piled high with luggage, and Maddy could hear a couple of lads shouting, vying with one another as to who could shout the loudest.

'Half price lodgings, only five minutes' walk away...'

'You come along wi' me, sir, madam. Me mam runs t' best boarding house in Blackpool...'

Maddy looked questioningly at Percy who was standing beside her. 'They're touting for custom,' he told her. 'It's quite a common custom hereabouts. A lot of visitors arrive "on spec", as they call it, and the landladies know they want to find digs as soon as possible. So they send their husbands – or, more likely, their sons – to grab what business they can.'

One of the lads had a handcart onto which he was piling the luggage of a man and woman and their two children, who were dancing up and down with excitement.

'No thanks, lad,' said Percy, waving his hand at another youth who had accosted him with an offer of the best lodgings in Blackpool. 'We're fixed up, ta very much.' They had already booked their lodgings for the fortnight at a boarding house on Albert Road. For once, Henry Morgan had managed to procure rooms for them all at the same place. 'Right, lads and lasses,' Percy called to his troupe. 'Let's get moving, shall we? It's not very far, only a few hundred yards up the road opposite us.'

'Far enough with these heavy cases to carry,' said Queenie Colman with a petulant frown, and Susannah Brown nodded her agreement.

'I'm lucky though,' she said, preening herself a little. 'Frank's carrying my case as well as his own.' All that Susannah had to carry was her big circular hatbox, which contained a selection of elegant headgear. She changed her large-brimmed hats, bedecked with flowers, fruit, ribbons and lace, at frequent intervals throughout their performances.

'And Carlo's carrying mine an' all,' retorted Queenie. 'But he's not as young as he used to be. His arms'll be pulled out of their sockets if he has to carry these more than a few yards.'

Percy and Henry always tried to get lodgings near to the station in each town they visited, and near to the theatre too, if possible. Sometimes the landlady's husband or son would meet them with a cart to assist with their luggage, or they might hire a couple of cabs. On this, their first visit to Blackpool for a few years, it seemed that they must fend for themselves.

'Aye, I see your point,' agreed Percy. Indeed, all the men would be carrying two cases, their own and that of their wife; and then there was young Maddy to consider. 'Here, lad; d'you think you could come and give us a hand?' He called to a lad of about fifteen who was standing at the side of his handcart, not shouting, as the others were doing, but looking a little lost and unsure of himself. 'We'll make it worth your while if you'll take this lot up Albert Road for us. We've already got lodgings, but we'd be glad of your help.'

'Ooh, ta, mister,' said the lad. 'Me mam's sent me out to tout for custom, but it's me first time this weekend, an' I'm not right used to it. I don't suppose she'll mind though, if I'm earning a bob or two.'

He set to with a will, piling the suitcases and bags onto the handcart, with Susannah's hatbox on the top. 'Righty-ho, folks; we're ready to go,' he called to the little group clustered around him. 'You're all going to t'same place? Up Albert Road? Very well then, follow me.'

They crossed Central Drive and set off up Albert Road, and Maddy had her first real glimpse of the rows and rows of boarding houses. This was only one of many such streets in the town; long terraces of three-storeyed houses, built in Victorian times to cope with the increasing number of visitors from the inland towns of Lancashire, and further afield, who were taking advantage of the one week in the year, known as 'Wakes Week', when the mills and factories closed down and the workers had a chance to spend their hard-earned wages. There were many such boarding houses in Maddy's native Scarborough, which prided itself that it had been a popular seaside resort – a spa resort – long before anyone had heard of Blackpool. But she soon realised that this Lancashire resort was on a much bigger scale than her hometown across the Pennines, much larger, too, than the nearby towns of Filey and Bridlington, with which she was quite familiar.

All the boarding houses looked alike, at least at a first glance; all with donkey-stoned front steps and window sills, iron railings fronting small paved or grassed garden areas, and a bench, on which the visitors could sit, beneath the front window. Some of the houses had names: Sea View, which surely must be a misnomer unless the sea was visible from a topmost attic window; Tower View, which was more likely; Bella Vista, or Rest-a-While; or names borrowed from the Royal Family – Balmoral and Windsor House. Some names were derived, so it seemed, from the names of the owners: Wilmar or Kenlyn or Bertrose, whilst the majority just had numbers. By the side of some of the front doors there were framed notices declaring, 'Mrs Ethel Brown is pleased to welcome visitors from Rochdale', or some such epithet, indicating that this was the town from which the said lady had hailed. No doubt, though, she would be pleased to welcome visitors from other towns as well.

Maddy found herself walking alongside the lad who was pushing the handcart. He was a pleasant round-faced youth with unusual greenish eyes and curling ginger hair, from what she could see of it beneath his flat cap, which appeared to be much too large for him. He seemed to have lost much of his shyness since he had been offered the job.

He grinned at Maddy. 'Me name's Joe,' he said, 'in case you're wondering who I am. Joseph Murphy, but everybody calls me Joe. Me mam runs a boarding house in Adelaide Street, that's the next street to this.'

'Hello then, Joe.' Maddy smiled back at him. 'I'm Maddy; Madeleine Moon, but I'm usually called Maddy... Not all the time though,' she added. She was always billed on the posters and in the programmes as Madeleine Moon. Percy had said that the name had a memorable ring to it. But she wouldn't say that to Joe, whom she had only just met; it would seem like boasting.

'Like I was saying to that feller...' Joe cocked his thumb in the direction of Percy, 'it's the first time I've tried this touting lark; well, nearly the first. We only moved here last back-end, to the boarding house, I mean, and me mam's trying to rustle up as much business as she can.'

'Then I'm afraid we're not much use to you,' replied Maddy. 'We've already got our lodgings booked.'

'Ne'er mind,' said Joe. 'I'll try again later.' His eyes took in the group of people accompanying him and his handcart up the street. 'Are you lot actors, or summat o' t'sort?' he asked. 'You have that look about you, somehow.'

'Yes, as a matter of fact, we are,' said Maddy, not without a feeling of pride. 'We're a concert party, and that man you were talking to, he's Percy Morgan, our leader.'

'So...you're doing a show in Blackpool, are you?'

'Yes, so we are – for the next two weeks.'

'And where is it, like?'

'We're appearing at the Eastern Pavilion at the end of the North Pier; the promenade end, I believe,' Maddy told him.

'Just as well.' Joe nodded. 'There's another theatre up at t'other end, the Indian Pavilion. You'd get blown to bits walking t'length o' t'pier every night. And what is it that you do then?'

'I'm a singer,' she added modestly. 'I wonder if you might like to...?' She was just starting to ask him if he would like to see the show – there were always complimentary tickets to be handed out – when Percy and Pete Pritchard came to walk beside them.

It was Pete who spoke. 'Hang on, lad,' he began. 'Just have a rest for a minute and listen to me. We've got another job for you, if you're willing, haven't we Percy?'

'We have indeed,' agreed Percy. 'We've just been saying that you seem to be a hard-working lad.'

'We've left all our props and stuff back at the station in the left luggage place,' Pete continued. 'We're artistes, you see – we just heard a bit of what Maddy was telling you – and we need somebody to shift it for us to the Eastern Pavilion. Would you be willing? I'll come along with you – I'm always in charge of the props – to help you to load and unload it.'

'I'll say I'm willing,' said Joe, a wide grin spreading all over his rosy-cheeked face. 'It's a darned sight better than touting. I reckon I'll have to do that an' all, though, to keep on t'right side of me mam.'

'We'll make it worth your while,' said Percy, 'like I told you before. How about ten bob in all, for this job and for moving the props?'

'Gosh, that's grand, mister,' said Joe. 'Ta very much.'

'And I think we might throw in a couple of free tickets for the show,' Percy went on. 'Happen you could take your girlfriend along, eh, Joe? It is Joe, isn't it? I heard you saying so to our Madeleine.'

Joe blushed crimson. 'Aye, I'm Joe. But I haven't got a girlfriend; I'm only fifteen. I could ask me brother to go with me, though.'

'Take whoever you like, Joe,' said Percy. 'It's all the same to us. I tell you what; we'll let you have another couple of tickets for your parents. It's a shame to leave them out. Er…you do have both your parents, do you?' he asked, knowing it was sometimes widow women who ran the boarding houses.

'Yes, 'course I have. But me dad's got a job; he has nowt to do wi' t'boarding house. Thanks again, mister... D'you think their tickets could be for a different night, though? We can't all be out at once in case the visitors want summat.'

'Certainly,' agreed Percy. 'Anyroad, you don't want to be with your mam and dad all the time, do you? Come on then, let's get on our way. It's not much further, is it, to our lodgings?'

'No, I think the number you said is just the other side of Coronation Street,' said Joe, taking up the handles of his handcart again. 'Follow me...'

Maddy found herself sharing a room once again with Susannah Brown and Nancy Pritchard. Two of the married couples – Percy and Letty, and Carlo and Queenie – had rooms to themselves, leaving the others to fit into the available rooms the best way they could. Not one of them complained, especially as Mrs Jolly, the landlady, had not objected to accommodating Nancy's dogs. Moreover, she had agreed to cook a midday meal for all of them each day in addition to their breakfast, and snacks and cups of tea at other times if they required them.

'We're not right busy at the moment,' she told them when they arrived. 'The season hasn't got started properly yet. We could've been full twice over for the Easter weekend, mind, but I was only too thankful that I'd got you lot booked in. Come Whit week and after, the town'll be bursting at its seams. We've got some more pros staying later on, appearing at t'Winter Gardens, I believe. Anyroad, come on in and make yourselves at home. And Sid'll show you to your rooms. Sidney…' she shouted, and a tall thin man appeared from the rear of the house. He had a striped apron tied round his waist, which he hastily pulled off and hung over the banister rail.

'See these good folks up to their rooms, would you, Sidney love? We've got four rooms ready, so just sort yourselves out; some of 'em are big enough for three or four. Make yourselves at home,' Mrs Jolly repeated. 'Our place is a real home from home; at least we hope it is, don't we, Sid?'

'Aye, we do that, Rosie love,' agreed her husband. 'Now, I'll give you an 'and wi' these cases.' He picked up one in each hand as though they weighed only a couple of pounds, leading the way up the first flight of stairs.

'There'll be a cup of tea ready for you in the dining room when you've unpacked,' Mrs Jolly called up to them. 'And we'll make you a spot of dinner an' all – well, "high tea" I should say, round about five o' clock. Will that suit you? Don't suppose you've had much at dinner time, have you, and there's nowt much open in town on a Sunday.'

'No, just a sandwich,' replied Percy. 'Thank you very much, Mrs Jolly. We'd all very much appreciate something to eat…

'Looks as though we've landed on our feet, lass,' he whispered to Maddy as they followed their host up the stairs.

Mr and Mrs Jolly – Sid and Rosie, as they all soon began to call them, at the couple's request – looked a well-matched pair and it seemed as though they worked well together. Rosie Jolly was, indeed, a jolly person; shortish, plumpish, fiftyish, pink-cheeked and with greying hair, which was cut and curled to its best advantage. She was by no means the archetypal Blackpool landlady – except perhaps in stature – portrayed on the now popular comic postcards, reputed to be harridans with a permanently sour expression and a heaving bosom encased in a floral apron.

It was a common music hall joke, too, that the landladies' husbands were henpecked little men who spent their lives in the kitchen, peeling potatoes and washing mounds of greasy pots. The members of Percy's company soon discovered that this was not the case with Sidney, even though he had made his first appearance wearing one of his wife's pinnies. He had a job with a firm of joiners throughout the week but was pleased to help his wife at weekends. Most of the time Rosie ran the boarding house on her own, apart from Peggy, the young chambermaid-cum-waitress, who came in to help for a few hours each day.

'By heck, that was grand!' exclaimed Henry Morgan when they had all eaten Mrs Jolly's home-cooked steak and kidney pie and chips, followed by cream trifle; and they all agreed with him.

'Now then, how about a bit of fresh air?' said

Percy. 'Let's go and see what Blackpool's got to offer us, eh?'

They put on their hats and coats and mufflers too – they had already discovered that the Blackpool breeze could be chilly – and then set off en masse, with Nancy's two little dogs trotting along beside her.

The Big Wheel loomed above them as they walked along Coronation Street and then made their way through the town. The streets were quite deserted at six-thirty on a Sunday evening and, of course, all the shops were closed. The town was quite familiar to most of them, but it was Maddy's first visit and she stared around her in wonder. They had spread out a little now, walking in twos and threes, Maddy with Henry Morgan.

'There's the Winter Gardens, see...' He pointed to the impressive entrance and the glass dome, 120 feet high, which topped the building.

'And the Grand Theatre, see...' as they walked along Church Street, heading for the promenade. That was a smallish theatre, tucked away in a corner. This theatre, also, had a domed roof, a green one, with ornate brickwork surrounding it.

They crossed the wide promenade and the tramtrack. 'Look over yonder,' said Henry, pointing to the right. 'That's the North Pier, see, and that's the Eastern Pavilion where you'll be performing for t'next two weeks.'

They walked up to the entrance and Maddy

stood in awe, looking at the poster advertising their very own show, Morgan's Melody Makers. And there was her own name, 'Madeleine Moon, Yorkshire's own songbird'.

She stood a little away from the rest of them, leaning against the iron railings and watching the incoming waves lapping against the sea wall. She breathed in the fresh tang of the sea and the salty air for which Blackpool was renowned, experiencing a sense of deep contentment. She had a feeling that these two weeks in Blackpool would be memorable ones.

Chapter Six

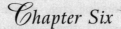

Daniel Murphy didn't go to the theatre very often. In fact, he very rarely went to any of the places of entertainment in Blackpool, where the visitors and the local folk went to enjoy themselves. He worked as a part-time sales assistant in a gentlemen's outfitters on Church Street, and also helped his mother in their boarding house on Adelaide Street. Daniel waited at the tables and saw to the visitors' requirements in the evening, serving the late night cups of tea and biscuits. His younger brother, Joseph, was what might be called a general 'dogsbody'. He lent a hand wherever it was needed, in addition to his work as a delivery lad at a nearby grocery store.

Daniel's part-time occupations, however, were only a stop-gap. He was studying hard so that he might go to college sometime in the near future. His mother, Anna, made sure that he kept his nose to the grindstone. And Daniel knew, deep down, that it was more for her sake than his own that he continued with his studies. She had high aspirations for her elder son and he did not want to disappoint her. For his part, he would be quite content to work full-time as a sales assistant, or to take up a training position in the office of a solicitor or estate agent. The opportunities in Blackpool were many and varied, but his destiny was secured, at least as far as Anna Murphy was concerned.

It had been so ever since she had set eyes on her first-born child, her first-born live child, that was, because she had already had two stillborn babies. He had been the very image of herself with the selfsame gingerish hair and green eyes. His eyes had been an indeterminate greyish bluey-green at first, but they had soon changed to the clear green that betrayed their Irish heritage, so Daniel's mother had told him many times, along with her ambitions for his future. How could he ever think of disappointing her?

He knew, though, that he really should go out and about and enjoy himself a bit more; he was missing out on quite a lot of the things that young men of his age liked to do. And so he had agreed at once to accompany his brother to the show at the North Pier Pavilion. It would make a pleasant change, and Joe deserved a night out just as much as he did. Joseph was a rather shy lad, but his dealings with his grocery customers and the visitors at the boarding house had helped to bring him out of his shell. He had never been much of a scholar and had been glad to leave school at thirteen and find a job. They had been living in Liverpool at that time and he had worked as an odd-job lad in all sorts of places. Joe was a hard worker; there was no doubt about that.

As for Daniel, he had a more outgoing disposition than his brother and had never found it difficult to make friends with either sex. He had subjugated his feelings, however, to a certain extent, knowing that years of study lay ahead of him; he knew he must develop the trait of single-mindedness and not allow himself to be sidetracked.

'Good for you,' he said to Joe, when his brother told him about the tickets he had obtained. He had come back in great excitement from his trip out with the handcart; it was empty, however, and he had not brought any visitors back with him. 'Where did you get the tickets, though?' Daniel asked. 'Don't tell me you've bought them?'

'Don't talk daft!' replied Joe. 'I got talking to this girl, see…'

'What girl?' asked Daniel, surprised. His brother did not usually bother with girls; he was covered with confusion whenever he met any. He, Daniel, could talk to them easily enough, but he never allowed himself to think any further about them; there would not be much point. 'Don't tell me you've got yourself a girlfriend?' he asked, laughing, but not unkindly. He thought the world of his young brother.

'Don't talk daft!' said Joe again. 'Course, I haven't, but she was real nice and friendly. I was carting their cases for them, see, to their lodgings, an' she told me she's a singer in the show. Then the boss man came up to me and asked if I'd take their props round to t'theatre, so I did. It's real posh inside, Dan, the Eastern Pavilion. You should see it! Well, you will, won't you, if you go with me. He gave me these tickets, see. They're for Monday night. I asked if we could have second house; you know, with us having to see to t'visitors' teas, and he said yes. And he gave me two for Mammy and Daddy as well. D'you think they'll go?'

'I don't see why not,' replied Dan. 'Go and ask Mammy; she's in the kitchen; well, they both are. I'll go with you, Joe, on Monday. I'm ready for a night out.'

'Aye, our mam's a slave-driver, isn't she?' said Joe. 'Making sure you study all t'time.'

'You could say that,' smiled Dan. 'But I don't mind...most of the time. Her heart's in the right place.'

Joe was relieved that his parents seemed pleased about the tickets as well.

'Well done, lad,' said Thomas Murphy. 'What a nice surprise. It's ages since we had a night out, isn't it, Anna? We'll look forward to that.'

'That's all very well,' said his wife, 'but what about the visitors you were supposed to be finding for us, Joe? A couple of tickets for a theatre won't put any money in our pockets.' Joe could see just a glint of annoyance in her green eyes.

'Aw, leave the lad alone,' said Thomas. 'I'm sure

he's done his best, haven't you, son? Sunday's not a good day; most of 'em arrive on a Saturday.'

'That's true,' said Anna, relenting a little. 'And maybe four couples are as many as we can manage this week. It'll break us in gently before the Easter weekend. We're pretty nearly full up then.'

'And I keep telling you, Anna, you've got to learn to walk before you can run,' said her husband. 'I think we're doing jolly well, considering we only took over here last back-end.'

'You're right, so you are.' Anna managed a grudging smile. 'Sure, the Lord's been good to us and I mustn't forget it. And thank you for the tickets, Joe,' she added, to his surprise. 'Yes, I expect we'll enjoy a night out, your Daddy and me. So long as you and Dan hold the fort for us.'

'Now, don't they always?' said Thomas. 'We couldn't have two better sons.'

'You're right,' said Anna again. 'Two grand lads, so they are.' Just so long as we toe the line, thought Joe, listening to the exchange of words between his parents. His father was always ready to stick up for them, but his mother was not quite so fulsome in her praise of himself and Dan. He shuddered to think of her reaction should one of them try to oppose her.

'That's her,' said Joe, nudging his brother as Madeleine Moon came onto the stage. 'That girl I was talking to; Maddy, she's called. She's pretty, isn't she?'

'Yes, very…' replied Daniel. He wasn't sure what he had expected. Some flibbertigibbet – as his mother might say – with brassy blonde hair and a cheeky grin. But this girl was not of that ilk at all. He leant forward in his seat to get a better view, although the seats were very good ones; five rows from the front and in the centre.

'Good evening, ladies and gentlemen,' she began. 'I would like to sing for you an old Irish song…' She nodded to the pianist at the side of the stage who played just one note. Then the girl began to sing, unaccompanied.

> *'I know where I'm goin'*
> *And I know who's goin' with me;*
> *I know who I love,*
> *But the dear knows who I'll marry…'*

Was she Irish? Daniel wondered. Her voice had a lovely lilting quality with just the trace of an accent that could be of Celtic origin; but maybe it was just her interpretation of the song. She was billed as 'Yorkshire's own songbird', and that was certainly true. There was not a murmur in the house as the audience listened, enraptured, to the sweet-toned lyrical melody ringing out across the rows of seats. She stood motionless, her hands clasped gently in front of her, a charming picture in her simple dress of cream-coloured silk and lace, which fell to her ankles, her golden hair, worn loose, waving softly almost to her shoulders.

There was a silence for a few seconds when she stopped singing, and then tumultuous applause. Dan and Joe clapped as loudly and enthusiastically as anyone.

'She's good, isn't she?' Joe nudged his brother again. 'It might've been better with the piano though, don't you think?'

'No, I don't.' Daniel shook his head. 'Not at all. Hush now...' He knew that this type of song, a traditional air, was meant for the voice alone, especially for such a thrilling voice as he had just heard. Now the girl, Madeleine, was going to sing again.

'And now for a complete contrast...' She smiled at the audience, and this time the pianist struck up with the strains of a song that they all knew.

'*In the twi-twi-twilight,*

Out in the beautiful twilight...' she began to sing.

As she said, it was a complete contrast to the previous song, but just as well received by the audience. She revealed in this number that she was not only a sweet and demure young girl, but that she had vitality and more than a spot of gaiety and humour. And Dan decided that she was not Irish; she most probably hailed from Yorkshire. She raised her hands, inviting the audience to join in with the second chorus.

'*...and many a grand little wedding is planned*
In the twi-twi-light.'

They sang with gusto, applauding wildly as the girl curtsied and tripped off the stage, then reappeared to take a final bow.

'That was good,' said Joe. 'I liked that song better than the first one. That was what she was like when she was talking to me, all happy and friendly.'

'Yes, she certainly does seem to be a...very nice sort of girl,' replied Dan. In point of fact he felt quite overwhelmed by his immediate attraction to her. He did not know her, of course. She was a stranger to him, an unknown girl who sang on the stage. But the moment he saw her, and especially when she started to sing, Daniel knew that he wanted to meet her and talk with her. Some quality in her had reached out to him in a way no young woman had ever done before. Indeed, he had never before allowed himself to be affected in this way.

'Fancy me knowing a girl like that,' Joe was saying. 'A real proper singer on t'stage. And them two funny fellers that were on before – you know, them that did "There's an 'ole in my bucket" – well, they were the ones that asked me to move their props.'

'Well, fancy that,' said Dan. 'Hush now; the next act's starting.'

It was a dancing duo, billed as Barney and Benjy; two men dressed in tight black trousers and red and white striped shirts, with flashing feet and wide grins revealing pearly-white teeth. He did not know which was which, Barney or Benjy, but one of them, the blonde one, he termed to himself as a 'pretty boy', whilst the other one was dark and more suave in appearance. Dan could not help but admire their expertise as their shiny patent-leather shoes darted in and out like lightning to the music of a fast staccato tune. Then came a slower dance to the strains of 'Lily of Laguna', which the men sang along to, inviting the audience to join in.

There was a lot of audience participation in the show, and Dan found he was joining in and enjoying himself as much as anyone. He and Joe agreed at the short interval that it was a first-class show, much better than he had expected as far as Daniel was concerned. Dan enjoyed all kinds of music and was saving up to buy a gramophone.

There had been some good singing: a baritone – 'That's the boss man, Percy Morgan,' Joe had whispered to him – singing 'Silver Threads among the Gold'; and Carlo and Queenie, the duettists singing 'The Old Rustic Bridge by the Mill', followed by 'None Shall Part Us From Each Other', a song from Gilbert and Sullivan's *Iolanthe*; quite expertly sung, although it was difficult to imagine them as a shepherd and shepherdess.

Susannah – now, there was a coquette if ever there was one – and her partner, Frank, sang a song about the honeysuckle and the bee, with flirtatious overtones; and Frank proved to be a good turn on the banjo and the concertina. Dan was surprised at how versatile they all seemed to be.

In the second half a woman called Nancy did an act with performing dogs. It was not entirely to Dan's taste as he did not like to see animals being exploited. On the other hand, the little dogs seemed contented enough, wagging their tails and appearing to grin, and he could not imagine anyone in this happy little troupe being anything other than kind and considerate; that was certainly the impression they gave.

When Madeleine Moon sang again, this time 'The Lark in the Clear Air', another Irish song, he was just as captivated as before. He could feel his brother's eyes upon him, and when he glanced at him there was a knowing grin on Joe's face. When she appeared at the finale with the rest of the troupe, Dan scarcely noticed anyone but Madeleine.

He was quiet at first as they walked home, along the promenade and then through the streets of the town, just saying 'yes' and 'no' in answer to his brother's chatter.

Joe gave a chuckle. 'You were quite smitten, weren't you, with that girl?'

'Which girl?' said Dan, putting on a show of innocence.

'You know very well which girl. Maddy – Madeleine Moon. She's what our daddy would call a bobby-dazzler, isn't she?'

'Yes, Joe, so she is. Although I don't think that is how I would describe her. She's...she's lovely,' Dan said simply, no longer able to feign indifference. 'Lovely to look at, and I'm sure she's a very nice person as well.'

'I know where she's lodging,' said Joe. 'I know which house it is in Albert Road. D'you want me to show you?'

'Oh no...no, I don't think so.'

'Ne'er mind what our mam says about keeping on with yer studying, or about anything else. You could go and see her – Maddy, I mean – and tell her how much you enjoyed the show. We could both go; she knows me, and I could introduce you, like.'

Dan smiled. 'No, thank you; I don't think so,' he replied. 'Anyway, what about you? You like her, don't you?'

'Yes, but she's too old for me,' said Joe. 'I reckon she's about eighteen or so; she might even be nineteen, same as you. Anyroad, I'm not all that used to girls.'

'Neither am I,' said Dan with a wry smile.

'No, but I don't see any reason why you can't be. I've told you; never mind what Mammy says. She's got a one-track mind where you're concerned.'

'Don't I know it!' said Dan. 'Just leave it, Joe. I don't think it's a very good idea to go running after her...or after any girl for that matter. But for heaven's sake, don't say anything to Mammy.'

'D'you think I'm stupid?' said Joe, laughing.

'No...' Dan sighed. 'But I think it might be best to leave things as they are.' Nevertheless, his brother's suggestion stayed with him.

After a few days had gone by, however, he had still not acted upon it. Joe did not say anything further; but Daniel, of course, had asked him to leave it alone and maybe his brother thought that he had decided the lovely girl he had seen on the stage was not for him. His parents, who went on the Tuesday evening, said they had enjoyed the show and how very good it was for a pier entertainment; but they did not comment on any individual act.

His mother was busy preparing for the Easter weekend. They were expecting the largest number of visitors they had entertained since they had taken over the boarding house last October. The guests would be arriving on Saturday, which was generally changeover day in the resort, although visitors who arrived on spec on other days usually managed to find accommodation. The beds of the departing guests would need to be changed, and all the bedrooms made spick and span to give the very best impression.

Daniel would not be working at the gents' outfitters on Friday, as it was Good Friday and all the stores were closed on that day. As well as assisting with the sales he was responsible for the bookkeeping and the ordering. Mr Jonas Grundy, the elderly gentleman who employed him and who owned the shop, would have been only too pleased to give him a full-time position, but he understood that Daniel, in time, would leave and move on to an entirely different career.

'So, on Friday he would be assisting his brother, preparing the house in readiness for what was officially the beginning of the spring season. There might, then, be a lull of a few weeks before the summer season began in earnest at the Whitsuntide weekend. His father might even lend a hand as well as he, too, would not be working on that Good Friday. Thomas Murphy was employed by a local building firm and did not often take much part in the running of the boarding house. That was almost solely his wife's concern. Soon after they had arrived in Blackpool, Anna, following the example of many of her fellow landladies, had put up a framed notice outside the front door. 'Mrs Anna Murphy, late of Liverpool and of Galway, welcomes guests from all regions.' That was a question of expediency, Anna's desire not to show discrimination. After all, Liverpool folk sometimes chose to go to Southport, and there might be only a few who would make the journey from Dublin, across the Irish Sea to the fishing port of Fleetwood, just north of Blackpool. Anyway, time would tell, and this would be their first full season.

Daniel was thoughtful as he walked along the promenade, near to the North Pier, on Thursday afternoon. He had finished his morning's work in the shop at one o'clock and was supposed to be on his way home. He had not been able to resist, however, taking a roundabout route, passing the pier entrance and seeing the name of the girl he admired on the poster: Madeleine Moon, Yorkshire's own songbird. What did he expect? he mused. It was not likely that she stayed near to the pier all day, and the first house did not start until five-thirty. He chided himself for being such a fool and kept on walking briskly. When he came opposite the Tower, approaching the spot where he could cross the tramtrack and make his way home, he stopped dead in his tracks.

He stared at the girl who was leaning against the railings, looking out across the expanse of sand towards the grey-blue sea. He wondered for a moment if his thoughts had conjured up a vision, or, more likely, if he was mistaken and the girl was just someone who bore a resemblance to Madeleine Moon. But as he continued to watch her from a distance of a few yards he realised that it was, indeed, the girl he had been longing to meet. Her golden hair was drawn back from her face and she wore a close-fitting little hat. She suddenly turned, as though aware of his glance, and looked at him. And then she gave a tentative smile, as though she recognised him…

Chapter Seven

Maddy turned round, suddenly aware that someone was staring at her. She gave a smile of recognition, stepping towards the young man. 'Joe...' she said. 'Fancy seeing you...' Then she stopped, putting her hand to her mouth in confusion because it wasn't Joe; just someone who looked very much like him, maybe a little older though.

'I'm sorry,' she went on. 'I mistook you for someone else, a young man I met the other day. I only saw him once and so...'

'And would that be Joe Murphy, by any chance?' asked the youth, smiling at her in a most friendly way.

'Yes...' she nodded, a little puzzled.

'Then I'm not surprised that you mistook me for him. Folks tell us we're very much alike. Joe's my brother, my younger brother; the only one I've got, in fact. And I'm Dan, Daniel Murphy.' He held out his hand. 'And I know that you are Madeleine Moon. I'm very pleased to meet you, Madeleine.'

She took hold of his outstretched hand, smiling back a little unsurely into his green eyes, which were shining with interest and good humour. 'Yes, I'm pleased to meet you too,' she said. 'But how did you know…? Oh yes, of course. You must have seen the show. Joe said he might take his brother along with him.'

'And so he did,' laughed Daniel. 'On Monday night. And a very good show it was, too. I must say how much I enjoyed your singing, Madeleine… You don't mind me calling you Madeleine, do you?'

'Of course not, but I'm usually called Maddy. That's what most people call me. But I decided I would be Madeleine when I'm on the stage. It sounds – well – more grown-up, more distinguished, sort of.'

'So it does,' agreed Daniel, with a more serious air. 'And I will call you Madeleine, if you don't mind. It's a lovely name. Do you mind if I join you for a little while? You're not meeting anybody, or doing anything special?' he enquired tentatively.

'No, not at all. I decided I'd have a couple of hours enjoying the sea breeze before the first house starts. That's at a quarter to six – five-forty-five, I suppose I should say – and the second house is at eight-thirty. But I don't mind if you join me.' She had decided that she liked the look of this young man. He had the same green eyes and dark gingerish hair as his younger brother, with an open, honest-looking face and an engaging smile; quite a handsome lad in a homely sort of way. But it was not just his looks that attracted her. She had felt at once that there was something about his personality that reached out to her, and she knew she would like to get to know him.

'You're certainly kept very busy,' Dan commented. 'Er...shall we walk on? Which way were you going?'

'Same way as you were, I suppose,' she replied. 'I thought I might walk as far as the next pier, Central Pier, isn't it? I haven't been that way before.'

'Have you eaten?' asked Dan. 'Your lunch, I mean, or do you call it dinner at midday? I know most northerners do, including my family since we came to live here.'

'Yes, I've had my dinner,' she laughed. 'I'm a true Yorkshire lass – dinner at dinner time, tea at teatime. As a matter of fact, Mrs Jolly, our landlady, makes us a cooked meal at quarter past twelve, so it has time to settle before we go on the stage. Then we might have a sandwich later, sometimes between the first and second house. What about you? Have you eaten, Dan?'

'Yes, I took a sandwich with me and ate it before I left the shop.' She looked at him enquiringly. 'Oh, of course you don't know do you?' he continued. 'I work part-time at a gents' outfitters on Church Street, and the rest of the time – well, some of it – I help my mother in the boarding house.'

'Yes, Joe told me about that. Adelaide Street, isn't it, the next street to where we're staying? So...were you on your way home?'

'In a roundabout way. I try to get an hour or so

to myself in the afternoon, and we're not very busy this week. It's on Saturday that we will start in earnest, for Easter week. Then we'll be rushed off our feet; Mammy will be at any rate, and our Joe, but I just help out part-time. We serve a cooked breakfast, midday dinner and then 'high tea' at five-thirty. It will be Mammy's first full season. We only moved here last back-end, and I guess she'll have to get some extra help for the summer season – a chambermaid and a waitress maybe.'

'Yes, the visitors certainly get good value for money in Blackpool,' Maddy commented. Walking along Albert Road each afternoon, on her way to the pier for the first house, she had seen the tables near the windows all laid ready for 'high tea'. There was usually a three-tiered cake-stand with a silver handle, the bottom plate holding white bread and butter cut in triangular pieces, the middle plate buttered scones, and the top plate an assortment of cakes, known as 'fancies'. Sometimes the meal would be ready and waiting on the plates; a slice of boiled ham or tongue, with lettuce, tomato and cucumber at the side, with the cruet, a jar of salad cream and a jar of pickled onions in the centre of the table.

'I'm sure they get good value in Scarborough as well,' she added. 'That's where I come from. But I've never had anything to do with the boarding house trade. My father has a very different sort of business,' she added with a wry grin, determined to be truthful about it.

'Oh, and what is that?' enquired Dan. 'May I ask?'

'Yes; he's an undertaker,' replied Maddy. 'It's a family business. My grandfather, my dad and my brother, they run it. And we have a shop as well. We sell clothes for funerals and for all sorts of other occasions. My stepmother is in charge of that.'

'I see,' said Daniel. 'And what about you then, Madeleine? You left Scarborough to go on the stage, did you?'

'Yes, two years ago...' She told him about the Pierrot shows where she had started singing, and how her father had allowed her to join the travelling company when she was fifteen.

Dan looked at her in some surprise. 'So you are...how old? Seventeen?'

'I'll be seventeen in June,' she replied. 'Why? You look surprised.'

'I thought you might have been...eighteen, perhaps. But it doesn't matter, does it?' He grinned at her. 'And I will be twenty next September.' He hesitated a little before continuing and she thought he looked at her a little regretfully. 'I might be going to college then. At least...well, that's the idea at the moment.'

'What for?' asked Maddy. 'I mean...what will you be doing at college? Are you going to be a teacher?'

'Sort of...' He nodded. 'Yes, that's right – a teacher. But I'm not terribly sure about it, you see.

I'm quite happy where I am, or I've been thinking about getting a job in an estate agent's office and working up from there. The...er...teaching, that's really my mother's idea.'

'But surely you should be able to choose your own job, your own...career?' said Maddy. 'Oh, I'm sorry,' she went on when he did not answer. 'That was rather rude of me, wasn't it?'

'No, of course it wasn't,' replied Dan. 'You are quite right. But it's rather complicated. Let's not think about it at the moment, eh? Tell me some more about yourself, Madeleine.'

'I don't know what there is to tell really,' she said. She felt, suddenly, a little shy, as she saw the warmth shining in Dan's eyes as he smiled at her. 'I'm just an ordinary sort of girl who is lucky enough to be earning a living doing what I love best, and that is singing.'

'I don't think you are an ordinary girl,' replied Dan. 'Far from it; and you certainly have an extraordinary voice. Did you have singing lessons? Somehow I don't think you did,' he went on, answering his own question. 'Your voice has such a clear, unaffected tone, so perfectly natural.'

'Thank you for the compliment,' smiled Maddy. 'You're quite right. I've never had singing lessons, but I did learn to play the piano, after a fashion, and so I do understand the – what do they call it? – the rudiments of music, and that has helped me a lot. And I used to sing in the chapel choir at home before I started with the Melody Makers. Not a proper choir; just a few men and women – all of the others were older than me – who like to sing. Methodists love a good sing,' she laughed.

He was looking at her keenly, a little oddly, she thought. 'You are a Methodist then?' he asked.

'Well, yes, sort of,' she replied. 'That's what my family are, Methodists. A lot of folk in Scarborough are. My grandfather's always telling us how the great John Wesley used to preach there, not very far from where our undertaker's yard is. He doesn't remember him, of course; it's ages ago. But his own grandfather used to listen to him, to John Wesley, and so it's become a family tradition to attend the Methodist Chapel.'

'Yes, I see,' said Dan, nodding thoughtfully.

'What about you?' asked Maddy. 'I take it that you're not...?'

'No.' He shook his head. 'I'm not a Methodist. But I do go to church, a different sort of church, though.'

'That's all that matters then,' replied Maddy. 'My grandad says it doesn't matter where you worship – that's what he always calls it, worship – because we're all heading for the same place and following the same God.'

'A very sensible way of looking at it,' replied Daniel. 'Would that everyone saw it that way...' he added quietly, almost to himself.

'I've never really thought much about it to be

honest,' said Maddy. 'Not to worry about it, at any rate. My father sometimes goes to the Church of England now because that's where my stepmother likes to go. And my grandad, well, he's not narrow-minded like some of 'em are. He said he signed the pledge when he was a lad – they were all forced to by their parents – but he likes a drink of beer now and again. And I'm afraid I haven't been to chapel for ages because we're usually travelling on a Sunday. I expect I shall go on this Sunday though, on Easter Sunday. I noticed there's a chapel near to Central Station…'

'Oh look, there's a Punch and Judy show,' she called out, noticing the red and white striped box on the sands below them. 'That reminds me of home. I loved watching Punch and Judy when I was a little girl, when I wasn't watching the Pierrot shows, of course.'

They stopped, leaning against the iron railings, looking out across the wide expanse of sand. 'Seven golden miles' was Blackpool's boast regarding the length of its beach, and certainly, looking northwards and southwards, it did seem to go on for ever. The tide was well out but the beach on this Thursday afternoon before the Easter weekend was not at all crowded. A few children and adults were clustered in front of the Punch and Judy booth. It was fairly near to the sea wall and Maddy could make out the writing on the front of the box, 'Prof J Green, est. 1880'.

She read the words out loud. 'An old Blackpool family, I suppose,' she commented. 'It's the same in Scarborough. The Punch and Judy men are very proud of their heritage.'

'Yes, I believe so,' replied Dan. 'We haven't been here very long, as I told you, but our next-door neighbours have always lived here and they've told us a good deal about Blackpool's history. The Green family, apparently, was a famous circus and music hall family at one time.'

'Look at Dog Toby,' said Maddy, 'sitting there so patiently. He must be very well trained.' The white dog with brown patches on his back and brown ears, and with a red and white ruffle round his neck, was sitting motionless, whilst near to him Mister Punch was banging around with his stick and calling out in his squeaky nasal voice, 'That's the way to do it...'

It was rather a dull day with a fitful sun doing its best to shine, and there was a stiff breeze. A group of three donkeys was standing forlornly near by, their heads bowed and their bells jingling softly in the breeze as they waited for customers.

'You should see this stretch of beach at the height of the season,' observed Dan. 'It gets so crowded you can scarcely find room for a deckchair or a towel. We came here a couple of times last summer, before my parents actually bought the boarding house, and I was amazed at the number of folk on the sands. The donkeys have their run, usually nearer to the sea, but nearer to the prom and the sea wall you can hardly move for the crowds. It's the herd instinct, I suppose. Some people feel happier when they're in a crowd. I prefer a bit of solitude sometimes, or the company of just one other person.' He turned to look at her and she nodded.

'Me too,' she said quietly, 'some of the time.'

There were a few brave souls sitting on deckchairs and some even braver ones paddling at the edge of the sea; men with their trousers rolled up to their knees and women with their skirts held high, holding a little child by the hand. But they didn't linger for more than a few moments.

'Let's walk as far as Central Pier, shall we?' said Daniel. 'Then we can cross over and walk back along the other side of the prom.'

Central Pier, the middle one of Blackpool's three piers, looked pretty similar to the North Pier from the frontage. But whilst the North Pier boasted two entertainment pavilions, the Central Pier had a large area devoted to open-air dancing or, alternatively, roller skating. A poster outside the pier entrance stated that the Blackpool Steamboat Company Ltd had daily excursions to Douglas, Llandudno, Bangor, Liverpool, Southport, and Morecambe, on their fine saloon steamers, the *Queen of the North*, the *Bickerstaffe* and the *Wellington*. And there was the *Bickerstaffe*, moored near to the jetty.

'That's another old Blackpool family,' Dan told

her. 'John Bickerstaffe was the first chairman of the Blackpool Tower Company, so I believe.'

'I would love to go for a sail,' said Maddy, just a little regretfully. 'I noticed that there are steamboat sailings from the North Pier as well. But I'm not on holiday, am I?' She gave a shrug and laughed. 'I'm here to provide the entertainment – well, some of it – not to be entertained.'

'Never mind,' said Dan. 'There's always another time. Perhaps, sometime, you might be able to have a holiday here, who knows?'

'Who knows?' she echoed, and they smiled a little shyly at one another.

'But you do have some free time, don't you?' asked Dan. 'When you're not on the stage... I would love to show you some of the other parts of the town. That is, if you would like me to?'

'Yes...yes, I would. Thank you very much.' She nodded, but not as eagerly as she might have done. She was, in truth, delighted at the prospect, but she had only just met this young man and she knew it would not be seemly to appear too enthusiastic.

'But aren't you busy as well,' she enquired, 'with your job in the shop and the boarding house? You said it would be a busy week.'

'Ye-es, but I am allowed a little time to myself, at this time of the day, for instance. Sometimes I go to the library to study for a couple of hours, but you know what they say about all work and no play?' He gave a sudden grin. 'And what the eye doesn't see the heart doesn't grieve about – that's another good old cliché – and I doubt if Mammy will be any the wiser.'

'Oh dear!' Maddy laughed, looking at him quizzically. 'I don't want to be responsible for you neglecting your studies. I wouldn't want you to get into trouble with your…er…mother.'

'Don't worry, I won't,' he replied. 'I noticed that you smiled before when I referred to her as Mammy,' he went on. 'I know it sounds a little odd to some people, but it's because we're Irish, you see. Well, my mother is, so that makes me half Irish; but my brother and I were born in Liverpool.'

'I'm sorry,' said Maddy. 'I didn't mean to offend you.'

'You didn't,' he assured her. 'It's what she's always liked to be called, and so it's what we've got used to, Joe and me.'

'I shouldn't have smiled though; it was tactless of me. But it did sound a little strange. In Yorkshire, and in Lancashire too, we usually say "me mam". But I've been trying to speak more…"proper like",' she laughed, 'since I went on the stage.'

'Come along,' said Dan, holding her elbow and guiding her towards the tramtrack. They waited whilst a huge Dreadnought tram trundled past, and then waited again at the kerbside, which separated the tramtrack from the road, for a couple of motor cars and a horse-drawn landau to pass by.

'My mother was from Galway originally,' Dan

continued as they started to walk back northwards. 'Her family – quite a large family – moved "across the water", as they call it, when she was a little girl, and they settled in Liverpool, like a lot of Irish folk do. That was where she met my father, eventually.'

'And does your father help to run the boarding house along with your mother?' Maddy asked.

'Oh no, Daddy's a builder,' replied Dan. 'He got a job as foreman with a local firm soon after we arrived here. It was Mammy who was hankering after moving here and running a guest house, and Daddy gave in to her. People usually do,' he added. 'She's a very strong-willed woman.'

'It's usually the women who run the boarding houses, isn't it?' said Maddy. 'Where we're staying Mrs Jolly is in charge, and Mr Jolly has a job as a joiner. He just helps out now and again.'

'Yes, that's generally the way of it,' replied Dan. 'This area here…' he pointed to the right-hand side of him, 'it is what you might call the – er – not quite so salubrious part of Blackpool.' The long gardens of the houses, it appeared, had been taken over by stalls of different kinds. 'They used to call this part South Beach,' he continued, 'but now folks are starting to refer to it as the "Golden Mile".'

Maddy stared, fascinated, at the various booths and stalls they were passing. Stalls selling rock, oysters, ice cream, or mugs and cans of strong tea; 'Quack' doctors proclaiming the efficacy of pills to cure all ailments, and hair restorer which would make hair grow on the baldest of scalps. There were sideshows where skittles were knocked over, hoopla games, and coconut shies, and a gaudy tent in which sat a fortune-teller.

'Apparently a lot of these stalls used to operate on the sands,' Dan told her, 'but then the Town Council stepped in and made it illegal, so now they've all moved over here. With the consent of the house owners, no doubt, but it is becoming the more seamy side of Blackpool. Another day we could walk further north, perhaps, towards the cliffs at Bispham?'

'Yes, that would be very nice,' agreed Maddy. She was looking forward already to meeting Daniel Murphy again, but a niggling thought had come into her mind. She hoped that his mother – his 'mammy' – would not step in and spoil her son's plans. She sounded a real tyrant if ever there was one!

The Golden Mile ended near to Central Station, and it was there that they turned off the promenade to make their way back to the boarding house area of central Blackpool. Maddy needed to collect her thoughts and to have a rest before setting out again for their first-house performance. Daniel walked with her to the house on Albert Road, where they said goodbye.

'Until Sunday then,' he said. 'If I pull my weight on Friday and Saturday, then Mammy can't object to me taking an hour or two off on Sunday. Our shop – Mr Grundy's shop, I should say – is closed for Good Friday, so I will be able to spend more time at home. And you have a matinée performance on Saturday, don't you, Maddy?'

'I'm afraid so,' she replied, 'but only one house in the evening.'

He took hold of her hand and held it for a moment. 'Till Sunday then,' he said quietly. 'I'll be waiting by this gate at half past two. Goodbye, Maddy. It's been lovely meeting you, and I've enjoyed our time together.'

'Me too,' she said, as he gave her hand a gentle squeeze, then quickly walked away.

He was there, waiting, as he had promised, at two-thirty on Sunday afternoon. Maddy had tried to warn herself not to be disappointed if he did not turn up. She had a funny feeling, somehow, about that mother of his. But there he was, and she felt her heart give a leap and a broad smile spread over her face at the sight of him.

'Madeleine…' He took hold of both her hands, his green eyes looking intently into her own. 'I've been looking forward so much to seeing you again.'

'Yes…so have I,' she murmured.

'Come along then, let's go.' He crooked his elbow and she, a trifle hesitantly, tucked her hand inside it. He was a few inches taller than herself, though by no means a very tall young man; five foot seven or so, with a jaunty spring to his step that matched well with her own.

'You managed to get away without any trouble, did you?' Maddy enquired. 'You've done your duty at home?'

'Yes, in more ways than one,' replied Daniel. 'I helped with the breakfasts, and with the midday meal, and in between I managed to go to Mass...to church,' he added, as if correcting himself.

Maddy, however, had already come to the conclusion that Dan must be a Catholic, a Roman Catholic, to be more precise. Her grandfather had told her that the word 'catholic' meant broad or wide-spreading, and that the term 'the Catholic Church' really meant the worldwide church and did not just refer to those people who called themselves Catholics. There were, indeed, some members of the Church of England who called themselves Anglo-Catholics, so it was all very confusing. With regard to Daniel though, everything had pointed to it. His mother was Irish, from a large family, and probably his father's family was from Ireland too, way back, as they had an Irish name; she had heard that there were many of that faith in Liverpool. It did not matter to Maddy though; it did not matter two hoots what religion he was; but she guessed that it might matter a great deal to that mother of his if she were to discover that her son was hobnobbing with a Methodist. 'Mammy', no doubt, was looking forward to the time when her son would be teaching in a Roman Catholic school. All these thoughts had been running through her mind since Thursday, when she had first met Dan, and so his admission had come as no surprise to her.

'Yes, I realised you were probably a Catholic,' she said now, in quite a matter-of-fact way. 'Which church do you attend?'

'The Church of the Sacred Heart on Talbot Road,' he told her. 'It's a very beautiful church; it was designed by the famous architect, Pugin.'

Maddy nodded, although she had never heard of him. 'I've been to church too,' she said. 'Well, chapel, I should say. I went to the one near Central Station. It's called the Central Methodist Chapel, not very original, but it's a very friendly welcoming place. They sang some of my favourite hymns and I took Communion as well. So I feel much better, sort of, inside myself.'

'And that is how you should feel.' Dan smiled at her, pressing her arm a little closer to his own. 'I have been thinking quite a lot about what your grandfather said, Madeleine. You told me, you remember, how he said we were all serving the same God? And he is quite right. I believe there is far too much dissension between folks who call themselves Christians…

'Anyway, let's not worry ourselves about that at the moment. Where shall we go? Have you any ideas?'

'Northwards, you said, didn't you? I haven't seen very much of Blackpool yet, apart from the town itself and the area around the North Pier,' said

Maddy. 'Nor have I ridden on a tram. I must do that sometime before we move on.'

'And that will be next Sunday, I suppose?'

'Yes, that's right. We'll be off to the inland towns of Lancashire. A week in Wigan, then Burnley and Bolton, before we go back to Yorkshire. And then, at the end of May, we'll be starting our summer season in Scarborough. We'll all become Pierrots again then,' she laughed.

'I would love to see that,' said Dan. 'I shall have to see if I can sneak away for a day, or a couple of days...' He sounded doubtful though. 'Anyway, we've got a week, haven't we, to acquaint ourselves with the delights of Blackpool, before you go? There's a lot I haven't seen myself yet; I'm still what you might call a newcomer. So...let's head off for the cliffs. Are you ready for a good walk?'

'Yes, of course,' agreed Maddy. The sun was shining and the clouds riding high in the sky boded no threat of rain. There was a fresh breeze, which she had come to realise was almost always present in Blackpool, especially on the seafront. 'God's in His heaven, all's right with the world.' The words of a poem she had learnt at school came into her mind as she strode along briskly at Daniel's side, but she kept her thoughts hidden away. All was well, though; all was very much right in her little world at that moment.

They headed for the promenade, passing the North Pier which had become very familiar to

Maddy during the past week. To the north of the pier a good deal of work had been done, widening the promenade area and strengthening the sea defences. The Hotel Metropole, an impressive red brick building with turrets and balconies, stood in solitary splendour, the only hotel to have been built on the sea side of the promenade.

'That's one of the oldest hotels in Blackpool,' Dan told her. 'It was called "Bailey's" at one time and it's been there since the mid eighteenth century.'

'Mmm, fancy that,' said Maddy, knowing she must try to show that she was impressed or, at least, interested, which, of course she was. She could have told him, though, that Scarborough's history went back much further than that. It had been a popular spa resort since the seventeenth century; and many moons before that Richard the Third was said to have stayed there – in the public house which was now known as King Richard the Third's House – when he was not in residence at Scarborough Castle. But she did not say any of this.

They passed many large hotels, in particular the magnificent Imperial Hydropathic Hotel, although Maddy felt that they could not compete with the famous Grand Hotel at Scarborough.

Their walk took them along what was called the Middle Walk, a wide promenading area built below the level of the road and the tramtrack. Further down was the Lower Walk, where a strong sea wall had been constructed to keep the tide at bay. But this did not stop the waves cascading over when there was a particularly high tide, drenching everything and everybody in close proximity. It would have been thought that the stormy weather would not be agreeable to visitors, but there were some, so Dan told Maddy, who came especially to view the raging sea. Indeed, one of the postcards she had bought to send to the folks at home in Scarborough was of a 'Stormy sea at Blackpool'.

The sea was relatively calm though, on that sunny Sunday afternoon. The tide was in and they could hear the waves beating against the sea wall, but it was a pleasant sound, accompanied by the cries of the seagulls wheeling high above them. Blackpool was justly proud of its three-tiered promenade, and also of its cliffs at the north end of the resort, which were completely man-made. They had turned off the main promenade onto the cliff path, which was becoming gradually steeper as they climbed.

'I found it hard to believe at first that these cliffs were the handiwork of man,' said Dan, '...and not of God,' he added. 'But I suppose the whole of Blackpool is a tribute to man's ingenuity. I must admit that there is no natural beauty here, apart from the sea and the golden sand, of course. Blackpool, in its early days, must have been very flat and featureless. I've never been to Scarborough, only seen pictures of it, but I should imagine it had a head start as a resort, didn't it, with regard to the contours of the land?'

'I hadn't really thought about it,' replied Maddy. 'But yes, of course you are right.' She had, in fact, been comparing in her mind the two resorts. She reflected on the appeal of her own hometown with its two magnificent bays, one on either side of the headland, and its attractive woodland walks and gardens that had been constructed on the cliff sides to the south of the resort. Compared with all that scenic beauty, Blackpool seemed stark and bare. A mass of concrete and red brick, and she had been struck by the absence of trees near the seafront. Maybe the fierce winds would have destroyed them, but the trees in Scarborough had managed to survive the gales.

'Yes, Scarborough is lovely,' she said, 'but then I would say that, wouldn't I? I'm sure to be prejudiced. I find it rather confusing. We're walking northwards, but in Scarborough, with the sea on our left, we'd be walking south.' She laughed. 'I know it's because we're right at the other side of the country here, as far west as we can go...but my sense of direction was never very good.'

'Well, I'm here to guide you,' smiled Dan. 'And if you look back you must admit it's a magnificent view.'

And so it was. Far away in the distance the tall structure of the Tower pointed to the sky; to the left of it stood the Palace building, the Big Wheel silhouetted on the skyline, and a long long row of hotels and boarding houses facing onto the promenade. The sea, catching the rays of the sun, was a shining sheet of silver, shifting and shimmering with the movement of the breeze. Maddy, comparing it with the view of Scarborough she had seen so often – the sweep of the South Bay, the fishing boats in the harbour and the ruined castle perched high on the clifftop – realised that Blackpool, although it was so different, had a grandeur that was all its own.

'Yes…it is magnificent,' she breathed. 'In its own way, it's quite beautiful.'

Dan gently put his arm around her shoulders as they stood there taking in the view, and they looked at one another and smiled. It seemed natural, then, to hold hands as they continued their walk.

'You say these cliffs are entirely man-made?' asked Maddy.

'So I've been told,' replied Dan. 'They're made from massive boulders of rock encased in clay, but they're not indestructible. They are gradually eroding, being worn away by the tide. See the building up there on the top of the cliff? That's Uncle Tom's Cabin.'

'Yes, I've heard of it,' said Maddy. 'It's a popular place for entertainment, isn't it?'

'So it was, but it won't be for much longer,' said Dan. 'See how near the cliff edge it is? In fact, very soon it will have to be closed down and the buildings demolished, before the sea puts paid to it altogether. It used to be a popular place for dancing and there's a good refreshment room.' One or two people could be seen sitting at tables or walking around the site.

'What a pity,' said Maddy. 'You've been dancing there, I suppose, Dan?'

'No…actually, I'm not much of a dancer,' he replied. 'Look up on the roof, Madeleine.' He seemed anxious to change the subject. 'Those wooden statues are Uncle Tom, Little Eva and Topsy, from the book *Uncle Tom's Cabin*.'

'Yes, I've heard of it,' Maddy nodded. 'It was written by a lady called Harriet Beecher Stowe, and it's about the slave trade.' She wanted Dan to know that, even though she had left school at thirteen, she was not unintelligent or uneducated. She was somewhat fazed by the knowledge that he would be going to college to train as a teacher…although he didn't seem very keen on the idea. She liked him, though, she liked him a lot, and she guessed that he liked her too.

'Come along then,' he said. 'Let's go and have a closer look at them, and I think we deserve a cup of tea after all that walking.'

As they sat on the wooden bench, near to the railings which separated the café grounds from the clifftop path, it was not hard to imagine that, quite soon, the whole structure might well go crashing down into the sea. The waves pounding against the bottom of the cliff looked perilously close. The drink of tea refreshed them, but Dan decided that they would ride the couple of miles back to town on a tramcar. They made for the nearest stop and boarded a huge cream and green Dreadnought tram. It was a double-decker and Maddy insisted on going upstairs to have a better view.

She found the ride exciting although she had ridden on tramcars before, in Scarborough, and in Leeds and Bradford. It was the pleasant company, though, on that Sunday afternoon, and the blissful freedom of the day that were causing her to feel so light-hearted and so dazed with happiness. She loved everything about it, as though she were a little girl again: the clanging of the wheels against the iron rails, the 'ting-ting' of the bell, and the occasional 'toot-toot' of the hooter when pedestrians wandered too near to the track, as visitors to the resort were inclined to do.

They alighted near to Central Station, the stop nearest to Dan's home and Maddy's lodgings. He had to be back to assist with the visitors' teas, and Maddy, too, was expected to return, although the day was their own to do with as they liked. She was sad that the afternoon was coming to an end, and hoping against hope that Dan would ask to see her again.

She was surprised, though, as they stood at the gate, to hear him say, 'Would you like to come out again this evening, Madeleine?'

'This evening?' she repeated. 'Well, yes, of course I would but...'

'But what?' He raised his eyebrows in a question.

'Well, I was wondering about you. It's my day off, but won't you be needed to help with the suppers?'

'Oh, I'll have a word with my brother,' said Dan. 'He's a very obliging lad, and he knows how to keep mum when needs be. He'll cover for me.'

'All right then,' agreed Maddy. 'Yes...I'd love to.'

'Seven o'clock then,' said Dan. He leant forward and kissed her cheek. 'Goodbye, Madeleine, till then. And thank you for a lovely afternoon.'

'Thank you, too,' she replied. As she watched him walk away she felt that it was all so very unreal. When was she going to wake up? she wondered.

But it was no dream. The rest of the company had noticed her absence, and Susannah and Nancy were quick to remark on it. 'I've been for a walk on the cliffs with a young man,' she told them. 'We met by chance, and he recognised me from the show. He's Joe's brother; you know, the lad who helped us with the props when we arrived. And...I'm seeing him again tonight,' she added, making up her mind to be truthful about it.

'Mmm...' Nancy looked at her seriously before saying, 'You're a sensible girl, though, aren't you, Maddy?'

'Of course she is,' said Susannah, giving her a sly wink. 'You enjoy yourself, love.' They exchanged meaningful glances. After their tête-à-tête in

Roundhay Park, Susannah had learnt enough about Maddy to trust that she could take care of herself. And Maddy recalled Susannah's remark that she would meet quite a few young men before she met the right one. She wondered, though, about that. Already it seemed as though Daniel was...rather special.

Chapter Eight

'I want to show you one of the most wonderful sights to be seen anywhere in the world,' said Dan as they walked along Albert Road. 'Well, that might be a slight exaggeration, but certainly one of the most wonderful sights in the country.'

'In Blackpool?' queried Maddy.

'Yes, right here in Blackpool,' said Dan, grinning at her. 'Just you wait and see.'

On reaching the promenade, they crossed the road and the tramtrack and stood by the railings opposite the Tower, in almost the same spot where Dan had been standing when they had met for the first time on Thursday, three days ago. Could it really be only three days? Maddy pondered. She felt as though she had known Dan for ages.

It had been a fine day, not overwarm, but the sun had shone all the time, and now it was beginning to set in a slow descent over the sea. And as they gazed across the sand to the silver-blue expanse of the ocean, Maddy realised what Dan had meant. Never had she seen a more glorious sunset. Earlier in the day the sea had looked grey and choppy, but now the wind had died down and all was calm. As the sun's rays caught the slight movement of the waves, the shimmering sheet of turquoise blue was set ablaze with a million golden coins dancing on the surface. The sky was a glory of darkening blue streaked with rose, orange and vermilion and each cloud was rimmed with gold.

'Yes, I see what you mean,' said Maddy, in a quiet voice because she was awestruck. 'It's…so beautiful.'

'And unique to the west coast,' said Dan. 'I've watched the sun setting over the hills and rooftops in other places. It's always beautiful, but the sea adds that extra touch of wonder. I come to see it from time to time when I'm able. I find it so very restful and soothing.'

Maddy nodded silently. God's in His heaven, all's right with the world… The words came into her mind again. But what she said was, 'This can't happen in Scarborough, can it? Over on the east coast the sun sets over the land, doesn't it?' It was something she hadn't considered before.

'Yes,' agreed Daniel. 'So it does. But it rises over the sea, and I'm sure that must be just as beautiful a sight. Don't tell me you've never been up early enough to see it?' he laughed.

'I'm afraid not,' smiled Maddy, 'but maybe I will, one of these days.' She felt Dan's arm steal around her shoulders as they stood there, not speaking, for several moments. And it felt so very right and natural.

They both seemed to know without mentioning

it that they must not stay out too late. As they strolled along the promenade the sky grew darker and the electric lights came on over the tramtrack and road. They found a solitary café open in the town where they drank tea and held hands across the table. She told him about Jessie with whom she had been best friends long before her father had married Jessie's mother. And about the twins and Aunty Faith, her father and Grandad Isaac. And then, because Dan seemed so very interested in everything, about some of the other members of the concert party. And in exchange Daniel told her…really very little.

She did not wonder if he would ask to see her again because she knew it was inevitable. As they said goodnight at her gate he held her shoulders and kissed her, very gently, on the lips.

What Maddy did not know was that it was the first time ever that Daniel Murphy had kissed a girl. He could not quite comprehend what was happening to him. He had never felt anything like this before. He was happy – he could not remember ever feeling so happy – but it was more than that. There was a feeling of rightness about it. He had been experiencing doubts about his future for quite some time, and now, meeting Maddy was forcing him to come to a decision. There was no doubt in his mind that he wanted to go on seeing her. And he also knew that very soon he must tell her the truth about himself.

His mother had not questioned him about where he had been that afternoon and she did not enquire about the evening either. She appeared preoccupied and scarcely spoke to him at all.

Maddy and Dan continued to enjoy one another's company over the following days. They walked to the end of the North Pier, rode on the Big Wheel and, on a rainy afternoon, they visited the various delights of the Tower buildings.

'I've heard tell that John Bickerstaffe – he's the chairman of the Tower Company – that he prays for rain,' Dan told Maddy, 'because then all the visitors flock to the Tower.'

There was certainly plenty to see. On the ground floor was the Aquarium, an eerie place with limestone pillars and dim lighting, where strange and exotic fish swam around in glass tanks bathed in a greenish glow. Upstairs was the Menagerie which housed lions, tigers, monkeys and a noisy hyena, as well as producing a very strong and malodorous smell. By contrast, the roof gardens were a source of pleasure with cool shady corners where you could sit and marvel at the palm trees, vines, and plants of every kind and colour, to the accompaniment of orchestral music. On the same floor was 'Ye Olde English Village' where you could buy souvenirs to take home; and from this floor, too, was the lift that ascended to the top of the Tower.

Dan persuaded Maddy that this was something

they really must do and so, despite her trepidation, she agreed. She had already had a ride on the Big Wheel, and that had turned out to be not so scary as she had imagined, but the Tower was much higher. The glassed-in viewing platform, however, was not at the very top and afforded stupendous views in all directions. They could see across to the hills of Barrow and the Lake District in the north, south to the resort of Southport across the Ribble estuary, and along the stretch of the Fylde coastline, from Lytham St Annes to Fleetwood.

Before they left the building they took a peep into the ballroom, which had been described as the finest in Europe. 'Gosh!' exclaimed Maddy. 'It takes your breath away, doesn't it?'

From the wooden floor, inlaid with a pattern of mahogany, oak and walnut blocks, up to the frescoed ceiling, which had been painted by talented artists of the day, the ballroom was a magnificent sight. It was surrounded by roomy balconies with red velvet seating, supported by massive marble pillars. A few couples were dancing to the strains of a light orchestra, but it would be at night that the place truly came alive. Maddy wished that she might see it. Maybe she would, sometime; but her two weeks in Blackpool were already turning out to be far more wonderful than she could ever have imagined.

The rain had stopped so they stood in a now familiar spot near to the promenade railings. It was

Friday afternoon. They both knew that their time together would soon come to an end. Maddy had a matinée performance on Saturday afternoon followed by one at seven-thirty in the evening. And on Sunday the Melody Makers would be off on their travels again.

'Madeleine,' Daniel began, putting his arm around her shoulders, 'you know how much I have enjoyed being with you over this past week, don't you?'

She nodded, breathing an almost inaudible, 'Yes...'

'And I do so hope that we might be able to go on seeing one another...'

She nodded again. 'Yes, and I hope so too, Dan,' she said softly.

'But there is something that I have to tell you,' he continued. 'I'm afraid I haven't been entirely honest with you...'

'Oh?' she queried. She could see the shadow of uncertainty in his eyes, and she felt the first faint stab of apprehension.

'You remember how I told you that I might be going to college, sometime soon, and you assumed that I would be training to become a teacher?'

'Yes, that's right.'

'And that is what I let you go on believing. But the truth is...I should say the idea was...that I should train to become...a Catholic priest.'

She gave an involuntary gasp as she drew a step

away from him. She felt the colour drain from her face and all she could do was utter an incredulous, 'What…? No…!'

He shook his head. 'But I'm not going to do it, Madeleine. I'd been having doubts, and I know now that it was never what I really wanted to do. Not with all my heart and soul…'

'But you mean…because of me?' She stopped then, aware that what she was about to say might sound very presumptuous, very conceited of her to suggest that she could have had any bearing on his decision. She was only seventeen – well, nearly – and although she knew already that she was growing very fond of him, and she had even wondered if there might be a future for them together, it was still far too soon. They had known one another for only a short time, and now Dan was considering turning his life around completely. She shook her head. 'No, of course it isn't because of me,' she went on, 'and I wouldn't want it to be. But I wish you had told me…'

She had drawn away from him, but he stepped nearer to her again, placing his hand over hers as it lay on the railing. 'Yes, it is partly because of you, Madeleine. It must be, don't you see? Meeting you has made me realise all the more that I don't want to take that enormous step. If I'd told you the truth straight away, you wouldn't have gone on seeing me, would you?' She could not answer. 'And I would have felt that I was doing something wrong.

I knew as soon as I met you that I wanted to see you again like…like any ordinary lad wants to go on seeing a girl he's met. And it's not wrong to want that. As I said, I'd been having grave doubts, and this – meeting you – was the catalyst, you might say, that made me realise I was heading in the wrong direction. It was never entirely my idea, you know, to become a priest. Well, if I'm honest, it wasn't my idea at all. It was Mammy…er…my mother.'

'Yes…your mother,' breathed Maddy. 'And what is she going to say when you tell her you've changed your mind?'

'I've already told her,' said Daniel.

Indeed, it had been a stormy encounter. He had known the previous evening that it was time he had a frank discussion with his mother. Not about Madeleine; there would be time enough later for her to know about that. But he must tell her about his change of heart, the decision he had arrived at that the priesthood was not for him. He was a devout Catholic, although he preferred to think of himself as a Christian and not first and foremost as a Catholic; and there were other ways in which he could serve God and lead an honest and virtuous life.

He decided to speak to his mother as soon as the family meal was over and the dishes had been washed and put away. It was the usual procedure for the family to dine after the visitors, then they had a short respite before starting on the job of resetting the tables, in part, for breakfast the following morning.

Dan was thankful that his father had gone into the backyard, as he often did of an evening, to have a smoke of his pipe and a time of quiet contemplation. And Joe was chatting by the front gate to the waitress-cum-chambermaid, a young girl by the name of Myrtle, whom they had engaged only that week. Dan had never seen his brother so animated before in the company of a girl.

'Could I have a word with you, Mammy?' he said. 'Just you and me at the moment, although I shall talk to Daddy and Joe later. There's something I want to tell you.'

His mother nodded curtly. She sat down in the family living room at the back of the house, not in a comfortable fireside chair, but in a wooden one near to the table, which was covered with a maroon chenille cloth when it was not in use. Dan sat opposite her, but she did not give him the chance to speak. She placed her clenched fists on the table, leaning forward in an aggressive manner.

'Yes, and I'm not at all surprised that you've something to tell me. Who is she?'

His mouth dropped open with shock. He knew what she meant, of course; someone must have seen him with Madeleine. But all he could answer was, 'What...? How did you...?' He was well aware that he sounded stupid, but there was no thought in his mind about denying it. Anyway, why should he?

'How do I know? Because you've been seen...
And I'm not going to tell you who it was,' his
mother went on as soon as he opened his mouth.
'Who is she? That's what I want to know,
this...floozy that you've been gadding around the
town with all week?'

'Be careful what you are saying...Mother,' said
Dan, feeling immediate anger at such a wrongful
description of Madeleine. 'Yes, I have been out with
a young lady, quite a few times during the past
week. But she is certainly not a "floozy". She is a
most respectable young lady, and one that you have
met. Well, Joe has met her anyway, and you and my
father have seen her.'

'Don't tell me it was one of the girls from our
congregation? If it was then she should be ashamed
of herself. All the young women at the Sacred Heart
know that you are destined for the priesthood. And
more fool you if you've let your head be turned by
one of them; although I know it wouldn't be the
first time that a young novice priest has been led
astray by a girl who should know better.'

'Will you please listen to me,' cried Daniel. 'No,
it isn't anybody from the church, and as for me
becoming a priest – and everyone knowing about
it,' he added pointedly, 'that is exactly what I want
to talk to you about. The young lady in question is
the singer from the North Pier show, Madeleine
Moon. If you remember, she had a lovely voice.
And she's a lovely girl too.'

'A showgirl?' Two high spots of colour blazed on Anna Murphy's cheeks and her green eyes flashed with the brilliance of an emerald. 'It gets worse. Not only do I find that you've been lying to us, to your daddy and me, now I find that you're consorting with a common showgirl!'

'She is certainly not common!' Dan thumped his fist on the table, then, realising that on no account must he lose his temper, he clasped his hands together in his lap, the tension he was feeling making his knuckles white. He forced himself to speak in a normal voice.

'Madeleine – that is her name – is a very respectable, well-brought-up girl, who happens to have a remarkable voice and – yes – she sings on the stage. I met her, quite by chance, on the promenade. She had already met Joe, and so we became friendly. And that is all, apart from the fact that I do intend to go on seeing her. And now I would like to know what you mean by saying that I have lied to you. When have I ever lied to you, or to my father?'

'By pretending that you were at the library, and that you were studying with Father Fitzgerald when you were out gallivanting with...that girl! I met the Father in town yesterday, I'll have you know, and he said he hoped you were feeling better! "Feeling better, Father?" I says. I wasn't aware he'd been poorly. "Ah well, maybe it's me that's made a mistake then," says the Father. He said a note was pushed through his door saying that you would not be going for your tuition at all this week, and that you would let the Father know when you were able to start again. And so he assumed that you were ill. What do you have to say about that, eh?'

'I wasn't ill,' replied Dan, 'and nor did I say so. He misunderstood, that's all. And you and my father assumed that I was at the library, or with Father Fitzgerald. At no time have I lied to you, although I admit I may not have told you the absolute truth. Which is what I intend to do now…

'Mammy…' He put his elbows on the table, leaning forward and clasping his hands together. 'I have decided, after hours and hours of thought – and of prayer, too, I must say – I have decided that I am not going to enter the priesthood. I realise now that it is not for me. I do not want to be a priest.'

'What!' His mother sat back with such force that the chair rocked. 'You meet a young lass, you take a fancy to her, and then you decide that you'll turn your back on God? You'll forget about what He has been calling you to do all your life, ever since you were a tiny baby in your cradle?'

Dan gave a thoughtful smile. 'Are you sure that God has been calling me, Mammy? Or…was it you? It was what you wanted, wasn't it?'

'Of course it was,' replied Anna. 'And it was what I promised as well. We had two stillborn babies, you know, your daddy and me, two sons, before you came along. We'd almost given up hope of having a live child, and I promised God that if my next baby was all right, then I would give him back when he was old enough, to serve the Lord. And you were not just all right, you were perfect, Daniel, and I had to keep my promise.'

'Supposing I'd been a girl, Mother?' asked Dan. 'Would you have forced me to become a nun?'

'I don't know, Daniel!' Anna shook her head vexedly. 'Maybe I would, yes... But I don't like the way you say forced. I am not aware that I have forced you to do anything that you didn't want to do. I remember, when you were old enough, how we used to talk together about a life of service and what it would mean. And you became an altar boy, didn't you, and a server? And you did so well at school, staying on until you were seventeen and studying theology. And Father Fitzgerald has been so good to you since we moved here, taking you under his wing and coaching you. I thought you were happy with him.'

'I am,' replied Daniel. 'He's a great fellow as well as being an excellent priest, and I've learnt a good deal from him. But during the course of my studies I have also learnt that...well, that it is not for me. There are other ways in which I can serve God, and I don't intend to give up on my faith, if that is what you are thinking.'

'I am only thinking what a fool you are, Daniel, to have your head turned by a pretty young woman.'

'Actually, it has very little to do with meeting

Madeleine,' said Dan, very calmly. 'But it did start me thinking. Or, I should say, it finally brought my soul-searching to an end. I want to lead a normal sort of life; to enjoy the friendship of girls as well as lads, and not to think that it is wrong and that I'm in danger of committing a mortal sin.'

He could see that his mother was looking tearful now, more than angry. 'I am so disappointed,' she said, dashing away a tear that had formed in the corner of an eye. 'Whatever will Father Fitzgerald say? And all the other people...' Yes, all the other folk that you have told, Mammy, thought Dan. 'You have let me down, and yourself, to say nothing of letting God down. And I still think it is all because of that girl. You are making a big mistake, Daniel.'

'I would be making a bigger mistake if I went ahead with it,' he replied. 'Believe me, Mammy. Now, just you think about it. Whose idea was it, when I was a little boy, when I was encouraged to go to church and Sunday school, and then to become an altar boy? It was your idea, wasn't it, your plan for me? Yes, I went along with it and – yes – I grew to love it all; the mystery and the sanctity and the feeling of holiness. There is something about it all that compels you to become part of it. But I know now that it was not my idea to take it so far. I can't do it, Mammy. I just...can't do it.'

Anna did not answer at first. She sorrowfully

shook her head. Then, 'You will change your mind,' she said in a whisper.

'Don't delude yourself, Mother,' he replied gently. 'I won't change my mind, I can assure you of that. And as for Madeleine...well, she's a nice respectable girl, as I've told you. And she does go to church.'

'She's a Catholic then?' asked Anna, looking up with just a glimmer of hope in her eyes.

'No, as a matter of fact she's a Methodist,' replied Dan.

'I've heard everything now,' yelled his mother, standing up with a force that made her chair topple over. 'A Methodist of all things!' She stormed out of the room.

'I must admit it didn't go awfully well,' Dan went on to tell Maddy. 'But then I didn't expect it to. I knew my mother wouldn't understand.'

'Does she know about me?' she asked.

'Yes, of course,' replied Dan. 'I told her about you, how we'd met on the promenade, and that I've been showing you some of the sights of Blackpool.'

'And I can imagine how she would feel about that...' Maddy sounded as though she were close to tears and Dan felt an upsurge of affection for her. The poor girl. It was all his fault; she hadn't asked for any of this.

'That wasn't the main issue with Mammy,' he replied carefully, in an attempt to reassure her. 'What she is upset about is finding out that I'm not going to enter the priesthood.' On no account would he tell Madeleine that his mother was laying all the blame on her for leading him astray.

'I explained to her that I had already been having doubts before I met you, and you must believe that too, Madeleine.' He placed his hand over hers and she did not pull away. 'And I do want to go on seeing you, even though you are leaving in two days' time.' She was looking at him thoughtfully, sorrowfully, and much of the sparkle had gone from her eyes.

'Madeleine,' he begged, 'please tell me that I can come and see you in Scarborough. You will be there all summer, and I don't want this to end for us.'

'No, I don't want it to end either,' she replied. 'But it's been such a shock, hearing all this; and it's a tremendous step you're taking, changing your mind about everything.'

'It would have been a tremendous step if I'd gone on with it, as my mother wanted me to do,' he replied. 'What is more, it would have been wrong, because I was never sure about it. I tried to explain this to Mammy but at the moment she's too angry and upset to listen to me properly.'

'So what are you going to do? About your job, I mean, and your studies? You say you've been having tuition from a priest?'

'Yes, Father Fitzgerald. I shall go and see him soon and try to explain. He has said to me, more than once, that I must be very sure of my calling –

it's quite possible he had realised that I was not absolutely certain – so I think he will understand. And I shall start working full-time for Mr Grundy at the shop, until I have a definite plan in mind. He will be pleased; he has asked me many times to consider it. And I do believe that you can serve God in whatever walk of life you happen to be,' he smiled. 'Even if it's selling trousers and shirts.'

'You will still go to church, won't you?'

'Of course. I tried to explain that to mother as well, that I'm not turning my back on everything. I work with a group of young people at the church, boys and girls of thirteen and upwards. We meet on a Saturday night and have a game of rounders or cricket, on the sands if the tide's out. Then we go back to the Sunday school hall and have a chat about…well…theological matters, or anything that might be puzzling them.'

'And they know, do they, about you studying to be a priest?'

'Some of them; well, most of them, I suppose. But it shouldn't make any difference…' In point of fact, some of the young folk with more enquiring minds had almost tied him in knots about several of the doctrines of the Roman Catholic Church, making him wonder if he really believed wholeheartedly himself in such things as the Infallibility of the Pope, or the Bodily Assumption of the Virgin Mary. And these doubts in his mind had played a part in the decision he was now making.

'Listen, Madeleine,' he said. 'Meet me just one more time, will you, please, before you leave? What about Saturday night? There's only one house, isn't there?'

'Yes, we should finish at about a quarter to ten...'

'Shall I wait for you then, by the pier entrance?'

'Yes, all right Dan. I'll meet you there... I must go now to get ready for tonight... No, don't come with me.' She put her hand on his arm to stay him as he started to walk along with her. 'I'll walk back on my own if you don't mind. I'd like to be alone for a little while.' She hesitated, then turned and gently kissed his cheek. 'Goodbye, Dan,' she said.

He wondered if the 'goodbye' meant goodbye for ever; that she didn't want to meet him again. It seemed to him, in his anxious state, that it had a ring of finality to it. But she could hardly avoid him, could she, if he stood at the pier entrance? She had to come out that way.

He need not have worried because she greeted him cheerfully on the Saturday night. He felt his heart give a leap as he saw her trim figure hurrying towards him along the pier. She was dressed in a close-fitting green suit with a neat little matching hat with a long feather. He was pleased to see that her eyes had regained their sparkle as she smiled at him.

'Hello, Dan. I got away as quickly as I could. The rest of them will be having a bit of a do back at our lodgings, with Mr and Mrs Jolly. I said I would join them later…I mustn't stay out too long,' she added.

'Of course not,' he said. 'We'll just have a little walk away from the crowds.'

Most of the people coming away from the pier and from the other shows that were on in the town were walking on the busy stretch of promenade near to the Tower. Maddy and Dan walked the other way, past the Metropole Hotel, towards the quieter end of the resort. They spoke very little, each of them, it seemed, waiting for the other one to start. Eventually, Dan stopped in a spot where there were few passers-by.

'Have you forgiven me, Madeleine?' he asked.

'There is nothing to forgive,' she replied. 'I am trying to understand. I realise this is difficult for both of us. I have grown…fond of you, as I'm sure you realise, and I do want to go on seeing you, when we can…if we can,' she added, a shade doubtfully.

'Madeleine…' He put both his arms around her, drawing her close to him. 'I…I love you,' he whispered. 'We haven't known one another very long, but I know that I do.' He lowered his head and their lips met in the first real kiss that they had shared; a kiss full of tenderness and sweetness, and wonder, too, about what the future might hold. Daniel hoped and prayed that there might be a future for them.

She did not reply that she loved him, but he could

see the depth of feeling there in her eyes. They turned to walk back home, chatting more freely on the way. Maddy told him how well the show had gone that evening, with an enthusiastic audience who had wanted encore after encore. Dan would have liked to have been there, but he was biding his time at home, anxious not to distress his mother any more than he had done already.

Maddy gave him her father's address – she was not sure of the lodgings in the Lancashire towns they would be visiting next – but he promised her that there would be a letter awaiting her when she arrived in Scarborough at the end of May. She promised she would write back and they would arrange a time for him to go and see her there.

He kissed her once more at the gate. 'Goodbye, Madeleine...my darling,' he added in a whisper. It was the first time he had murmured words of love, but it felt so right.

'Goodbye, Daniel,' she said, smiling at him, but he could see the glimmer of a tear in the corner of her eye. 'I'll see you soon... It won't be very long.' Then she turned and hurried away up the path.

But Dan felt at that moment that the end of May was a lifetime away.

Chapter Nine

Maddy unpinned her straw boater and threw it on the grass at the side of the picnic basket. Then she lay down, stretching out full length on the clifftop overlooking the North Bay.

'It's heavenly to feel the sunshine,' she called out, closing her eyes and lifting her face to the warmth. 'What bliss!' She gave a deep sigh of contentment. 'And it's so lovely and peaceful up here.'

'It's all right for you,' retorted her friend, Jessica, who was unpacking the basket and placing the items carefully onto the plaid rug. 'If I let the sun get to my face I would have more freckles than I have already. Anyway, young ladies are supposed to be pale and fragile looking, aren't they?'

'I suppose so,' agreed Maddy. 'I remember my mother making me keep my sun bonnet on when we went on the beach.' She sat up again. 'But be blowed to all that. I'm far too hot. I'm going to take this off as well.'

She unbuttoned her Norfolk style tweed jacket to reveal a high-necked, long-sleeved blouse with a slim ribbon necktie. A gored skirt, not too narrow, but not too wide to catch in the spokes of a bicycle wheel, completed the bicycling costume that she was wearing. It was almost identical to the one that Jessie wore except for the ribbons on the hat and at the neck; Jessie's were blue and Maddy's were green.

'Leave that, Jessie,' she called, 'and come and sit down. We don't want to eat just yet, do we? Not after that enormous lunch.'

They had cycled from Scarborough along the road that eventually led over the moors to Whitby, as far as the hamlet of Scalby Mills. The grass-topped cliff overlooked a sandy beach and beyond was the wide sweep of the bay with the ruined castle perched on the clifftop.

Jessie joined her on the rug, taking off her jacket as well but keeping her hat on. Her hair had darkened a little from the fiery orange it had been when Maddy had first met her. She had worn it in two bunches or plaits then, but it now waved gently around her ears, her centre parting revealing a high freckled forehead. She had tried to tone down the sun spots with emollient creams and lotions but with no great success. But to Maddy, and to others who were fond of Jessie, the freckles were part of her charm. She was the same age as Maddy; they would both be seventeen within a week of one another at the end of that month, June. Jessie was now the taller of the two by a few inches. Her long arms and legs resembled the limbs of a young foal, but she was not graceless, having learnt to move with the dignity that enhanced her height, as her mother had always done. Faith Moon was a beautiful woman, the passing years only adding a maturity to her loveliness. Jessie, who resembled her to a certain extent, could never be called beautiful, but she was a striking-looking girl and, more importantly, she had a friendly and sympathetic nature.

One of the best parts of Maddy's homecoming had been the resuming of her friendship with her best friend, now her stepsister. It was a Sunday afternoon at the beginning of June and Maddy had been at home for just one week. Uncle Percy's Pierrots, as the troupe was called during the summer season, had given a few preliminary shows the previous week but were to start in earnest the following day in their usual pitch on the North Bay.

To Maddy's great delight there had been a letter awaiting her from Daniel. Not a long letter, but enough to tell her that he was thinking of her and looking forward to seeing her again. He said very little – nothing, in fact – about the situation at home, but had mentioned that he was now working full-time at the gents' outfitters and that they were getting busy with the onset of the summer season.

She had written back to him the next day, suggesting that he should come to Scarborough during the third week in June. She would turn seventeen at the end of that week – on the Friday – and she felt that the extra year would add more weight to her announcement to her father and Faith that a young man was coming to see her. Seventeen sounded so much more grown-up than sixteen. She hadn't plucked up the courage to tell them yet, although she was not sure why. In fact, she hadn't told anyone about Dan, but she intended to tell Jessie that very afternoon.

'I've got something to tell you,' she began, unable to keep the delight out of her voice, 'but promise you won't say anything to my dad, or to Aunty Faith just yet. I'm waiting for the right moment to tell them myself, you see.'

'No, of course I won't tell,' said Jessie. 'Not if you say I mustn't. You know you can trust me. But what is it that I haven't to tell? Is it something to do with the Pierrots?'

'No, nothing like that,' Maddy replied shaking her head. She sat hugging her knees and looking out into the distance with a dreamy smile on her face. 'I met a young man, when I was in Blackpool,' she began. 'He came to see the show and...well...we happened to meet, and we liked one another. A lot,' she added. 'And he's going to come over to Scarborough to see me. Soon, I hope.'

'Gosh!' Jessie's blue eyes were agog with excitement. 'What is he called? How old is he? What does he do?' The questions poured out of her with scarcely a breath between them.

'Not so fast,' laughed Maddy. 'Give me a chance. He's called Daniel Murphy, but everyone calls him

Dan, and he's nearly twenty, and he works…well, at the moment he's working in a gents' outfitters in the town…I really do like him,' she added, turning to look eagerly at her friend. 'But…'

'But…what?' asked Jessie. 'Do you think there might be a problem with our parents? He's a few years older than you, of course.'

'Only three years,' said Maddy.

'Yes, I know, but you've not had a boyfriend before, have you? D'you think they might say that you're too young?'

'No, it's not that,' replied Maddy. 'Anyway, they don't know what I'm doing when I'm away all through the winter, do they? I might have had any number of boyfriends for all they know. But I haven't,' she added. 'There was nobody at all until I met Dan.'

'What about Samuel?' asked Jessie, looking at her closely. 'I know you liked him a lot; I could tell. And I've seen him looking at you as well. And I know he took you out for supper when you were in Leeds, didn't he?'

Maddy could feel her cheeks turning a little pink. 'Oh no, there was nothing like that,' she said. 'We went out for supper, and…it was very nice seeing him again. But – well – he's my stepbrother, isn't he, like you're my stepsister, and that's all there is to it.'

'I'm glad to hear it,' said Jessie. 'I know he's my brother, but there are times when I don't like him very much. I'm relieved to hear that you're not keen on him anymore. Your brother, Patrick, now, he's much nicer.'

'Yes, you used to like him, didn't you? You know, really like him,' said Maddy, giving her a sly look.

'Yes, so I did. We were both a bit silly about each other's brothers when we were younger, but we've grown up now, haven't we?' said Jessie. 'Patrick's just another brother to me now, and he and Katy seem very happy together. They're talking about getting married next spring. Anyway, that's enough about all that. You were telling me about this Dan. So…what's the problem?'

Maddy was silent for a moment. Then, 'He's a Catholic,' she replied, 'and I'm a Methodist. At least I am when I go to church; I haven't been going all that much recently with being away. And…well, there are always problems, aren't there?'

'I don't see why,' said Jessie, carefully. 'I was C of E, and so was my mother, but we all go to the chapel with your dad and Grandad Isaac sometimes. The twins go to the C of E Sunday school because Mother wanted them to, but we never have any arguments about it.'

'But being a Catholic is rather different, isn't it?' said Maddy. 'I mean, there was a lot of trouble in the past – King Henry the Eighth and all that – and some people have never got over it. Not that I've ever really understood it properly. I don't know much about them, the Catholics, except that they have a Pope and they have to believe everything he says, and that they worship the Virgin Mary as well as God and Jesus.'

Jessie nodded. 'We learnt all about the Reformation at school, about Henry the Eighth making himself head of the English Church and breaking away from Rome. But it was only because he wanted to divorce Catherine of Aragon and marry Anne Boleyn, so that he could get a male heir to the throne.'

'And she got her head chopped off, didn't she?' said Maddy.

'So she did, and she didn't give him a male heir anyway,' said Jessie. 'Only a daughter, who became Queen Elizabeth.'

Maddy knew that Jessie's historical knowledge was greater than her own. Jessie had attended a private school in York and then continued her education in Scarborough before going on to the commercial college, whereas Maddy had left school at thirteen. There were certain gaps in her knowledge, which she had tried to rectify by reading books on all manner of subjects.

'So it was all because of Henry the Eighth, was it?' she asked. 'That's why we have the Church of England?'

'I think that was the crux of the matter,' said Jessie. 'But I'm sure there's a great deal more to it than that. I know it has caused a great deal of discord and dissension over the centuries.' Jessie had used important-sounding words ever since she was a little girl, but Maddy knew she was not showing off and she had long since learnt to accept it without comment. 'But hasn't this young man, Daniel, explained it to you?' asked Jessie. 'He obviously doesn't mind that you're not a Catholic, or he wouldn't be coming to see you... He does know that you're not, doesn't he?' she added, looking at her friend keenly.

'Of course he does,' replied Maddy. 'But we didn't talk much about religion; in fact, he hardly mentioned it at first. And then...he said there was something he had to tell me.' She paused. 'You see, the point is...he was studying to be a priest,' she went on, speaking quickly, 'and then – well – he changed his mind. And his mother is furious with him, and it's causing a lot of trouble in the family. He hasn't said much about it, but I know it is and...that's what I'm worried about.'

Jessie's eyes were wide with amazement, tinged with something that amounted to horror. 'Good gracious!' she said. 'No wonder you're worried. You mean – he changed his mind because he met you?'

'No, not really,' said Maddy. 'At least, he said it wasn't because of me. He was already having doubts about being a priest. But I feel as though I'm to blame for him falling out with his mother. I had a nice letter from him, though, and he still wants to come and see me.'

'When is he coming?'

'I've suggested the third week in June.'

'And where will he be staying? At our house?'

'I don't know. I haven't got round to thinking about that yet. Like I said, I haven't told my dad yet, or your mum.'

'You've written back to him?'

'Yes, nearly straight away, and now I'm waiting for another letter from him.'

'Well then...' Jessie paused, frowning as though she was concentrating hard. 'I think you should wait until you hear from him again, and then you'll have to tell our parents, won't you?'

'Yes, I suppose I will. But I don't need to tell them everything, do I? About him going to be a priest, I mean, because he's not, not anymore.' Maddy was beginning to have doubts herself as she looked at Jessie's worried face, and some of the joy of looking forward to Dan's visit was receding.

'No, perhaps you don't need to tell them that,' said Jessie, doubtfully. 'But you'll have to tell them about his different religion, won't you?'

'I didn't think it would matter,' said Maddy, feeling perplexed, 'but now I'm not sure. You think it's wrong, don't you, me being friendly with him? I can tell you do.'

'No...of course I don't.' Jessie placed a consoling hand on her friend's arm. 'I was surprised, that's all. But if you like him then I'm sure my mother and Uncle William will like him too. What does he look like? Tell me all about him...'

And so Maddy told her friend more about Daniel as they ate the salmon sandwiches and fruitcake, made by Mrs Baker, and drank the hot coffee from the Thermos flask. But she no longer felt quite so blissful about it all. She could see problems on the horizon, which, in her euphoric state, she had been trying to forget. All she could do at the moment, however, was to wait until she had another letter from Dan.

'So what about you?' she said to Jessie. 'Tell me what you have been doing. You will be finishing your college course soon, won't you? Have you started looking for a job?'

'Yes, as a matter of fact, I have,' replied Jessie. 'Actually, your father asked me if I would consider going to work for him; in the office of course, not…anything else.'

Maddy grinned. 'No, you've never been keen on the idea of dead bodies and all that, have you? I remember when I first met you, you thought it was very strange, my dad being an undertaker. You used to be scared stiff there'd be corpses all over the place when you came to see us.'

'No, I didn't!' said Jessie indignantly. 'I wasn't used to it, that's all, and you'd been brought up with it, hadn't you?'

'That's true,' replied Maddy. 'So what have you told my father? You wouldn't come into contact with coffins and all that side of the business if you were working in the office. Have you agreed to do it?'

'No, I haven't given him an answer yet. I don't want to offend him – I'm very fond of Uncle Will, as you know – but I think I would prefer to work somewhere completely different. Not because of the connotations with death, but I feel it might be rather restricting. There are already quite a few members of the family working in the business, aren't there? Patrick went into it straight from school, and now my mother is in charge of the shop. I'd rather spread my wings and do something else. You didn't work there, did you? You never wanted to.'

'No, I worked for Aunt Louisa, learning the dressmaking trade, and then I joined the Pierrots and...here I am, an "artiste" or a "showgirl" or whatever you want to call me.' Maddy laughed. 'Anyway, why does my dad want someone else to work in the office? They've managed all right between them, haven't they, with the office work, with the bills and bookings and everything?'

'Your grandad is slowing down,' said Jessie. 'He doesn't do nearly as much as he used to in the workshop, or attending funerals. You must have noticed that he's getting frailer?'

'Yes, I've seen quite a change in him,' agreed Maddy. 'It's sad, isn't it? I thought Grandad Isaac would go on for ever.'

'Most of the work is falling on your father and Patrick,' said Jessie. 'Joe Black is a good carpenter, but I don't think he's all that competent at office work, and Patrick has never had much to do with that side of the business. So Uncle Will really does need an extra pair of hands. I shall have to tell him, though, that I'd rather he appointed someone else. As a matter of fact, I have an interview next week. I'll tell him and Mother before then.'

'You clever thing, you!' said Maddy. 'So what's the job? Where is it?'

'It's at a new store that's opening soon in Castle Road,' replied Jessie. 'A furniture and carpet store, and they're looking for office staff. I saw the advertisement in the evening paper so I applied and, as I said, I've got an interview on Wednesday afternoon.'

'What about your college course?' asked Maddy.

'Oh, they'll let me miss an hour or two at college. Several of us are applying for jobs right now. I might not get it, of course, and it might be quite a menial job if I do; running errands and making the tea, but I have to start somewhere.'

'Don't underestimate yourself,' Maddy told her. 'You stand as much chance as anyone else; more, I would say. Don't be afraid to blow your own trumpet.'

'I've never been very good at that,' said Jessie. 'I hate showing off. Do you remember when we went in for that talent contest at the Pierrot show? I said I'd rather die than appear on a stage, but you persuaded me to do it; and it wasn't nearly as bad as I expected once I got up there.'

'And you won a highly commended prize for your recitation,' said Maddy, remembering how reticent her friend had used to be. 'You never know what you can do until you try.' It was she, Maddy, she recalled, who had been far more outgoing when they were children, but Jessie had blossomed quite a lot recently, especially since she had been at the commercial college.

'But you won the first prize, didn't you?' Jessie reminded her. 'Everybody was enthralled when you sang "Scarborough Fair". Is that song still in your repertoire?'

'Yes, I sing it sometimes,' said Maddy. 'But I include more modern ones as well, quite a lot of music hall songs; the audience always enjoys those. You won't be able to come and watch us during the day, will you, while you're at college?'

'No, but you can be sure I'll be there on the front row at the evening performances,' said Jessie. 'We're all coming tomorrow night, you know, to the show at six-thirty. Mother and Uncle Will, Patrick and Katy and the twins, and Grandad Isaac said he was coming as well. We're expecting a first-rate performance.'

'And that's what you'll get,' laughed Maddy. 'Mind you, it's not really all that different from what it was a few years ago. The same old acts...' She hesitated. 'I shouldn't say that, should I? It sounds as though they're hackneyed and "old hat", and of course they're not... Well, I suppose some of the older ones might be getting a bit stale,' she added truthfully. 'I know Percy would like to inject some "new blood", as he calls it, but he's always careful not to offend anyone.'

'Percy Morgan's a grand fellow, isn't he?' Jessie remarked. 'I remember all the children used to love him, and he's so friendly and courteous to the adults as well.'

'Yes, he's one of the best,' agreed Maddy. 'Far too nice to be a showman, really. He's not ruthless enough, but he keeps the loyalty of his troupe and that's the important thing... So what do you do with yourself when you're not at college?' Maddy went on to ask her friend. 'I take it you're still a member of the cycling club?'

'Oh yes; we're out and about quite a lot, now that the lighter evenings are here. And Saturdays and Sundays, too, sometimes. You would be very welcome to come with us, Maddy, whilst you're here, but I wanted you all to myself this afternoon, and that was why I didn't go with them today. There are some lovely rides around Scarborough. We've been to the Forge Valley, and the Mere, and out towards Flamborough Head.'

'It's ages since I went to those places,' said Maddy, rather wistfully. 'Of course, I've been away from Scarborough for a couple of years and during the summer I'm always so busy... I shall have to try and get a bit of time to myself, though, when Dan comes,' she said.

If he comes...she added silently to herself, wondering why she suddenly felt so unsure.

Chapter Ten

Maddy dashed to the door on Monday morning on hearing the rattle of the letter box. She was hoping there would be a letter from Dan in reply to the one she had written, in which she had suggested a possible date for their meeting. But, alas, the only mail consisted of a couple of brown envelopes addressed to her father and a rather larger white one for Mr and Mrs W Moon. She felt her heart plummet in a spasm of disappointment, but she told herself that it was possibly too soon to be expecting a reply. It was, after all, less than a week since Dan would have received her letter. There was sure to be one tomorrow, or the day after.

There was no time to brood, however, because it was today that Uncle Percy's Pierrots were to start in earnest with their summer season performances. Three shows a day, morning, afternoon and early evening, weather and tides permitting, of course. The notice 'If wet, under the pier' had become something of a standing joke amongst the Pierrots in former years, those belonging to Percy Morgan's troupe and to the rival troupes who performed on the South Bay sands at the other side of the headland. But now the pathetic little notice regarding the wet weather was no longer applicable, because Scarborough Pier was no longer there. On the 8th of January in 1905, the pier and the pavilion had been blown away overnight in a particularly vicious storm. So since then, having no shelter to run to, they had carried on stoically and cheerfully in all kinds of weather: blazing sunshine, strong wind or drizzly rain; only the heaviest of showers would cause them to abandon the show altogether. The tides, too, were out of their control. If there was no sand, then they moved their pitch to the promenade at the top of the cliff path.

It was good to be back, Maddy reflected later that same morning as she donned her Pierrot outfit; the white tunic with the large frilly collar and red pompoms, the white skirt that came down to her ankles, and the conical-shaped hat. The only difference between the male and female Pierrots was that the men wore baggy trousers and the women wore skirts. It was a traditional costume that had been derived originally from the French characters of Harlequin and Pierrot, and was worn by all the troupes, not only in Scarborough and the East Coast but in other parts of the country as well. For Pierrots were to be found almost everywhere where there was a beach. The only variation was in the colour of the pompoms on the hats and tunics.

Some troupes still kept to the old tradition of

employing only male performers. Percy Morgan's biggest rival, Will Catlin, who had had a pitch in Scarborough for many years, was still keeping to his strict rule of men only. Maddy found that hard to imagine. Women, in her opinion, added a touch of originality, of lightness and frivolity and diversity. Certainly the five women in their own troupe could not be more different, both in appearance and in the content of their performances. The thing they had in common, though, and which Percy insisted upon, was their adaptability and their willingness to help out – to 'muck in', as he put it – wherever they were needed.

There was no theatre dressing room here such as they had been used to during their autumn and winter tours, although several of those had been far from luxurious, or even comfortable. They dressed, on Scarborough sands, in two tents, one for the men and another for the women, on either side of their stage of wooden boards which was laid down every time they performed. The piano that Letty played was wheeled down to the beach each day on a handcart or 'barrer', by an odd-job man in the town who was known as the 'Barrer Man'.

Maddy peeped through the flap of the tent. There was not a very big crowd there as yet, but there were still five minutes to go. The day was chilly; fine but with a grey sky and a stiff little breeze; not the sort of weather that was conducive to sitting around on the beach. The children on the front benches and the adults, seated on deckchairs further back, were all wearing their coats, and a few of the grown-ups looked far from happy. The children, though, were chattering excitedly and Maddy remembered how she had loved the Pierrot shows when she was a little girl. And she was sure that the infectious humour and light-hearted banter, and the magic of the songs and dances would coax a smile from even the most miserable face.

There was a ripple of applause as they all tripped onto the stage for their opening number.

'Here we are again,
By the silver sea,
Lads and lasses, one and all
As happy as can be...'

It took a little time for them to get into their stride and for the audience to respond as enthusiastically as they might have wished, but there was a gradual improvement as the show continued.

There were one or two unfortunate little incidents that made the audience laugh, in sympathy, fortunately, rather than in derision. Daisy, one of Nancy's little West Highland terriers, who was usually very well behaved, cocked her leg up against her stool and would not jump onto it and 'sit up and beg' until she had finished what she was doing. Nancy decided that the best thing to do was to laugh along with the audience, then Pete, her husband, made a great show of coming on with a mop to wipe up the stream that was running across the platform.

Then Barney's bow tie was knocked askew when Benjy flung out a hand rather too energetically.

'Hey, mister, yer tie's all crooked,' called a cheeky lad on the front row of the audience, at which Benjy stopped in the middle of the dance and fussed around straightening his partner's apparel.

Susannah, to her consternation, muddled up the words when she was singing 'In the Shade of the Old Apple Tree', although she had sung it dozens of times before, but like a true pro she turned it to her advantage. It was far better, sometimes, to admit that you had slipped up rather than try to disguise it. 'Oh, come on, you lot, help me out!' she cried, and the audience good-humouredly joined in with her.

'I could hear the dull buzz of the bee
In the blossoms as you sang to me,
With a heart that is true I'll be waiting for you,
In the shade of the old apple tree.'

As for Maddy, she felt that she performed reasonably well, but it was strange singing in the open air again after being used to the cosy intimacy of many of the theatres in which they had played. Not that all of them had been ideal; some of them had been great barns of places, and others were functional church or civic halls with few amenities. The sound was confined, though, when you sang indoors, whereas here it tended to drift away on the breeze. Her unaccompanied song, in particular, did not get the applause she was used to. It can only get better, she told herself, and tonight she would be singing especially for her family.

Nobody could help but notice that Queenie's top notes were decidedly wavy, and her voice cracked as she strained for a top F in 'Poor Wandering One', a favourite Gilbert and Sullivan number which she had sung on many occasions. Seaside audiences, however, were not as critical as those in a theatre and no one winced – at least not noticeably – or jeered. On the contrary, she received a good round of applause, although it could have been out of sympathy for a brave performance, in view of the fact that she was getting a little 'past it'. Indeed, there had been a few catcalls and boos from the gallery in a couple of the inland towns in which they had played. Percy had not commented on it, but Maddy felt sure that he was aware of it. She saw him frown a little as he listened to Queenie. She knew of his concern and could foresee that there might be difficulties ahead.

'Well done, everyone,' he said after the performance. 'A few minor hiccups, but nothing that can't be remedied, I'm sure.'

Not a great deal of money had been collected, though, when Pete, the bottler, had gone round at the interval with his wooden box to collect contributions – halfpennies, pennies or threepenny bits as a rule – from the children on the front benches, or the grown-ups who had chosen to stand. They charged a shilling now for the privilege of sitting on a deckchair, and most adults considered the price to be well worthwhile. There were still a few, though, who would stand, and even some who would walk away when the bottler appeared. 'Bottling' was an old tradition in the Pierrot troupes. It had derived from the fact that the proceeds of the collection had, in the early days, been placed in a large bottle so that they were not easily removable. At the end of the week the bottle would be broken and the money shared out fairly between the members of the company. Nowadays, though, they had more sophisticated ways of earning their money. Seats that had to be paid for; programmes and song sheets to be bought at twopence a time; and sepia postcards of all the Pierrots, in groups or in separate poses, for sale at the end of each performance.

The afternoon performance went ahead without any mishaps and there was a larger audience, which was encouraging. The bigger the audience, the better the show, was the usual way of things. Artistes responded more enthusiastically to a goodly crowd than to a handful of people.

By the time of the evening performance the tide had come in, and so the show took place at a spot halfway up the cliff known as Clarence Gardens. It was an ideal venue with a little bandstand, where the Pierrots congregated before going onto the stage for their various acts. There were forms aplenty which were permanent fixtures at the site, and grassy banks where those not wanting to pay for a seat could recline, as well as the deckchairs and benches for the children, which had to be transported from the beach. It was quite an undertaking, shifting everything around, but there were always local chaps and visitors to the resort who were willing to lend a hand for the price of a pint of ale.

The evening show turned out to be the best of the day and Percy declared that he was well satisfied with the takings and with the way the troupe had rallied round and given it their all. Maddy was delighted that all the members of her family had come to watch. Tilly and Tommy beamed at her from their seats on the front row, and sitting a little way back were her father and Aunty Faith, Grandad Isaac, Jessie, and Patrick and his girlfriend – now his fiancée – Katy. And, to her surprise, there on the row behind was Miss Muriel Phipps, the senior assistant from the store; Martin Sadler who was in charge of the gentlemen's clothing, with his wife at his side; and even young Doris, the thirteen-year-old who had recently started as a trainee sales assistant. And Joe Black, too, who was on the undertaking staff, with Alice, his new wife whom he had married a few months ago.

Maddy was moved almost to tears at the sight of

them all. They smiled at her, not without an air of propriety that she was their very own daughter, or sister, or friend, and applauded loud and long at the end of each song. She knew it would be most unprofessional to wave at them, as children did at school concerts, but she nodded her head slightly in their direction to acknowledge that she valued their support.

Then, on an impulse, she said, 'Ladies and gentlemen, this next song is for all of you who love Scarborough. And especially for my family, who live here and who are all in the audience. It happens to be the very first song I sang for the Pierrots, and it is my favourite song of all…'Scarborough Fair'. She did not say that it was the one she had sung when she won the talent competition at eleven years of age, but there were many people there who would remember that.

Letty played a single note on the piano, because this was the song that she always sang unaccompanied.

'Are you going to Scarborough Fair?
Parsley, sage, rosemary and thyme;
Remember me to one who lives there,
For he was once a true love of mine…'

'You're getting better and better, lass,' her grandad told her later that evening when they were back home, 'and that song never fails to bring a tear to my eye. It's grand to have you back with us for a while, it is that. We've missed you; aye, we've missed you, lass.'

'It's lovely to be back, Grandad,' she told him, 'and I miss you too, all of you, when I'm away.'

Grandad Isaac had aged a good deal during her last absence. His shoulders were stooped, whereas he had once had such an upright carriage, deep furrows creased his brow and cheeks, and his once blue eyes had a pale and rheumy look behind the spectacles that he now wore nearly all the time. She felt a stab of sorrow at the thought of her grandad not always being there. He seemed in good health though, if a little less agile, and was still quite alert in his mind. So he could well live to be ninety or more, she told herself.

It was good to be back in the bosom of her family again, and in the place she loved most in all the world. Not that she had travelled the world, of course; she had scarcely seen anything of England until she joined the concert party. Her thoughts flew involuntarily to Samuel, who would quite soon be embarking on his journey to foreign parts. He was the only member of the family who had been missing that evening.

There was only one thing that Maddy wished for to make her happiness complete. She hugged to herself the thought that there would soon be a letter from Daniel.

After a week had gone by and she still had not

heard from him she was starting to feel worried. She had not yet told her parents about him; there was really no point in doing so until she received his letter, but she knew that she had to confide in Jessie.

'Yes, I know,' said her friend, looking concerned. 'I know you haven't had a letter from Dan yet; you would have told me if you had, but I didn't want to mention it until you told me yourself.' Jessie put an arm around her stepsister as they sat on one of the single beds in the room they shared when Maddy was at home. 'Never mind. It's only a week, isn't it, and I'm sure there's a good reason for it. Letters go astray sometimes, you know. I'm sure the Royal Mail isn't always infallible.'

'I think he's changed his mind,' said Maddy. She sighed and shook her head. 'Probably his mother has been on at him again; I think she has a big influence on him. And we had only known one another for such a short time…'

'But you seemed so sure,' said Jessie. 'And he doesn't sound the sort of person who would give up so easily. Everything will be all right, you'll see. Just wait another day or two.'

Maddy knew that all she could do was wait. One consolation was that she was busy and had little time during the day to worry about what might have gone wrong. And at night, in spite of herself, she usually managed to fall asleep straight away, tired out by giving her best – as she always tried to do – at three performances. It was an exacting life, but one that she loved. Sometimes it seemed that her time with Daniel had been only a dream, a transitory thing; just a week out of her life which was meant to be enjoyed and then forgotten. But at other times she felt dejected, and she tortured herself with the thought that he had never really cared about her.

She pulled herself back from her meandering thoughts to give Jessie a hug. 'You're a great friend,' she said. 'D'you know, the worst thing about being away from home is not seeing you for so long? And I'm really pleased about your good news this week. You must be thrilled to bits. Aren't the other students green with envy?'

Jessie had attended the interview on Wednesday at the furniture store on Castle Road, which would soon be ready to open, and she had been offered a position of shorthand typist there and then. There were six applicants, out of which two had been chosen: Jessie, and another young woman who was moving from her position at a less prestigious store in the town.

'Not really,' replied Jessie. 'We all get along well together and are pleased at one another's successes. Some of the students already have jobs to go to, at their own family firms, as I would have done if I had taken up your father's offer.'

'He didn't mind, though, did he, when you told him about the interview?'

'No; and he was just as pleased as Mother was

when I told him I'd been successful. I think he's quite philosophical about it all. He says he'll wait awhile and probably something will turn up.'

'Like Mr Micawber,' smiled Maddy. It was Jessie who had introduced her to the works of Charles Dickens and *David Copperfield* was one of her favourites.

'Exactly,' said Jessie. 'And something will turn up for you in a day or two, I feel sure, so "keep yer pecker up!" That's what Grandad would tell you, isn't it?'

'Yes, if he knew about it,' replied Maddy. 'On the other hand he might well disapprove of Dan. They all might...' she added gloomily. 'Ohh...' She gave a long shuddering sigh. 'Sometimes I wish I'd never met him.'

No letter turned up, but something else did the very next day. Not something, though, but somebody; it was Henrietta Collier, William Moon's elder daughter.

William had known of her existence but had never set eyes upon her until two years ago, when she had come to Scarborough to find him, following the death of both her adoptive parents and her real mother, Bella Randall. She had visited them occasionally since that time and had always fitted in well with the rest of the family. It was mainly due to Faith, William's sympathetic and understanding wife, that the young woman had been so well received, because the circumstances of her birth and subsequent adoption were regarded by William as shameful episodes in his life.

It was Sunday afternoon, midway between dinner and teatime, when Maddy, who had just been coming down the stairs, opened the door to find her half-sister standing there.

'Hetty!' she cried in surprise. 'Whatever are you doing here?' Then, aware that that might have sounded rather impolite, she went on, 'I mean, it's lovely to see you, but we didn't know you were coming…did we?' She realised that her father might well have known, but the news had not been passed on to her.

It was always something of a shock to Maddy whenever she saw Hetty. She was the very image of her mother, Bella, the woman whom Maddy had disliked so much when she was a child and who had caused so much havoc in the family. But all that was in the past and best forgotten. Henrietta – who was usually called Hetty – was a very different person from her mother; she had a much kinder and gentler disposition. The two half-sisters, with nine years separating them, had formed a cautious friendship, but one that could develop if they were to see one another more often.

'No, you're right, I'm not expected,' replied Hetty, stepping over the threshold as Maddy held the door open. 'It was a spur of the moment decision. I do hope it's not inconvenient.' Maddy noticed she was carrying a holdall as well as a capacious handbag.

Faith and William appeared in the hallway on hearing voices and they greeted her warmly. 'Hetty, my dear, how lovely to see you.' Faith kissed her gently on one cheek then the other, then William, too, gave her a brief kiss. 'Yes, good to see you, Hetty. What a surprise, eh?'

'Yes, I'm sorry, William,' she said. It had never been considered appropriate to either of them, William or Hetty, for her to address him as Father. 'I was just saying to Maddy that I should have let you know I was coming, but it was an impulse. I just knew that I had to come…'

Maddy noticed then that Hetty was not her usual bright and sparkling self. Her dark brown eyes had shadows beneath them and she looked apprehensively at William and then at Faith. 'I would be very grateful if I could stay here tonight, and then…well, I'll have to make up my mind about what would be the best thing to do.'

'Come on in then, lass, and tell us all about it,' said William, putting a protective arm round her and guiding her into the sitting room, where he, Faith and Isaac had been enjoying a relaxing afternoon.

Maddy decided she had better make herself scarce. It looked as though Hetty was in some sort of trouble and she did not want to appear nosey. Besides, there was something that she needed to do. She had decided to write another letter to Dan. It might well be, as Jessie had suggested, that the letter had gone astray, but it couldn't happen a second time. Anyway, what did she have to lose? If she hadn't heard from him in another week or so in answer to a second letter, then she would know that he had had a change of heart and that she must try to forget about him.

Maddy discovered what was troubling her half-sister later that day when Hetty confided in both her and Jessie about the circumstances of her sudden arrival in Scarborough. They had had tea when Jessie returned from her afternoon jaunt with her cycling club, and then the three young women met together in the room that Maddy and Jessie shared.

Hetty had recovered a little by that time. She had been tired after the train journey and was clearly distressed about something, but the jollity around the tea table had cheered her up considerably. Patrick and his fiancée, Katy, had been there too; and Faith had remarked, as she often did, that the only member of the family who was missing was Samuel.

Maddy and Jessie perched on a bed and Hetty sat in a basket weave chair. 'I've been jilted,' said Hetty, with no preamble. She was trying to smile, but then her lip quivered and she stopped and took a deep breath before continuing, whilst the two girls looked at one another anxiously, not quite knowing what to say.

'Oh dear! How...awful,' said Maddy, and Jessie

nodded in agreement, but it seemed such a feeble response to something that was a serious issue once a ring had been given to cement the betrothal.

'You knew I was engaged, didn't you?' asked Hetty, and the two girls nodded. She had told the family about her forthcoming engagement when she had visited some six months before, and soon afterwards she had started to wear a ring. 'We were planning to get married sometime next year but...well, it's all over.' She shrugged her shoulders. 'He's been seeing someone else, not only seeing her, but I'm afraid he's "got her into trouble", as they say.' She managed a wry smile. 'Obviously she was willing to...er...give him what he wanted, something I refused to do,' she added. Jessie and Maddy exchanged startled glances at the bold admission. 'So...he's marrying her instead of me. Her parents have insisted on it. She's only seventeen, the same age as you two; the baby's due in four months' time. So...that's what's going to happen.' She shook her head dejectedly. 'People are trying to tell me I'm better off without him.'

'And so you are,' said Jessie with a decided nod. 'It's a dreadful situation for you to be in, though, isn't it?'

'Who is she?' asked Maddy. 'Do you know?' They knew who the fiancé was – or had been – although they had never met him. His name was Alec Tempest and he was one of the undermanagers at the colliery in Ashington, where Hetty worked in the office.

'It doesn't matter,' replied Hetty dismissively, in answer to Maddy's question about the girl. 'The less said about her the better. I don't want to think about her if I can help it. And I won't say her name. Actually, she's the daughter of one of the other bosses; and he's insisting that they get married, as I told you. If she'd been the daughter of a pit worker then maybe he'd have got away with it – Alec, I mean – with a suitable payment. As it is he's got a noose round his neck whether he wants her or not. My guess is that he doesn't, not really.'

'It serves him right,' said Maddy hotly. 'Did you know, though, what was going on?'

'I noticed a certain coolness, but I thought it was because I wouldn't…you know. Then I heard rumours – everybody seemed to know except me, of course – and eventually he had to tell me. I gave him his ring back…'

'Threw it at him, I hope!' said Maddy.

'No…I managed to behave with decorum. But I gave my notice in the very next day. I couldn't go on working there, seeing him every day as I would have had to. They're getting married next weekend, so I heard on the grapevine.'

'Oh…poor you!' breathed Jessie.

'But you've done the right thing coming here,' said Maddy. 'Good for you! Are you going to stay? I suppose you've not decided yet.'

'I wasn't sure at all what to do, as I told you,' replied Hetty. 'I just knew that I had to get right away from the area. I have no family in Ashington now, since my ma and da died, and Bella, of course. You are my family now, aren't you?' She smiled a little sadly, but wistfully too, at Maddy and Jessie.

'Of course we are,' said Maddy, in a show of loyalty to her half-sister to whom she already felt she was drawing closer.

'Yes...' agreed Jessie. 'I know I'm not really your sister, like Maddy is, but we're all part of the same family now, aren't we?' She smiled. 'It's lovely, isn't it, how we've all come to know each other?'

'Indeed it is,' said Hetty. 'You two will be a great help to me, I'm sure, whilst I'm trying to sort myself out again. And William and Faith are being so kind and helpful. I'm staying here for a night or two, and then they're going to help me to find a flat. And there's the sale of my little cottage up north to see to... So many problems to sort out, but I'm feeling better about everything now.' The light had returned to her eyes again and her sadness had disappeared, for the moment at least, as she leant forward eagerly. 'And...guess what? William has asked me if I would consider working for him, in the office at Isaac Moon and Son. What do you think of that?'

'It's very...fortuitous,' said Jessie, smiling knowingly at Maddy.

'So it is,' agreed Maddy. 'He didn't have to wait

long, did he, for something to turn up?'

'Yes, a real Mr Micawber situation,' said Hetty, who was following their train of thought exactly. 'He told me, Jessie, that you were not very keen on the idea of working there. So it is, as you say, very fortuitous. And I jumped at the chance of finding an office job so quickly. Don't worry; coffins and corpses hold no fears for me.' She gave a wry smile. 'It's the living that you need to beware of!'

Chapter Eleven

When another week had passed and Maddy had still not received a letter from Daniel, she was finding it increasingly hard to keep up her pretence of cheerfulness. She had to force herself to do so during the performances; it would never do to show the audience anything other than a happy smiling face.

She did, however, confide in Susannah, but her older friend, although she listened sympathetically enough, had problems of her own to contend with. She and Frank wanted to get married; but Frank was already married and it seemed as though there was little likelihood of him being able to free himself. He and his wife, Hilda, had lived apart for ages and Hilda appeared to be quite contented with the situation. Frank would be quite willing for her to divorce him; after all, he and Susannah were unashamedly 'cohabiting', as the official language termed it.

'But she can't do it,' Susannah told Maddy, 'and she probably wouldn't want to, anyway. Divorce him, I mean. Frank's been to see a solicitor, and apparently it is quite acceptable for a man to commit adultery, but not a woman. An awful word, isn't it, adultery? But I suppose it's what we're doing, Frank and me, although it doesn't feel like it. So it looks as though we'll have to go on as we are…

'Frank could divorce her,' she went on, 'if he found out that she was…doing that, but it's not very likely that she is. She's not terribly interested in that sort of thing, from what Frank says. And he hates the idea of getting a private detective to spy on her to find out if she's up to anything. And I admire him for that. It's a funny how-d'you-do, isn't it, when a man is allowed to have a lover and a woman isn't…?

'I'm sorry, Maddy, I'm going on about myself, aren't I? I really am sorry that you've not heard from that nice young man, but I'm afraid you'll have to try and forget about him. From what you've told me, it seems as though there would be quite a few problems; and it isn't as if you've known him for ages, is it?'

'No, I suppose you're right,' Maddy was forced to agree. There was a good deal of sense in what her friend was saying, but she still found it hard to accept that Dan had let her down. It was a Saturday afternoon during the second week in June, and the two of them were enjoying a walk on the promenade overlooking the North Bay. They had been to a meeting of all the members of the troupe, held at the digs where Percy and Letty and a few more of the Pierrots were staying, in order to discuss future plans and to assess how the performances were going so far. They did not give a performance on a Saturday afternoon, because it was change-over day and the visitors were busy sorting themselves out after their arrival.

'What we need is more variety in the acts,' Percy had said. 'At the moment it seems to me that we are rather overloaded with singers and dancers and…er…not much else.'

Barney and Benjy glanced meaningfully at one another, raising their eyebrows, and Queenie Colman tossed her head and looked most annoyed.

'Please don't think that I am singling out anyone in particular,' Percy went on hastily. 'I appreciate what you do, every one of you, and I have no intention of getting rid of anyone, if that is what you are thinking. But we all do need to look at ourselves and at our acts and see if there is any way in which we can introduce an element of originality, some sparkle and imagination, instead of going on in the same old routine.'

'But tradition is good, isn't it?' said Carlo, after glancing sideways at his wife who was still looking exceedingly peeved. 'It's what Pierrot shows are all about, the old traditions. The audiences know what they like, and they expect it to follow the same pattern. There haven't been any complaints, have there? I haven't noticed anyone walking away, apart from those stingy beggars who won't pay for a seat and disappear when the bottler appears.'

'Tradition, yes; we thrive on tradition,' said Percy. 'I agree with you, to a point. But just think about it; apart from singing, and dance numbers, and musical items – and we do have a good variety of instruments as well as the piano – and a few comedy routines, what else do we have? Nancy's performing dogs, of course; I'm not forgetting them.'

'And Carlo's monologues,' said Queenie, who was by now quite red in the face. 'You were only too pleased to take us on when that other character man you had retired. And then you started mucking about with Carlo's act. I know he was quite upset when you took his jolly policeman out of the programme, and his Chelsea pensioner.'

'It was time for a change, Queenie, that's all,' sighed Percy. 'We must all look to changing our routines, that's what I'm trying to say. Anyway, you might as well know; I have put an advertisement in the *Stage* magazine inviting artistes – of any kind – to come for an audition.'

'What sort of artistes?' asked Frank Morrison, sounding a little dubious.

'I've just said – any kind,' replied Percy. 'I'm hoping we might get some different sorts of acts.

'Who knows? Ventriloquists, jugglers, magicians… It's variety that we need.'

'On the other hand you might just get the same old singers and dancers and funny men applying,' said Frank.

'And then some of us may well have to start thinking about ourselves,' said Queenie. 'Loyalty is all very well, but it does work both ways.' She gave a self-satisfied nod.

'Let's just wait and see what happens, shall we?' said Percy, a trifle wearily. 'I'm saying no more about it at the moment, but I do like to keep everyone informed about my intentions...

'Now, let's move on to the money raising... We have to pay the rent for our pitch whilst we're here in Scarborough, and that amounts to about four pounds a week at the moment. Very reasonable, I know, but it is rumoured that the Corporation might increase it soon, and quite drastically, too. So it may well be that the old tradition of "a bob a nob a day" will not be in force for very much longer.' This quaint turn of phrase referred to the rent charged by the Corporation; one shilling a day, which amounted to six shillings a week per man (or woman) in the troupe.

'We are doing well with the sale of programmes and songbooks, and the picture postcards, of course,' Percy continued. 'Now, how about some more activities for the children? Competitions with, perhaps, a more realistic entrance fee, say a shilling a head...?'

'Aye, it'd make sense to charge a bit more than we've done in the past,' agreed Pete, 'or else we'll end up giving it all away in prize money. We'll have the usual sandcastle competition, I suppose, and the talent show. And how about a Fancy Dress Parade? Kiddies love dressing up, don't they?'

'What a brilliant idea!' exclaimed Susannah, clapping her hands like a little girl. 'We could have three categories: the prettiest, and the funniest, and the most original. How about that?'

'A very good idea.' Percy nodded his approval. 'Thank you, Susannah, and to you as well, Pete. Any more ideas...?'

It was decided that they should hold a slap-up Gala Performance one evening during their last week in the resort, that would be mid-September. All the artistes would perform in evening dress, rather than their usual Pierrot costumes, and everyone agreed that it would not be unreasonable to ask double the amount for seats on that evening. The show would be widely advertised on posters displayed around the town, which, hopefully, would attract the local people as well as the holidaymakers.

'And perhaps a special souvenir programme,' suggested Nancy Pritchard. 'Folks love mementoes, don't they? And I'm sure they'd be willing to pay – what should we say, sixpence, maybe? – for one that's bright and colourful.'

Dates were decided upon for the various children's events, with particular reference to the tide's table for the sandcastle competition. Most of the troupe members seemed happy enough as the meeting ended, apart from Queenie, who had hardly let her face slip all afternoon, and Carlo, whose expression as he looked at his wife was one of consternation.

'Methinks that our Queenie is decidedly put out,' Susannah remarked as she and Maddy, after their walk along the promenade, had turned round and were heading back towards the castle. 'And poor old Carlo daren't do anything other than agree with her.'

'So I've noticed,' said Maddy. 'You don't think they'll leave, do you?'

'I doubt it,' replied Susannah. 'They wouldn't get treated any better anywhere else. Percy has been very fair with them, considering...' She didn't say what the consideration was, but Maddy knew that she was referring obliquely to the older woman's dodgy top Fs. 'Queenie likes to have her say and to make sure they're both appreciated, but I think they know on which side their bread's buttered.'

'And Barney and Benjy as well,' said Maddy. 'I noticed them exchanging glances when Percy remarked that we had a surfeit of singers and dancers. But that could apply to all of us, couldn't it, not just to them?'

'Quite so,' agreed Susannah. 'But I'm sure you don't need to worry, and nor do Frank and I. The two boys put on a bit of an act now and again, hinting that they might have had a better offer elsewhere. But it's just a game to try and get Percy worried, and he knows it only too well. I can't see them ever leaving. We just have to accept that they both have more than a touch of artistic temperament. Because of the way they are, of course,' she added. 'You know...'

'Yes,' replied Maddy, although she didn't really understand what her friend meant about Barney and Benjy.

They walked up the slope towards the castle, turning left when they reached Blenheim Terrace. Maddy recalled that that was where the Barraclough family had used to stay during their summer holidays; Faith and the four children, with Edward, even then, being very much an absentee husband and father. The undertaker's premises, Isaac Moon and Son had been – and still was – situated on North Marine Road, only a few minutes' walk away. And so Maddy and Jessie, during that summer of 1900, had cemented their friendship, which had lasted to that day.

She said goodbye, for the moment, to Susannah – they would be meeting again that evening for the performance – at the junction of Castle Road where Susannah and several of the other members of the troupe were lodging. Maddy decided to walk home a rather longer way round, passing St Mary's church and graveyard. It was not a church that was familiar to her as a place of worship. The Methodist chapel where the Moon family had worshipped when they lived in the North Bay area was not very far away. Even now, Isaac and William still made the journey across from their South Bay home, most Sunday mornings, to the place that was so dear to them. But Maddy loved the tranquillity and the feeling of holiness that she always experienced in the vicinity of St Mary's church. The old graveyard was full and was used no longer, but it was as though the spirits of the men and women – and many children, too – who had been buried there had imbued the place with an aura of sanctity and peacefulness.

And it was there, in a quiet corner in an annexe just off the main graveyard, that Anne Brontë was buried. Anne had loved Scarborough and it was the place she had chosen to visit for her last outing from Haworth. She had come there with her sister, Charlotte, in the final stages of her fatal illness, tuberculosis. They had stayed in lodgings on St Nicholas Cliff, on the site where the Grand Hotel now stood. And it was there, on the 28th of May, 1849, that Anne had died at the age of twenty-nine. Her age had been wrongly recorded as twenty-eight on the gravestone, and had never been rectified. No matter though, thought Maddy, as she stood there in contemplation. It was tragic that the talented young woman should have died so young. Maddy confessed to herself that she had not read *Agnes Grey* nor *The Tenant of Wildfell Hall*, although she had read some of the works by the other two sisters, *Jane Eyre* and *Wuthering Heights*'. But as she stood there she made a pledge to herself and to the ill-fated Anne that she would, one day, make good her omission.

She stood awhile, taking in the view of which she never tired, one of her favourite views of the town. St Mary's church stood on the headland between the two bays, and looking down through the trees one could see the whole sweep of the South Bay: the stretch of golden sand and the sparkling sea, the fishing boats in the harbour and the lighthouse on the quay, the Grand Hotel, and the Spa Bridge leading across the ravine to the hotels on the clifftop. She made her way then down the steps to Church Stair Street, and thence to the main street of the town. It was still a fair walk to the family home, but one that she was getting used to, having to take the route two or three times each day. Sometimes, if she felt inclined, she rode to the entertainment place on her bicycle, and sometimes she took sandwiches with her to eat between the morning and afternoon performances, or, alternatively, the afternoon and evening ones. But it was worth the inconvenience of the long walk to be staying with her family for the whole of the season. It was only to Maddy that the place was home; to the rest of the troupe it was just the resort where they were performing for the summer season. She had not heard any of them, however, complain about coming back to Scarborough year after year.

Maddy and Jessie both celebrated their seventeenth birthdays during the third week in June, and the occasions were celebrated on the

Sunday – Maddy's only free day – by a family tea party. She tried to smile and laugh and enter into the jollifications, but her heart was not in it. After the tea they had a sing-song around the piano; Maddy played whilst Grandad Isaac entertained them with some of the old music-hall songs that he loved: 'Two Little Girls in Blue', and 'After the Ball'. They all joined in the chorus with him, singing lustily,

> *'Many a heart is aching*
> *If you could read them all;*
> *Many the hopes that have vanished,*
> *After the ball.'*

Jessie noticed that Maddy was not singing, only playing the piano in a rather mechanical fashion, without her usual enthusiasm and flair. And she could not be persuaded to sing on her own, saying that it was quite enough for her to perform three times a day, and that Sunday was her rest day. Jessie was the only one who knew how Maddy was feeling. She knew that her beloved friend's heart was, indeed, aching, and that her hopes, as the song said, were beginning to vanish. Jessie knew that her stepsister had still not had a letter from Daniel, the lad she had met in Blackpool, who seemed to have captured her heart.

Jessie was not the only one who had noticed Maddy's unusual lassitude and the unhappiness that lay beneath her attempts at cheerfulness.

Faith waylaid her when she entered the house after the evening performance on the following day.

'Come and have a chat with me, Maddy,' she said, leading the way into the sitting room. 'Your father and Grandad Isaac have gone out for a drink, and Jessie has gone up to her room to read. So we will be on our own for a while. I'll just ask Mrs Baker to bring us a pot of tea.' She rang a bell and Mrs Baker came at once from her little bed-sitting room at the rear of the house, where she had her own comfortable living quarters: her bed, dining area and easy chairs.

'I wonder if I could trouble you to make a pot of tea, just for the two of us?' asked Faith. She was always extremely polite with the woman whom she regarded almost as much as a friend as a servant. 'And a few of those delicious shortbread biscuits you made this morning, please, Mrs Baker.'

'Certainly, madam.' She returned in a few moments with a laden tray. It was only when the tea had been poured out, and Maddy was sitting with the china cup and saucer on her lap, and a shortbread biscuit that Faith insisted she must try, that Faith broached the subject that had been bothering her.

Maddy was not surprised to hear her stepmother say, 'What is the matter Maddy? I know that something is troubling you. You are not yourself at all, and I would like to help, if I can... That is, if you would like to tell me about it. I'm not forcing you, of course, but I do realise that there's something wrong. There is, isn't there?'

Maddy gave a deep sigh. 'Yes, you're right, Aunty Faith,' she replied. It was a great relief to her to know that she could confide in the woman she had come to love so much, who had become almost, possibly just, as dear to her as her own mother had been. 'I met a young man in Blackpool,' she began. 'He's called Dan, Daniel Murphy. I know you will say that I'm very young, and so I am, but I did become very fond of him, and I thought he felt the same way about me. Well, he did; I know he did. But he's only written to me once, and I haven't heard from him since then, since I first came back to Scarborough. And I've written to him twice. I know I can't write again. And I'm so afraid that he's changed his mind about me...'

Once she started to tell the story, the words just poured out of her. She told Faith everything; that Daniel was a Catholic, that he had even been studying to become a priest, but had decided not to go on with it. 'But not because of me,' she insisted. 'He assured me that that was not the reason. He had already been having doubts before he met me...'

She went on to tell Faith about Dan's mother, how she had a great influence on her son, and how she, Maddy, believed that in the end his mother's determination had been too much for him to withstand, and that he had finally succumbed to the pressure she put on him. 'I'm afraid he's changed his mind,' she said again.

'Oh dear,' said Faith. 'Oh, dearie, dearie me! I can understand how you must be feeling, Maddy, my love. I know that first love can hurt, so very, very much. And that's what it is, isn't it; your very first love?'

Faith didn't know about Samuel, but Maddy knew now that she had never really been in love with him. 'I knew you would say that,' she replied. 'That's what everyone will say, that I'm young. And that's what I thought myself at first. I told Dan that I was very young – only sixteen – and that it would be difficult. We both knew that. But he seemed so sure, and so did I, Aunty Faith, after I'd seen him several times. He's a lovely young man and I'm sure you would think so, if you met him.'

'Yes, my dear, it is very sad,' said Faith. 'But you do realise, don't you, that there would always be problems? Even if he did give up on the idea of being a priest, his family – especially his mother – would find it hard ever to accept you. I'm very sorry, my darling,' she continued, seeing Maddy's crestfallen face, 'but it really is so. I know of the influence that Catholic mothers can have on their sons, especially the Irish Catholics, and that is what she is, didn't you say? So many of them have an ambition for their sons to go into the priesthood. There was a girl I knew in York; her brother became a priest, and it was the mother who was the driving force. The girl was called Veronica, I remember, and her mother would dearly have loved for her to become a nun as well, but Veronica was made of sterner stuff than her brother. So much so that she married a young man who was not "of the Faith" as they say. He belonged to the Church of England; quite a devout young man, from all accounts, but her mother never really forgave her. So you see, my dear, there would be sure to be problems...'

Maddy nodded sadly. 'Yes, I'm beginning to see that. Then you are telling me, aren't you, that I should try to forget about him?'

'I'm very much afraid so,' said Faith. She crossed the room and sat on the sofa. She put her arm around her. 'You are young, my love,' she said. 'So very young, and you have plenty of time to meet lots of other young men. Dan sounds a grand young man; I'm sure he is, and I'm sure he really was fond of you. But you must try to accept it, that he's been forced to...to think again.'

'I'll try,' replied Maddy. 'I must admit that I think you're right. It's hard, though. It really is hard, Aunty Faith. I can't believe that he would let himself be influenced, and that he hasn't even let me know that it's...all over.'

'It had hardly begun, my dear,' said Faith gently. 'How long had you known him? Only a week? Well then...I know it hurts, but it will pass. Believe me, it will pass...'

Maddy tried. She really tried very hard to put all thoughts of Dan to the back of her mind, suppressing them when they rose to the surface by thinking of something else. She looked for new songs – new to her, at least – to add to her repertoire, bearing in mind what Percy had said to them all about livening up their acts and adding some different numbers. She decided to include 'After the Ball', remembering how her grandad had sung it so poignantly on the occasion of the birthday party; it was a plaintive little song that would go down well with the audiences. And 'Joshua, Joshua (Nicer than lemon squash, you are)', a comical little song about a shy young man courting his lady friend; not quite her usual style, but one that would show Percy how adaptable she was, able to be amusing as well as pensive.

But it was an unaccompanied song that she was singing – a new one to her programme – one night in mid-July, when she noticed a once familiar face in the audience. The song was a haunting one, an old Somerset air, usually known as 'O, Waly, Waly'.

'The water is wide,' she sang,
'I cannot get o'er;
Give me a boat
To take me home.
My true love waits
On yonder shore,
So far away,

So long alone…'

Her eyes were scanning the faces of the audience, mostly smiling a little and listening intently. She did not expect to see anyone she knew that evening. Her family had been to see the show earlier that week, to hear her new songs and see the revitalised acts of some of the other members of the troupe.

She almost stopped singing when she saw the face of a young man on the back row, smiling at her. It was Dan! But of course it couldn't be. It just wasn't possible; it showed how thoughts of him were still filling her mind, even though she had tried to push them to one side. Her voice faltered for just a second, then she looked again. Yes, it really was Dan! There was no doubt about it, and as she stared at him, bewildered and incredulous, he lifted one hand, not waving, but motioning gently to her.

It was her first appearance, during the first half of the programme. It was not the thing, really, for the artistes to go and chat with the members of the audience during the interval, apart from the bottler, doing his round. But Maddy could not wait until the end of the show. As soon as Barney and Benjy had brought the first half to an end with their toe-tapping number, she ran from the dressing tent, across the stretch of sand to where Dan was waiting for her. The next moment his arms were round her as they greeted one another.

'Dan, oh Dan! I thought I'd never see you again.'

'Maddy! I just couldn't wait any longer.' He

kissed her gently, then she heard him say, 'But why didn't you write? I've been going frantic. I thought you'd changed your mind about me coming to see you. But I knew I had to find out for sure. So…here I am. You still…you do want to see me, don't you?'

'Of course I do,' she cried. 'But I did write to you, Dan. I wrote you two letters, then I decided it was no use. I thought you'd changed your mind.'

'Never,' he said. 'As if I would.' His face was serious. 'You wrote to me, you say? But I don't understand…' He frowned. 'But perhaps I do,' he added slowly. 'Yes…I think I'm beginning to understand, only too well.'

'I must go now, Dan,' she said. 'We're only halfway through the show, and I have to change for the second half. You will wait, won't you?'

'What do you think? I would wait for ever,' he replied. Reluctantly he let go of her hand and watched her run back into the dressing tent.

Chapter Twelve

'Dan's there, in the audience!' Maddy cried in great excitement to Susannah.

'Who? You mean...the young man from Blackpool?' said Susannah. 'Well, I never! And what does he have to say for himself?'

'I'm not sure yet,' replied Maddy, 'but it's all very mysterious. He says he didn't get my letters. Anyway, I'm seeing him afterwards. He's waiting for me. Oh! Isn't it exciting?'

'Yes, love; I'm very pleased for you,' said Susannah, sincerely. But she had a word of warning for her young friend when the show came to an end and a starry-eyed Maddy was ready to dash off to meet her young man.

'Don't rush into anything, love,' she said. 'Remember what I told you before. You are still very young and there may be all kinds of problems ahead of you.' She smiled, though, at her friend's enraptured face. 'But I really am happy for you. Surprised, though, I must admit, that he's actually turned up at last. But off you go and enjoy yourself. Don't do anything I wouldn't do!' she added with a cheeky grin.

'We won't,' replied Maddy seriously. 'You have no need to worry, Susannah. There will be…none of that.' Deep down, Maddy didn't really approve of her older friend's 'goings-on', behaving as they were before they were married. But Susannah, of course, had much more experience of the ways of the world, and of men, than she had. She knew, though, that her friend was concerned for her, and it pleased Maddy that someone cared about her problems.

It was still broad daylight, a balmy summer evening, as Maddy and Dan, arm in arm, made their way up to the promenade, and then through the streets of the town.

'So tell me why you're here,' she said.

'To see you, of course,' he replied.

'Yes, but…it's been such a long time. I really thought I would never see you again. And you say you didn't receive my letters. I wonder why?'

'I'm afraid I can guess why,' replied Dan in a grim tone. 'I don't want to think so, but I very much fear that they might have been intercepted by…well, you can guess who, can't you?' Maddy looked at him in horror.

'You mean…your mother? Oh, surely not, Dan. She wouldn't do that, would she?'

'I'm afraid she might. She's always up long before any of the rest of us in the morning, and she makes it her business to look through the letters. Oh! What a fool I've been. What a complete idiot! But I trusted her, you see. I believe that all relationships should be based on trust. And I never thought for one moment that she would…'

'Didn't you ask her if there was a letter for you? Didn't you tell her that you were expecting one?'

'No, I didn't. I thought the less said the better. You know how disapproving she's been…about you and me.'

'So does she know you've come here this weekend?'

'I just told her that I was going away for the weekend, that's all. I'm afraid I'm spending less and less time at home, helping in the boarding house, and more and more time at the shop. I'm full-time there now, as I told you. Mr Grundy agreed for me to take a long weekend off, so I'll be going back on Monday morning.' It was Friday, so Maddy was overjoyed that they would be able to spend the whole weekend together, when she was not performing, that was.

'But why didn't you write to me again?' she asked. It was something that had been puzzling her. 'When you didn't get a letter? You said you were worried.'

'And so I was,' replied Daniel slowly. 'It's difficult to explain, Madeleine. I feared I might have rushed you, you see. I wasn't sure that you felt the same way as I do. I know we haven't known one another very long, but…I love you, Madeleine.' They stopped by the railings of the Spa Bridge, and he turned towards her, looking deeply into her eyes.

'I love you very much. But I know how young you are, a few years younger than me. And I know you lead a very busy – exciting – life. I wanted to know that you were very sure. And then, when you didn't write – or I thought you hadn't – I started to think that I might have been mistaken about your feelings for me.'

'I do feel the same, Dan,' she said quietly. 'I love you too. I'm very sure about it.' He kissed her gently, but without a great deal of passion; a kiss of deep affection and tenderness. They both felt, at that moment, that they had all the time in the world ahead of them. Then suddenly, he laughed.

'Where are we heading anyway?' he asked. 'I'm not really sure where we are. I'm relying on you to show me the way back.' Maddy laughed too.

'Oh, how silly of me! I haven't even asked where you're staying. You've found somewhere, I suppose?'

'Yes, I arrived this afternoon, and I managed to find lodgings at a little boarding house near to the railway station. Just off…Westborough, is it called?'

'Yes, that's the upper part of the main street that leads through the town, from the harbour up to the station. This is the Spa Bridge, where we are now. I always stop whenever I cross it to look at the view. Just look, Dan. Don't you think it's a wonderful view from here?'

Looking back in the direction from which they

had come they could see the wide curve of the bay, with the now diminishing stretch of sand as the tide advanced; the harbour with the yachts and fishing boats at anchor, and the lighthouse; and dominating the scene, the impressive bulk of the Grand Hotel. Standing out against the skyline, above the trees and the huddle of rooftops, was the grey-stone tower of St Mary's church, and above it all, on the very top of the cliff, the ruins of the ancient castle.

'And down there, on the lower promenade, that's the Spa,' Maddy said, pointing in the other direction. 'It's an entertainment place. They have concerts and dancing there, and brass bands playing in the Pavilion. Some of the other Pierrot troupes have their pitches on the sands down there. But we've always been on the North Bay.'

'Yes, I can see that Scarborough is a lovely town,' agreed Dan. 'I am very impressed. So different from Blackpool, but it isn't really fair to compare the two places. One always has a soft spot for one's home town,' he added loyally. 'I'm still lost, though. I hope you're going to tell me how to get back to my digs.'

'Of course,' she laughed. 'Come on now, and I'll show you where I live. It's not very far from here... Would you like to come in and meet my parents? My father and my stepmother, I mean; my Aunty Faith, as I always call her.'

Her question was tentative, though, and she was rather relieved when Dan said, 'No, I don't think so. Not tonight. They're not expecting me and it wouldn't be fair. You've told them about me, though, haven't you?'

'I've told Aunty Faith,' she replied honestly, 'and Jessie, my stepsister. Not my father, though...with you not writing, you see. But I will tell him now, of course.'

'Yes, I understand,' he said. 'I'll leave you to explain everything, and then, perhaps, I might come and meet them?'

They continued over the bridge and up the steep slope to the South Cliff, passing the Crown Hotel, the first of the prestigious hotels to be built on the South Bay. Maddy's family home was on Victoria Avenue, one of the streets leading off the Esplanade. Dan was impressed by the large detached house with its own carriage drive, and the attractive garden with tall trees, ornamental bushes and flower beds.

'So where do I go from here?' he asked.

She pointed him in the right direction. 'Walk in a more or less straight line from here, and you will come to the railway station. About ten minutes' walk, I would say, that's all.'

'And...when shall I see you?' he asked.

They agreed to meet after the Saturday morning show and spend the afternoon together.

Dan put his arms around her and kissed her, very gently. 'I'm so glad I've found you again,' he whispered.

'So am I,' she replied. She kissed his cheek, then ran up the path, turning at the door to wave to him. He was still standing there, watching her as though he couldn't quite believe that she was real and not a dream.

Only Faith and Jessie were in the sitting room when Maddy rushed in. She guessed that her father and grandfather had gone out for what Grandad called their 'nightly constitutional'. Not every night, but on a few nights a week, the father and son would go for an evening walk followed by a drink – but only one, they both insisted – at a local public house before returning soon after ten o' clock.

'You're a bit later than usual, Maddy,' said Faith, then she noticed her stepdaughter's flushed face and her air of excitement.

'Yes, I know, Aunty Faith,' replied Maddy. 'I'm sorry…'

'There's no need to apologise,' said Faith. 'I'm not complaining. I'm just stating a fact, that's all… What is it, dear?' she asked, looking at her more closely. 'Has something exciting happened?'

'Yes, very exciting,' replied Maddy, taking off her straw hat and throwing it onto an easy chair. She flopped down on the sofa next to Jessie. 'You'll never guess!'

'I think I might,' said Jessie, smiling knowingly at her friend. 'Would it be something to do with a certain young man from Blackpool? It's all right,' she added. 'I know that you've told my mother about him. What is it? Have you had a letter from him at last?'

'Better than that,' laughed Maddy. 'Anyway, you would know if I'd had a letter, wouldn't you? I'd have told you this morning. It's much, much better than that. He was in the audience tonight! I just happened to glance at the back row and there he was! I could hardly believe it.'

'Gosh! That's wonderful,' said Jessie. 'I don't wonder you're excited.' The look of delight on Jessie's face told Maddy that her friend was very happy for her. But when she looked at her Aunty Faith's face she saw quite a different expression there. There was a guarded look in Faith's eyes, and although she smiled it was a little uneasily.

'Well then, I'm glad you're happy, dear,' she said. 'It's good to see you looking so cheerful again. But...why hadn't he written? Did he say? It has been quite a long time.'

'He didn't get my letters,' said Maddy. 'And he didn't write again because...because he thought I might have had second thoughts. As if I would! I told him that I'd been thinking just the same about him. Anyway, like I said, he didn't get my letters, and he's got an idea that they might have been intercepted. Well, he's convinced they were...by his mother! Can you believe that any mother would behave like that, Aunty Faith? It's terrible, isn't it?'

'Indeed it is, if it's true,' replied Faith. 'But you shouldn't really jump to conclusions before you

226

know the facts. You told me though, didn't you, about his mother. And I would say that this doesn't bode well for the future if it's true. And…well, yes…I must admit that I fear it might be true. I daresay that woman had great expectations for her son and, to her way of thinking, he's let her down badly.'

'You sound as though you agree with her,' said Maddy, a little heatedly, but carefully at the same time. It was the first time she had ever had reason to argue, even mildly, with her dear stepmother.

'Yes, you do, Mother,' Jessie added. 'You surely can't think it was right for a mother to do such a despicable thing as to steal her son's letters.'

'If she has done,' sighed Faith. 'And we don't know definitely, do we? Yes, I agree it would be awful, and I'm really sorry about it. But I did warn you, didn't I, Maddy love? When you first told me about this Daniel I said it wouldn't be all plain sailing.'

'But he still feels the same,' cried Maddy. 'And he's come to see me, to find out what was wrong. Oh! Please don't spoil it for me. I was feeling so happy. And I thought you would want to meet him. He's staying for the weekend and he's not going back till Monday morning.'

'Then of course we shall meet him,' said Faith. 'Your father and I will be very pleased to meet him. You know that any friends of yours are always welcome here.'

'Father doesn't know anything about him yet,' said Maddy, a little apprehensively. 'You haven't said anything, have you, Aunty Faith?'

'No, of course not, dear. I thought it best, under the circumstances, not to mention it, especially as...'

'Especially as you thought it was all over, didn't you?' retorted Maddy. 'Because it had hardly even started, that's what you said, didn't you?'

'Oh, my dear, please don't let's quarrel,' said Faith. 'We never have done, and we mustn't ever. I'm just concerned for you, as I would be for Jessica or for any of you. And I know your father will feel just the same.' Faith's lovely blue eyes were clouded with anxiety, and Maddy knew that her stepmother did, indeed, care about her, just the same as if she were her own daughter. Maddy jumped up from the sofa and went across to her. She gave her a hug.

'I'm sorry, Aunty Faith,' she said. 'It's just that I was feeling on top of the world and then...well...I started to see the problems again. But it'll be all right, I know it will... I'm going to make us all a cup of tea now. We don't need to trouble Mrs Baker, do we?'

'Very good dear,' said Faith. 'Make a big pot, will you? I expect your father and grandfather will be back soon. Then you'll be able to tell your father about Daniel, won't you?'

Maddy looked a little fearful. 'I was hoping that you might do that, Aunty Faith,' she said.

'No,' said Faith, quite firmly. 'I really think it's up to you to tell him.'

'He'll say I'm too young, won't he, like you did?'

'Yes, maybe he will. But he knows, as I do, that you're a sensible girl and that we can trust you. All you need to say is that you met a nice young man in Blackpool and that he's come to see you this weekend. And we'll invite him to come and have lunch with us on Sunday, shall we?'

'Poor lad!' said Jessie. 'What an ordeal, eh?'

'No, we'll all be very kind and welcoming,' said Faith, 'as we are with all our guests.'

'I don't think I'll tell Father about him being a Catholic, and all that,' said Maddy. 'Not yet anyway. What do you think?'

'No, perhaps not,' replied Faith. 'Don't worry, dear. Leave that to me. I'll try to explain to your father later on, about the – er – complications. First things first, eh?'

Her father and grandfather had returned by the time the tea was ready. William's reaction was predictable. He didn't say a great deal, apart from that he didn't know that Maddy had a young admirer; she had kept it quiet; why hadn't she mentioned it before? And she was, of course, only seventeen. But he agreed that the young man should come for what he preferred to call Sunday dinner, rather than lunch. William still thought of lunch as sandwiches that you carried to work in a tin box.

Maddy and Dan spent a happy two days

together. They lunched on fish and chips at a little café near to the harbour after the Saturday morning performance. This was a meal just as popular – and just as well cooked, Dan agreed – in Scarborough as it was in Blackpool. They walked back to Maddy's home where Dan, for the first time, met Faith and Isaac. William was busy in the office on North Marine Road, as was Hetty; she was adapting well to her new position, but still required a little guidance now and then. Maddy was pleased at the welcome Dan received from her stepmother and her grandfather, and she started to feel a little less apprehensive about the family meal the following day.

Dan borrowed Jessie's bicycle and they rode southwards, along the coast road that led eventually to Filey and Flamborough Head. They stopped on the clifftop near to Cayton Bay from where there were panoramic views to the north and the south. As they sat on the springy grass, listening to the sound of the sea as it lapped against the rocks far below, and the cry of the seagulls wheeling in the cloudless sky above them, Maddy felt an overwhelming sense of contentment. At that moment she was convinced that nothing could ever spoil the happiness she knew when she was with Daniel. He put an arm around her, kissing her softly on the cheek, and then, more daringly, on her lips. She responded to him and they shared several more kisses before drawing apart.

'I love you, Madeleine,' he told her. 'I can't believe I waited so long before coming to find out what was wrong. I'm trying not to think about what my mother has done,' he went on. 'I don't want anything to spoil our lovely weekend.'

'Are you going to ask her about it? And are you going to tell her where you've been this weekend?'

'Of course I am. Don't worry, darling. I've made up my mind that she is not going to control me anymore. I'm finding it very hard to forgive her, although I know I have to try. And the point is, she very nearly got away with it. I had almost convinced myself that you must have changed your mind. But she can't – she won't! – rule my life. And if it means that I have to move away, then…so be it.'

'Leave home, you mean?'

'Yes… Please don't worry, Madeleine. Everything will be all right in the end, I promise.'

A small dark cloud passed, momentarily, over the sun, and Maddy shivered a little. 'I do hope so,' she said. 'I really didn't want to do anything to upset your family life. I know I would feel dreadful if it was me. I have had such a happy life with my family – apart from the time when we lost my mother, of course – and I wouldn't want anything ever to spoil it.'

'Neither did I,' replied Dan, looking solemn for a moment. Then he smiled again. 'Cheer up, love,' he said. 'I've told you, I'm not going to let anything spoil our time together now, and not in the future either. Now…shall we see what your nice Aunty Faith has prepared for us? I thought I'd not be able to eat another morsel after those fish and chips, but the sea air is making me quite hungry.'

There were dainty salmon sandwiches, two small meat pies, and two pieces of Mrs Baker's delicious fruitcake, and a bottle of home-made lemonade with two unbreakable bakelite cups. It was just enough, as Maddy could not sing well after a big meal. By the time they had cycled back, then walked to the promenade, it was almost time for the evening performance to begin. As the tide was in, it was held in Clarence Gardens that evening.

Dan, of course, was in the audience, in the second row this time. At his request, she sang once again, the haunting Somerset air, 'O Waly, Waly'.

'My *true love waits*
On yonder shore,
So far away,
So long alone…'

As her eyes met his, she wished so fervently that there would be a time when they would be together, for always.

The routine on a Sunday morning was that Mrs Baker would stay at home and cook the dinner whilst the Moon family attended church or chapel. Mrs Baker attended her own Methodist chapel in the evening, and the arrangement suited them all very well. They usually alternated, week by week, between St Martin's Church of England on the South Bay, quite near to where they lived, and the Methodist chapel on Queen Street, much further away, but the one that the Moon family had always attended before their move to the other end of the town.

As it was a Church of England morning, the family arrived home before twelve noon, and were greeted as they came through the door by the appetising aroma of roast beef, and what smelt like one of Mrs Baker's specialities, rhubarb and apple crumble.

Maddy opened the door to Dan at twelve-thirty, and introduced him to the members of her family he had not met previously.

'This is my father, William Moon... Daddy, this is Dan...'

William shook hands cordially, and laughed when Dan addressed him as sir.

'Nay, we'll have none of that, lad. I'm William, or Will, whichever you prefer. We don't stand on ceremony here.'

'And this is my best friend, Jessie; my stepsister, actually. I've told you a lot about her, haven't I, Dan?'

'Many times,' agreed Dan. 'I'm so pleased to meet you, Jessie, at last. I've heard so much about you that I feel I know you already.' Jessie blushed a little, as she always did when she met someone new.

'And the twins, Tommy and Tilly...' They grinned and said hello, Tommy first and then Tilly following his lead.

'And then there's my brother, Patrick,' said Maddy. 'But he's having dinner with his fiancée's parents today. I expect you'll meet him sometime.' She didn't mention Samuel, or Henrietta, although she had told Dan a little about them. The family was quite complicated enough as it was.

'Now, tuck in, lad, and don't be afraid,' said Isaac, after Dan had helped himself from the china dishes to roast potatoes, mashed carrot and swede, and garden peas, to accompany the thick slices of roast beef with rich gravy and a touch of horseradish sauce. And a square-cut piece of Yorkshire pudding, golden brown and crispy at the edges.

'Mind you, this is not the proper Yorkshire way of serving it,' Isaac informed Dan. 'When my wife made Yorkshire pudding – God bless her – she used to serve it before the meal on separate plates, to whet the appetite, you might say. But Mrs Baker allus does it this way, and we're not complaining.'

'I should think not,' said Dan. 'It's delicious. This is the way we serve it in Lancashire, as part of the main meal.'

'Aye, I reckon so.' Isaac sniffed, but he grinned at Daniel as he said, 'There are some Yorkshire folk who say that the only good thing to come out of

Lancashire is the road that leads over t'Pennines. But I think we can make an exception with you, lad. Aye, I'm sure we can. You're very welcome and we're right pleased to get to know you. Our Maddy's kept it all very quiet, mind. But we're real glad to have you here with us.'

'Thank you; it's very kind of you to say so,' replied Dan. His eyes twinkled. 'Lancashire folk say the same thing, you know, about the road leading from Yorkshire. But the Wars of the Roses are long gone, aren't they?'

'Aye, life's too short to quarrel,' agreed Isaac.

Maddy had guessed it was inevitable that religion would be mentioned, if only in passing. It came out in the conversation that Daniel had attended Mass that morning at a Catholic church in Scarborough.

'Yes, Maddy told us about that,' said William, although it was, in fact, his wife who had told him about the young man's religious persuasion. 'But we won't hold that against you, Dan, you can feel sure about that. Each to his own is what I say, and I know that my father agrees with me. There has been a good deal of bigotry here in the past, though.'

'Aye, Scarborough was a real hotbed of Methodism,' said Isaac. 'John Wesley preached here, you know, umpteen times; it was one of his favourite places for preaching the gospel. My own grandfather heard him preach many a time. And the chapel we attend, it can hold up to two thousand folk.'

'Not that we get so many there now though, Father,' said William, with a warning look at Isaac to tell him that that was enough.

'What sort of a season are you having in Blackpool?' asked Faith, to change the subject.

'The town is crowded, as usual,' replied Dan. 'My mother's boarding house has been fully booked all season. She's very pleased because it's her first full season there.'

All told, it was a comfortable meal time, and Maddy was relieved that it had all gone so well.

The rest of the day flew past, and Maddy was to look back afterwards at an idyllic time when every hour, every minute and second, was filled with joy; joy in one another and in their certainty that their love was growing and would last for a lifetime. Nothing had been said; neither of them had given voice to their feelings that this would be for ever. Maddy knew in her heart of hearts that it was too soon to speak of a lifetime commitment. Neither she nor Daniel could make such a pledge, not yet. She was still only seventeen, just on the brink of adulthood. It was only yesterday that she had been a young girl, not believing that she would soon fall so deeply in love. She knew now that what she had thought was love – her silly infatuation for Samuel – had been nothing at all; a foolish notion which embarrassed her even to think of it now.

They listened to a brass band concert at the Spa Pavilion on Sunday afternoon, then wandered through the Valley Gardens, along the woodland paths that meandered up and down the cliffside of the South Bay; then they picnicked again in a quiet spot on the clifftop.

They strolled back to the town hand in hand, aware that their time together was fast dwindling away, but neither of them wanting to say goodbye to what had been a wonderful two days. Both of them felt sure, though, that there would be another time, lots of times when they would be together.

They stood eventually on the path looking down on the Spa Pavilion, just as the sun was beginning its descent behind the trees and the rooftops of the town above them.

'I'll come and see you again before very long, I promise,' said Dan. 'Shall we say in a month's time? Mid-August or thereabouts. I shall write first, but you can be quite sure that your letters will not disappear again.' He looked at her troubled face, drawing her close to him and kissing her forehead. 'It will be all right, believe me. You and me...you know that I won't let anything come between us, don't you, Madeleine...my love?'

'Yes, I know,' she answered quietly. He kissed her tenderly and longingly, then they drew apart and started to climb up the last slope to the promenade, near to the avenue where the Moon family lived.

'Will you come in and have a cup of tea, and say goodbye to my family?' she asked. She was not surprised when he refused and she knew, too, that she was relieved. She did not want their last moments together to be spent in the company of others. It was far better this way. He kissed her again by the gate, but neither of them wanted to linger; it was too painful.

She stood for a few moments on the doorstep before taking her key from her purse and letting herself into the house. 'Hello there,' she called, with an assumed gaiety. 'I'm back...'

She knew they would talk about Daniel. It was unavoidable and she knew she must not react too much to anything they might say. She guessed, though, that he had already made a favourable impression. They were all there in the sitting room – her father, Aunty Faith, Jessie and Grandfather Isaac, all except the twins, who had gone to bed.

'I thought Dan might have come in with you,' observed Faith.

'No... He's catching an early train in the morning,' said Maddy, although that, of course, was not a sufficient reason. Faith smiled and nodded and Maddy felt sure that she understood.

'He's a very pleasant young man,' said her father. 'Yes, we liked him very much.'

'Aye, I must admit that he's a grand young feller,' agreed Isaac, 'especially when you consider he's a left-footer,' he added with a grin.

'Father, really!' said William, and Faith, too, frowned a little.

'What d'you mean?' asked Maddy. She could

guess but it was an expression she hadn't heard before.

'I don't mean any disrespect to the lad,' said Isaac. 'Keep yer hair on, all of yer. It's just a nickname for a Catholic, that's all. Don't ask me why.'

'A derogatory term all the same,' said William. 'Like the Catholics sometimes refer to us Protestants as Proddies. I suppose it all came from Ireland in the beginning. There's always been a lot of bitterness there between the two religions.'

'Aye, it dates right back to the battle of the Boyne,' said Isaac. 'When William of Orange defeated James the Second and his Irish army. T'Catholics have never forgotten it. Aye, the Irish have long memories. I reckon there'll be more trouble there afore we're done.'

Maddy knew only too well that the Irish had long memories, well, some of them at any rate; Dan's mother was a case in point. 'But surely it doesn't matter now, does it?' she said. 'Not to us?'

'Of course it doesn't,' said her grandad. 'Don't mind me. I speak me mind, happen too much at times. I've told you; we liked your young man, Catholic or not. But it isn't as if you're going to marry him, is it?'

'No indeed,' added William. 'I've no doubt he'll be the first of many young men that our Maddy'll bring home.'

'Don't say that, Father.' Maddy couldn't help

defending herself. 'I'm not a flirt, you know. I happen to be rather fond of Dan, and he's fond of me.'

'Yes, I've no doubt about that,' said William. 'But you must take your time, love, that's all I'm saying. You're far too young to be thinking of settling down. Anyroad, you've got your career, haven't you? Not the one I might have chosen for you at one time, but we're real proud of you, all the same.'

Maddy glanced across at Faith, and she could see the concern and compassion in her stepmother's eyes as she smiled at her. Aunty Faith understood perfectly how she felt even if nobody else did. She always would.

Chapter Thirteen

Dan was determined to waste no time before tackling his mother about the subject that was uppermost in his mind. He arrived back at Blackpool Central Station in the early afternoon and his long-legged strides, urged on by his determination, took him in a matter of minutes to the boarding house in Adelaide Street where 'Mrs Anna Murphy...welcomes guests from all regions'.

He let himself into the house, dumped his bag in the hallway and walked purposefully into the kitchen at the back, where he guessed his mother would be washing up after the midday dinner. She was there at the large sink, her arms immersed almost to the elbows in soapy water, piling plates onto what already seemed a considerable mountain of crockery on the wooden draining board. Myrtle, their 'maid of all work' – waitress, chambermaid-cum-kitchen maid – stood at her side, wiping the plates with a striped tea towel before placing them on the pine table in the centre of the room.

'Myrtle, would you please leave us alone for a few minutes?' said Dan politely. 'I have something rather important to discuss with my mother.'

'Certainly,' said the girl, quite deferentially, although she did not bob a curtsy as some maids had been trained to. After all, from what he had noticed, she had already become more than a little friendly with his brother, Joe, and so regarded Daniel as an equal rather than as the son of her employer.

'And who do you think is going to wipe these pots if she disappears?' Anna Murphy turned round indignantly. 'You should mind your own business, my lad; gadding off for the weekend, then coming back and throwing your weight about.'

'What shall I do then, madam?' asked Myrtle, rather pertly, Dan thought.

'Oh, go and find something else to do, I suppose. Go and make sure the dining room's been left tidy.' Anna turned to her son. 'And I'll thank you not to interfere in matters that are nothing to do with you.'

'Like you interfered in mine, do you mean?' retorted Daniel. What an appropriate opening she had given him, to be sure.

'If you are still on about the way you have let me down by turning your back on God, then I've heard enough, Daniel. I told you, I wasn't interfering; I was guiding you in the right direction. I'm your mother and I know what is best for you.'

'And you thought it was best, did you, to steal my letters?' asked Daniel, with an assumed politeness.

His mother turned a little pink, but, to her credit he supposed, she did not try to deny it or to bluff by asking him what he was talking about. 'I thought it was for the best, Daniel,' she replied. 'I've told you, I do know what's best for you. I always have…and I've got to do whatever I can to put things right when I can see that you're heading off in the wrong direction.'

'How dare you, Mother?' He found that he was no longer able to contain his anger, and he was unable, also, to address her as Mammy, the childhood name that he and Joe had always used. 'How dare you try to control my life? Where do you think I have been this weekend?' She did not answer.

'Go on, answer me,' he persisted. 'Where have I been?'

'I should imagine that you've been to see her…that girl,' said Anna coolly, but, he noticed, a little apprehensively.

'Yes, you are quite right. I have been to see Madeleine Moon in Scarborough, a young lady I am very fond of. And who you so very nearly managed to…to get rid off. Because that is what you wanted, didn't you, Mother?'

'I thought it would be for the best,' Anna said again, but in a rather less aggressive tone. 'That sort of a girl… She's not right for you, as well as…everything else.'

'What "sort of a girl"? I've told you before,

Madeleine is an extremely well-brought-up and most charming girl. By "everything else" I suppose you mean that she is not a Catholic. Well, no, she isn't, but I was made to feel most welcome by all her family this weekend. I will be seeing her again, quite soon, and if you think for one moment that anything you can do will split us up, then you are wrong, Mother.'

'Don't be so silly, Daniel!' Anna had managed to regain a little of her confidence. 'You are not twenty-one. You are not even twenty yet, and until then you are under the control of your parents. You can't get married without our permission.'

'Have I said anything about getting married?' replied Dan. 'The word has never been mentioned. What I want – and what I am going to have – is the freedom to go out with a girl of my choice, or several girls if I so wish. That is what most young men of my age do. But as it happens, Madeleine is the only one that I want. I have not asked her to marry me, if that is what you are thinking. We haven't discussed the future, not the distant future, that is, although I do believe that she and I will have a future together, and I believe that she thinks so too. Did you really imagine, Mother, that I wouldn't find out about what you had done?'

Anna shrugged a little sheepishly. 'I suppose I hoped she might forget about you, or think that you had forgotten her. It can't last anyway, Daniel. She's a showgirl, isn't she? All over the place, a different town each week. She's sure to meet all kinds of young men. Do be sensible, love.' Her voice was taking on a wheedling tone now. 'You've never been out with a girl before, have you, because of…well, because of the way things were, so you're bound to be fascinated by her. She's very pretty, I must admit…'

'And you think I'm so shallow as to be captivated by a pretty face, do you? Madeleine is not only beautiful, she is kind and considerate and warm-hearted, and I happen to believe that she is the girl for me.'

'Well, we shall see,' replied Anna, quite calmly.

'Yes, we shall see, Mother, as you say. But you won't be seeing me for very much longer. I always believed that I could trust you, and it's come as a great shock to me to find out that I can't.'

'But I didn't mean… I've told you, I thought it was for the best,' pleaded Anna.

Dan went on as though he hadn't heard her. 'So I have decided that I am going to leave and find somewhere else to live. I have already had the chance of somewhere else and I feel, to quote your words, Mother, that it would be "for the best".'

'But you can't… You're not twenty-one. You can't just go and do as you please.'

'Oh, I think you will find that I can, Mother,' replied Daniel. 'Let's do this sensibly, shall we? We don't want the whole town knowing our business, do we? Talk it over with Daddy. I think you will find that he will agree with me.'

It was Mr Grundy, Dan's employer, who had already offered him a place to live, should he ever need it. The elderly shopkeeper had been aware of his assistant's preoccupation and guessed that something was troubling him. Dan had confided in him that he was not too happy at home at the moment – not the whole story, though, out of loyalty to his mother – and Mr Grundy had suggested, at once, that it was high time he got round to making more use of the rooms above the gentlemen's outfitters. They were used mainly for stock, although at one time they had been rented out to a young couple who had left to move into a small house when their first child arrived. So there was already a small kitchen, as well as a cubbyhole with a sink and lavatory. It would be an easy matter to move the stock to the smaller of the two remaining rooms, and convert the larger room into a bed-sitting room.

When Dan returned to work on the Tuesday morning he told Mr Grundy that he would be pleased to take up his offer and to move in as soon as it was possible.

Jonas Grundy was delighted, just as he had been when the young man had asked, a couple of months previously, if he could work full-time at the shop instead of part-time. He and his wife, Emmeline, were now in their late sixties, and Jonas was coming, more and more, to regard Daniel as the son he had never had. He and Emmeline had courted for many years before marrying at the age of forty. They had both had elderly parents to care for and had, therefore, left it too late to have a family of their own. They lived in the house that had belonged to Emmeline's parents, in the district known as the Raike's Hall estate, within easy walking distance of the shop on Church Street.

On Wednesday afternoon, which was half-day closing for the Blackpool stores, Jonas accompanied Daniel to a second-hand saleroom where they purchased the necessary items to furnish a bed-sitting room. A fold-away bed, a small oak dining table and two chairs, a bookcase and two easy chairs, somewhat shabby but clean and comfortable. The room was already carpeted, and Mrs Grundy was only too pleased to be able to supply the young man with some of the more essential smaller items: crockery, cutlery, towels, bedlinen and a few cooking utensils. During a marriage of nearly thirty years she had acquired far more things than she needed.

If it had been a more amenable parting Dan would have asked his mother for help with equipping his new home, but under the circumstances he knew it would not be advisable. Nor did she offer to do so, although she was well aware of what was going on around her.

'What has brought this on?' Thomas Murphy asked his wife. 'Our Daniel moving out?' It was

Thursday evening and the two of them were relaxing for a little while in their private sitting room. In a few moments Anna would go and attend to the visitors' supper requests. This had formerly been one of Daniel's tasks, but he no longer took any part in the running of the boarding house.

'He's told me about it,' Thomas continued, 'but he wouldn't say too much, only that he thought it was time he had a little place of his own. And Jonas Grundy wants somebody living above the shop for security reasons, at least that's what Dan says. But I reckon there's more to it than that. There's summat he's not telling me.' He looked keenly at his wife. 'You and Dan have had a bit of a falling-out, haven't you?'

'Well, sort of.' Anna shrugged. 'It's something and nothing really. It'll soon blow over, I'm sure. But I thought it might be better if he went his own road for a while. I've talked till I'm blue in the face, but he won't listen to me, he's that stubborn.'

'So...are you going to tell me what it's all about?' asked Thomas.

Anna sighed. 'It's about that girl, you might know.'

'You mean...the one that we saw in the show at the North Pier? Aye, I remember that he'd got friendly with her. That's what caused all that upset a couple of months back, isn't it? But I thought it had all fizzled out. We've not heard anything about her lately.'

'Yes, I was hoping that we'd heard the last of her, but no such luck. That's where he was last weekend, in Scarborough, chasing after her. Didn't you realise that's where he might have gone?'

'No, I never gave a thought to the girl. I thought happen he'd gone to visit a schoolfriend. I don't believe in prying too much, Anna, into what the lads are doing. They're both old enough – and sensible enough an' all, I reckon – to know what they're about.'

'Huh! Then I'm afraid I don't agree with you. It's up to us to guide them, especially if we think they're going astray. And that's what I thought Daniel was doing, mooning around after that girl. I tried to put a stop to it, but...'

'But what, Anna?' He looked closely at his wife's face. She had gone rather pink and there was a wary look in her eyes. He guessed that she had been interfering and not for the first time either. 'Come on, Anna; tell me what you've done.'

'I thought it was for the best, Thomas, really I did. And that's what I told Daniel, but it's only gone and made things worse than ever. That's why he's moving out...'

'What have you done?' he asked again firmly, but quietly because he could see his wife was close to tears. Tears of guilt, maybe, but he didn't want to be too hard on her. She was hot-headed was Anna, stubborn and determined at all costs to have her own way. He had known that, of course, when he married her, but he had fallen in love with the red-haired, high-spirited and passionate girl; and nothing that she had done since, wrong or ill-advised though it might have been at times, had caused him to regret his decision or to alter his deep affection for her.

'She wrote to him, that girl,' she said, 'from Scarborough. 'And...and I found the letters,' she added quietly.

'What do you mean, you found them? You mean...you kept them from him? You didn't give them to him?'

Anna nodded. She was silent for a few moments, then she said, 'I thought he might think she had changed her mind about him. A few weeks went by...and I thought it was all going to be all right. But then he went to see her, and he found out. And that's why he's leaving home, because he's angry with me...'

'And I can't say I blame him,' said Thomas. 'That was a wicked thing to do! You should be ashamed of yourself!' At that moment he felt angrier with his wife than he had ever been. Anna always had to be right and would ride roughshod over anyone who got in her way. But it hadn't worked this time, and he was glad. 'It was a despicable thing to do, and to your own son. I just hope he can find it in his heart to forgive you...sometime; although it might take a long time, Anna.'

'But I love him,' insisted Anna, with tears in her

eyes. 'I tried to make him see that that was why I did it. I still think he's done wrong to turn his back on God, the way he has done. And it's her, that girl, who's the cause of it all.'

'For pity's sake, Anna, he hasn't turned his back on God!' Thomas almost shouted. 'He still goes to Mass, doesn't he? Our son is a very devout young man – even if he has decided he doesn't want to be a priest – and we should be very proud of him.'

'But does he still go to Confession?' asked Anna.

'I really don't know, but it's his business, not ours. And what about you, Anna? Do you still go to Confession? I should imagine you have a great deal on your conscience right now, haven't you? You certainly ought to have.' He could not tell whether or not he had touched a raw nerve. Anna's face was impassive as she answered.

'That is between myself and the Lord. Anyway, the Father knows how I feel about everything.' Thomas knew that she was not referring to the Almighty Father but to the parish priest. He, Thomas, was not at all sure that their priest would agree with Anna about the way she had tried to dominate their son. As for himself, he had never agreed with her about the matter of the priesthood, and he was not afraid of telling her so, yet again.

'Daniel has made the right decision,' he said, 'in deciding not to become a priest. Whether you like it or not, Anna, it is his life and his choice. You can't force someone into a way of life that is wrong for them.' Of the two of them, himself and Anna, his wife had always been the more zealous about her religion. When they had first met, Thomas had lapsed somewhat in his faith, but Anna had soon dragged him back on to the straight and narrow pathway. He was his own man, though, and had never been afraid to stand his ground with her.

'Daniel will find his way back,' Anna persisted now. All trace of tears had gone from her eyes and there was a look almost of exaltation on her face. 'I feel sure of it. I don't know how or when, but I know in my heart that my son is destined to become a priest. You will see that I am right, all of you.'

'Aye, happen we will, happen we won't,' replied Thomas. 'Now...are you going to get the visitors' supper orders, or shall I do it?'

'I'll do it,' said Anna, cheerily. 'You go and put the kettle on.' He could see that she was back to her normal self, bossy and determined to be right.

Chapter Fourteen

Maddy received a letter from Dan a few days after his return to Blackpool. She was a little concerned that he had done as he had threatened and left home. He was moving during the weekend to a flat above the shop where he worked. He did not say very much about his mother; Maddy admired him for being as loyal to her as he was able to be. She guessed, though, that they would have had quite a heated argument, resulting in his decision to leave. He assured her that he had no regrets. He was looking forward to having a little place of his own and intended to make it as comfortable as he could.

And, of course, he was longing for the time when he would see her, Madeleine, again. The following month, August, would no doubt be a busy time at the shop, but he hoped he would be able to manage a long weekend in the near future, especially as they now had a junior sales assistant at the gentlemen's outfitters, a fourteen-year-old boy who had recently left school.

And so Maddy was well content. She wrote back to his new Church Street address on Sunday afternoon.

She, too, was longing for their next meeting, but for the moment she was pleased to receive his letters and to sustain herself with the memories of the happy time they had shared together.

Her thrice daily appearances with the Pierrots occupied much of her time and thoughts, increasingly so as the summer progressed. There were additional events at which all the members of the troupe helped: a sandcastle competition for the children, which brought back memories for her of the time when her team, with Samuel as the leader, had won the first prize; a fancy dress parade; and a talent contest. It was six years since she had won the event herself, although it seemed to her to be far longer. During that time she had grown from a little girl into a young woman...and she had fallen in love.

Other things were happening, too, during that summer of 1907, some of which would have a lasting effect on Uncle Percy's Pierrots.

On the Tuesday morning of the first week in August a bouquet of flowers – roses, sweet williams and sweet peas – was left outside the tent where the male members of the cast dressed for the shows. Percy, who was the first to arrive, picked it up and grinned as he read the words on the card.

When Benjy arrived, with Barney close behind him, Percy thrust the bouquet into his hands. 'Here you are, Benjy; you've got an admirer.'

'Ooh, well, fancy that!' said Benjy. He looked at the attached card and read it out loud. '"For Mr

Benjamin Carstairs, from an ardent admirer".' He grinned at his partner. 'Not just an admirer, you see; an ardent one!'

A frown creased Barney's forehead. 'Are you sure that's all it says? Doesn't it say my name as well? You haven't read it properly.'

'Oh yes I have! You're not mentioned,' said Benjy. 'I'm right, aren't I, Percy?'

'Yes, you're quite right,' smiled Percy. 'But don't fall out about it, there's good chaps.'

'I wonder who it can be?' said Benjy, his pink and white complexioned face turning a little pinker. 'My eyes will be scanning the faces in the audience tonight.'

'You watch your footwork,' retorted Barney, 'or you'll find yourself falling arse over tip. And it'd serve you jolly well right, an' all! Pride goes before a fall, you know.'

'You're only jealous!' Benjy gave an exaggerated shrug and started to put on his costume.

Word soon got round to the ladies' dressing tent that Benjy had an admirer who had sent him flowers.

'Well, I suppose he's quite handsome really, isn't he?' observed Maddy. 'Of course it all depends on whether you like dark men or fair men.' Benjy was the blonde-haired, blue-eyed one, whereas Barney was dark-haired and more swarthy looking.

'Your young man is neither, is he?' remarked Susannah. 'He's ginger-haired and green-eyed. A real Oirish laddie, straight from Killarney's lakes and fells.'

'Not quite,' laughed Maddy. 'And I'm certainly not looking elsewhere. Benjy doesn't appeal to me.'

'It would make no difference if he did,' replied Susannah. Maddy gave her an odd look.

'There must be some lady who's pining for him, though,' said Maddy. 'I wonder who it is?'

'It might not be a lady. Haven't you thought about that?' said Susannah with a mischievous little gleam in her eye.

'What? You mean...a man? Oh, don't be silly, Susannah. It can't be a man. Or perhaps you mean it might be a little girl, do you? No, it'll be a middle-aged lady, you can bet.'

'Yes, you're probably right,' agreed Susannah. She knew that Maddy hadn't understood her remark at all.

The next night a box of Cadbury's chocolates was left outside the tent, again for Benjy, and this time the wording was rather bolder.

'To Benjy, How I love your dazzling smile,
To see you I would walk a mile;
Yet here you are, so close to me,
I'm waiting for you, can't you see?'

Benjy was amused, more than anything. He opened the chocolates and passed them around the tent.

'No, thank you; it would choke me,' said Barney.

He even went so far as to take a coffee cream and throw it onto the sand, stamping it underfoot.

'Don't be so childish!' sneered Benjy. 'Honestly! As if I cared!'

Percy could see, though, that it was causing discord between the two men and he didn't want the situation to get any worse. He, like Susannah and Maddy, assumed that it was probably an unmarried lady who had fallen for the – undoubtedly – handsome young man. But if she were to reveal her identity, which he guessed might be the next step, the situation might prove rather awkward. All the members of the troupe knew about Barney's and Benjy's proclivities, but they kept the knowledge to themselves and it was never mentioned to outsiders. Percy confided in Susannah, the woman in the troupe most likely to know how to deal with such a delicate problem. She agreed to come to the beach early before each performance, and to watch and wait.

She did not have to wait long. On the following day, which was Thursday, as she waited a fair distance away, she saw a woman approaching, looking cautiously around her, although the sands were, in the early evening period, almost deserted. She looked, Susannah thought, about forty years of age, possibly more, and was reasonably attractive, at least she could have been if she had bothered to take more care with her appearance. She was of medium height and build and expensively, but not stylishly, dressed. Her costume, of a drab serviceable dark grey, was not at all suitable for the summer weather. The only touch of lightness was in the pale mauve high-necked blouse, and the only concession to the warmth of the day was the large-brimmed straw hat, decorously trimmed with mauve ribbon. Mourning colours, thought Susannah, as she quickened her steps and walked towards the woman. She watched as the stranger opened a capacious black handbag and took out a book, a leather-bound one with gold edging.

'Excuse me...' Susannah stepped right up to her. 'That book, would it be for Benjy, by any chance? Mr Benjamin Carstairs?'

'Yes, as a matter of fact it is,' replied the woman. She pressed the book closely to her bosom and stared at Susannah. Her face was turning quite pink and her grey eyes were wary. 'Who are you?' she asked. 'No...wait a minute. I know who you are. You're Susannah, aren't you? The one who sings those amusing songs. And sometimes you're with the one called Frank...'

'Yes, that's right,' said Susannah. 'I'm sorry to butt in like this, but...I'm here to try and stop you from making...well, rather a fool of yourself.'

'Oh dear! Yes, I suppose I am,' said the woman. 'I've never done anything like this before. I don't really know what's come over me, but I do so admire that young man. And I thought, perhaps, if I could meet him, if he would agree to meet me, that is…that we might become…well, friends. I'm very shy, you see, and I guess that he might be, too, under all that jollity and the showing-off that he does. I'm a pretty good judge of character, you see…'

'Well…yes,' said Susannah, guardedly. 'Benjy isn't always as he seems to be on the stage. None of us are. A lot of it is an act; it has to be. But I had better tell you right away that…that Benjy is married.' She crossed her fingers tightly behind her back, something she had done ever since she was a child whenever she was telling a lie. 'Very happily married,' she continued. 'In fact, he and his wife have a three-year-old boy and I believe they are expecting another child very soon.' Please God, forgive me, she pleaded inside her head. It was only a white lie to save this poor woman from even more unhappiness.

'Oh…oh dear!' The woman let out a tremendous sigh. 'What an absolute fool I am! Why didn't I think of that? Do you know, I could have bet anything that he was not married. He looks so young and carefree. And so does his partner, Barney. I suppose…?'

Susannah answered her unspoken question. 'Yes, Barney is married as well.' She crossed her fingers even more tightly. 'But please don't worry about it. Benjy took it all in good part. In fact, he was very flattered, but I thought I'd better step in to stop you any further embarrassment.'

'Yes, thank you,' said the woman. 'I'm glad you did. Like I say, I don't know what came over me. I used to come and watch the show on the sands ages ago, when I was a little girl. They were black-faced minstrels though, at that time; the Pierrots came later, didn't they?'

'You live in Scarborough, do you?' asked Susannah.

'Yes, I've always lived here; I was born here. We live near St Mary's church. I say we, but there's only me now. My father died last year, and I lost my mother, too, this spring, so I'm on my own now. I was rather lonely and feeling at a loose end. I'd been looking after them both for so long, and then…well, I found myself on the beach one day and there was a Pierrot show going on. I stayed and watched, and then I started coming down every day and…well, you know the rest. Oh dear! I feel such a fool now. You won't tell him – Benjy – will you, about me?'

'No, of course not,' said Susannah. She was not quite sure what she was going to say to Benjy. It would be best, maybe, not to mention it at all, then he would think that his unknown admirer had got cold feet. 'I don't know who you are anyway, do I?' But whoever she was, Susannah felt sorry for her. Poor lady, living in a dream world like that.

'I'm Emily,' she said. 'Emily Stringer, not that it matters much who I am. I'm comfortably off, and I don't need to go out to work. I suppose I'm very lucky really, compared with some folk. But we all have our dreams, don't we?'

'Yes, maybe we do,' replied Susannah.

Emily held out the book she was carrying. It was a small volume of love poetry, lettered in gold leaf. 'I was loath to part with this really,' she said. 'It belonged to my mother, but I didn't come across it until after she died. It is inscribed to her, "With all my love from Robert", in the year of 1855...but Robert was not my father's name.' She smiled sadly. 'It seems that she must have had another life that I knew nothing about. It's hard to believe that now. I'm afraid she became a rather crabby and selfish old lady. I should hate that to happen to me.'

'There's no reason why it should,' said Susannah. She realised she was getting quite involved in Emily Stringer's affairs, although she had met her only a little while ago. She seemed a very gentle, unassuming person and Susannah guessed that, despite her foolish fantasies, she was intelligent and normally quite sensible. 'But you must forget about Benjy right away,' she told her. 'There is no future in that at all, and besides, there are plenty more fish in the sea, as the saying goes. And you certainly must not think of parting with that precious little book.'

'No...I suppose not. I was thinking I might get it back, that it would only be on loan...if I got to know him, that was. Oh! What a stupid fool I am! I had even picked out one of the poems.'

Emily opened the page at the silken ribbon marker, showing it to Susannah. The poem was 'Love's Philosophy', by Shelley. Susannah's eyes scanned the lines and some of the words leapt out at her.

> 'Nothing in the world is single,
> All things by a law divine
> In one another's being mingle...
> Why not I with thine?'

'Yes, but having a husband – or a lover – is not the be all and end all of everything,' she said. 'I hope you won't mind me saying so, Emily...but I feel that you need something else in your life, instead of...well, indulging in dreams that are...just that. You might not even like Benjy Carstairs if you were to meet him. He's not everybody's cup of tea. As you said yourself, most of us are nothing like we appear to be on the stage. Don't you do anything else? I'm sure you must have some friends?'

'One or two. Two girls I was at school with, but they are both married. I'm godmother to some of their children. And I go to church, to St Mary's.' Susannah had guessed that she probably did. 'The bottom dropped out of my world when I lost my parents,' she went on. 'I thought I might be glad of the freedom, but it's hard picking up the pieces again.'

'Yes, I can see that. But you need something –

other than Pierrot shows – to occupy your mind. I'm sure you're talented, aren't you?'

'I can do all the usual ladylike things,' smiled Emily. 'Needlework and crocheting and knitting – I love knitting – and I can cook and bake – Mother made sure of that – and I play the piano a little. And I'm quite good with children, though I haven't any of my own and I'm never likely to have.'

Susannah was tempted to ask her to come along and help with the children's events that were organised by the Pierrots. There would be another sandcastle competition soon and an afternoon of games and races. But that would not be a good idea, as it would mean coming into closer contact with the artistes. And Emily might well discover that she, Susannah, had lied to her about Benjy's marital status. No, it would not do.

But why am I involving myself? she wondered. It was really none of her business, but by her intervention – interference it was, really – she had inevitably made herself party to the woman's problems. Besides, she had taken a liking to Emily and felt sorry for her. She was far too able a person to stagnate at home, turning into an old spinster and dreaming about what might have been.

'I've even considered going out to work,' said Emily. 'Just a part-time occupation, I mean. Most of my friends had jobs when they left school, but we were rather more "'well off", you might say, than some of the others, and Mother insisted that I should stay at home. So here I am, forty-two years old and I've never done a day's work in my life; paid work, I mean; I've worked hard enough at home.'

Susannah knew that there were many such women in the same situation, and she rejoiced in her own independence. 'It's never too late,' she said. 'I think that would be a splendid idea, Emily, and you have such a lot to offer. Look…I'm very pleased to have met you, and I hope I've been able to help you a little. But hadn't you better be going? Unless you intend to stay and watch the show?'

'Do you know, I think I might,' replied Emily, much to Susannah's surprise. She put the book back into her bag. 'I'm not going to skulk away as though I've done something wrong. I've just been foolish, that's all. Yes, I'll stay and watch. I love all the acts anyway: you and Frank, and the performing dogs, and that lovely girl called Madeleine. She has the voice of an angel, hasn't she?'

'Yes, and she is a lovely girl,' said Susannah. 'Now, she is one person who is just as she seems to be.'

Emily smiled. 'I promise I won't do anything silly. And…you won't say anything, will you? Not to Benjy, or anybody?'

'No, cross my heart and hope to die,' said Susannah.

'Thank you very much. I feel much better for talking to you. I'll just take a stroll along the prom until it's time for the show to start. Goodbye, Susannah. I feel quite proud to know one of the artistes.'

Some of the other members were beginning to arrive as Emily made her way up to the promenade. Susannah caught sight of Percy going into the tent and she hurried to meet him.

'It's all sorted out,' she said, 'all that business with Benjy. Don't ask me to tell you all about it,' she touched her nose, 'because I promised not to say anything. Just a lady – a very nice lady – who took a fancy to him. I told her he was happily married.'

'Oh, that'll be the day!' laughed Percy. 'Anyway, thank you, Susannah. Let's hope that'll end the friction between the boys.'

Percy noticed, though, that Benjy, on arriving, cast an expectant glance at the entrance to the tent, which did not go unnoticed by his partner.

'Ha ha!' exclaimed Barney. 'Nothing there tonight, midear. Looks as though she's deserted you. What a shame!'

'D'you think I care?' retorted Benjy. 'At least I know that somebody appreciated me. She's probably gone back home now. Well, I'm glad I brightened up her holiday, whoever she was.'

Percy was aware, though, that a little of the sparkle had gone from his performance, as it always did whenever he had words with his partner; and that, inevitably, affected Barney as well. He hoped they would soon sort out their petty little quarrel.

Susannah didn't consider that she would be breaking Emily's confidence too much by telling Maddy what had happened. She took her to one side at the interval.

'Well, I've sorted out Benjy's little problem,' she said. 'We were right; it was a middle-aged lady – well, youngish really, I suppose. In her forties, that's what she told me – who had developed quite a passion for him. She was actually bringing a book of love poems for him tonight. Would you believe it? I feel quite sorry for her, poor lady.'

'You mean...you've talked to her?'

'Yes; I waylaid her just as she was leaving her latest gift for him. She came early and there was nobody around but her and me. Anyway, I put her off him good and proper. I told her it was no use because he was married.'

'Oh, Susannah!' cried Maddy. 'Why ever did you say that? It's not true!'

'Well, I couldn't very well tell her the truth, could I?'

'The truth? What do you mean?' Maddy looked bewildered and Susannah realised that she was still a rather naive and innocent girl. She had little idea of the ways of the world, and although it was a pity to disillusion her, Susannah knew that she would be bound to discover some of the more unusual facts of life during her travels with the Melody Makers. Better sooner rather than later, she decided.

'Well, Barney and Benjy are very good friends, aren't they?' she began.

'Yes, of course. I know that. But it doesn't mean that they won't meet somebody they might want to marry, does it? They are both quite handsome men, and very friendly. I'm surprised they haven't met somebody already.'

'And you thought, maybe, this lady might fit the bill, did you? And now I've gone and spoilt it?'

'Well, you never know, do you?'

'No, Maddy love. Barney and Benjy will not get married, not ever, because...well, they are partners, and I don't mean just dancing partners. They're...they're very fond of one another, and I suppose they regard themselves as being married – sort of – to one another.'

Maddy's eyes opened wide with shock and disbelief. 'You mean...two men? Like...a man and a woman? As though they were married?'

'Yes, that's what I mean,' replied Susannah. 'Don't ask me to explain it to you though, because I can't. I remember talking to you about what goes on between a man and a woman, but this is something I can't talk about because I don't know. I can only guess and I find that I don't want to think about it. Anyway, it's their business, Barney's and Benjy's, and although we all know we never talk about it.'

'But I'd no idea at all about that sort of thing,' said Maddy. 'I didn't know it was possible... Yes, of course, now I think about it, they are rather possessive and jealous of one another, aren't they?'

'I'm surprised that Emily – that's the woman's name – hadn't realised that Barney and Benjy were that way inclined,' said Susannah. 'But I daresay she's led a very sheltered life. Maybe it's best she doesn't know. That's why I said they were married; both of them. "Hell hath no fury like a woman scorned", as they say; although I don't think Emily would be vindictive.'

'What do you mean?' asked Maddy, looking puzzled again.

'Well, it's a punishable offence, what those two get up to, if anybody was to find out and report them, that is. Did you never hear of Oscar Wilde?'

'Yes, I've heard of him. He was a writer, wasn't he? He wrote plays; "The Importance of Being Earnest". And I know he went to prison.'

'But you didn't know why?'

'No, actually I didn't.'

'Well, it was because of his friendship with a young man; Lord Alfred Douglas, he was called. One of the gentry, and his father was a very important man. And it was the father who accused Oscar Wilde of…well, something that has a dreadful name that I'd rather not say. Anyway, he was found guilty and sentenced to two years' hard labour in prison.'

'And can men still be put in prison for…that?' asked Maddy.

'Yes, I believe so, although I don't suppose it often happens. People know to keep quiet about it.'

'It seems rather drastic, doesn't it,' said Maddy, 'just for being fond of someone? Although I must admit I find it...peculiar, to say the least.'

'Mmm... It can be a very puzzling world at times,' observed Susannah. 'And a cruel one, too. Anyway, I don't want you to worry your head about it, love. Try to put it out of your mind. But I thought it best you should know about these things.'

'I've learnt a good deal since I got to know you, Susannah,' smiled Maddy.

'Yes, you can always rely on Aunty Susie to put you right,' laughed her friend. What Susannah did not tell her young friend was that the same sort of thing could happen between two women as well, but this, for some odd reason, was not considered to be a punishable offence.

Maddy had other things on her mind, however, before very long. She had been looking forward to Dan's next visit in mid-August, but a couple of days before he was due to arrive she received a letter from him saying that he would be unable to come. His employer, Mr Grundy, had been taken ill very suddenly with appendicitis and had undergone an emergency operation. He was now in hospital where he would have to stay for a week or more, and then he would recuperate at home. As he was elderly it would be several weeks before he was able to return to the shop. Daniel had been put in charge and could not possibly take any time off until Mr Grundy was well again.

'I am so disappointed,' he wrote, 'and I know you will be, too. But I hope and pray I will be able to see you in Scarborough before you set off on your autumn and winter tour. If not, then I will travel to Halifax or York or wherever you happen to be. Just let me know your itinerary and we will sort out when I can come to see you. Remember that I love you, and I always will, my darling Madeleine.'

And with that she had to be content, although she began to feel that Fate – or something – was against them. Their last performance in Scarborough would be in mid-September when the last of the visitors were departing. Then they were to have two weeks' break before starting off on their travels again at the beginning of October.

It was during the second week in August, round about the time that Dan should have been visiting, that Percy auditioned three hopeful artistes who had answered his advertisement in the *Stage* magazine. The audition took place on Saturday afternoon at Percy's digs in Castle Road, where he and his wife and some other members of the troupe had stayed for many years. Mrs Ada Armstrong made the house a real home from home for them and was pleased to allow Percy the use of her parlour, where there was a piano.

One of the would-be artistes was a singer, by the name of Dora Daventry, and Letty accompanied her as she sang, very sweetly, 'The Old Rustic Bridge by the Mill', and then more coquettishly, 'Daddy Wouldn't Buy Me a Bow-wow'. She was good, there was no doubt about that, but possibly her act would be too much like Susannah's, and they were trying to add more variety to the shows. Then there was a young man in his twenties. He introduced himself as Jeremy Jarvis but he did not say whether that was his real name or a stage name. He produced a gaudily painted dummy figure from a large wooden box. It could not be called lifelike, but then it was not meant to be. It had wide staring eyes and ruddy painted cheeks and lips and was dressed in a tailcoat and black trousers, complete with bow tie and top hat.

'I'm Tommy the Toff, the toast of the town,' declared the ventriloquist's dummy on Jeremy's arm, and Percy, watching him carefully throughout his act, could scarcely see the young man's lips moving. He was even more impressed when Tommy the Toff said, 'I've brought my lady friend along. Would you like to meet her?'

And out of the box came Belinda, the belle of the ball, with dazzling blue eyes, long golden tresses, and a low-necked evening dress of vivid scarlet. The two of them, one on each arm, sang a duet about, 'The Man who Broke the Bank at Monte Carlo'. Percy and Letty decided, there and then, that they must sign Jeremy Jarvis up right away for the autumn tour.

The last young man to perform was a conjuror called Freddie Nicholls. Percy looked at him keenly.

'I've seen you before, haven't I?' he said.

'Yes, you have, Mr Morgan,' replied the young man. 'I took part in your talent contest six years ago when I was thirteen. Actually, I won second prize.'

'Yes, of course; so you did,' said Percy. 'I remember you now. Well then, let's see how much you've improved, shall we?'

His sleight of hand was truly impressive as he produced yards and yards of silken scarves, as it were from nowhere, and made cascading fountains of playing cards, as well as doing ingenious tricks with them. He performed tricks with ropes and with seemingly empty boxes, and the usual white rabbit – although not a real one! – that popped out of a top hat.

'And I'm working on a sequence with white doves,' he told Percy. 'But I haven't perfected it yet. Do you think that would be permissible?'

'I think it would be wonderful, lad,' replied Percy. 'Yes, you've certainly come on by leaps and bounds. How old are you now? Nineteen? Yes, I could see when you performed six years ago that you had great potential. So…are you performing now?'

'When I can,' replied Freddie. 'As an amateur, of

course. I work in a bank, actually, in Halifax – that's my home town – and I perform at clubs in the evening, or local church halls and that sort of thing. But I'd like to do it professionally, if I can.'

'Well, we'll certainly give you a try,' said Percy. 'Won't we, Letty?' He turned to his wife, who nodded enthusiastically. 'Could you be ready to start a tour with us at the beginning of October?'

'I'll say I could,' answered Freddie. 'You mean to say…you're willing to give me a try? That's wonderful; thank you ever so much.'

'It'll be hard work, lad,' Percy told him. 'Make no mistake about that. And I can't promise you riches untold. But we don't do too badly. We get some pretty full houses in the inland towns. Our little company is getting to be quite well-known now, and we get asked back year after year. We've been on the road for six years now. We started touring soon after that contest you mentioned. And we're always back here in the summer… God willing,' he added. 'Our rents are going up, but it's the same for all the other troupes. I expect we'll manage.'

'That suits me fine,' said Freddie. 'I'm always pleased to spend some time in Scarborough. I'm staying here for the weekend, and I shall be coming to see the show tonight.'

'Good,' said Percy. 'You'll be very welcome, and the other two if they would like to stay. I'd better call them in and tell them what we've decided, Letty and me.'

The other two artistes had been waiting in what was the residents' dining room. Percy felt sorry, and rather embarrassed, too, about the decision he and Letty had made. It seemed mean to take two out of the three. He had been tempted to take the singer as well, but he knew the ill feeling that that might cause amongst some of the other singers in the company. Dora Daventry, however, didn't seem too put out at the news.

'Never mind,' she said. 'It's only what I expected. I watched the show this morning and I could see that you already have quite enough singers. Very good ones, too. I know I'm only an amateur, but I hope I might get a chance to go professional, sometime.' Like Freddie Nicholls, she performed at local events in her home town, Huddersfield, where she worked as a shop assistant.

'I hope so too,' Percy told her, 'and we wish you every success. Leave your address with us just in case we need to contact you. You never know in our business how things are going to turn out.'

Jeremy Jarvis was delighted to have been taken on. He had done a little professional work but was 'resting' at the moment and had returned to his other occupation as a barman, in the neighbouring town of Whitby. As all three of them were staying the night in Scarborough they agreed that they would attend the performance that evening. They left together, the best of pals already, it seemed, saying that they would go and have a fish and chip tea before watching the Pierrot show.

Percy wondered whether it would be a good idea or not to introduce the newly appointed artistes to the rest of the troupe. He decided that perhaps it might not be, not yet. There were sure to be murmurings amongst some of the members; not many, maybe, but it might be better to wait a while before breaking it to them, tactfully, that in October they were to have some new colleagues. The trouble was that they had been the same little select troupe for so long, and some of them had grown complacent and inward-looking. Even though they had been told about the advertisement, it would come as a shock to be asked to curtail their acts a little to accommodate the newcomers.

As it turned out, however, the matter was taken out of Percy's hands to a certain extent. At the end of the performance Freddie Nicholls excused himself from the other two, saying that there was someone in the troupe he had met before, to whom he would like to go and say hello. Dora Daventry and Jeremy Jarvis seemed to have struck up quite a friendship and didn't appear to mind at all. And if they thought it strange that Percy Morgan had not offered to introduce them to the members of the troupe, they did not say so.

Freddie waited outside the tent that he had seen the lady artistes enter until Madeleine Moon came out. She seemed surprised when the tall, dark-haired young man stepped up to her and said, very politely, 'Hello, Madeleine. Do you remember me?'

She was startled for a moment. Nobody, except Dan, ever called her Madeleine. She looked at him more closely. He was quite attractive in an odd sort of way. His nose was a shade too long and his mouth too wide, but there was an appealing glint of humour in his grey eyes.

'I'm Freddie Nicholls,' he said, 'although I was Frederick then, actually. But Freddie sounds better for a stage name. The boy conjuror? You know, when you won the talent contest, and I was second?'

'Why, yes, so you are!' she said in surprise. She smiled at him. 'How nice to see you again. Of course I remember you. So...what are you doing here? Well, that's a silly question; I expect you're on holiday, aren't you?'

'Obviously you don't know,' he replied. 'I've been for an audition this afternoon with Percy Morgan and – guess what? – I'm joining the company in October for the autumn tour.'

'Are you? Well, that's wonderful,' she said. 'I knew Percy had put an advert in the *Stage*, but he's kept very quiet about the auditions. Anyway, congratulations! I'm sure you'll enjoy being with us.'

'I was surprised to see you singing with them,' said Freddie. 'But then again, perhaps I wasn't. We all knew you would win, that afternoon. How long have you been with them?'

'Two years,' she replied. 'I live in Scarborough, you see, so I was able to keep in touch with them. I did a few appearances as a guest artiste, and then when I was fifteen my father agreed that I could join them.'

'And you're glad you did?'

'Yes, I've never regretted it.'

'Listen, Madeleine... What are you doing now?' he asked. 'Would you like to come for a stroll with me, and perhaps we could stop and have a drink somewhere? Then you can tell me all about the...Melody Makers. That's what they're called in the autumn, isn't it? Or...perhaps you're meeting somebody?'

She hesitated for a moment before replying. 'No...as a matter of fact, I'm not. Yes, Freddie, that would be a nice idea.' Of course, if Dan had been there, as he should have been, it would have been different.

'Aha, I see you two have met,' said Percy, appearing suddenly from his dressing tent. 'I guessed you might remember one another.'

'Yes, Madeleine's going to tell me all I need to know,' said Freddie.

'Don't frighten him off then, will you?' laughed Percy. 'Off you go and enjoy yourselves.'

He watched them, Maddy and Freddie, as they walked across the sands and up the steps to the promenade. Those two make a very nice couple, he mused.

Chapter Fifteen

Something else of note that happened in the month of August was the return of Samuel Barraclough to Scarborough. He had been awarded a first-class degree in Geology at Leeds University, and after a few weeks' holidaying with his fellow students, all now ready to make their way in the world, he had decided, at last, to visit his family. His expedition to Peru was due to begin in the second week of September.

William pretended to share his wife's enthusiasm for her son's visit. Obviously, she was delighted at the prospect of having her eldest child at home for a few weeks. But William knew that it was only a duty visit. He was sure the young man was fond of his mother; he must give him credit for that, but he knew that Samuel only came to see them when he had nothing better to do. This was his home, though, whenever he returned to Scarborough, and he must be accommodated. It meant that the twins, Tommy and Tilly, would have to share a room. Faith had decided it was no longer appropriate for them to occupy the same room as a rule, but now, with Maddy home as well, there was no alternative.

There were mixed reactions when Faith broke the news to the rest of the family, over the dinner table on Sunday, that Samuel was coming to stay. He would be arriving in two days' time and was staying for about three weeks. And he would be sleeping in what was usually Tommy's bedroom.

'He'd better not mess about with my things, then,' said Tommy. 'I've got my engines and everything laid out just the way I want them.' He was mad about anything to do with railways at the moment. In his bedroom he had a circular railway track on a tabletop, on which he ran his Bassett-Lowke clockwork engines, as well as goods waggons and passenger coaches. He also had a station and miniature figures of passengers, railway guards and porters. Every Christmas and birthday his collection grew a little larger.

'Put them all back in their boxes then,' suggested William, but Tommy said he would rather not.

'I shall still want to run them when I come home from school,' he said. 'Samuel can't have my room all the time. He can sleep in it, but I'm allowed to go in whenever I want to. Anyway, he'll be out most of the time, won't he?'

'We must make him welcome whilst he's here,' said Faith. 'You don't often see your big brother, do you?'

'And you'd better not mess with my things either,' said Tilly to her twin brother, on hearing that she had to share her room with him. 'I shall have to move all my dolls, and Teddy as well, onto the window sill.'

'Huh! Why should I want to mess around with a lot of silly old dolls!' scoffed Tommy. 'I'm only sharing with you because I have to. And I hope you don't still snore, that's all.'

'I don't snore!' retorted Tilly. 'Listen to what he's saying, Mummy! I don't snore, do I? Shut up, Tommy!'

'Stop it, you two,' said Faith. 'It will be lovely to see Samuel again. He'll be able to tell you all about what he'll be doing in Peru. That's exciting, isn't it?'

'S'pose so,' said Tommy. Then with a little more enthusiasm, he added, 'I looked it up in my atlas. And it's miles and miles away, right at the other side of the world.'

'No, it's not,' retorted Tilly. 'It's Australia that's at the other side of the world, isn't it, Uncle William? Our teacher said so.'

'Yes, that's right, Tilly,' agreed William. The twins' knowledge of geography seemed to be rather better than his had been at a similar age, although he did remember the map of the world, with all the red parts showing the countries that belonged to Great Britain. He was very pleased at the way the twins were developing and how they were both engrossed in the things they learnt at school. They were not his children, but he took a keen interest in them. And he was pleased at the way they had accepted him as a surrogate father. 'Australia is at the opposite end of the world, that's what we've always been told, although I don't suppose many of us will ever go there. But Peru is a very long way away, too. It's in South America, isn't it, Tommy?' He knew very well that it was, but he guessed that Tommy would like to air his knowledge.

'Yes, that's right,' Tommy answered. 'And the capital city is Lima.' But to William, all these places – Australia, South America, Africa – had about as much relevance as the moon. And were just as impossible to get to, for such as him.

Maddy and Jessie looked at one another, but made no comment about Samuel's impending visit. Maddy intended to keep all her thoughts to herself. She had not set eyes on her stepbrother since that awful time in Leeds and she was not looking forward to meeting him again. She doubted, though, that she would see him very much. She would be working most of the time and most probably he would not condescend to go and watch a Pierrot show.

But that was where she was wrong. Samuel arrived on the Tuesday and Maddy saw him only briefly until the Wednesday, when Faith had organised a tea party for the whole family, in honour of his arrival. The clothing emporium that Faith managed was closed on a Wednesday afternoon, as was the office where Hetty worked, and the furniture store where Jessie was now employed.

It was quite a gathering of folk around the table that teatime, to partake of a rather earlier than usual meal. Faith had insisted that Maddy must be there. Her evening performance started at six-thirty and, to Maddy's surprise, they were all going along to watch. In addition to William, Faith and Isaac, Maddy, Jessie and the twins, Faith had invited Patrick and Katy, and Hetty Collier. And Samuel, of course, was the guest of honour.

Maddy wondered what he thought about it all. She had changed her opinion of Samuel drastically and imagined that he would be viewing them all with a sardonic eye, wishing that he were somewhere else, far away from the family that he only condescended to visit once in a while. She was surprised, however, at how chatty and charming he was with everyone. He took an interest in Tommy's trains and in Jessie's new job and told her, Maddy, that he was looking forward to seeing her in her Pierrot costume, and was she going to sing the 'Scarborough Fair' song again? She found she was able to speak to him quite normally and she was relieved to think that what had happened between them appeared to have been forgotten. But she knew that she still did not entirely trust him.

It was the first time that Samuel and Hetty had met. Her visits had never coincided with his, and this was the first time he had returned since she had been living and working in Scarborough. She now had her own flat in a road leading off the

Esplanade, quite near to where her father and family lived. Maddy noticed that the two of them seemed to be getting along very well indeed. They were sitting next to one another at the tea table, and she was aware of a few whispered comments and giggles going on between the pair of them. And later, at the performance, she noticed that, again, they were sitting together, and from the way they exchanged remarks and smiled at one another it would appear that they had known one another for ages.

She wondered if she should warn Hetty about him, but on reflection she decided that that might seem spiteful and vindictive. Besides, Hetty was plenty old enough to look after herself. In fact, she was several years older than Samuel.

'Shall we go and have a drink?' said Samuel to Hetty when the show had finished.

'Yes, thank you. I would like that very much,' she replied.

They distanced themselves from the rest of the party who were heading towards the dressing tent to wait for Maddy; nobody appeared to notice their absence. The two of them made their way up to the North Bay promenade and from there to North Marine Road which ran parallel to the promenade and was where the undertaker's business and shop were situated.

'So you're working for my stepfather?' said Samuel as they walked past the premises.

'Your…father, of course, isn't he? Goodness me! What a complicated family we have, you and I. All these stepbrothers and half-sisters and God knows what. It's hard to get the hang of it sometimes.'

'Yes, I agree,' laughed Hetty. 'And me arriving on the scene as I did two years ago, it quite took the wind out of William's sails. But I'm pleased to say that everything has worked out well between him and me. I liked him straight away. He's a decent fellow.'

'Yes, he's all right is William,' replied Samuel. 'Not that I've seen a great deal of him and Mother since they were married. I've been away at university, and I'll be ever further away before very long. I was flabbergasted, I must admit, when the news broke – about you, I mean. Well, the crafty old devil! I thought. But I'd always suspected there'd been something between him and Bella Randall. Sorry, Hetty – your mother, of course. I hardly knew her, but I remember she was a very attractive woman. You are very much like her, as I expect you know. William must have thought he was seeing a ghost when you turned up out of the blue.'

'Yes, it was rather a shock for him. I gather there had been some bad blood between her and William at one time. A good deal of resentment, but by the time she died I think she had managed to come to terms with most things. And your mother, Faith; well, she's been wonderful about it all. What a lovely person she is.'

'Yes, I must agree that my mother is very patient and understanding. Quite saint-like, in fact. Now, what about this place?' He stopped at a small public house on St Thomas Street, the street that led to the town centre.

'Yes, that looks like a respectable place,' said Hetty. 'We'll just have one drink, shall we? It's quite a long walk back to South Bay.'

'Oh, don't worry about that. We'll call a cab when we're ready,' said Samuel with an air of nonchalance. He held open the swing door, inclining his head graciously towards her as she entered.

There were a few people at the bar and Hetty studied Samuel as he stood waiting to be served. She knew that he was a few years younger than herself, twenty-one to her twenty-six, but no one would imagine, seeing them together, that there was any age difference at all. Samuel had the appearance and bearing of a man in his mid-twenties or even more. The old cliché of 'tall, dark and handsome' fitted him perfectly. He sported a small moustache, which made him look older than his years, and he was the picture of sartorial elegance in his well-cut light-coloured sports jacket, grey flannel trousers and the straw boater which he now held casually in his hand. He did not smile very much except when something amused him, although he seemed to have smiled more than usual whilst in her company; and when he did his dark brown eyes lit up with a humorous, although faintly sardonic, gleam.

She had gained the impression that Maddy was not too keen on him, and Jessie, too, did not speak about him very much. It seemed to Hetty that Samuel had not been as overjoyed at the marriage of William and Faith as the rest of the family seemed to be, and he appeared to be something of an outsider. But she had decided that she liked him and was ready to give him the benefit of the doubt. He was a personable young man and she knew she would be pleased to have his company for the next few weeks until he departed for South America. That was, of course, if he wanted to go on seeing her, as she guessed he might.

'There we are – one port and lemon,' he said, returning to the table in the corner of the saloon.

'Cheers, Hetty,' he said, lifting his tankard of ale. 'Here's to us, and to the rest of our various family members. But chiefly…to us.'

'Cheers, Samuel,' she replied.

'Let me see,' he began, putting down his glass and looking intently into her eyes. 'You and I, we are not related, are we? We're not…brother and sister, in some complicated way?'

'No, I don't think so,' she replied, smiling. 'I don't see how we can be. William is not your father. I'm half-sister to Maddy, and to Patrick. But I'm not related to Jessie and the twins, although Jessie claimed me as an extra sort of sister when I came to live here. You and I, we could possibly be called stepbrother and sister, I suppose, but that's stretching things a bit far.'

'Just as I thought, ' he replied. 'Then you and I can be friends, Hetty, without worrying about what anybody might say. And I hope I might have the pleasure of your company whilst I am here in Scarborough.'

'That would be very nice,' she replied, quite sedately. Samuel, studying her appraisingly across the table, decided that he liked what he saw. Henrietta Collier would do very well to keep him amused before he departed on his expedition. She was a good-looking lass; the very image of that Bella who, from all accounts had been, 'no better than she ought to be'. A daft expression that didn't make any sense at all, but that was what he had heard folks say about her and he knew what they meant. It was another way of saying that she was a woman of easy virtue. Not that he imagined for one moment that Hetty was like her mother in that respect. She appeared to be a most respectable and well-brought-up young lady. But she might well have inherited some of her mother's tendencies...or her father's, for that matter. William had risen somewhat in Samuel's estimation after the news of his philanderings as a young man had come to light, two years ago. Who would have thought it, the randy old dog!

Hetty was a few years older than himself, and

Samuel rather liked older women. He guessed that, with a little persuasion, she might not be averse to his amorous advances, not like that mealy-mouthed half-sister of hers. He had only agreed to go along to watch the Pierrot show so that he could get to know Hetty a little better. But he knew that he would have to proceed with caution.

The Melody Makers' autumn tour started at the beginning of October; and Dan had still not managed to get to Scarborough to see Maddy. They corresponded, though, and she looked forward to receiving his letters at least twice a week. The shop had been extra busy, he told her, and he was unable to take any time off as the new assistant was by no means capable of being left in charge. And Mr Grundy was taking longer than had been anticipated in recovering from his operation.

Maddy found she was looking forward to going on tour again, seeing different towns and cities and, this time, working with some different people. She was aware that the troupe had got into something of a rut, and new artistes would bring new ideas and a feeling of freshness to the show. Although Freddie Nicholls and Jeremy Jarvis had been engaged because of the originality of their acts, she knew that Percy would want them to be versatile and to take their part in sketches and in chorus numbers, as did the rest of the company. It would be interesting to see what the new members had to offer.

She had enjoyed the short time she had spent with Freddie, finding him to be good-natured and friendly, and with a keen sense of humour. They had had a drink together after the performance and she had told him about her fellow artistes, all of whom he remembered from the time when he had taken part in the talent contest. The troupe had not changed at all since that time, so they were, indeed, ready for an infusion of new blood. He had seen her home safely, and had then walked the mile or so back to his digs near the railway station.

Maddy had then pushed Freddie Nicholls to the back of her mind. He was a pleasant young man and she felt sure he would be good fun to work with; her thoughts, though, were still largely centred on Daniel, wondering when she would see him and imagining how wonderful it would be when she did.

Freddie, however, found he was unable to stop thinking about Madeleine Moon. She had blossomed from a pretty little girl with a silver-toned voice into a beautiful young woman, chatty and charming and friendly and such fun to be with; and her singing voice had improved immensely. It had matured, of course, as she had, and whereas it had been silvery and light, it was now pure gold. He was looking forward to working with her and, if it were possible, getting to know her much better. He had had one or two girlfriends, but nothing serious, and there had been no one who had captivated his heart and his mind in the way she had done.

They travelled, with all their props and bags and baggages, from Scarborough, in the early afternoon of the first Sunday in October. They were bound for Manchester, where they were to play for two weeks at a provincial theatre, the Empire, in the suburb of Gorton, not too far from the city centre.

The Empire was typical of many small theatres on the outskirts of towns and cities – the Empires, Palaces, Alhambras and Hippodromes – insignificant, sometimes drab, little theatres on the whole, but with imposing names. The digs, too, did not vary very much. Maddy, this time, was sharing a room with just Susannah and Nancy. Carlo and Queenie had been allotted a room to themselves, Percy being aware that the couple needed to be kept sweet; they were not too happy about the newcomers and the subsequent changes to the programme. Barney and Benjy and the new young men, Freddie and Jeremy, were sharing an extra large room. Fortunately Mrs Finch, the landlady, had rooms enough for them all; and a bonus was that she was prepared to put on a midday meal at twelve noon, which would give them time to get ready for the matinées on Wednesday and Saturday. They were performing twice nightly, at five-thirty and eight o'clock, but with one evening show only, at seven o'clock, on Wednesday and Saturday. This was the routine in most of the towns they visited, with slight variations.

Freddie, by the second week of their Manchester stay, had decided that it was time he plucked up courage and asked Madeleine if she would go out with him; for supper, perhaps, after the show on Wednesday evening. He was not usually so backward in coming forward, but he had received no encouragement whatsoever from the girl he admired so much. She had spoken to him in a friendly manner, but that was the way she was with everyone. He suspected, to his dismay, that she had scarcely given him a thought since the time they had met in Scarborough; that he was, to her, just another member of the company, of no more significance than those two tap dancers or Jeremy, the new ventriloquist.

However, nothing ventured, nothing gained, he told himself. But before speaking to Madeleine he decided he would have a word with Susannah Brown. He had noticed that the two of them were friendly and they were sharing a room. He had found Susannah to be a straightforward sort of person who always spoke her mind. She would be able to tell him, he hoped, whether or not he might stand a chance in his pursuit of the fair Madeleine.

He chanced to meet her on the corridor outside her room on the Monday night of the second week of their stay. 'Susannah...have you a moment?' he began.

'Certainly, Freddie,' she answered in her usual coquettish manner, although he knew it was an assumed impudence, a continuation of the way she flirted with an audience. He had already realised that she and Frank Morrison were what might be termed a 'couple'. 'So, what can I do for you, young man?'

'I wanted to ask you about Madeleine,' he began. 'I...well...I like her very much, and I was wondering if she might agree to go out with me; on Wednesday, I thought. I'd like to take her out for supper after the show.'

'Well, it's no use asking me, is it, lad? Ask her yourself; she can but say no. But I've a feeling she might say yes. Go on, chance your arm; why don't you?'

'Is there anyone else though? I mean...she's such a lovely girl. I wondered if she already had a boyfriend. I haven't seen any sign of anyone, though; and, of course, she is quite young, isn't she?'

'To be quite honest, Freddie, there is someone,' said Susannah. 'A young man she met while we were in Blackpool. But there are...complications.' She didn't intend to tell him what they were, but she had thought all along that things would never be easy for Maddy and Daniel. And she knew that he hadn't been to see her yet, in spite of his promises. She thought, now, that it might be a good idea for Maddy to widen her horizons. 'Ask her,' she said again. 'How could she refuse a handsome young man like you! And I wish you the best of luck.'

'Don't tell her I've spoken to you, will you?' he insisted.

'Of course I won't. Now, make sure you go ahead, and don't dilly-dally on the way!'

To his great delight Madeleine agreed to go out with him on the Wednesday evening. He had asked her on the Tuesday morning, and at her answer, 'Yes, why not? Thank you, Freddie, that would be very nice,' he had dashed into Manchester on Tuesday afternoon and booked a table for two at a little restaurant on Market Street.

They took a tram from Gorton as soon as the performance ended. Freddie could hardly believe his good fortune as he shared a seat with Madeleine on the tramcar, and later, as he gazed at her across the table. She looked enchanting, as always. The tawny feathers on her little hat and her russet-coloured jacket with the fur collar enhanced her colouring: her reddish-gold hair and her warm brown eyes. He made up his mind to proceed carefully, not to do anything to spoil these precious moments.

To Maddy, the restaurant was reminiscent of the one in Leeds where Samuel had taken her on that ill-fated occasion; the red-shaded lights and oak panelling, the snowy white cloths and the gleaming cutlery. But, to her relief, the menu was less complicated, not nearly as posh, to her mind, and it was all written in English.

The fare was more down to earth and after they

had enjoyed chicken soup they both chose beef steak and chips with mushrooms and tomatoes. Their chatter was inconsequential, about their fellow artistes in the main, as might be expected. Freddie had struck up quite a friendship with Jeremy Jarvis, who was a few years his senior. She was interested to hear that that young man was still corresponding with Dora Daventry, the singer who had not been successful at the audition and who lived in Huddersfield.

'We will be in Huddersfield in a few weeks' time,' said Freddie, 'so he'll be able to see her then. I sense romance in the air with those two.'

'It's rather a pity she wasn't taken on at the same time as you and Jeremy,' said Maddy. 'I haven't met her, but she sounds very nice from all accounts. Although we do have a fair number of singers, of course. I can think of a couple of them, though, who are not too happy at the moment.'

'You mean Carlo and Queenie, I presume?'

'Yes, that's right. I guessed you might have noticed. I think we all have.' Carlo's and Queenie's mutterings had become more audible during their stay in Manchester. One of their duets had been cut out, and Carlo's monologues were no longer required at all, to make room for the conjuror and ventriloquist.

'Now, Madeleine,' said Freddie, when they had both eaten every last morsel on their plates. 'How about a dessert? Do you think you can manage one?'

'I don't see why not,' she replied. He was glad she was not one of those fussy, faddy young women, forever worrying about putting on an ounce or two by eating the wrong things. She obviously enjoyed her food; in fact, she seemed to enjoy every aspect of life. 'What about Manchester tart, seeing that we're in Manchester?' she suggested. 'My mother used to make Yorkshire curd tart. My real mother, I mean; she died when I was ten. Perhaps Manchester tart is a similar sort of delicacy; I think I'll try it anyway.'

'Yes, and so will I,' he agreed. 'I didn't know about your mother, Madeleine. I'm sorry to hear about that. It must have been sad for you, losing her when you were only a little girl. There was a lady at the station with your father, when we were leaving Scarborough. So, of course, I assumed…'

'That she was my mother?' Maddy smiled. 'That was Faith – I still call her Aunty Faith – and she's been a wonderful stepmother to me. She was a family friend, and she and my father got married four years ago. Yes, it was dreadful, very sad as you say, losing my mother at such an age; but I guess it's dreadful however old or young you are. I still think of her, but not with the same agonising grief. By the way, why don't you call me Maddy, like everyone else does? I wish you would.'

'Oh, all right then,' said Freddie. 'I'll call you Maddy, if that's what you prefer. It's just that

Madeleine is such a lovely name, and it suits you very well.'

That was exactly what Dan had said to her; and he, Dan, was the only one now who used the full version of her name; and that was the reason she did not want Freddie to call her Madeleine. It was special; it was Daniel's way of addressing her.

'My mother makes curd tart too,' Freddie told her. 'I must admit I'm missing her cooking now I'm away from home. But Mrs Finch is a jolly good landlady, isn't she?'

'Make the most of it,' laughed Maddy. 'She's the exception, rather than the rule. We might get somebody not nearly as good a cook, nor so obliging, next week.'

The Manchester tart, when it arrived, was nothing like curd tart. It was a custard mixture in a pastry case, with a layer of jam underneath and shreds of coconut sprinkled on the top. Very palatable though, and they both enjoyed it.

Whilst they were waiting for the coffee to be served, Freddie decided to pluck up courage and try to proceed a little further with his courtship – if he could dare to call it that – of Madeleine.

Her hand lay on the table, and he reached out his own and gently took hold of hers. 'Madeleine...' he began. 'I mean... Maddy; I have really enjoyed being here with you tonight. And I'm hoping we might be able to do it again...soon. In fact, I would like to go on seeing you; I mean, not just seeing you when we are performing, but all the time. I realised as soon as I met you again that I wanted to get to know you better, a lot better. Would you...would you go out with me again?'

'Oh, Freddie...' she replied, looking at him with such tenderness in her lovely brown eyes, but with a touch of pity too. She gave a sad little smile. 'I've enjoyed it too, I really have. But if you mean what I think you mean then...I'd better tell you right away; I've got a boyfriend. He lives in Blackpool. That's where I met him, when we were performing there earlier this year. And we...well, I suppose you could say we fell in love straight away.'

'Oh...I see.' Freddie squeezed her hand lightly, then let go of it. 'I'm sorry; I understand.'

'You weren't to know, were you? He hasn't been to see me lately. He works in a shop, a gentlemen's outfitters – Dan, he's called – and he's been extra busy lately with his boss being ill. But I shall be seeing him soon.' Her face lit up in a glowing smile. 'I'm sorry, Freddie, but I hope we can go on being friends. There's no reason why we shouldn't, is there?'

'No...no, none at all,' replied Freddie, with an assumed cheerfulness, although he was, in truth, feeling utterly deflated. He had thought he might have had a slight chance with her, even though Susannah had warned him that there was someone already in Maddy's life; she had also said that there were 'complications', which had given him an added hope. But Maddy obviously did not intend telling him what they were. However, he was not going to let her see how downcast he was.

He put on a brave face, hiding his disappointment very well beneath a bright smile and a flow of trivial chatter. After all, he was a real artiste now, a 'pro', and it was well-known that all true stage folk were able to conceal their aching hearts and carry on.

They did not linger over the coffee as the hour was getting late and they must return to Gorton. As they sat on the homebound tramcar Maddy turned to him and said, 'Thank you, Freddie. I've had a lovely evening. And I do hope we can go on being friends.'

'Of course,' he replied with the cheeriest grin he could muster. The loveliness of her face and her radiant smile brought a pang of sadness as he thought of what might have been. This Dan, whoever he was, was a damned lucky fellow, that's all he could say. He only hoped he realised how lucky he was.

'How did your date go?' Susannah asked Maddy the next morning.

'I enjoyed my meal with Freddie, if that's what you mean,' she replied. 'You could hardly call it a date. Well, I suppose Freddie hoped that it might be, but I put him in the picture about Dan. I mean, it wasn't fair to let him think that I might go on seeing him; just in case he was getting ideas, you know.'

'And how did he take it?'

'Oh, he was fine about it. I think he just saw me as a nice girl to take out for the evening, but when I said it couldn't go any further, that I couldn't go out with him again, he backed off straight away. He'll soon forget about me and find somebody else. I really like him – just like him, you know, as a friend – and he's a real asset to the troupe, isn't he? Those magic tricks of his; he has the audience spellbound.'

'Yes, he's a grand lad,' said Susannah, 'and I'm sure he won't stay unattached for long. A nice lass'll come along and snap him up, you'll see. Have you heard from your Dan lately, by the way?'

'Yes, as a matter if fact I had a letter this morning,' said Maddy, with just a hint of defiance.

'He's coming to see me in two weeks' time. His boss, Mr Grundy, is back in the shop now, and provided he keeps as well as he is now – Mr Grundy, I mean – Dan should be able to get away.'

'That's good news then,' said Susannah. 'I'll keep my fingers crossed for you.'

The fortnight in Manchester was followed by a week in Rochdale and then a week in the nearby town of Oldham, both of them being Lancashire cotton towns. The next week would see them back across the border with Yorkshire, in the town of Halifax, one of the smaller woollen mill towns. Both Susannah and Freddie were looking forward to that week, as Halifax was their home town. They would not be staying in digs with the rest of the company, but at their own homes; Freddie with his parents and his younger brother and sister, and Susannah with her sister and brother-in-law, whose home she shared when she was not on tour.

'And Frank will be staying there as well,' she told Maddy. 'My sister's got used to the idea now, of me and Frank being together, so she says he can share my room. She's pretty broad-minded, is our Flo. And she knows we'd get married if we were able to.'

'So there's no chance of that yet, for you and Frank?' asked Maddy.

'No, 'fraid not. Frank keeps trying to find a loophole in the law, but he can't see any. Like I told you, he's allowed to carry on with me and his wife can't divorce him for it. If she was up to the same game, though, it'd be different, but she's not, and Frank won't spy on her. Your stepmother was divorced, wasn't she, Maddy? Did they have any problems, do you know, when she and your father wanted to get married?'

'I never knew the ins and outs of it all,' said Maddy. 'I was too young at the time for them to explain it to me, I suppose, and it wasn't the sort of thing that was talked about. But I do know that Faith's ex-husband, Edward, was quite an influential businessman, a banker, and I daresay he had friends who were lawyers and barristers and whatnot.'

'I see…and money talks, doesn't it?' observed Susannah. 'Well, ne'er mind, eh? Frank and me are quite content as we are. Things might change one of these days, you never know.'

Freddie was looking forward to seeing his family again and having them come to watch him on the stage at the little variety theatre in the town centre. He was even more relieved to be on home territory when he discovered it was the week that Maddy's boyfriend was coming to visit her at long last. Her excitement was visible to everyone, in her extra pink cheeks and her bright eyes and the elation in her voice when she spoke of him.

It was good to be home again, to be fussed over by his mother and to enjoy her delicious home cooking and baking. And to bask in the admiration of his brother and sister who, unlike many siblings, did not scorn him but were delighted to have a brother who, they said, was a famous conjuror. He had entertained dreams, at one time, of taking Madeleine home with him to meet his family. What a fool he had been!

He realised how well he must have hidden his dismay at his dashed hopes, when Maddy invited her boyfriend backstage after the Saturday evening performance and introduced him to everyone. 'And this is Freddie,' she said. 'We've become good friends, Dan, Freddie and me, because we knew one another from the talent contest years ago. Isn't that amazing?'

She was more animated than Freddie had ever seen her. He shook hands with the ginger-haired, green-eyed young man – a touch of the Blarney there, unless he was very much mistaken – and found it was impossible to dislike him. He was an amiable chap, friendly and unassuming, with a look of candour, innocence almost, in those Irish eyes.

'How do you do, Freddie?' he said. 'Madeleine has mentioned you in her letters. I'm glad she has someone nearer her own age in the company now; you and…Jeremy, isn't it? Look after her for me, won't you? And I must congratulate you on your marvellous act. Very well done. You had us all mesmerised.'

'Thank you,' replied Freddie. 'Just wait till you see my flight of doves. I hope they'll be ready to perform with me by Christmas.'

'I shall look forward to it,' said Dan. Then he and Maddy linked arms and made their way out of the theatre.

And Freddie returned home to his last evening with his family and his dole of docile doves. They lived in a large cage in the garden and he had spent a good deal of his time that week in perfecting his act with them. He hoped to include it as his finale when they returned to Scarborough for the Christmas week. He could see, now, that he must put aside all thoughts of Madeleine. That was what Dan had called her, and he guessed that it was only Dan who did so. That was why she had asked him,

Freddie, to call her Maddy, just as everyone else did. If ever there was a young woman in love, it was Madeleine Moon.

Maddy and the rest of the company, minus Freddie, Susannah and Frank, had digs near to the town centre, just off Hopwood Lane. She had managed to book a room for Dan in the next-door house, from Friday till Sunday morning. He would be returning home on the Sunday when the Melody Makers moved on to their next booking in the nearby town of Huddersfield.

Halifax was a bustling little town in the daytime, but almost deserted in the evenings when the mills had closed, especially during the winter months. Apart from the pubs, of course, and the occasional restaurant. Maddy had managed to find one that stayed open till quite late, and they dined there on the Saturday evening. Dan had attended both performances on the Friday, then there had been time only for a few hugs and kisses on the pavement before they returned to their separate rooms in the adjoining houses.

They had been able to spend Saturday morning together, wandering around the little town, enjoying the hubbub of the busy market and seeing the magnificent Piece Hall, where manufacturers met to display their pieces of cloth woven in the mills.

Dan clasped Maddy's hands tightly inside his own, gazing at her across the tabletop in the tiny restaurant. It could be more accurately described as a café, not a very salubrious place, but at least it was clean and the food, though commonplace, was well cooked. They were the only customers at that late hour and they were only too happy to be together.

'I've missed you so much, my darling,' he said. 'It mustn't be so long before I see you again, Madeleine. I wish I could see you all the time...' His eyes clouded over with sadness, and she wanted so much to be able to say, So do I, Daniel... She wished she could tell him that she would leave the Melody Makers and join him in Blackpool, and find any sort of a job, just so that she could be with him. But it was not possible. She knew it and so did he.

And so she said, 'Cheer up, Dan. Let's enjoy the time we've got together. You'll be able to come and see me again soon, won't you?'

'I hope so,' he answered, 'but weekends are difficult. Saturday's a busy day in the shop. But I should be able to wangle another weekend before long, before we start getting busy for Christmas. Where are you off to next?'

'Well, let me see... Huddersfield, then Bradford, Leeds, York, Malton, Bridlington,' she counted on her fingers, 'and then we'll be back in Scarborough for the Christmas week. You could come and stay with us then; I'm sure it would be all right with my father and Faith.'

'Oh dear! I can't wait so long,' said Dan. 'I certainly will come to Scarborough, though. Perhaps not Christmas Day, but sometime that week…' He paused. 'I'm hoping to extend the olive branch to my mother before Christmas. It's a family time, isn't it? I ought to be with them. Surely, by then…'

'How is your mother?' asked Maddy tentatively. 'I mean…how are things with her?' He had scarcely mentioned his family all weekend.

'Oh, she's still being stubborn and unforgiving. She hasn't been to my flat, although Joe and my father have both visited me there. And when I go…home, she keeps out of my way. But she'll come round in time; I'm sure she will.' Maddy could see, though, that this estrangement from his mother was affecting him deeply.

They agreed that he would visit her when the troupe was in York, if that were at all possible. That would be the last week in November. It was harder than ever that night, kissing him, then leaving him at the front door. And even worse the next morning as they said goodbye at Halifax station, then boarded trains going in opposite directions.

Would it always be like this? Maddy began to wonder. It was the first time she had allowed such a negative thought to take root in her mind, but it remained there for the whole of the journey to Huddersfield.

Chapter Sixteen

Maddy was not the only member of the company who was thoughtful on the journey to Huddersfield. Barney had not turned up at the station and they had been obliged to board the train without him.

'Where is he?' Percy asked Benjy. 'Really, this is too bad! He knows the time of the train and he might have to wait ages for the next one. Anyway, I thought he'd be with you.'

'Don't blame me,' retorted Benjy, with a petulant shrug. 'We've had a tiff, if you must know, and he stormed out in a huff. I don't know where he is, and I don't much care neither!'

It was common knowledge amongst the Melody Makers that relations had not been too good just lately between the dancing duo, ever since Benjy had received those mysterious gifts and messages. They had stopped abruptly with no one being any the wiser, at least, that was what most of them had been led to believe. But the friction between the two young men had continued. Percy had become anxious because their bickering was having an adverse effect on their performances; and now he was furious.

'He'd better damned well turn up!' he stormed. 'It's high time you two sorted out your petty little quarrels. You're not irreplaceable, you know; neither of you!'

'Oh, he'll turn up like a bad penny,' said Benjy. 'Don't fret yourself. He's a big boy and he can take care of himself. He's got the address that we're going to in Huddersfield. He'll probably be on the next train.'

'Whenever that is,' said Percy. 'Sunday travel's pretty grim.'

'Well, serves him right then,' snapped Benjy. 'See if I care!'

But Barney did not turn up that day, nor the following morning. In fact, by the time of the first-house performance he had still not shown up and Benjy was in a rare old panic.

'Oh, whatever shall I do?' he wailed. 'I can't go on without him. Whatever will the audience think? We're a couple. I can't manage without him.'

'Yes, you can and you jolly well will!' said Percy. 'You get on that stage and you perform the numbers on your own. We'll make an announcement that Mr Barnaby Dewhurst is indisposed, and nobody need be any the wiser.' Then he added, more kindly, 'Come along, Benjy. Nobody is blaming you, you know. And you're a real trouper, aren't you? Go on there and give them all you've got, there's a good chap.'

'Yes, I suppose so,' said Benjy with a sniff. 'The show must go on and all that.'

And of course the audience rose to the occasion and Benjy received tremendous applause and even cheers at both houses.

'There you are, you see. You can do it,' Percy told him. 'Well done! I shall have a few harsh words, though, for Barney – well, more than a few – when he turns up.'

'If he ever does,' said Benjy glumly.

'Oh, he will, when he comes to his senses,' said Percy. 'I know Barney, at least I thought I did. He's a decent chap at heart, just like you are. He won't leave us in the lurch without an explanation.'

The explanation, such as it was, came in the post the following morning. A letter arrived at the digs in Huddersfield addressed to Mr Benjamin Carstairs, and the landlady handed it to him at the breakfast table.

'And about time too,' he declared, almost snatching it from the lady, but remembering at the same time to say thank you. Benjy hardly ever forgot his manners. His eyes scanned the first page of the letter, then, to the consternation and embarrassment of the rest of the company seated around the table, he burst into tears.

'He's left me,' he wailed. 'He's gone and left me! He's gone back home to Rochdale. Oh, dearie me! Whatever am I going to do?'

'You're going to manage without him, that's

what,' said Frank Morrison, always one to speak his mind. 'Come along, old chap. You did splendidly last night and we were all very proud of you.'

'Yes, but it's not just our act, is it?' cried Benjy. 'He says he doesn't want to see me anymore. He says it's time we parted company.'

'Well then, perhaps it is,' said Percy gently. 'What else does he say...or is it private?'

'No, why should it be?' retorted Benjy. He thrust the letter across the table to Percy in a dramatic gesture. 'Here, read it for yourself.'

The message was quite brief and to the point. Barney was returning to his home town of Rochdale to think things over. He and Benjy had come to a parting of the ways, he wrote, and would his partner please give his apologies to Percy for walking out on them so abruptly. He was sure that Benjy would manage perfectly well without him.

'Hmm, I'm very annoyed with him,' said Percy when he had read the letter. 'Oh, come along, Benjy. Do stop snivelling. We've got to sort out what we're going to do. As Frank said, you did very well last night, but some of your songs and dances – well, most of them really – are arranged for a duo, aren't they? How would you feel about it if we were to advertise for another partner for you?' Percy felt, however, that Benjy might not like that idea at all.

'I don't know,' replied Benjy in a small voice. 'It would take some getting used to. And we might not get on in the same way as Barney and I did…if you see what I mean.'

'Yes, I do see what you mean,' said Percy, 'but that is something you would have to sort out for yourselves, isn't it?'

'Wait a minute,' said Jeremy Jarvis. 'I've got a good idea. Well, you might not think it's good but…how would you like a female partner for a change? Does it have to be another man?'

'No, not necessarily,' said Benjy in a sulky voice. 'Sometimes men can be more trouble than they're worth. Why? Have you got something up your sleeve, Jeremy?'

'I might have,' said Jeremy. He turned to Percy. 'You remember Dora, don't you? Dora Daventry, the young lady who auditioned at the same time as Freddie and me.'

'Well, of course I remember her,' said Percy. 'And I believe you are still quite friendly with her, aren't you?'

'So I am,' grinned Jeremy. 'She lives here in Huddersfield and I shall be seeing her quite a lot this week. But what you may not know is that she is a dancer as well as a singer. She's a very good tap dancer, apparently. She passed all her exams when she was younger, but then she decided to concentrate on her singing.'

'Why didn't she tell me then, at the audition, that she could dance?' asked Percy.

'Well, she'd seen Barney and Benjy perform and

she knew you wouldn't want another tap dancer. And then it turned out that you didn't want any singers either.'

'It wasn't that we didn't want her,' replied Percy, 'as I explained to her at the time. I could see she was very talented but – yes, you're right – I felt we didn't need anymore singers…not at that time,' he added meaningfully. Carlo and Queenie, sitting next to Percy, exchanged significant glances, of which he was well aware. 'How would you feel about a lady partner, Benjy?' Percy asked him. 'Do you think that it might work, that you might…consider it?'

'I don't see why not,' said Benjy. 'I'm too upset at the moment to think straight, but I know you have to do whatever is best for the company. And I'm not a solo act, am I, not really?'

Percy rubbed his chin thoughtfully. 'You're seeing Dora today, are you, Jeremy?' The young man nodded and agreed that he was. 'Well then, would you ask her if she would like to come and see me at the theatre this afternoon, if possible? Two-thirty, shall we say? And you too, Benjy. Would you agree to that?'

'Yes,' he said in a quiet voice. 'But you won't mind, will you, if I'm not at my sparkling best? I promise I'll be there, though.' He sniffed audibly and turned his head away.

'That's good then,' said Percy. 'We'll see what Dora thinks about it; she may not agree, of course. But I'll keep my fingers crossed. I thought at the time that she could be an asset to the troupe, so here's her chance, if she wants it.'

Dora was delighted at the suggestion that she might join the Melody Makers, provided she and Benjy could adapt the act accordingly, and provided, of course, that they thought they could work together amicably.

With Letty at the piano and Percy watching and making suggestions, they ran through a few routines on the Tuesday afternoon. She was, indeed, a very competent tap dancer, and it was clear that after a few more practices she would be ready to become the second half of the dancing duo. It was agreed that she should wear a short black skirt to match Benjy's black trousers, with a similar white shirt and red bow tie and she already had black patent leather tap shoes. She complemented Benjy in appearance, as his former partner, Barney had done. She was dark-haired and brown-eyed, and an inch or two shorter than Benjy.

When they had finished their rehearsal that day Benjy threw his arms around her and kissed her on both cheeks. 'Thank you, thank you, my darling girl,' he enthused. 'You have saved my life. I thought I would never be able to carry on without Barney, but now I know that I can manage perfectly well without him.' The spasm of pain that showed on his face, however, after he had made this brave statement, revealed to the others that he was still hurting. There was little doubt that Dora would be a satisfactory dancing partner, but it was not likely that Benjy would be able to forget Barney and their long-standing friendship so easily.

'What about our name?' he went on. 'Barney and Benjy had quite a nice ring to it, I always thought. But Benjy and Dora, the Dancing Duo doesn't sound too bad, does it? We've got the alliteration with all the Ds, haven't we? Unless you would like to change your name to Betty or Bella or...something?'

'No, I wouldn't,' she replied.

'No, of course not, no more than I would like to be Don or Dick or Dave!' said Benjy. 'Righty-ho then, Benjy and Dora it is.'

Percy thought that after a few more practices, Dora should be ready to make her debut with Benjy at the Friday performances, followed by the matinée and one evening performance on Saturday. Next week they were moving on to Bradford and Percy would make arrangements to have the names changed on the programmes and posters as soon as possible.

Word had got around the company about the possibility of a new member. It was hardly a secret because the idea had been mooted by Jeremy at the breakfast table. Percy made a formal announcement before the Wednesday matinée that Dora Daventry would be joining them before long and that he knew, of course, that they would all make her very welcome.

Everyone smiled their agreement and there followed a buzz of conversation about how fortunate they had been to find a replacement for Barney so quickly. Some of them had met Dora and they thought she would fit in with the rest of the company very well. Jeremy, naturally, was delighted that his suggestion had been acted upon and had proved successful.

'You lucky old dog, Jeremy!' said Frank Morrison, with a nudge and a wink. 'A lady friend on tap all the time, eh? Just like me.'

'Hey, steady on, Frank,' said Jeremy. 'We're not at that stage yet.'

'Or maybe it's not so lucky then,' teased Frank. 'You'll have to watch your step, won't you, lad?'

'Oh, I'm lucky all right,' replied Jeremy. 'Dora's a grand girl, and I'm real pleased she's joining us. I'm not going to rush things, though. And I've promised her mam and dad that I'll take care of her.'

The only faces that were not smiling were those of Carlo and Queenie Colman. Percy knew that they saw Dora as a threat, as she was a singer as well as a dancer. Especially as Percy had had occasion to speak to Queenie after the Monday night performances, concerning the wobbliness of her top notes in her solo song.

'Choose another song,' he told her, 'in a lower key. Or else ask Letty to transpose that one a tone lower, at least. I'm sorry, Queenie, but your voice doesn't have the same timbre that it used to have to

315

reach those top Fs and Gs. It happens to all of us in time.'

'Are you saying that I'm getting old, that I'm past it?' she snapped.

'No, not at all, but the quality of your voice is changing. Choose something that is more in keeping, that's all I'm saying.'

Queenie had tossed her head in answer, but she had done as he requested and sang a different song the following night: 'The Moon and I', from *The Mikado*, instead of her usual 'Poor Wandering One' from *Pirates*. The audiences of late had winced or giggled at the tremulous, 'Ah! Ah! Ahs...' as the woman's bosom heaved and her face turned red. Percy hated any of his troupe to be a laughing stock. With a less polite audience it might result in a deluge of rotten tomatoes. He had gone out of his way to compliment her on her new choice of song, but he knew that she and Carlo were still not happy.

The company moved on to Bradford the following week, and it was at the end of their time there that Carlo and Queenie announced to Percy that they were leaving.

'We're giving you a week's notice,' said Carlo, 'and we will be going at the end of next week.' The company was moving from Bradford to the nearby city of Leeds for their next booking. 'We'll do the week in Leeds, and then we're off, Queenie and me...to pastures new.'

'That's very short notice,' said Percy. 'I thought it was usual to give a month's notice if you intended leaving.' Although he knew that there had never been a hard and fast rule in their troupe about how long the period should be. It was a very long time since anyone had wanted to leave, apart from Barney, of course, who hadn't given any notice at all. Percy realised that he hadn't a leg to stand on. Besides, he was growing increasingly weary of Queenie and her complaining, and there was no doubt that their singing was no longer of the quality he expected. He knew, in truth, that he would be glad to see the back of them.

'We can't wait a month,' said Queenie. 'Like Carlo's just said, we're off to pastures new.'

'Very well then; a week's notice it is,' agreed Percy. 'Fortunately, we've got a new artiste, and I'm sure she will be able to fill in the space you'll be leaving, for a little while.'

'Oh, yes, I'm sure she will,' said Queenie with a knowing glance at her husband. 'That's what we thought. I said to Carlo, we won't be missed, especially now they've got another young lass on board. I can see she'll be only too ready to step into my shoes as well as Barney's. So it'll be a case of off with the old and on with the new.'

'Now, don't say that…' Percy knew that he must make some placatory noises. After all, Carlo and Queenie had been with the troupe for several years and had played an important role at the start, if not now. 'Of course you will be missed. You have been loyal members – real troupers – and we do appreciate all that you've done. Where are you going...may I ask?'

'Oh, we've got a permanent position at a little theatre down south,' replied Carlo, showing a little more grace than his wife had done. 'It's a friend of mine from way back that runs it. Part repertory and part vaudeville, week and week about, we understand. I expect Queenie and I will find a niche there. We're both pretty adaptable. There might be some character parts, and that's what I like doing most of all. And we're both getting a bit long in the tooth for this Pierrot lark in the summer months; all that dressing up in fancy costumes. It's all right for the youngsters, but not for us anymore.'

'Yes, and we're getting a bit weary of all the travelling,' admitted Queenie. 'It's high time we put down our roots somewhere. And these Yorkshire winters are no good for me and my chest. It'll be a good deal warmer down on the south coast, we hope.'

'We'll miss you,' said Percy, 'and I wish you well. So will the others when they hear about it.'

He knew he couldn't let them go without some sort of a farewell, and he was glad they were not leaving under a cloud. Queenie had taken umbrage, he knew, at the curtailing of their act and his criticism of her singing; and she had been vociferous in her complaints about all the youngsters who were joining the company. But by the time it came to the end of their week in Leeds she had become more amenable and kindly disposed to the artistes that she and her husband were leaving.

They all congregated at a public house near to City Square after the Saturday evening performance and the couple were given a rousing send-off. Queenie was presented with a bouquet of flowers and they were handed a cheque, which was the result of a whip-round amongst their fellow members.

'Let's raise our glasses to Carlo and Queenie,' said Percy. 'We wish them every success in their new venture.'

'Carlo and Queenie...'

'All the best...'

'Break a leg...' they all echoed.

And Queenie cried into her milk stout. 'Oh dear! Oh, dearie me! I shall miss you all...so very much. I've never had such good friends as you lot. Carlo...why are we going?'

'Because it's time to move on,' said her husband, putting his arm around her plump shoulders and drying her tears. 'Come on, old girl; cheer up. I tell you what – how about a song? Just you and me, eh?'

'Why not?' said Queenie. She rose unsteadily to

her feet and together they sang, unaccompanied, about the ivy on the old garden wall. All the Melody Makers joined in the chorus.

'As you grow older
I'll be constant and true;
And just like the ivy
I'll cling to you.'

Chapter Seventeen

The Sunday afternoon train rattled along the tracks, taking the Melody Makers from Leeds to York where they were to stay for not one, but two weeks.

'How would you feel about doing a solo singing spot?' Percy asked Dora Daventry, suddenly appearing in the compartment that she was sharing with Jeremy, Freddie and Maddy.

Dora looked startled. 'Oh! Well…I'm not sure to be honest.' She glanced apologetically at Maddy. 'You already have two first-rate singers, haven't you? Maddy here, and Susannah. I don't want to tread on anyone's toes. You told me at the audition, didn't you, Percy, that that was the reason you couldn't take me on.'

'Well, yes, so I did. But with Carlo and Queenie leaving so suddenly it's put a different complexion on things. We're an act short, aren't we? I know I could give one or two of the others a longer spot, but I feel that everyone already has quite enough to do.'

'And I haven't?' asked Dora with a grin. 'I'm already partnering Benjy. I don't want to be accused of stealing the limelight.'

'You wouldn't be,' Percy told her. 'The good thing about our little troupe is how we all muck in and help one another. I shall be roping these two lads in before long to take part in our sketches.' He nodded towards Freddie and Jeremy.

'Maddy's already taking part, aren't you, love? Although she took some persuading at first.'

'Yes, that was because I saw myself as a singer and nothing else,' said Maddy. 'But it's surprising what you can do when you try; and if you're used to appearing on a stage then you usually find out that you're pretty adaptable.'

'Carlo and Queenie were a double act, though,' Dora remarked, 'with just the occasional solo. I don't feel that I could carry the act on my own. Besides, as I've said, you already have Maddy and Susannah.'

'But you could aim at something different,' said Percy. 'A little bird tells me that you are really a classical singer. You've taken exams, haven't you, and sung in the church choir and amateur operatics?'

'Yes, that's true,' smiled Dora. 'And I can guess who the little bird is.' She nodded reprovingly at Jeremy. 'I suppose my repertoire does veer more towards the classical type of song. But when I did the audition I was giving you what I thought you would want.'

'There's nowt wrong wi' a bit o' class,' said Percy with a laugh. 'It'd be something different. I always think of Susannah's act as being a bit naughty and coquettish, and as for Maddy, she's the girl next door, isn't she, with her sweet plaintive songs. Think it over, Dora, there's a love, and perhaps during our second week in York... As far as this next week is concerned, we're putting in an extra sketch and two more songs in the finale, ones the audience can join in with.'

'But what about you, Percy?' said Maddy. She still felt a mite uncomfortable at addressing him by his Christian name; when she was a child he had always been 'Uncle Percy' to her and to all the other children. 'When I first started watching the Pierrots, you used to sing solos, didn't you? You had a very good voice – a baritone, weren't you? – and I expect you can still sing very well.'

'Yes, you're right,' replied Percy. 'I was quite a passable baritone; I could sing tenor, too, if it wasn't too high. But I've not done much lately. I've been concentrating on the managing and producing side of things, and doing the funny men acts with Pete. He's a singer too, of course, but he prefers the comedy routines. Why, what are you suggesting?'

'That you could pair up with Dora,' said Maddy. 'You'd be a darned sight better that Carlo and Queenie...but I suppose I shouldn't say that,' she added with a guilty smile.

'No, you shouldn't,' said Percy with a frown of mock reproof. 'Dear old Queenie. I do hope she settles down in the south of England. I suppose we northerners were a mite too common for her at times.'

'But she was a northerner, wasn't she?' asked Maddy. 'I thought she came from Yorkshire.'

'So she did: from Wakefield,' said Percy, 'But she tended to forget her working-class roots. Something of a social climber, was our Queenie. Anyway, I do hope she'll be happy. And we have to fill the gap they've left behind. Aye, maybe that's not a bad idea, for me and Dora to have a bash at singing duets. How about it then, Dora?'

'I'd rather do that than have a solo spot,' replied Dora.

'Very well then; we'll have a go, shall we?' said Percy. 'And thanks for the suggestion, Maddy. Happen it's not such a bad idea to start using my vocal cords again; they're getting a bit rusty. Pick out some of your favourite songs, Dora, and I'll do the same. Then we'll get Letty to have a run-through with us. It'll be a weight off my mind if we can construct another act between us.'

They started rehearsals on the Monday morning, with Letty at the piano, and by the end of the week they had put together a performance that was rather more highbrow in content than were the other acts in the show. As Percy had remarked, there was nowt wrong wi' a bit o' class. They aimed to cater for the varying tastes of all the members of the audience, and there would be some, Percy guessed, who might enjoy music that was a little more serious in content.

He and Dora decided to announce their act as 'Percy and Dora, bringing you a touch of class'. He explained to the other members of the company that this description was not decrying in any way the more lowbrow acts that, until now, had been their mainstay; but he was aiming for greater variety in their programme. There was not one member who disagreed. They remembered how Carlo and Queenie had aimed at a similar type of act; but that of late it had become, albeit unintentionally, more of a comedy routine.

By the beginning of the second week in York the new act was ready for its debut. It consisted of two solos and three duets. Percy and Dora had discovered that their voices, baritone and soprano, blended well together. Dora had no problem in soaring up to the top Fs and Gs in 'Cherry Ripe', and Percy's 'Come into the Garden Maud', suited the mellow quality of his voice. But it was their final duet, 'On Wings of Song', that earned the most applause and shouts of 'Bravo!' and 'More, more!' But there was never time for encores in a show that needed to keep to a strict timetable, especially when there were two houses a night.

Percy and Dora had reason to be well pleased with their first performance. Percy hugged her and kissed her on the cheek when they left the stage. 'We've done it, lass,' he said. 'Thank you for helping me to find my voice again.'

Jeremy, whose act was next, had been standing in the wings watching the debut performance of the young woman who was beginning to mean so much to him. He, too, flung his arms around her. 'Well done!' he cried. 'That was marvellous...and you too, Percy. The audience loved it, didn't they?'

'Aye, I think they did, lad,' said Percy. He was more than satisfied with the way things were going. Taking on the two new lads, and then Dora, was proving to be a turning point in the fortunes of the Melody Makers. 'I've a feeling we're going from strength to strength,' he said. 'Off you go now, Jeremy, you and Tommy the Toff. It's a good audience tonight and they'll just lap it up.'

'From the sublime to the ridiculous, eh?' said Jeremy with a grin and a grimace, as he walked onto the stage with his big black box. And his act, too, with Tommy the Toff and his lady friend the buxom blonde Belinda, was a rip-roaring success.

On the whole it was a happy and profitable fortnight for most of the members of the company, in the city of York. But for Maddy, alas, there was a bitter disappointment.

It was not always easy to maintain contact with Dan because, quite often, she did not know the address of the digs for that particular week or fortnight until they actually arrived there. She wrote to him as soon as they arrived in York, telling him how much she was looking forward to seeing him, although that went without saying. He had promised he would come to York at the end of the first week of their stay there, if it were at all possible.

A letter arrived, however, on the Friday morning, the very day on which he was expected, saying that he was dreadfully sorry – in fact, he scarcely knew how to find the words to tell her – but he could not come after all. The young lad, Cedric, who had been employed as a junior assistant, had been taken ill with a severe cough and cold, which had turned to bronchitis. Moreover, the affliction had been passed on to Mr Grundy, as Cedric had kept on working for several days before he finally succumbed to the illness. And Mrs Grundy had insisted on her husband staying in bed; she had taken extra care of him since his operation earlier that year. Dan, therefore, was in charge of the shop and there was no possibility of his being able to get away. He would be with her at Christmas, though, he assured her; not on Christmas Day but at some time during the Christmas period, when the company would be at Scarborough for a fortnight. He would move heaven and earth to be with her and nothing would keep him away. He loved her more than ever. He was longing to see her. And, after all, it was only a few weeks until Christmas. That was the time now on which they must focus their hopes and longings…

Maddy's eyes had misted with tears as she read the letter at the breakfast table, but she had blinked them away and made an excuse to leave the room as soon as possible. She knew she must not give way to a bout of weeping and wailing which was what she felt like doing. Crying only made your eyes red and puffy and everyone would notice. Travelling with the Melody Makers was teaching her to be more stoical and in control of herself, and always she tried to give heed to the familiar adage that the show must go on.

She did something, though, that she had never done before, something that she would never have dreamt she would do. She screwed up Dan's letter and flung it into the empty firegrate in her room, because she was angry as well as disappointed. For the first time ever she was starting to wonder if their love could survive these long periods away from one another. It was not the first time that Dan had been unable to keep his promise to her, and she doubted that it would be the last.

Then the memory of him surfaced: his radiant green eyes, by no means a warm colour, but how they shone with tenderness and sincerity, and how his face lit up in a smile of sheer delight whenever they met. Yes, she loved him, and she trusted him. It was not his fault that he could not come. She would just have to try and forget her disappointment and look forward to the next time. As Dan said, it was not too far distant...

Freddie Nicholls was one person who noticed Maddy's change of expression at the breakfast table. Since she had told him that they could never be more than friends he had tried, not to forget her – that was impossible with them working so closely together – but to channel his thoughts into other directions. He worked on new tricks for his act and on perfecting his already remarkable sleight of hand, and on visiting, usually alone, the parts of the cities and towns that he had not seen before. In York there were many such places. He delighted in the narrow streets and alleyways, where the wooden framed houses leant towards one another, their rooftops almost touching; the vastness and solemnity of the Minster church; and the ancient walls that encompassed the city and along which one could walk for miles.

It was on one of those walks, on the Thursday afternoon of the second week of their stay in York, that he met Maddy, coming towards him from the opposite direction. He was always able to speak to her quite normally, just as he did to all the other members of the troupe. No one could tell from his ease of manner towards her that he still harboured feelings for her that were other than those of a casual friend. Maddy, herself, was convinced that her word to him had done the trick and that he now regarded her as just another fellow artiste. So she did not hesitate when he suggested that they should descend from the wall and spend some time together over a cup of tea.

They walked over the Lendal Bridge, which was

where they alighted the wall, and found a cosy tea shop near to the Minster. They chatted of this and that, and agreed how well the new act with Percy and Dora was being received by the audiences.

'A very versatile young woman,' remarked Freddie. 'Singing as well as dancing. I hadn't realised, until I actually joined the Melody Makers, how adaptable one has to be. Our show is not just a series of isolated acts, is it, like the usual variety shows? I didn't know that I might be called upon to be an actor as well. Percy is determined to get Jeremy and me into the latest sketches.'

'Oh, you'll be fine,' replied Maddy dismissively. 'You don't have to be Sir Henry Irving, you know. It's only a bit of fun, and I'm sure that if I can do it, anybody can. You never know what you can do until you try. Percy runs the winter tours as a continuation of the Pierrot shows, more or less, with everybody "mucking in", as he puts it. Apart from dressing up in our Pierrot costumes, of course.'

'I suppose Jeremy and I will have to wear them too, when we're in Scarborough next summer?' queried Freddie.

'Oh, I expect so,' said Maddy. 'Not for your individual acts, but certainly for the chorus numbers at the beginning and the end. Then you'll feel that you really belong.'

'I do already,' Freddie told her. 'Everybody has made us so very welcome. I'm really enjoying it all.

It's a great experience, being on the road, and it's good to have so many new friends.'

'Yes, the companionship can be a great comfort sometimes,' said Maddy, 'especially when you're feeling down in the dumps…as I was last weekend.'

'Oh?' said Freddie questioningly, not wanting to let on that he had noticed, and that, moreover, he had made a guess at the reason for it. He knew it was connected with the letter she had received a little while ago, probably from that absent boyfriend of hers. 'What has been the matter, Maddy? May I ask?'

'I don't see why not,' said Maddy. She felt no compunction about telling him. It was good to talk sometimes, and she had bottled it up after her initial outburst, apart from confiding in Susannah. 'I had a letter from my boyfriend – you remember Dan; you met him, didn't you? He was supposed to be coming to see me last weekend, but he couldn't manage it.'

'Oh dear! What a shame,' said Freddie. 'You must have felt terribly let down.' He assumed a sorry expression, although he could not help feeling, deep down, a surge of elation.

'He didn't mean to let me down,' said Maddy. She explained the reason for him cancelling his visit. 'And he's promised he'll be in Scarborough some time over Christmas. So I'll just have to look forward to that, won't I?'

'I daresay you will,' said Freddie. He wondered if

there was more to this than met the eye. Whether, maybe, this Dan fellow had met someone else and was trying to let Maddy down lightly. If so, then there might still be a chance for him, Freddie; but he knew he must not divulge his feelings, not in the slightest degree. 'It's only a few weeks, isn't it?' He smiled sympathetically at her.

'So it is,' agreed Maddy. Then, as though she had read his thoughts, she went on to say, 'I trust him, you know. He hasn't got somebody else or anything like that. No...' She smiled ruefully. 'I know that if Dan were ever to leave me it wouldn't be for another girl. No, it would be something entirely different.'

'Oh?' said Freddie again, eyeing her quizzically. 'And what is that? Or maybe I shouldn't ask. Don't tell me if you don't want to.' Susannah had hinted to him that there were complications in Maddy's relationship with Dan. Now, perhaps he was about to find out the nature of the problem.

Maddy sighed. 'There's no reason why you shouldn't know, I suppose.' She suddenly felt like talking about it, and Freddie was a good listener. 'My rival would not be another girl... It would be God.'

'What!' Freddie looked at her in amazement, so she went on to explain that when she had first met Daniel, he had been studying to become a Roman Catholic priest.

'I see...and he gave it all up when he met you, did he?'

'Not exactly,' said Maddy. 'He had already been having doubts and meeting me...well, that finally made him realise that he wanted a more normal sort of life and that he wasn't destined for the priesthood. It had been his mother's idea anyway, so it's caused ructions with his family as well, I'm sorry to say.'

'So it's not proving easy?' asked Freddie.

'No...but they say that the course of true love never runs smoothly, don't they?' Maddy gave a wry smile. 'Anyway, thanks for listening, Freddie. I feel a lot better for having talked to somebody...to you.'

'Don't mention it,' he said. 'That's what friends are for. Now we'd best be getting back to our digs, hadn't we? It'll soon be time for our first house.'

He settled the small bill and they walked back companionably to their digs near the railway station.

He's nice, thought Maddy. But only as a friend, of course. She was glad to see that he had got over his idea that he might be rather more than that. He had seemed so genuinely concerned about her problems, and she hoped he would find a girl who deserved him.

Chapter Eighteen

J oe Murphy was deep in thought as he walked
along Blackpool promenade one afternoon in
mid-December. Christmas was fast approaching
and he did so hope and pray that there might be a
reconciliation between his mother and Daniel in
time for the celebration of Christ's birth. Christmas
would not be the same without Dan, whether at the
Midnight Mass, which they all attended as a family,
or at the festive meal the following day, a dinner at
which Mammy always excelled herself.

Once or twice lately he thought he had glimpsed
a hint of regret in her eyes when his brother's name
was mentioned; for Joe had been determined that
he would go on talking about him even though
Mammy had tried to insist that his name should not
be spoken. Then he knew she had hardened her
heart again, refusing to speak of him, and keeping
out of the way when he called at the house. Dan
called only infrequently, and the reason he called at
all was because Thomas Murphy had been adamant
that the door should not be closed against their
elder son, as Anna had threatened to do. Joe called
to see his brother from time to time at his flat above

the Church Street shop, and he knew that his father visited him as well. But Anna had not set eyes on Daniel since there had been that terrible row about the letters, which had resulted in Dan leaving home. That was months ago, and how his mother could prove so obdurate filled Joe with sorrow, and anger, too, especially when he knew that she had been the one to blame.

Dan was of a far more forgiving nature, and Joe knew he would be willing, now that time had passed, to extend the olive branch, as he put it, to his mother. But it remained to be seen whether or not that would happen before Christmas. All that Joe could do was to hope and pray. And he did pray, although he knew that his faith had never meant as much to him as it had to his brother.

From an early age both he and Dan had gone along to Sunday school and church and had gradually become steeped in the doctrines of the Roman Catholic religion: the confession and the Mass; the elevation of the Host, the burning of incense, the choral responses and the litany; and they had grown to appreciate the wonder and mysticism that surrounded it all. His brother, though, far more so than himself. Daniel was the one with the superior brain power. Joe was well aware of that and bore his brother no grudge for being so much cleverer. He was the best brother any lad could have and the two of them had always been the best of pals.

It was inevitable, therefore, that Daniel should be the one who had had thoughts of entering the priesthood. He, Joe, would not have had the cleverness or the knowledge that it required. From the time he was in his early teens it was clear that that was the direction in which Dan was heading. Although Joe knew, as did his father and Dan himself, that the idea was largely that of their mother. It was the ambition of many devout Catholic mothers to have a son enter the priesthood, and therefore this mantle had fallen upon Daniel.

But Joe, with a perspicacity that few knew he possessed, was aware that his brother was not entirely happy about the decision that had been made for him. And Joe, also, had begun to think that it was unfair. His brother was a good-looking lad and personable, too; far more handsome and likeable than he was, or so Joe believed. He had seen the looks that the girls in the congregation cast in his brother's direction, but such dalliances were forbidden to Dan. Joe had wished at times that he could attract such soulful glances. And then Madeleine Moon had come along.

It was he, Joe, who had met her first, and he still remembered with pride how helpful he had been to her and the rest of the touring company when they had arrived at Central Station. And he had been thrilled to receive tickets for the show. Then it had happened: Dan had fallen hook, line and sinker for the delectable Madeleine…and landed himself in a whole lot of trouble.

What a dratted nuisance religion could be, thought Joe. He was sure that God didn't intend it to cause all that trouble. What did it matter that Madeleine was a Methodist? And why should it matter that Dan had decided not to be a priest after all, but to follow the dictates of his heart? There would always be plenty of young men to answer the call, so surely Daniel would not be missed.

Then he, Joe, had met Myrtle, the girl who had come to work at the family boarding house. She was the first girl who had ever taken much notice of him – apart from Madeleine, of course, but she belonged to his brother – and Joe had soon decided that he liked her very much. She was not as shy as he was and had brought him out of his shell in ways he had never dreamt of. And, as luck would have it, she was a Catholic. Not that it would have mattered, he told himself, but it had meant that Mammy approved of her. She was already accepted as being almost one of the family. But he was only sixteen, the same age as Myrtle; it was too soon to be thinking so far into the future, but they were very happy together and Joe was content with that.

Myrtle would be there at the Murphy family Christmas tea, after spending the earlier part of the day with her own family; and Joe did so hope that Dan might be there as well.

His head was full of thoughts of Myrtle and Dan

as he turned away from the promenade to cross the tramtrack. With his head down and the peak on his cap obscuring his view – although he had not, in fact, bothered to check – he failed to notice the huge Dreadnought tramcar approaching. Trams did not travel at an alarming speed, but the glancing blow that it struck him sent him flying into the air before he landed in a crumpled, seemingly lifeless heap at the side of the track.

It was early evening when Daniel answered the knock at the door of his flat. His father stood on the threshold and Dan could tell at once that there was something seriously amiss.

'It's your brother,' said Thomas. 'He's had an accident. He's in hospital…he's in a bad way, Dan. You must come now, at once. Your mother's there, waiting for news. We're not at all sure that he's going to make it… You will come, won't you, lad?'

'Of course I'll come,' said Dan. 'Come in for a minute and I'll get my coat.' He managed to comprehend, from his father's somewhat incoherent telling of the tale, that Joe had been knocked down by a tramcar when crossing the tramtrack near to the Tower. The first that his parents knew of it was when a policeman arrived at their door towards teatime. Fortunately Joe had had means of identification on his person in a diary that he always carried, containing his name and address. Indeed, Joe often behaved with a good deal more common sense than people gave him credit for.

Passers-by had called for an ambulance and he was taken as quickly as possible to the hospital on Whitegate Drive, where he was, at that moment, undergoing an emergency operation.

'It's not far to walk,' said Dan. Whitegate Drive was, in fact, a continuation of Church Street, where the shop and Dan's flat were situated. 'We could take a tramcar, but we'll get there nearly as quickly if we walk.'

'I don't want to see another tramcar as long as I live,' said Thomas as they set off walking briskly through the gathering darkness of the December evening. 'The silly lad! What on earth was he thinking of, wandering onto the track like that? Head up in the clouds, I daresay. Happen thinking about that sweetheart of his.'

'Yes… Myrtle,' said Dan. 'Does she know about this?'

'Not yet,' replied Thomas. 'Our priority was to let you know, son. We'll tell Myrtle by and by. I only hope we'll have some better news by then.'

Dan was aware of the break in his father's voice. 'Our Joe's a strong lad, Daddy,' he said. 'He'll pull through… We must pray that he does,' he added, realising that he had no idea, yet, of the extent of his brother's injuries. He had noticed, also, his father's use of the pronoun 'our', indicating that his mother must have been in agreement about contacting him.

'How is Mammy?' he asked, returning to the

once so familiar mode of addressing her. 'She was all right, was she, about you coming to tell me?'

'You know your mother, lad,' replied Thomas. 'She's very upset, naturally. Neither of us can think straight at the moment, but she did say that I was to come and tell you. "It's his brother after all," she said. "He's got a right to know."'

Dan had prayed that there might be some way in which he could heal the breach between himself and his mother, but this was certainly not a way he would have envisaged. He wondered, now, what her reaction would be on seeing him again.

Anna was sitting in a waiting room off the main ward. Joe had still not been brought back from the theatre. Dan went towards her, stooping to kiss her cheek and embrace her. 'Hello, Mammy,' he said. 'This is a bad do, isn't it? But I'm sure our Joe is in good hands. We'll have to trust in God, won't we, to…to bring him back to us?'

Anna did not return his embrace. She pulled away from him, and when she looked at him her vivid green eyes gleamed with a venom that verged on hatred. 'Don't you dare talk to me about trusting in God!' she raged. Her voice was not loud; it was more of a vengeful whisper. 'This is your fault. This is God's punishment because you turned your back on Him. But why it should be your brother I don't understand. It should have been you, under the wheels of that tram, not our Joe.'

'Anna, that's a wicked thing to say!'

remonstrated her husband. 'Of course it wasn't Daniel's fault; it was an accident, pure and simple. I hate to say it, but it was probably Joe's own fault for not looking where he was going.'

'And why?' retorted Anna. 'Why wasn't he looking where he was going? Because he was worried, that's why. I know he wanted things to be right with Daniel again. But now they never will be.'

'Mammy, you're upset, and I don't blame you,' said Daniel. 'You have every right to be upset...and angry with me as well, if it helps. But it's not my fault; it's not anyone's fault. It was a tragic accident. You know how dozens of people are knocked down every year by trams. We're always reading about it in the newspapers. They seem to creep along so quietly and there's no barrier by the tramtrack... And I meant what I said; we'll have to trust in God to make Joe well again.'

At that moment a doctor appeared in the room. 'Mr and Mrs Murphy...' he began. 'I am pleased to say that your son has survived the operation. We have done all we can, but he is still very poorly.'

'Can we see him, Doctor?' asked Anna.

'You may see him for a few minutes, but he is still unconscious. It may be quite a while before he comes round from the anaesthetic... I have to tell you that there were a few internal injuries and bleeding, as well as a broken arm and a severe blow to the head. But I assure you that we will do everything we can. Now, if you would like to come with me...'

Joe was on his own in a small room at the side of the main ward. His eyes were closed, his head swathed in bandages, and there was a mask over his face to assist with his breathing, as well as tubes attached to other parts of his body. He was deathly pale and it seemed to them all, at that moment, that it would be a miracle if he were ever to come round.

'Just a few moments, now,' said the doctor. 'He won't regain consciousness for a while yet.'

'Oh, my poor baby,' said Anna, taking hold of the hand that lay on top of the counterpane. The other hand and arm were encased in plaster. 'Joe...oh Joe, please come back to us.' She did not hurl anymore acrimonious words at her elder son, but she looked at him keenly as he stood at the other side of the bed.

'Pray that your brother recovers,' she told him. 'And if he does, then you know what you must do, don't you, Daniel? To put things right and to show that you are thankful? You must turn back to God. It's all been a lot of foolishness, giving up on your studies, but He will forgive you. Promise me that you will. Make a promise to God that you will, if He answers your prayer. I know you believe in the power of prayer, at least you used to.'

'Mammy...you don't know what you are asking!' he cried. 'You can't make bargains with God. It isn't right.' He shook his head. 'Of course I will pray that Joe recovers. But as for anything else…I'm sorry, but I can't do it.'

Anna did not answer. She turned to her husband. 'Come along, Thomas. I want to go home now.'

'Mammy…' said Dan. 'You must see that I made my decision ages ago. It doesn't mean that I've turned my back on God. That's what I've been telling you all along. It can't possibly make any difference to whether or not Joe recovers. But he will; if we pray hard enough, he will.'

Anna ignored him. She went over to the bed and gently kissed her younger son's cheek. Then she walked from the room with Thomas following her.

He turned to say goodbye to Daniel. 'She's upset,' he said, which was a great understatement. 'She doesn't really mean it…'

But Daniel knew only too well that she did. He stayed for a few moments after his parents had gone. He took hold of his brother's hand, looking down on his waxen pale, but untroubled face. Joe had never been one to worry unduly about anything, but Dan knew he had been anxious about the ill feeling caused by his decision to live his life in the world and not wholly in the service of God.

He prayed, in a whisper, 'O Lord, please make Joe well again…if it be Thy will,' he added, knowing that in all things he should submit to God's will. That was the thing his mother had accused him of failing to do. He was deep in thought as he made his way back to the solitude of his flat. There were times when he appreciated his privacy, but there were other times when he felt lonely, missing the companionship of family life.

His employer, Jonas Grundy, was saddened to hear what had happened to Joe, and he insisted that Dan should take time off each day to visit the hospital. There was no change in his brother the following day, nor the day after that. Dan prayed each night and morning; he prayed as he stood by Joe's bedside, but it seemed that his prayers were to no avail. There was no change at all in Joe's condition, and when Dan put his fingers to his brother's wrist he could tell that the pulse was very weak. He feared that Joe was gradually losing his hold on life.

During his lunch break from the shop he went into the Church of the Sacred Heart, which he still attended each Sunday. As he had done twice before he lit a candle, one amongst many that were burning on the table to the side of the chancel, each of them signifying a plea to God to answer a heartfelt prayer, or to give thanks for blessings that had been received. Dan, alone now in the church, knelt at the chancel steps. He looked up at the crucifix with the bleeding figure of Christ; at the much more comforting statue of Mary, the mother of Jesus, in her blue robe; at the diffused light shining through the stained-glass windows; and at the altar, the symbol of sacrifice to Almighty God.

He recalled the sacrifice that Abraham had been

ready to make, of his beloved son, Isaac, and how God had intervened, just in time, with the ram caught in the thicket. He thought of the many sacrifices that had been made in Old Testament times, and then of the supreme sacrifice that Jesus Christ had made when he died on the cross, dying so that mankind might believe and live.

The words of his mother returned, involuntarily, to him. 'You know what you must do, Daniel...' And it seemed, at that moment, to be not such a tremendous sacrifice for him to make. He wanted so much for his brother – his little brother, Joe, whom he loved so dearly – to be made well again. But from the way he had looked that morning it seemed that there was little likelihood of that happening. Even the doctor had looked grim, shaking his head and refusing to comment when Dan had spoken to him.

'Dear Father in heaven,' he found himself saying, in his own simple words, not the ponderous words used in the Church litany. 'I am sorry if I have grieved You by turning away from You. Please make my brother well again. I believe You are able to do this... And I promise that I will pledge my life once more to Your service. I will serve You and obey You all the days of my life...Amen.'

He rose from his knees in a daze. In those few moments he had not been thinking of Madeleine, only of his brother and the estrangement from his family. How he longed to be part of it again. A little while later, however, as he returned to his duties at the shop, his thoughts returned to Madeleine. He loved her, there was no doubt in his mind about that, and he would always love her. But now, all he could do was to wait. He knew that he must continue to pray for his brother's recovery, even though it might mean turning his back on what he had once thought was so precious to him.

He had decided not to visit the hospital during the evening. That was the time that his parents chose to visit and there was no point in upsetting his mother any further. But the reality of the situation had not quite dawned upon him yet. If God were to answer his prayer, then the bitterness between himself and his mother would soon be a thing of the past, that was if he honoured his promise to commit himself wholly, once again, to a life of service to the Lord.

Daniel was in a state of limbo. His future was uncertain; it all hinged on whether his brother would live or die. How he fervently hoped and prayed that Joe might live. But was there, also, that flicker of doubt in his mind? He could hear the voice of his conscience asking him if he had, perhaps, made his promise believing, deep down, that he might not have to fulfil it, half expecting that Joe might die?

He stayed away from the hospital the following day, nor did he visit the church during his lunch break as he had been doing whilst Joe was in hospital. He performed his tasks, at the shop and at home, in a perfunctory manner. His thoughts were all over the place; he was finding it increasingly hard to concentrate or to focus his mind on one problem. All he could do was wait; the answer would be revealed to him in God's good time.

Five days had passed since Joe's accident. It was quite late on Saturday evening when he answered the knock at his door. He knew at once from the look on his father's face that the news was good, or at least more hopeful.

'He's come round,' said his father, giving him a hug. 'Joe's opened his eyes, just now, only half an hour ago when we were there, your mother and me. Mind you, I don't suppose he's out of the woods yet, but the doctor seems pleased. Isn't that good news, eh, Dan?'

'I'll say it is,' replied Dan. His answer came automatically, and the smile on his face showed his joy and relief that his brother was recovering. But his mind had not yet started to focus on the implications that would arise from this momentous turn of events.

'Did he say anything?' he asked. 'I mean...his brain's not been affected by the accident, has it?' That was one thing that Dan had feared might have happened, if Joe should recover.

'He said "Hello..." replied Thomas, and "Where am I?" So we told him, briefly, like, what had happened to him. He didn't say much else, but he knew who we were, right enough. So I don't think there's anything to worry about on that score.'

'Well, that's good then,' said Dan. 'I'll go and see him tomorrow.'

'I'll not stop now, lad,' said Thomas. 'I'd best get back to your mother. I just had to come and tell you the news. Happen things might be sorted out between you and her now, eh?'

'I hope so. It's gone on far too long. Tell her...' Dan hesitated, then he said, 'No, on second thoughts don't tell her anything. I'll see her tomorrow. I'll come round after morning Mass. In fact...I'll come home to stay, if she'll let me.'

'Will you?' Thomas's eyes shone with happiness. 'Eeh, that would be grand, son. I'm sure she'll be ready to make her peace with you.'

'We'll see,' said Dan evasively. 'There's a lot to consider...'

'I won't let on,' said his father. 'I'll leave it to you to tell her yourself. Goodnight then, Daniel, and God bless.'

'Goodnight, Daddy,' said Dan.

As he knelt at the altar, receiving the sacrament from the priest, Dan knew that there could be no turning back. He had made his promise, not to any earthly being, but to Almighty God. Now, what must be, must be.

As he rose from his knees he was sure in his mind what he had to do. His heart might well be telling him something else, but he must try to subdue, now, the feelings of his heart, however strong they might be.

When his mother opened the door her glance, at first, was wary. Then, as he smiled at her she could see that this was a different Dan, and she smiled at him in return.

'I've come home, Mammy,' he said. 'That is...if you will have me.'

'Of course I will,' she answered, drawing him into a close embrace. 'Oh, you have no idea how much I've prayed for this to happen. And now our Joe's getting better. We'll all be together again. Oh, thanks be to God and to all His saints...'

Chapter Nineteen

His mother did not ask him any questions about Madeleine or, indeed, about anything at all. She just seemed glad to have him back in the fold. For his part, Daniel felt a certain relief at being home again and knowing that the discord in the family was at an end. Or, at least, had been put to one side.

The three of them, plus Myrtle, Joe's girlfriend, went to visit him in hospital after their midday meal on Sunday and were happy to find him very much improved. He was, as Anna put it, 'sitting up and taking notice', which was a very good sign. The doctor said that it was a minor miracle and that they were very pleased with his progress. He would need to stay in hospital for quite a while yet, but the signs were hopeful.

'And our Daniel's back home,' Anna told her younger son. 'Isn't that good news?'

'Aye, I reckon it is,' said Joe, looking questioningly at his brother. 'You're back for good, are you, Dan?'

'Yes…yes, I suppose I am,' replied Dan, though he sounded a little unsure.

Joe smiled faintly. 'I missed you... Everything's all right then, now, is it...you know what I mean?' he said quietly, half nodding towards his mother who had just moved away to speak to a nurse.

'Yes...yes it is,' said Dan, a trifle abruptly. 'Don't you worry your head about it, Joe. Just you concentrate on getting well again. You gave us all an awful fright.'

'I can't remember owt about it,' said Joe. 'All I know is that I woke up here with a headache and a broken arm. But I reckon I'm lucky to be alive, aren't I?'

'So you are,' replied Dan, feeling his eyes growing moist. 'Just look where you're going in future, there's a good lad.'

Dan was still in a quandary. He felt as though everything around him was strange and unreal. He remembered about the vow he had made when he lit his candle and knelt to pray, but that now seemed to be far removed from reality. It was an awesome promise that he had made, or, rather, renewed, he reminded himself. He knew he could not turn back; he could not renege on his commitment again. But neither did he intend rushing headlong into anything. There were things that had to be sorted out.

Christmas was approaching, and with it the time of his intended visit to Scarborough to see Madeleine. He wondered if he should still go...to say goodbye? It would be painful for both of them, but maybe he owed it to her to explain, face to face, what had happened. But...no; reflecting on this he realised that it would be too much of a temptation. How could he possibly bear to part from her if he were to spend time with her again? It would be asking too much of both of them.

His mother seemed to be taking it for granted that he had 'returned to his senses', which is how he knew she would think of it, even if she did not utter the words. However, they did not speak about the situation for several days, and then only obliquely.

She asked him, tentatively, about his work at the shop. 'You will be getting busy, I suppose, with Christmas coming? I'll come in soon and choose a new shirt for your father and something nice for Joe. A pair of bedroom slippers perhaps? I expect it will be a while before he can go back to work. But he'll be home in time for Christmas.'

Then, more pertinently, 'Let me see... You work full-time for Mr Grundy now, don't you? Are you going to keep on with that...or might you go back to working part-time again?'

'I'm not sure, Mother,' he replied.

'And what about Father Fitzgerald? Will you be going back to your studies?' She broached the subject, daringly, after his first week at home.

'Quite possibly, Mother,' he said. 'But please don't rush me.' He looked at her unflinchingly. 'I need to do some serious thinking. Maybe after Christmas... I may go back then.'

'And what about Christmas?' she asked, even more boldly. 'Will you be going away...at all?'

'No, Mother; I will be at home all the time,' he answered resolutely.

'Then praise be to God!' She smiled lovingly at him, but there was a hint of self-satisfaction there, too. She paused for a moment, then she added, 'It would never have worked out, Daniel, with that girl. I'm so pleased that you are beginning to realise that.'

He could not answer her. He turned away and retired to the solitude of his bedroom. What have I done? said a small voice in his mind. Dear God, whatever have I done? But there could be no turning back, not again. He opened his notepad and unscrewed the cap of his fountain pen. He knew it was time for him to write to Madeleine.

Maddy was getting more and more concerned as she had not heard from Dan for well over a week. She was relieved, therefore, to receive a letter from him on the Saturday morning, the day before they were due to leave Filey. She had written to him as soon as they arrived there, as she did at every move, to tell him her address. It was the third week in December and on the following day, Sunday, they would be moving on to Scarborough. They would stay there for two weeks, over Christmas and the New Year. Maddy was looking forward to being with her family again, and, above all, to having Dan to come and stay with them for a night or two; they had not yet finalised the date.

She grew more and more anxious as she read the letter. She was shocked, first of all, to read of Joe's accident and of how they had all feared at first that he might not recover. But he had done so and he was due home from the hospital in a few days' time. But she was filled with misery again as she read that Dan would not be able to visit her in Scarborough. He could not possibly leave his family at such a time...which she supposed she could understand, although, at the same time she felt hurt by his decision. He had moved back home, he told her, and he had made up his quarrel with his mother. Maddy could understand that. Crises usually caused families to forget their differences.

When would he be coming to see her then? Her eyes anxiously scanned the final page, but there was no suggestion that he might do so. And – which was the most heartbreaking thing of all – he had not said that he loved her, or that he was looking forward to seeing her again.

Dan had been unable to find the words to tell Madeleine that he could never see her again. And so he had just written of how the situation was at that moment. A cowardly part of him hoped that she might begin to put two and two together. At least she would be in the bosom of her family at Christmas, and not alone; and she would be kept busy with the shows. Perhaps, in the New Year, he might have found the courage to tell her.

'Is there something the matter?' Susannah asked Maddy when they had returned to the bedroom they were sharing that week. She had noticed her young friend's face blanch and her smile disappear as she read the letter handed to her at the breakfast table. She had guessed it was from Daniel, the young man who seemed to be conspicuous by his absence at the moment. Maddy had told her very little about the situation, but Susannah guessed that she might want to talk, right now.

'Yes,' replied Maddy briefly. 'Here…read this.'

'Oh no; I can't do that,' said Susannah. 'I can't read your private letter. It's from Dan, isn't it? Just tell me about it…if you want to, that is.'

'No, read it,' said Maddy again. 'There's nothing in it that nobody else could read. I want you to tell me what you think.'

'All right then,' said Susannah. 'If you're sure.' She had had doubts right from the start about Maddy's friendship with the said young man. She was a young girl in love, there was no doubt about that. He seemed a nice enough lad and the affection appeared to be mutual from what she had seen of them together. But there were so many problems, apart from the fact that they were able to see one another so rarely. He was a Catholic, and she knew that that oftentimes boded ill when someone of a different faith was involved. And that mother of his sounded a real harridan. It was doubtful that she would ever forgive Maddy for taking her son away from his one-time commitment to his religion.

She read the letter, and understood how Maddy must be feeling. There was no word of love, no suggestion of another meeting, just the overriding concern about his brother – which was only natural, she supposed – and the news, which must have come as a blow to Maddy, that he was now home again, having made up his quarrel with his mother. She, Susannah, had a feeling that all was far from well, but she knew she must not be too pessimistic in what she said to Maddy.

'He's upset, love,' she said. 'He's had a shock and it's obvious that he's very fond of his young brother. No doubt he feels that he shouldn't leave his family over Christmas, especially now that they've come together again. I expect he'll write again soon... You'll just have to wait and see, won't you?'

'That's all I can do,' said Maddy. 'That's all I ever do with Dan, isn't it? Wait and see. I've got a funny feeling about it, Susannah. A premonition – sort of – that I'm not going to see him again. He's trying to let me down lightly, isn't he?'

'I don't know. Honestly, I don't know what to think,' said Susannah. 'But you know him better than I do. I'm sure he's a trustworthy young man and he'll write again soon. And you can be sure he'll be just as upset about this as you are.'

'He seems to be happy with his family again,' said Maddy, sounding far from joyful at the thought.

'And tomorrow you'll be with your family again,' said Susannah. 'That's the best place to be, isn't it, when you're feeling sad?' She gave her young friend a hug. 'Try and cheer up, darling. You've lots of friends here, you know, in the company, and we won't let you be miserable.'

'No, I know that,' said Maddy. 'We have to learn to smile through our tears and all that, don't we? To put a brave face on for the audience.'

'Yes, try to look for the rainbow in the sky,' replied Susannah. 'That's something my mother used to say when I was a little girl. The rainbow shines through the darkest clouds, that's what she said, and it's been a comfort to me many times.'

'My heart leaps up when I behold a rainbow in the sky...' said Maddy musingly. 'Now, where did that come from? It was a poem we read at school, I seem to remember. I think it's Wordsworth; my sister, Jessie, would know.' She sighed. 'What am I worrying about, anyway? He hasn't said it's all over between us, has he? Perhaps he's just feeling a bit down in the dumps. But thanks for listening to my troubles, Susannah. I don't know what I'd do without you.'

'No, nor I without you,' answered her friend, smiling at her fondly. 'You've grown up a lot since you first joined us, Maddy, and I'm so glad we're such good friends. Look, I'll have to go now; I'm meeting Frank and we're going for a last walk on the prom. Remember now, Maddy; keep on smiling.'

'I'll try,' said Maddy.

Poor kid, thought Susannah. Things did not look too good, but she was young; she would get over it. It was a true example of 'first love'. She doubted that it had even been consummated. No…knowing Maddy, and the religious scruples of that young man, she felt sure it would not have been.

But maybe, now, there might be a chance for that nice Freddie Nicholls. Susannah knew that he was still sweet on Maddy, although he was trying hard not to let his feelings show. But there was not much that went on in the company that Susannah Brown did not know about.

The Melody Makers were performing for two weeks at the Spa Pavilion in Scarborough. It was quite a prestigious booking, as Percy Morgan and his troupe of Pierrots were already very well known in the town. Maddy was pleased about the venue as the Spa was situated, on the lower promenade, quite near to Victoria Avenue, where her family lived. It was only a few minutes' walk to the theatre for each evening performance, and the more frequent matinées, which were put on so that the children of the town could attend. For these afternoon shows the troupe, at Percy's request, dressed in their Pierrot costumes for the finale. They encouraged the audience to join in with the singing, thus giving them a foretaste of the summer that was to follow, when Uncle Percy's Pierrots would be back, as usual, to entertain them.

Christmas Day fell on a Wednesday, a welcome respite in the middle of the week from the hurly-burly of the theatre. There was, of course, no show that day, but they would be back with a vengeance on Boxing Day, with both a matinée and an evening performance.

There were eleven of them seated around the dining table at midday to enjoy the dinner that Mrs Baker had prepared for them; with a little help from the ladies – Faith, Maddy, Jessie and Hetty – who assisted with the setting of the table and the placing of the crackers and decorations. Mrs Baker had been up since early morning in order to give the giant-sized turkey time to cook to a crackly brown perfection; and to see to the vegetables, many of which she had partly prepared the previous day; the apple sauce and sage and onion stuffing; and the succulent fruit pudding, laced with brandy, which would take more than two hours to steam. After all that had been cleared away and the pots washed – again with a little help from the womenfolk of the family – Mrs Baker would then be free to spend the rest of the day with her brother and his family, who lived over on the North Bay.

The party consisted of Faith and William; Maddy, Jessie and the twins; Grandfather Isaac; Patrick and his fiancée, Katy; Hetty; and Louisa Montague, an old family friend. The only member of the family who was missing was Samuel, and Faith, as was only to be expected, commented on his absence.

'I wonder if Samuel will be having a Christmas dinner?' she pondered. 'Do you think so, William?'

'Oh, I should imagine so,' replied William. 'It's a British expedition, isn't it? I'm sure they'll manage to get hold of a turkey, or the nearest equivalent. And some wine to go with it. You can be sure he'll be having a whale of a time, my dear. You don't need to worry about him.'

'But I can't help worrying,' said Faith, 'especially as I know he hasn't been well just lately.' In the last letter they had received, a few weeks previously, Samuel had written that he had been suffering from a sort of sweating sickness and a stomach upset. He feared that the climate was not suiting him awfully well, but he was now recovering. A few days ago there had been a Christmas card, but no further word as to his state of health.

'I'm sure he'll be tucking into his Christmas pudding with gusto,' said William, in an attempt to set his wife's mind at rest. 'Just as we are. I must say that Mrs Baker has done us proud with this.' He was savouring every mouthful of the rich dark brown – almost black – pudding and the brandy sauce.

He knew that Faith worried about Samuel, needlessly at times, in his opinion, and he knew that her thoughts centred on her elder son far more than Samuel's centred on her and on the rest of his family. He knew, also, that Samuel was corresponding with his own daughter, Hetty. He had been a little anxious during the weeks before Samuel departed for Peru, when he noticed that the two of them seemed to be friendly, and he was aware that they had been out together a couple of times, maybe more. But he had decided that it was really none of his business and that Hetty, at twenty-six years of age, was quite capable of taking care of herself. Besides, it would not be long before Samuel was far away across the sea. The top and bottom of it, of course, was that he did not like Samuel. He had never taken to the young man and he guessed that he never would.

'It won't be snowing, though, in Peru,' announced Tommy, with his usual aplomb. A few flakes of snow had fallen that morning, to the twins' delight, but unfortunately for them it had not settled. 'I've been reading all about it. Samuel is actually quite near to the Amazon Basin. It's a tropical climate there and it rains a lot.'

'Quite unhealthy, in fact,' observed Faith. 'I shall feel better when I know that he's all right.'

Jessie glanced at Maddy and raised her eyebrows expressively. She was not filled with sisterly love for Samuel and she knew that Maddy felt the same about him.

'Let's drink a toast to Samuel,' said William, magnanimously, after they had all eaten their fill of Mrs Baker's splendid meal. They all raised their glasses of brown sherry, and Tommy and Tilly their tumblers of lemonade, as William proclaimed,

'Here's to Samuel...and to all absent friends.'

'To Samuel...' they all echoed, but Maddy was thinking of her dear Daniel, a very absent friend.

'And to the king, God bless him,' said William.

'And to our lovely Queen Alexandra,' added Faith.

'To the king and queen...' They all joined in the loyal toast, knowing that thousands of other patriotic families throughout the land would be doing the same.

The three sisters, Hetty, Maddy and Jessie had agreed that Mrs Baker had done enough and so they had bundled her, laughing and protesting, out of the house, saying that they would see to whatever else needed to be done. They retired to the kitchen where, between them, they tackled the great mountain of pots and pans, washing and drying and then returning them to the cupboards and shelves.

'Well, thank goodness that lot's all out of the way,' said Hetty. 'I wouldn't like to do that every day.'

'Nor would I,' agreed Maddy. 'We don't always appreciate Mrs Baker as much as we should, do we? She has to do this every day and she doesn't often get any help.'

'She's not usually catering for so many, though, is she?' said Jessie. 'Eleven of us; that's quite a lot. And we'll have the same number to wash up for at teatime, don't forget.'

'So we will,' said Maddy. 'Oh dear! But it'll only be a simple tea, won't it? No greasy pans and dishes. I'm so full up at the moment, though, that I'm sure I'll never be able to eat another morsel.'

'So am I,' agreed Jessie. 'But replete is a more ladylike word,' she smiled. 'It sounds rather common to say that one is full up. I don't think Queen Alexandra would say that.'

Maddy laughed. 'You and your posh words! You sound as though you've swallowed a dictionary sometimes.' But she knew that Jessie was only having a bit of fun.

'I doubt that the king and queen will have had a nicer meal,' observed Hetty. 'And you can be sure the twins will be ready to start again at teatime. They're really enjoying themselves today, aren't they?'

'We don't need to think about tea just yet, though,' said Jessie. 'Let's go and sit in the dining room and have a bit of peace and quiet.'

The older members of the party – William, Faith, Isaac and Louisa – were taking their ease in the sitting room, the elder two no doubt having a postprandial snooze. Patrick and Katy had gone for a walk on the prom to work off the excesses of the meal, whilst the twins were playing with one of their new jigsaws in a quiet corner of the room.

Tea, or more likely early supper, would be just a simple meal, as Maddy had said: turkey sandwiches, which the girls had agreed to make, and then the ceremonial cutting of the Christmas cake. And in the evening, before the twins retired to bed, later than usual, the family would play games: charades, 'My Grandfather's Cat', a Christmas version of 'I Spy', and 'Hunt the Thimble' – or, more accurately, hunt the chocolate pennies, wrapped in gold paper, which Faith would have secreted throughout the house – this being a great favourite with the twins.

'Tommy and Tilly are great kids, aren't they?' said Hetty, as they sat at ease around the dining table, leaning on their elbows in a most unladylike fashion, which would be frowned upon at meal times. 'It's so lovely to be part of a large family, especially at Christmas time. I'm really happy that it has worked out so well; me coming back, I mean, and being accepted the way I have been by William and Faith, and everyone else. I know I've said so before, but it comes over me sometimes, how lucky I am.'

Maddy and Jessie looked at one another a little embarrassedly. Maddy remembered a time when she could have been less than welcoming to her half-sister, but she had managed to put all bitter thoughts behind her and she had become very fond of Hetty. She smiled at her, then made a joke of it. 'Yes, you are lucky – isn't she, Jessie? – to have two lovely sisters like us.'

Maddy had had reservations, though, about Hetty's friendship with Samuel. She didn't know how things stood between the two of them, but she had noticed that Hetty had remained very quiet and uncommunicative when Faith had been going on about her son.

Hetty spoke suddenly. 'I've been writing to Samuel; I don't know whether you know that. Well, I don't suppose you do…and I haven't mentioned it to Faith and William. Not that we have anything to hide but…I'm not sure how they would feel about it.'

'No, we didn't know that,' replied Maddy. 'Not that it's any of our business really.' Then, aware that she might have sounded rather abrupt, she continued, more concernedly, 'How is Samuel? Has he really been quite poorly?'

'Yes, I'm afraid he has,' said Hetty. 'I don't think he's said a great deal to his mother and William, but there has been some talk of him returning home. He was not adjusting to the climate as well as he might. But then he recovered and he seems to be all right just now.'

'Oh dear!' said Maddy. But she was thinking, not so much of Samuel's illness, but of his coming home again. She was afraid that no good would come of the friendship between him and Hetty. But that, she decided, was something that Hetty would have to find out for herself, as she had done. Unless, of course, he had changed a good deal.

'We'll just have to wait and see,' said Hetty.

As far as Hetty was concerned, she found that

she was missing Samuel far more than she had expected she would. She had enjoyed his company the few times they had been out together before he sailed for South America. He was good fun when he cast off his more sober image, they appeared to have quite a lot in common, and she had welcomed his kisses and the small intimacies they had shared. But when he had started to get overamorous – much too passionate and far too soon in her opinion – she had put a curb on their lovemaking. So that would be the end of that, she had thought, remembering how she had lost her fiancé to a girl who had been more willing than she was. But Samuel, to her surprise, had wanted to go on seeing her and had promised to write to her. And he had done so, quite frequently and in loving terms.

Now she realised that she was missing him. If he were to return home…well, she would have to see how she felt then, but she knew that she liked him a lot. It would be very easy to fall in love with him.

'Wait and see,' said Maddy, repeating Hetty's last words. She sighed. 'That's just what I'm doing at the moment, isn't it?'

She had told her father and Faith, of course, that Dan would be unable to come and stay for a couple of days during the Christmas or New Year period, as she had hoped. They had said they were sorry to hear about his brother's accident and that they understood that he was unable to leave his family at such a critical time. Apart from that, though, they had been very non-committal. They had not said that they hoped everything would go well for her and Dan; in fact, Maddy thought she had seen a look of relief on her father's face, and a faint smile of complicity pass between the pair of them. She could, though, have imagined it; she was feeling very vulnerable with regard to Dan at that time.

It was only to Jessie and Hetty that she had confessed her innermost fear; that it was more than likely that she would not see him again. She told them again, now, of her grave misgivings.

'He's back home again, isn't he, playing happy families?' she said, with a touch of bitterness that was not in character. 'And now that woman's got her claws into him again it's doubtful that he'll be able to escape a second time.'

She had received a Christmas card from him, sending kindest regards to all her family, with love to herself. He had, at least, sent his love, but only the sort of love that one often sent on a greetings card; no mention of how much he loved her, or a promise that he would see her again.

'Give him time,' said Hetty. 'Joe's accident will have been a shock to all of them, and they'll be rejoicing now that he's recovering. You said, didn't you, that they feared he might die?'

'Yes...they'll see it as God's answer to their prayers,' said Maddy thoughtfully. 'Which I'm sure it is,' she added. 'Don't think I'm being cynical because I'm not. I do know, though, that…this sort of thing means so much more to Dan than it does to me. I mean…I say my prayers and all that, but Dan is really devout. Not pious or sanctimonious – he likes a laugh and a joke – but deep down he's…well, I know it means a lot to him, that's all.'

'And he's all the better for that,' said Hetty. 'You can be sure he will do what is right.'

'But will it be what I want, what I'm hoping for?' said Maddy. 'I've got such a funny feeling about it all.'

'Like you said yourself, all you can do is wait and see,' said Hetty. She was thinking of Samuel, as well as of Maddy's absent love. She knew, to her slight consternation, that he did not possess the integrity or the innate goodness that Daniel had. It was possible, too, that Samuel might prove to be unreliable, that he might let her down. And in the case of Samuel it would be because he put himself and his own desires first. She knew all this, and yet she was looking forward to seeing him again. You could not choose with whom you fell in love.

'Try not to feel sad, Maddy love,' she went on. 'We've had a happy time today, haven't we, all of us together? And it'll be time for party games soon. The twins won't let anyone feel miserable.'

'And it's time for us to put on our pinnies now,' said Jessie. 'Don't forget we've promised to make the turkey sandwiches. You can cut the bread,

Hetty. I think you're better at it than Maddy and me. And we'll do the buttering. Then there's the turkey to carve... Oh dear! I think we'd better ask Uncle William to give us a hand with that. Come on then; let's make a start...'

Chapter Twenty

The Melody Makers continued their touring programme when they had completed their fortnight's booking at the Spa Pavilion. Maddy had been glad of the loving support of her family and friends, which had helped to assuage, to a certain extent, the sadness she felt at Daniel's absence. There had been no further message from him, and now, when she would be lodging first in one place and then in another, he would have no idea where she was. Unless, of course, she wrote to him again, which she was determined not to do. She had written just once, expressing regret at Joe's accident, but adding that she was pleased to hear he was recovering. Taking her cue from Dan, she, too, had sent no special message of love or of hope that they would meet again soon. The next move, she knew, had to come from him.

For the last two weeks in January, 1908, they were booked at a provincial theatre in Manchester. It was during the second week that a letter from Dan finally arrived, forwarded to her from her Scarborough address by her father and Faith. She did not open it at the breakfast table as she would normally have done, but waited until she had returned, as quickly as she could, to the seclusion of her bedroom.

'My dearest Madeleine,' he began, 'This is a very difficult letter for me to write…' Yes, it was as she had feared. Their brief friendship…courtship – it was difficult for her to find a word to describe it – was at an end. Dan explained that his brother's recovery had been nothing less than a miracle. He had been at death's door, and then God had answered their prayers and restored him to them again.

Reading between the lines she gathered that Dan had made a promise to God to serve Him again, in gratitude for answered prayers. She felt sure, though, that his mother must have had a great deal to do with his decision. She had got him back home again, under her sway, and it seemed as though he was powerless to do anything but obey her commands.

'I am not sure at the moment exactly what I shall be doing in the future,' he continued. 'I am still working full-time for Mr Grundy until such time as he can find another assistant. I have also returned to my studies with Father Fitzgerald, and he assures me that I will be able to start again from where I left off. I know this will be hard for you to understand, my dear Madeleine, but I know that it is something that I have to do.

'I will remember our time together as something very precious. But I know, deep down, as I am sure you do, that it might never have worked out for us. I fear that my family would never have come to terms with our friendship' – he means his mother, Maddy thought, feeling a deep bitterness towards the woman – 'and it would have been hard for me, and for you, to feel shut out from the family circle.

'There will always be a special place in my heart for you. I have loved you; I love you still, but I know that there is no future for us together...'

He had enclosed a copy of a poem by Christina Rossetti, who had died in the latter years of the nineteenth century; a very poignant poem called 'Remember'.

> *'Remember me when I am gone away,*
> *Gone far away into the silent land...'*

Maddy read it with tears in her eyes. She knew it was really referring to someone who was dying; but Dan might just as well be dead; she was sure she would never see him again. The last two lines were particularly apt.

> *'Better by far you should forget and smile*
> *Than that you should remember and be sad.'*

Her tears dropped on to the page, smudging the dark blue ink, as she read Dan's closing words. 'Please forgive me, Madeleine, and try to be happy. I am sure you will be. You have such a capacity for joy and delight in life, and that is how I will always think of you. With my fondest love, Daniel.'

She screwed up the letter in her hands, but not because she wanted to destroy it. It was more of a reflex action as her hands clenched together in a spasm of anger, as well as the sadness she was feeling. It could have worked, it would have worked, surely, if they loved one another enough... But it was clear that Dan's commitment to his God was greater than his love for any earthly being, such as her.

On second thoughts, she straightened out the pages of the letter and the poem and put them into her handbag. Then, suddenly, she rose from her seat on the edge of the bed. She glanced in the mirror to tidy her hair and brush away the stray tears, then she quickly put on her hat and coat. She didn't feel like talking to anyone at the moment. She would tell Susannah in her own good time, but not now... What she needed now was to be on her own, and she must get away before her friends came upstairs and started fussing around her. A brisk walk might help to clear her head, and she needed to be fully in control of herself before the matinée performance that afternoon.

No solace was to be found in the mean grey streets of Wythenshawe, but Maddy scarcely noticed where she was walking. She knew she would have to find the strength within herself to carry on.

And so she did. Not one of the audience listening to her that afternoon as she sang about the seeds of love could be aware that she was hiding a heart that was aching.

> '*I sowed the seeds of love,*
> *I sowed them in the spring…*'

But so often, in songs as in real life, love was found to be false.

> '*The willow tree will twist,*
> *And the willow tree will twine.*
> *How oft' I have wished I were in his arms*
> *Who once had the heart of mine.*'

The damsel in the song, however, was determined not to be downcast, and Maddy knew it was an example that she must try to follow.

> '*Come all you false young men,*' she sang,
> '*Do not leave me here to complain;*
> *For the grass that has once been trampled*
>   *underfoot,*
> *Give it time, it will rise up again,*
> *Give it time, it will rise up again.*'

Only Susannah, listening from the wings, knew how sad Maddy must be feeling. Her young friend had confided in her just before the performance began that she had received a letter from Dan saying that it was all over between them. First love, Susannah thought... How much it could hurt. But the sadness and the agony that it caused would be forgotten in time – she knew that from her own experience – and the first rapture would come to be remembered with tenderness and not regret. She hoped it would prove to be so for Maddy.

Meanwhile, waiting in the wings – metaphorically speaking as well as in reality – was that nice young man, Freddie Nicholls. Susannah believed that he still harboured warm feelings for Maddy, although he was trying hard not to let them show. There might be a chance for him, eventually. She knew that she must not tell him, not straight away, of Maddy's disappointment in love. It was not really her place to start spreading the word or to indulge in matchmaking. But it would become obvious before long, surely, that the lovely Madeleine was unattached once more.

She was young, of course, not yet eighteen; far too young, in Susannah's view, to be thinking of marriage. What was more, she had a promising future ahead of her. With a voice and a personality such as hers she could go far. No doubt there would be lots of young men, as well as Freddie, who would admire her and wish that they might become closer to her. Many would be able only to worship her from afar, but Freddie was right there, on the spot. And he was a far more suitable match for her than the heavenly minded Dan, in Susannah's opinion. Anyway, time would tell.

It had never entered Susannah's head to be envious of her young friend; not for her youth, nor her beauty, nor her glorious singing voice, which she knew was far superior to her own. She had enjoyed her years as an artiste, and although she had performed only in provincial theatres and had never had her name in lights, she knew she had brought pleasure to many audiences, who enjoyed her light-hearted singing and her saucy mannerisms. She had reached her own peak, she supposed; but since she had – surprisingly – fallen in love with Frank, whom she had known for years, ambition had ceased to be important to her. What they both wanted now was to be able to get married. Their relationship, in some quarters, was looked upon with disapproval. She knew that even Percy Morgan, who knew them both very well, would prefer it if they were able to tie the knot.

But now, at last, the situation was looking rather more hopeful. Hilda, Frank's wife, apparently had a gentleman friend. So a close friend of Frank had revealed to him, and he – the friend – was keeping his eye on developments. By this time next year, or even sooner, with a bit of luck, she might be Mrs Frank Morrison. Then she would be able to share a room with him openly, without pretence, or being dependent on the whim of an obliging – or more often a disapproving – landlady.

It was at the beginning of February that Samuel Barraclough was forced to return home from South America. The illness he had contracted previously – a sweating sickness and bouts of painful diarrhoea – occurred again; and after a spell in hospital it was decided that it would be in his best interests if he were to return home. It was obvious that the climate did not suit him.

It was with a feeling of relief, tinged with a certain regret, that Samuel boarded the ship, bound eventually for the port of Liverpool. What he had hoped would be a grand adventure had turned out to be a disappointment. He had not been given a position of authority, as he had hoped, but had been treated as little more than a minion, despite his first-class degree, which he had thought might count for something. But it appeared that he had to start at the bottom and prove his worth. He had been unable to do so due to the recurring bouts of illness, and he had come to be regarded as a liability who must be sent on his way as soon as possible.

He regretted that he had been unable to make a name for himself. And he knew that he would miss the camaraderie of some of the other members of the team, which he had enjoyed during the times when he had been feeling reasonably well. Despite his relief at being on the ship he found he was dreading the long journey home; but as it turned out, his cabin was comfortable, he took care with what he ate and drank, and the weather, fortunately, was fairly temperate.

One problem was that he had no home of his own to which he could return. He had gone, more or less, straight from his student lodgings in Leeds to the ill-fated expedition, apart from the visits to his father in York, and his mother and William in Scarborough. Also, he needed to find employment. And so his first port of call after disembarking at Liverpool was to the city of York. He had written to his father asking if he could stay for a little while, and Edward Barraclough and his wife, Gwendolen, were only too pleased to welcome him. Edward saw his other three children very infrequently; Samuel was the only one who had remained close to him, the one who bore no resentment for the break-up of his marriage to Faith. Edward realised that Samuel was very much 'a chip off the old block'.

Samuel had been very highly thought of at Leeds University. He had studied hard there and made the most of his opportunities, and he hoped that they might be able to offer him some guidance for the future. Fortunately for him, one of the junior lecturers in Geology had fallen ill and they had been unable, as yet, to find a replacement. Samuel was offered the post on a temporary basis, that was until the end of the spring term, with the promise that, if he proved satisfactory, there was a chance that he might be offered the full-time post. The previous lecturer, though junior in status, was really quite an elderly man. Samuel, indeed, remembered him as a bumbling old codger who knew his facts but was unable to communicate well with his students; Samuel, fortunately for him, had not been one of them. He had been persuaded to retire, to the relief of all concerned and to the especial delight of Samuel, who was determined, now, to prove himself worthy of the position. He had not envisaged, previously, that he might become a lecturer. He had, in the past, considered the old adage that those who can, do, and that those who can't, lecture. He had vowed that he, Samuel Barraclough, would always be a man of action and not of words. But circumstances altered cases and he was only too pleased, now, to have found a niche for himself; and in the city of Leeds, too, which he had come to regard as his home. Seeing that his plans for adventure had been thwarted, he considered he would be as well here as anywhere. There were a few friendships, too, of both sexes, that he would be pleased to rekindle.

Luck was with him and he found a flat to rent just off Woodhouse Lane, near to the university buildings. He paid a fortnight's rent in advance as security, returned to York to say goodbye to his father and Gwendolen, and then headed for Scarborough. He had been granted two weeks' grace to get acclimatised again and to ensure he was fully recovered before commencing his lectureship at the university.

Faith was delighted to see her elder son again. Although he looked pale and had lost a few pounds in weight, he seemed to be quite fit again after his debilitating illness. She had worried endlessly about him, although she had not always told William of her deep concern. She knew that the two of them would never be the best of friends, but that was the only very slight thorn in her flesh. Otherwise, her marriage to William was very happy indeed, with all the other members of their two families relating to one another with friendship and real affection.

Samuel had asked if he could stay with them for about ten days. Maddy, once again, was off on her travels, and so, with a little judicious planning, they made room for him. He lost no time in resuming his friendship with Hetty Collier. He realised that he had, quite genuinely, missed her. And the first time he took her out he realised that she, too, had missed him very much. He knew that, if he were to ever think of getting married and settling down, then he could do far worse than to make Hetty his wife. She was a good-looking lass, fun to be with, and very intelligent. He could never consider anyone who was not almost on a par with him intellectually, not for longer than an evening's dalliance, maybe. But marriage was something he did not intend to embark upon for ages.

He was surprised at how readily Hetty succumbed to his amorous advances. She had proved obdurate in the past, but he guessed, now, that she had been starved of real love – physical love – and affection for a very long time, as he had been.

As they lay together in her bed, Samuel felt a tenderness towards her, verging on love, that he had never experienced before. Perhaps he really did love her... He was not sure, afterwards, what words of endearment he had uttered, but he knew that he had meant them, at the time. They spent a few such times together. They promised to write to one another and to meet as often as they could. Leeds was only a short distance away, by train, and they would be able to see one another at weekends. Or so they promised...

As the harsh winter gave way to a cold spring, Maddy realised that the old saying that 'the show must go on' was very true. She threw herself into her work with what appeared to others to be a gay abandon. Her act on stage blossomed; her plaintive songs were even sweeter, and she laughed and smiled her way through the more light-hearted numbers, enchanting each successive audience.

Word had got around amongst the members of the company that her friendship with the young man from Blackpool had come to an end. Most people believed it was the time they had been forced to spend apart that had killed the romance. Only Susannah and Freddie Nicholls knew the truth; that Dan had decided to obey the dictates of his conscience and his dogmatic religion rather than follow his heart and his love for Madeleine. Freddie considered him to be no end of a fool. What a priceless chump he must be to turn his back on such a delightful girl. He was convinced that the fellow could never really have loved her, not as he, Freddie, would do if he were given half a chance. But Freddie knew that he must bide his time.

Maddy's family, of course, knew the truth. She had written a matter-of-fact sort of letter to her father and Faith explaining that she and Dan, by mutual agreement, had decided that their friendship could never come to anything and so they had parted; and that Dan was returning eventually to his studies for the priesthood. In that way, by saying that the decision was mutual, she was saving face a little. Her pride was forcing her to do so, although she was sure that her Aunty Faith would guess how much she was hurting. And Jessie would understand. Maddy was longing to see her again, to pour out her heart and all her pent-up feelings to her dearest friend. She would be home again in May once again, for their summer season as Uncle Percy's Pierrots. That had seemed a long way ahead during the bleakness of the dark winter days, but at long last spring, albeit a somewhat chilly one, had arrived.

For the last two weeks of their tour they were appearing in Leeds at a small theatre off the Headrow; the same one where, a year ago, Samuel had come to watch the show and had taken her out to supper afterwards. Could it really be only a year? Maddy pondered. It seemed, in some ways, more like a lifetime, so very much had happened. Strangely enough, she knew that Samuel was now back in Leeds, lecturing at the university following the curtailing of his expedition. She found that she bore him no ill will. The more generous side of her nature felt sorry for him; she knew he had been very ambitious and eager to make a career for himself in foreign parts. She doubted that he would be coming to watch the show this time. It was probable that he didn't even know that the Melody Makers were in the city, unless he had happened to see a poster advertising the show. Or maybe Hetty might have told him. Jessie had written in a letter that Hetty and Samuel had resumed their friendship during the time he had been in Scarborough, and that Hetty had looked like 'the cat that had got the cream'. That had been Jessie's way of describing it. Oh dear, oh dearie me! Maddy had thought to herself; but then she had decided, once again, that Hetty was quite old enough and sensible enough to take care of herself and that it was none of her, Maddy's, business.

Quite a lot had been happening recently in the touring company. One very successful act had been that of Percy Morgan and Dora Daventry presenting 'A Touch of Class'. They sang, together and individually, ballads of a romantic nature and some of the more popular arias from Grand Opera as well as Gilbert and Sullivan numbers. The trouble was that after a couple of months Dora had started to feel the strain. Not only was she singing with Percy, she was also dancing with Benjy as part of the tap-dancing duo. This had been intended, at the start, to be a temporary arrangement until such time as another partner – preferably a male one – could be found for Benjy. A couple of men of the right age and experience had been auditioned during the winter, but Benjy, each time, had raised objections. And Percy had known that it was no use going against his wishes. Benjy, even at the best of times, could be temperamental, and all hell would break loose if he were forced to work with someone with whom he was not compatible.

And then, when Dora was almost on her knees and Percy was tearing his hair out with frustration, a letter had arrived from Barney Dewhurst, begging for another chance. The letter had come to Percy, not Benjy; a heart-rending letter saying how much he had missed them all and how he regretted his rash departure. Could Percy ever forgive him? And, more pertinently, would Benjy welcome him back, or had he in the meantime found another partner? There had been no contact between the two one-time friends; but Barney must have followed the route of the Melody Makers, from stage periodicals, through the north of England. The letter arrived at the theatre in Bolton, where they were appearing in early March.

The first thing Percy did was to approach Benjy with the news. He was a little discomfited to see tears well up in the younger man's eyes, but the embarrassment was all on Percy's side. Benjy seemed to be unashamed of his tears, but after a moment he brushed them away and gave a radiant smile.

'I knew it!' he said. 'I always knew he'd come back to us. Barney likes to pretend he's tough, but he's as soft as a little kitten underneath it all.' He pouted slightly. 'I wish he'd written to me, though. I think he owes me that.'

'I'm sure he will, very soon,' replied Percy. 'But first of all he wants to know if I will have him back. It's a big decision, you know, Benjy. He let us all down and he'll have to promise that there will be no more shenanigans.'

'There won't be,' said Benjy. 'I'll make sure of that. Ooh! I'm so happy.' He clasped his hands together in delight. 'You'll write and tell him he can come back, won't you, Percy? I wonder what has made him change his mind?'

'Well, he misses us all,' said Percy. 'And I'm sure he's sorry that he quarrelled with you, Benjy. And I rather think, reading between the lines, that he hasn't been able to find any work, stage work, I mean.'

'Yes, it's his life,' said Benjy dramatically. 'He'd be lost without his stage career. You're a real pal, Percy. Thank you ever so much. I promise we will never let you down again.'

And the upshot of it all was that Barney rejoined the company a week later, to his own and everyone else's delight. It had seemed strange without him. The two friends appeared a little distant with one another at first, as though it was difficult for them to resume their close friendship. Their dancing, though, was as dynamic and sparkling as it had ever been and it was this that would bring them together again. Percy realised that, good as Dora had been, the act worked better with two men. By the time a few weeks had gone by, Barney and Benjy were as compatible as they had ever been. Benjy had been decidedly less chirpy during his friend's absence, but as the spring tour drew to its close he was once again his usual bright and breezy self.

Percy was pleased at the way the acts were progressing. Freddie Nicholls had quite a menagerie now: a real live rabbit that popped out of a top hat, and a flight of doves for the climax of his act. Percy had been afraid that the livestock might prove to be a problem during their travels, especially with certain of the landladies. But Freddie had everything under control. The doves were certainly docile, and Snowy, the white rabbit, was as tame and biddable as could be. She seemed contented in her special hutch, so long as she was kept well away from Nancy's 'westies', Daisy and Dolly. The merest whiff of Snowy was enough to send them tearing around and yapping loudly.

Jeremy Jarvis had a new character in addition to

Tommy the Toff and his lady friend, the buxom Belinda. This was Desmond the Drunkard, who drank – very convincingly – from a beer bottle and sang 'Show Me the Way to Go Home', whilst carousing unsteadily on Jeremy's arm. He went down a treat with the audiences, although Percy had warned Jeremy not to 'overstep the mark'. He was always anxious to ensure that the members of his company observed all the proprieties. They had a reputation for being a most respectable show, one that would appeal to children as well as to adult audiences. No parent need fear bringing their offspring to watch a performance by the Melody Makers.

Pete had found some new gags, to Percy's relief; he had not liked to tell his friend that some of his jokes were so old they were sprouting whiskers. And now that Percy was concentrating more on his singing than his 'funny business', one of the other men – Freddie, Frank or Jeremy – was called upon in turn to act as the 'stooge' or straight man to Pete. Jeremy and Freddie were proving to be adaptable and they both now took part in the sketches from time to time. Barney and Benjy were the only ones who did not 'muck in' wholeheartedly, but Percy was only too relieved to have them back together again.

By the time they arrived in Leeds, the last venue of their tour, Percy felt he had good reason to be proud of his company. He was, however, looking forward to a brief respite before they all met up again for their summer season in Scarborough.

Freddie had been waiting patiently 'in the wings' until he felt that the time was ripe for him to ask Maddy to go out with him again. She had spent a good deal of time in his company, but usually in a crowd or as part of a foursome with Jeremy and Dora. He had been pleased when she had confided in him about her break-up with Dan. He had listened sympathetically, making all the right responses, but trying hard to curb the elation he was feeling. He must have been convincing, because he was sure that Maddy believed he had put aside his desire to know her as more than just a friend. He had not betrayed in any way how he still felt about her, knowing that he must give her time to recover from her lost love.

When they arrived in Leeds he felt he could not wait any longer to make the first step. And so he asked her if she would go out for supper with him on the Wednesday evening, when they had only one performance. 'To celebrate the end of the tour' was what he said to her, and to his delight she agreed at once.

Maddy was glad that Freddie had realised the two of them could be friends without any romantic involvement. She found she was thinking of Dan less and less as the weeks went by, although on the occasions when she allowed herself to dwell on it, it still hurt badly. She was determined not to lose her heart again, at least not for a long time. But it would be good to go out with Freddie – she assumed it would be just the two of them this time – because she enjoyed his company and they always found plenty to talk about.

She hoped he would not have booked a table at the restaurant on Briggate where Samuel had taken her a year ago. To her relief he had not chosen that place, but a smaller venue, though just as posh, a little further from the town centre. She smiled at him over the large menu, and together they chose the simpler dishes that they both enjoyed; cream of mushroom soup, spring lamb with an assortment of potatoes and vegetables, and a medium-dry white wine – Freddie's choice – as an accompaniment. They would decide on a pudding later if they required one.

'This is lovely, Freddie,' said Maddy. 'Thank you so much for inviting me. It's a very stylish place, isn't it? Homely and comfortable as well, though.' She glanced round appreciatively at their surroundings; at the oak-panelled walls hung with pictures of Leeds in the Victorian era; the spring flowers in the centre of each table; the lights from the wall sconces casting a golden glow over the heads of the diners.

And then she saw him – Samuel...with a lady companion! She gave an involuntary gasp, hiding her face behind her large menu card.

'What's the matter, Maddy?' asked Freddie.

'Nothing much really...' she replied, trying to regain her composure. 'But would you mind changing places with me, Freddie...please? There's somebody over there that I know, and I don't want him to see me.'

'Yes, of course,' replied Freddie, looking puzzled. 'If that's what you want, we'll swap over.' She slipped cautiously into Freddie's chair and he into hers, but the other couple were right at the back of the restaurant and did not glance in their direction.

'Sorry about that,' said Maddy, breathing a sigh of relief once she had her back turned towards her stepbrother and his dining partner. 'I'm really sorry, and I do owe you an explanation. It's my stepbrother, you see. And he's with someone that I'm quite sure he shouldn't be with.'

'Oh dear! Playing away from home, is he?' grinned Freddie.

'It seems like it,' she said. She could still feel her heart racing. 'He's my Aunty Faith's son, Samuel,' she explained. 'I told you, didn't I, about my father marrying Faith? But Samuel...well, he's never got on all that well with the rest of us. And he was supposed to be seeing Hetty...a friend of mine.' It was far too complicated to explain that Hetty was a half-sister from the other side of the family. 'I'm sure he's still writing to her, and I know she's become very fond of him. Oh...I feel dreadful now; I knew I should have warned her about him...but I didn't.'

'Perhaps it's all quite innocent,' said Freddie. 'Like...you and me. Perhaps she's just a friend.'

Maddy shook her head. 'I don't think so.' From the glimpse she had caught of Samuel and his companion she had got the impression that the two of them were far more than friends. They had been leaning close together with their hands clasped, looking into each other's eyes. She was a blonde woman who bore no resemblance to Hetty and, what was more, she looked at least ten years older than Samuel. What her grandfather would have called a 'floozy'.

Freddie glanced now in their direction. 'Mmm...yes, I see what you mean. But you're not going to let it spoil our evening, are you?'

'No, of course not,' said Maddy. But she didn't feel comfortable until ten minutes or so later when Samuel and his lady friend rose and left the restaurant. They walked right past their table, but Samuel was far too engrossed in his companion to notice his stepsister, cowering behind her menu.

Chapter Twenty-One

'Phew! That was a close thing,' said Maddy, putting her menu down and leaning back in her chair with a sigh of relief. 'Now I can look forward to my main course.'

'It would have served him right, wouldn't it, if you'd gone and spoken to him,' queried Freddie, 'instead of hiding away?'

'Maybe,' she replied. 'But I was in such a flummox I didn't know what to do. It's complicated...' she added. 'Samuel and me...well, something happened between us, and I wouldn't want him to think I was being spiteful.'

'Oh, I see. Family problems, eh?'

'Sort of,' she replied. 'All right then, cards on the table.' She placed her hands flat on the table, leaning towards Freddie. She had decided it would be best to be truthful; Freddie was such a good friend. 'He's not to be trusted,' she began. 'I found that out for myself. I've known Samuel for ages, ever since I was a little girl when our families became friendly. And...well, I must admit I thought he was wonderful. He's four years older than me...and I fancied I was in love with him. He knew only too well how I felt and so…he took advantage of me. He…he tried it on – if you know what I mean – and when I wouldn't do what he wanted, he got quite nasty with me. And things have never been the same with us since then. I changed my opinion of him completely. Even his own sister – my friend, Jessie – knows that he's not a very nice sort of person. Although I've never told her about that – what I've just told you.'

'And all this happened before you met Dan, I take it?'

'Oh yes, of course. When I met Dan I realised how different it could be if you really loved somebody… Sorry,' she said, seeing a flicker of consternation pass across Freddie's face. 'I didn't mean to mention Dan. I'm trying not to think about him. In fact, I haven't really thought about him very much for ages.'

'That's good then.' Freddie smiled again. 'And you think that he – this Samuel – was supposed to be courting your friend, do you?'

'Not exactly courting,' she replied. 'But I know they've been out together several times and she was getting fond of him. That's another complication,' she added. 'You see, Hetty is my half-sister.'

And whilst they were enjoying their main course she told Freddie a little more about her complicated family. 'I shall have to see how the land lies when I get back to Scarborough. It might be all over between them, but if it's not, then I think I will have to tell Hetty. She doesn't deserve to be treated like that.'

'Well, don't worry anymore about it tonight,' Freddie told her. 'Now, how about a pudding to finish with?'

'I don't think I could eat another morsel,' said Maddy, putting a hand over her full stomach. 'Or maybe something very light.'

They both decided on vanilla and strawberry ices, and after a cup of strong coffee Freddie settled the bill, then they strolled back through the city streets to their lodgings near to the railway station. They chatted in a friendly manner and Maddy linked her arm through Freddie's; it felt good to be with him. He hesitated on the landing outside their bedroom doors, then he leant forward and kissed her gently on the cheek.

'Thank you for a lovely evening, Maddy,' he whispered.

'Thank you too, Freddie,' she replied. 'It's been ages since I enjoyed myself so much.'

And that was quite sufficient to send Freddie Nicholls off to bed a happy man. But he must tread carefully. He knew she was not yet ready for a romantic friendship, but he felt sure he would get there in the end.

When the Leeds booking finished there was to be a break of two weeks before they all met again in Scarborough. The Melody Makers went off to their respective homes and families in the towns of

Yorkshire or, for some, near to the Lancashire border.

There were all sorts of matters to be sorted out before the summer season began in mid-May. One task was to collect the Pierrot costumes for the newest members, Freddie, Jeremy and Dora. They had been ordered from Louisa Montague; she had been informed that all three were of a medium size, two men and one lady. Louisa had been making costumes for the troupe for several years. She was an old friend of the Moon family, well advanced in years now, but she still had given no thought to retiring. Maddy had worked for her for a couple of years after she had left school at thirteen, learning the dressmaking trade, until she had joined the Pierrots and the touring company. And long before that, Maddy's mother, Clara, had worked there for many years. Louisa Montague had been like a mother to the orphaned girl, and it had been there, in the little shop on Eastborough, that William Moon had met and fallen in love with his first wife, Clara. Louisa's friendship with the Moon family had continued right to the present day.

Susannah offered to go and collect the costumes. She and Frank had settled into their lodgings on Castle Road a few days before the shows were due to start.

The bell of the quaint little shop gave a friendly jangle as Susannah opened the door. She stepped forward to greet the assistant standing behind the mahogany counter, then she stopped dead in her tracks.

'I know you, don't I?' she said, frowning a little in puzzlement. Then 'Yes, of course I do!' she exclaimed as recognition dawned.

'You're Emily, aren't you? We met last summer...' It was the same woman whom Susannah had intercepted leaving love tokens for Benjy. But she didn't want to mention that, fearing it might be a source of embarrassment to the woman. And what a rumpus it had caused, to be sure, even though she, Susannah, had put a stop to it. She still felt guilty, though, about the way she had lied to the woman.

'Yes, I'm Emily Stringer,' said the assistant cheerfully. 'And you are Susannah Brown, of course. Do you know, chatting to you did me a world of good. I decided there and then that I must do something with my life. And the very next day I saw a notice in this window, about a position for a shop assistant. So here I am! And I'm helping Louisa – that's what she insists I must call her – with the sewing as well. Believe me, Susannah, I've never been happier, and it's all thanks to you.'

'I'm very glad to hear that,' said Susannah. 'It's wonderful news. I've come to collect the Pierrot costumes... I don't suppose you realised, did you, when you were offered the position, that Louisa makes all our costumes? Where is she, by the way?'

'She's gone across the road to the Market Hall to

buy her vegetables and fruit for the weekend. She should be back soon... No, I didn't know about the connection with the Pierrots. It was quite a surprise to me. Nor did I realise, until later, that Louisa is a great friend of the Moon family, that lovely Madeleine's father and his wife and son. I've met them all; they've been so kind to me, and I'm looking forward so much to meeting Madeleine. I've got over all that silliness, by the way...about Benjy.' She gave a wry smile. 'But you weren't exactly truthful with me, were you?'

'Telling you he was married?' Susannah shook her head. 'No, I wasn't, but I did it with the best intentions. I'm sorry. I didn't like lying to you, but Benjy...well, to be quite honest, he's not interested in ladies!'

'Yes, so I've heard.'

'Who told you?' asked Susannah. 'I didn't want to say too much – we all keep our thoughts to ourselves about Barney and Benjy – so that was why I took the easy way out and said he was married.'

'I understand,' said Emily. 'It was Louisa who told me that the two men were very close friends.' She smiled. 'She's a worldly-wise old lady and there's not much she doesn't know about what goes on in the town. She's full of titbits of news about the Pierrots, in the nicest possible way, of course. There's no malice in Louisa. And as for me, well, I may have led a sheltered life, Susannah, but I keep my eyes and ears open, and I have learnt to put two and two together. I've never told Louisa, though, how silly I was about Benjy. What a fool I was, wasn't I?'

Susannah laughed. 'You weren't the first, and I don't suppose you will be the last. I've had my share of admirers in the past; chocolates and flowers from deluded men in the audience. But I'll let you into a secret... I'm getting married soon!'

'Ooh, that's exciting!' said Emily, clasping her hands together in delight. 'May I ask who the lucky man is?'

'Yes, it's Frank. You know, the 'Music Man', the one who shares my act sometimes. We've been waiting for...well...for things to be sorted out. And we hope to get married here in Scarborough before the season ends. And you must come to the party, Emily!'

Emily's cry of joy was interrupted by the door opening as Louisa entered the shop. She was a bustling little woman, no more than five foot in height, still very agile and active in spite of her seventy-odd years; nobody was quite sure how old she was. Her bright eyes peering out from beneath her summer bonnet – for she was always fashionably dressed – missed nothing.

'Hello there, Susannah,' she greeted her. 'We've been expecting you. How very nice to see you back again. I trust everyone in the company is well?'

'Very much so,' replied Susannah, 'and raring to go.'

'That's good to hear. So you have already met my new assistant, Emily?' commented Louisa. 'She's a treasure. I don't know how I managed before she came, although perhaps I shouldn't let her hear me say that. She'll be asking for a pay rise!'

'Indeed I won't!' retorted Emily. 'I am highly satisfied, and very contented as well. I've just been telling Susannah what a stroke of good fortune I've had, coming to work here.'

'And what about the costumes?' asked Louisa. 'Have you parcelled them up for Susannah?'

'Sorry...no.' It was Susannah who replied. 'We've been too busy chatting. Emily and I have met before, you see, and I had quite a surprise when I found she was working here.'

'I'll see to it right away,' said Emily. She disappeared into the room at the rear of the shop, behind a curtain, and emerged a few minutes later with three costumes over her arm. Dazzling white Pierrot costumes: two sets of baggy trousers and one ankle-length skirt, and three tunics with ruffles at the neck, trimmed with bright red pompoms. The conical hats were made elsewhere. Percy kept a supply of them in a standard size and beneath the hats the men – but not the women – wore a tight-fitting black skullcap.

'Just the job,' said Susannah, as Emily cut a large sheet of brown paper and made a parcel of the outfits, securing it with string and sealing wax. 'Our new members will be thrilled to bits with these.' She settled the bill with the banknotes Percy had given her, and in addition to the money she handed over two tickets for the opening night of the show, to be held towards the end of May.

'We'll look forward to it,' said Louisa. 'Won't we, Emily?'

'Yes indeed,' agreed Emily. 'Especially since I've heard such a lot about all you Pierrots.'

'Please don't think that I gossip,' said Louisa with a twinkle in her eye. 'I haven't said a wrong word about any of you, but you are all such interesting people.'

'You don't know the half!' laughed Susannah. 'Come early, won't you, then you can get a seat on the front row.'

Percy had decided that Uncle Percy's Pierrots would need to charge more for the seats at the performances this season, in order to make ends meet. The rent for the pitches had been increased dramatically by the Corporation over the last year. Gone were the days of 'a bob a nob a week', which had not amounted, over the four months of the season, to a tremendous amount; certainly less than two hundred pounds a year. Now the rents had been more than doubled. They had increased their prices a little last year, but now they would need to charge even more for the deckchairs, also for the programmes and souvenir postcards, and for the entries to the various events, and hope that the members of the audience who chose to stand rather than sit would be more generous in parting with their pennies and sixpences when the bottler came round.

Percy Morgan and his troupe had reigned more or less supreme on the North Bay of the town over the years, but on the South Bay it was a quite different state of affairs. Will Catlin was becoming a force to be reckoned with. His all male troupe had been one of the first to perform on the Scarborough sands, although always on the South Bay, and over the years he had become more and more of an entrepreneur. There had long been rivalry between Catlin and another showman called Tom Carrick, who had already been established in the town when Catlin arrived in 1894. The two men vied continually for the prime pitches on the beach, which were auctioned each season by the Corporation. A couple of years previously Will Catlin had managed to secure all the pitches along the South Bay, causing his rivals to move on to other venues.

And now Catlin's reaction to the council's demand for a higher rent was a flat refusal to pay. To the anger of the town council he had moved his company to a new site near to the Grand Hotel; and when, subsequently, the council retaliated by declaring the site unsafe, he purchased a plot of land on the promenade, again quite close to the Grand Hotel; a prime position to attract visitors from the southern end of the resort. He had erected a permanent wooden structure with a roof to guard against the inclement weather, with scope for further expansion to stage more elaborate shows.

But Percy, despite the competition on the other side of the headland and the rising cost of the overheads, refused to be downhearted. He had his own faithful followers on the North Bay who returned year after year, and he was convinced that the improved show would attract larger and larger audiences.

The season started well, with a spell of warm late spring weather, which encouraged audiences to sit and take their ease. The new acts and the recently improved ones proved popular. Barney and Benjy received a spontaneous round of applause when they appeared on the stage the first few times. It seemed that word had got around that Barney had been absent for a while, but now the couple were back together again, which was as it should be. Audiences at Pierrot shows liked tradition as well as something new.

The summer audiences had not seen Freddie or Jeremy before, as the two young men had only joined the company in time to start the touring season. Freddie's conjuring act was immensely popular and he invited young members of the audience onto the stage to assist him with his card tricks. He had dispensed with his flight of doves whilst performing in the open air. Even though they were docile, he could not risk them taking wing and disappearing into the bright blue sky with the wheeling seagulls. Snowy, the white rabbit, was a great favourite, though, with the children.

Likewise, Jeremy's ventriloquist act was a novelty that was enjoyed by everyone. They sang along with Tommy the Toff as he 'Broke the Bank at Monte Carlo' and Desmond the Drunkard, 'Down at the Old Bull and Bush'.

They welcomed back the familiar acts as well: Madeleine Moon singing her plaintive folk songs, then, as a contrast, the more popular songs of the day; Nancy and her performing dogs, Daisy and Dolly, both looking a little older, but still behaving well and obeying commands. There would come a day, however, when they might have to retire and be replaced by younger and sprightlier dogs. Daisy had taken to sitting down, now and again, in the middle of an act, as though she was staging her own little protest; but Nancy was putting off the evil day for as long as she could. Frank, the 'Music Man' and Susannah, the soubrette, performed singly and as a couple. Word had clearly got around about them as well. Audiences cheered when they appeared together, seeming to know that they would soon be a couple in real life as well as on the stage. Then there was Percy Morgan; who would have believed he had such a splendid voice? He was usually seen in his role as stooge to Pete, or as a comedian in his own right; but he and his partner, Dora Daventry, another artiste who was new to the summer audiences, certainly did add a 'touch of class' to the show. And Pete Pritchard, Nancy's husband; the show would not be the same without Pete. He was tremendously popular in his roles as bottler and funny man; an all-rounder who held the show together, appearing in most of the sketches and popping up in whatever capacity he was needed.

At the end of the first week takings were up quite a lot compared with the same time the previous year, and Percy was thankful and hopeful. With regard to Frank and Susannah, their situation seemed to be common knowledge now. He had warned them, however, at the start of the divorce proceedings earlier that year, that he did not want any hint of scandal to touch the Melody Makers. They had a good number of faithful followers – older men and women, more 'Victorian' in outlook – as well as the younger generation they had attracted in recent years, and any talk of impropriety might prove damaging to the company. As it happened, the report of the divorce proceedings did not appear in the local papers. The couple were now awaiting the final decree to be made absolute, then they hoped to marry before the end of the summer season.

The marriage of Frank and Susannah was not the only one being planned at that time. Patrick Moon, Madeleine's brother, was to marry his fiancée, Katy, at the end of June. The wedding had been arranged for the last Sunday in the month, at the Methodist

Chapel on Queen Street, where Patrick and Katy and, indeed, all the Moon family, were regular attendees. It was an unusual day for a wedding, but Katy wanted Maddy as well as Jessie to be a bridesmaid and Sunday was the only totally free day for the Pierrots. Katy was the only daughter of rather elderly parents and she had been welcomed wholeheartedly into the bosom of the Moon family. She regarded Maddy, and Jessica too, as the sisters she had never had. Katy had already chosen her wedding dress, with the help of her mother and Faith, from an exclusive selection at Moon's Modes.

Katy wanted her dress to be kept a secret until the big day and so, after a slight alteration carried out by Miss Muriel Phipps, the wedding gown was hidden away in Katy's wardrobe. Simple ankle-length dresses of cornflower blue silken satin, a colour which would suit both Maddy and Jessie, had been ordered from the warehouse in Leeds that supplied much of the stock for Moon's Modes. It promised to be a happy occasion. The young couple had many friends in addition to family members. Katy was an only child, but apparently there was a plethora of middle-aged aunts and uncles to be invited to the wedding.

Maddy had been biding her time, waiting for a suitable moment to have a talk with Hetty. She wanted to find out, first of all, if the friendship between Hetty and Samuel had come to an end. If that was the case, then there would be little point in saying anything about what she had seen.

Her opportunity came when Hetty was invited to Sunday tea at the beginning of June. Fortunately Jessie went out as soon as they had finished their meal, for a bicycle ride with a few members of her cycling club.

'It seems ages since I saw you,' Maddy began as the two of them sat together in the bedroom she shared with Jessie.

'It is ages,' replied Hetty. 'It was Christmas time, wasn't it; and you were trying so hard to be cheerful and to put on a brave face in spite of not seeing Dan... I've only mentioned it because you seem to be quite all right again now. William and Faith told me that it was all finished between the two of you. I'm really sorry, Maddy; but you've got over it now, have you?'

'Yes, I have,' said Maddy. 'Well, most of the time; I try not to think about him. I'm very busy, of course, and I have lots of friends in the company. I have no time to be miserable. And...what about you? Are you still seeing Samuel? I hope you don't think I'm being nosey, but Jessie told me you were still writing to him and seeing him every now and again.'

'Yes, I've been over to Leeds a couple of times at the weekend since he started lecturing at the university. It was...very nice. We went out for a meal on the Saturday night, and once we went to

Roundhay Park on the Sunday. I had to come back, though, in the afternoon, to start work on the Monday.'

'And has he been over here to see you?'

'No...no, he hasn't. Apparently he has a lot of preparation to do at the weekends, although he did manage to take some time off when I went to see him. He's very keen to make a go of this lecturing, you know, after the disappointment over the expedition.'

'And he's quite well again now, is he, after his illness?'

'Oh yes, he seems to be. It was just the climate that didn't suit him.' Hetty's face suddenly took on a different expression. She had appeared, and sounded, quite normal and cheerful, but now she seemed anxious. She looked doubtfully and a little fearfully at Maddy. 'As a matter of fact, I'm not at all sure how he is at the moment. I haven't heard from him for...it must be three weeks, and he used to write every week at first. We weren't courting or anything like that, not seriously, I mean; but I was getting very fond of him, and I thought he felt the same about me. But now...I just don't know. You don't mind me telling you, do you, Maddy? I shall go mad if I don't talk to somebody.'

'Of course I don't mind,' said Maddy. 'You probably realise that...well, I'm not actually too keen on Samuel myself. I'm sorry to say this,

Hetty, but it might be as well not to get too involved with him. He's not the sort of person that you can trust entirely...or at least that's what I think.'

'He hasn't said that it's over between us,' said Hetty, 'but if he doesn't want to see me again, then I think he should have the courage and the decency to tell me. Don't you think so, Maddy? Dan was honest with you, wasn't he?'

'Yes, I agree,' said Maddy. She took a deep breath. 'Listen, Hetty. I didn't really want to tell you, but I think it might be better if I did. You see...I saw him, Samuel, in Leeds. I was with Freddie one night – you know, the conjuror? – and Samuel was there, in the same restaurant, with a...with a lady. Actually, I'm using the term reservedly. She was...well, she seemed rather common, and she looked quite a lot older than Samuel. And I could tell that they knew one another rather well.'

Hetty let out a tremendous sigh. 'To be quite honest, I'm not surprised. I guessed there might be someone else, possibly more than one. You were right to tell me, Maddy.' She shook her head sadly. 'I really have been the most absolute fool.'

'You weren't to know what he was really like,' replied Maddy. 'Samuel can be very charming when he wants to be. But now you can have the satisfaction of telling him that you don't want to see him again.'

'I'm afraid it's rather too late for that,' said Hetty. Her dark brown eyes filled up with tears. 'You see... I'm expecting his baby.' She covered her head with her hands and began to sob.

Chapter Twenty-Two

'Ohh...no!' Maddy realised immediately that her cry of surprise, verging on horror, could do nothing to help Hetty. Indeed, it would only serve to make her feel worse. But it had been an involuntary reaction, as a myriad of thoughts flitted through her mind. This was Hetty, the very moral young woman who had lost her fiancé because she had refused to give way to his too amorous advances. But now...this was dreadful!

'I know,' Hetty sniffed through her sobs. 'You must be shocked and thoroughly ashamed of me, behaving like that. And I know everybody else will be too.'

'No!' Maddy shook her head emphatically. 'Of course I'm not shocked or ashamed.' And that was the truth. Maddy was just amazed that Hetty could have allowed this to happen, and she felt worried for her, too, as the awful truth began to dawn on her. 'I'm surprised, perhaps. But then...maybe I'm not. I've just told you that I didn't trust Samuel. This just proves that I was right.'

Hetty gave a weak smile. She had stopped sobbing now; it was not really characteristic of her to give way to tears and to show her feelings so openly. 'You mustn't blame Samuel entirely. It takes two, you know, and I can't say that I was…unwilling. I lost Alec – you remember? – because I behaved rather prudishly. So this time…well, I didn't. I suppose I wasn't thinking about what the consequences might be. At times like that…you don't. And now…I'm in a right pickle, aren't I?'

'What are you going to do?' asked Maddy, feeling very helpless.

'I have no idea at all,' replied Hetty, 'especially now, after what you have just told me.'

'I'm sorry,' said Maddy. 'Perhaps I shouldn't have said anything.'

'Of course you should. Even more so, the way things have turned out. I know I could never trust him, so marriage would be out of the question. I doubt if he would agree to it anyway.'

'Yes, I certainly wouldn't want to see you married to that awful stepbrother of mine, but my father and Aunty Faith would be furious if they knew, and they would probably insist that he…well…made an honest woman of you, as the saying goes.'

Hetty smiled again, wryly. 'Aren't you forgetting something, Maddy? Our father has no room to talk, has he? Aren't you forgetting how I came on the scene?'

Maddy put her hand to her mouth. 'Oh…yes!

I'm sorry. I forgot, for the moment.'

'Yes; William and my real mother, Bella, let things go too far, and then he wouldn't marry her. The circumstances were rather different, of course. From what I've gathered, William was very young and quite innocent; and from what I learnt of Bella I'm sure she led him astray. No doubt he was scared to death, poor lad, when he knew what had happened. Anyway, she upped and went back up north, didn't she? And I was adopted.'

'But Samuel is older, and he certainly isn't an innocent young man, is he?' replied Maddy. 'Not by any means.'

'Quite so. He knew what he was doing. I knew I wasn't the first,' she added sagely. 'Although for me…it was the first time. No doubt he found that very satisfying. Another conquest, another notch on his bedpost.'

'Are you going to tell him?'

'No! No… I had been wondering what to do. I was trying to delude myself that he was busy and hadn't had time to write. But now, well, I know differently, don't I?'

'Are you quite sure, though…that you are having a baby? I mean, couldn't you be mistaken?'

'I'm afraid not. I've missed two periods and I feel…well, I just know. I shall go through with it, though,' she went on in a determined voice. 'To do anything else – to try to put a stop to it – would be foolish and dangerous, and very wrong as well. And

I certainly won't let him – or her – be adopted, like I was. I know there's a stigma attached to illegitimate babies, but I shall hold my head up high and face the consequences.'

'I think you're being very brave,' said Maddy. 'But Samuel will have to know sometime, won't he?'

'I suppose so, but let's not look too far ahead, eh? You are the only person I've told, but I know other people will have to know before too long. One thing I do know is that William and Faith would never cast me aside. I shall just wait a little while and see how things go. I feel much better, though, now I've told you.'

'Have you seen a doctor?' asked Maddy. 'Perhaps you should…'

'No, I haven't, not yet. But that's something I must do before long. Now…shall we go and join the family downstairs? They'll be wondering what we're doing.'

'Catching up with one another's news,' said Maddy. 'That's what we'll say. After all, we haven't seen one another for ages. I'll keep your secret, Hetty. I'm so glad you felt you could confide in me.'

'You're my sister, aren't you?' Hetty put an arm around Maddy and kissed her cheek. 'As I've said before, it was a lucky day for me when I came to find William, and found all of you.'

'In spite of what has happened?' asked Maddy.

'Yes, in spite of everything. It's at a time like this

that you need a family. And I know that mine won't let me down.'

One of them already has, thought Maddy, but she did not say it. Hetty was a strong young woman and Maddy knew that she would find her way through this problem. But if she, Maddy, could get her hands on Samuel, there was no telling what she wouldn't do to him!

It was a perfect day for a June wedding. The sun shone from a cloudless blue sky as Patrick and his new bride stood on the chapel steps posing for a photograph. A young man by the name of Bertram Lucas had recently opened a photographic studio on North Marine Road, near to the premises of Isaac Moon and Son. Patrick had been impressed by the selection of photographs in the window display, consisting of indoor and outdoor pictures, both in sepia and black and white, and had consequently booked the young man to take photographs of his forthcoming wedding.

After the one of the bride and groom had been taken they were joined by the bridesmaids, Maddy and Jessie, and the best man and groomsman, friends of Patrick from his school and Sunday school days.

Then a group study was taken with the family members of both the bride and groom gathered around the happy couple. Bertram suggested that a few chairs should be brought out from the nearby church hall – where the wedding breakfast was to be held – to help with the arrangement of the group.

Patrick and Katy sat on the two centre chairs, looking radiantly happy. Patrick was well-known for his jocular personality. He was always ready with a laugh and a joke whatever the circumstances, a trait he had developed as an antidote to his sombre career. Today, though, he was not laughing, and his smile as he gazed upon his bride was one of wonder and adoration.

Katy was a small girl, dark-haired and insignificant in appearance, until one looked at her lovely hazel-green eyes. They were her best feature, glowing with a radiance that revealed her inner beauty and the warmth of her nature. At times she seemed overshadowed by Patrick, not the sort of girl you would notice in a crowd. But today she looked as beautiful as any bride could be. Her dress of pale cream silk-satin – which Faith had suggested was more flattering to her than a stark white – was high-waisted with a deep V-shaped neckline inserted with lace and pleated silk, and a high stand-up lace collar of the style worn by Queen Alexandra (and all ladies who followed the fashions of the day). Her headdress of cream flowers held a hip-length silk-gauze veil.

Patrick's suit was medium grey; he had decided to have a change from the black he was forced to wear for funerals, and with it he wore a high-collared shirt and a cream silk tie that matched the cream carnation in his buttonhole and the cream roses and carnations in Katy's bouquet. On the chairs to his left were his father, who was similarly dressed, Faith, and at the end of the row, Grandad Isaac.

Faith looked truly beautiful, as she always did; her outfit today was the very epitome of elegance and caused more than a few heads to turn in her direction. This was never her intention – she was a very modest woman – but William, over the years, had grown accustomed to the admiring glances she attracted wherever they went. Her pale blue silk dress had a pleated cummerbund of a deeper blue, which matched her elbow-length gloves and her large wide-brimmed hat trimmed with ostrich feathers. The ankle-length skirt narrowed towards the hem and was split to just below the knee to facilitate movement.

Katy's parents, Mr and Mrs Hancock, sat to the right of Katy. Mrs Hancock was rather more soberly, but still smartly, dressed in a pale green tailored suit with a small-brimmed matching hat, topped with a cluster of cock's feathers in emerald green.

Behind the row of chairs stood Maddy and Jessie, the best man and groomsman, a middle-aged couple who were godparents to Katy, and at the end of the row was Hetty. She had seemed unwilling to be part of the family group, but William had insisted that she was a member of the family and must be included. And seated at the front, on the ground, were Tommy and Tilly. Tilly was very pleased with her appearance in the new deep pink dress she had been allowed to choose herself. Her mother had argued at first that pink was not a colour to be worn with ginger hair. But Tilly had insisted that that was the only dress she wanted, and it had to be said that it suited her and her colouring very well. Tommy was rather less pleased with his knickerbockers and short jacket, which felt stiff with newness. He hadn't particularly wanted anything new, but his mother had insisted that he must look smart.

Samuel, not surprisingly, was conspicuous by his absence. He had, of course, been invited to the wedding, but he had declined the invitation saying that he would be away that weekend on a potholing expedition to Derbyshire with a group of his students. It had been arranged several months ago, or so he said, and it was not possible for the date to be changed or for him not to accompany them.

Most probably it was only Faith who was really disappointed at his absence. Hetty had been relieved on hearing that he would not be there. She had written to him soon after her conversation with Maddy, telling him that it might be as well if they did not see one another again. She was sure he must have other commitments in Leeds? she queried. Maybe that was why he had not written lately?

He had replied, eventually, in a similar vein. Yes, he had been busy with all sorts of things and he simply had not had time to come to Scarborough. He had enjoyed her company, he wrote, but he agreed that it might be as well if they did not see one another again except, of course, as friends. It was inevitable that they should meet from time to time because of the family connection.

Hetty was relieved in a way. She and Samuel had managed to extricate themselves from a relationship that she knew, now, would never have gone anywhere. At the same time she was anxious and heartsore. She was expecting his child. A doctor had now confirmed this; he had assured her that she was fit and healthy and the child was due in six months' time, which would be sometime around Christmas. Her condition was not obvious to anyone yet, but she knew she would not be able to conceal it for much longer.

As she looked at the happy bride and groom she felt a pang of sadness and loneliness, although she was able, also, to rejoice with them. They were a lovely couple and she wished them every happiness. And she knew, too, despite her feeling of aloneness, that she was a part of this joyous family gathering. She felt, deep down, that they would all support, rather then condemn her when they knew the truth. But she could foresee difficult times ahead.

Maddy's eyes were upon Hetty as they all trooped into the church hall after the outside photographs had been taken. She was the only one who knew Hetty's secret and she was relieved to see how well her half-sister seemed to be coping with what must be, for her, something of an ordeal. She was smiling and chatting and behaving very normally, although Maddy feared that she must be agonising deep within herself.

Nobody could possibly have guessed that the young woman was pregnant. She had chosen her wedding outfit from Moon's Modes. It was a high-waisted silken dress with a fashionable narrow ankle-length skirt, in a shade of deep coral pink that suited her dark colouring. Her matching straw hat was trimmed with a large petersham ribbon bow. Like Faith, she looked the picture of elegance.

The ladies of the chapel had organised the wedding breakfast, which was really a tea, the wedding having taken place in the afternoon, well away from the times of the morning and evening services. As a special concession the Sunday school scholars were, this afternoon, meeting in the chapel itself instead of in the nearby hall.

It was, indeed, a chapel tea party, but on a grander scale. There were well-filled plates of boiled ham and tongue, new potatoes, mixed salad with boiled egg, and dishes of beetroot and pickled onions With a bottle of salad cream in the centre of each table. The band of six ladies – their best dresses covered with floral pinnies and still wearing their hats – cleared away quickly and efficiently, and then brought on the dessert in glass dishes. This was 'Methodist' trifle, as it was called in some quarters, made with fruit juice rather than sherry, in the chapel tradition, but bursting with succulent fruit and topped with fresh cream.

There was a 'top' trestle table covered with a pristine white cloth at which were seated, in a long row, the bride and groom, their respective parents and, at the end, Grandad Isaac. The rest of the guests were seated in groups of six around smaller tables. On the one nearest to the top table were the bridesmaids, Maddy and Jessie, the best man and groomsman, and Hetty. Occupying the remaining place was the photographer, Bertram Lucas. He had been invited to the reception because there was still one photograph to be taken, that of the ceremony of cutting the cake. Besides which, he was becoming quite a friend, as well as a neighbour, to the Moon family.

Maddy watched surreptitiously, but with interest, as Hetty and Bertram chatted together, appearing to get along very well and to have plenty to say to one another. They had, of course, met before, being near neighbours in their respective work places. Maddy knew that Bertram was a bachelor, around thirty years of age, she guessed, and that he lived in the flat above his studio premises. The thought passed through her mind that they made a handsome couple. What a suitable match it might have been, but there remained Hetty's problem...

After the trifle there were cups of strong tea,

without which no northern meal would be complete, poured from huge cream-coloured enamel teapots. Then it was time for the cutting of the cake and the toast to the bride and groom.

Katy and Patrick posed with the silver knife between their clasped hands, ready to plunge it into the bottom layer of the cake. It was two-tiered, a superb creation covered in pure white icing, decorated with pink rosebuds and, in the centre, small china figures of a bride and groom. The Moon family knew that it would taste just as delicious as it looked because it had been made and iced by their esteemed cook and housekeeper, Mrs Baker, who was an honoured guest at the reception.

Bertram Lucas disappeared behind his black curtain, there was a sudden flash, and Katy and Patrick were captured in a photograph for all posterity. When the applause had died down William rose, glass in hand, to propose a toast to the happy couple. They were not sticking strictly to the protocol as to how things ought to be done at weddings. This was a friendly family occasion and it had been agreed that William Moon was the one most able to make the speech, certainly more so than the shy and retiring Horace Hancock, Katy's rather elderly father.

'Now, will you all raise your glasses,' said William, 'and drink to the health of the bride and bridegroom, my son, Patrick, and his lovely wife, Katy.'

'Katy and Patrick…'

'Good luck…'

'Good health and happiness…' The voices of them all, united in their good wishes, echoed around the hall. The drink was blackcurrant juice, such as was used at the Communion services in Methodist chapels. William and Isaac, and Patrick, too, together with several of his friends, enjoyed a glass of beer from time to time – strictly on the qt! – but now they were adhering to the principles of their religion, especially as they were on the chapel premises.

William spoke of how happy he was to welcome Katy into the family, and how pleased he was to see all the friends and relations who had come to share in their celebration. Patrick replied, amidst cheers and laughter, that 'my wife and I thank you for being here with us and for all the lovely presents.'

There was not much 'speechifying' and the guests chatted amongst themselves, moving about the room to form and re-form in little groups whilst Katy, with her mother, retired to a side room to change into her 'going away' outfit. There was a cheer when she reappeared with Patrick at her side. His wedding suit, which he was still wearing, would be his best suit – apart from the funerals – for many years to come.

Katy looked just as lovely in the pink suit with the close-fitting jacket and broderie anglaise collar as she had in her bridal finery. A jaunty little brimless hat covered in pink feathers perched on top of her dark curls.

The couple were to spend their honeymoon in Blackpool, a place that neither of them had visited before. And Maddy had recommended that they should stay at Mrs Jolly's boarding house on Albert Road, where she had stayed with the Melody Makers on their spring tours. Patrick, unfortunately, could not be spared for too long away from the business. There had been two unexpected deaths in the town and the funerals had been booked for the end of the week. Also, Isaac had not been too well – he had been feeling much more tired of late – and so Patrick had agreed that they would spend only four nights in Blackpool and return home on Thursday morning.

They were to travel to the station in style, a very up-to-the-minute style. Patrick's friend, Arthur Newsome, who had acted as best man, was in possession of one of the new Fiat motor cars. In possession for the day only, however, as it actually belonged to his father, who was an influential solicitor in the town. A few of these motors, along with Renaults and Fords and the – very occasional – Rolls Royce were to be seen on the streets of Scarborough now, alongside the horse-driven landaus and hansom cabs. This car, unlike many, could seat four and it had the added advantage, especially on a windy day, of being a closed-in model rather than an open-top.

The guests crowded onto the pavement outside the chapel as Katy and Patrick climbed into the back seat. Jessie, still in her bridesmaid's dress, sat in the front seat. She knew Arthur from the cycling club and had eagerly accepted his offer of a ride. She was a keen cyclist, as was he, but this was much too exciting to miss.

'Mind you don't muck up your dress,' said Maddy who, surprisingly, had not yet ridden in one of the new petrol-driven motors. 'And take good care of that wedding bouquet!' She winked slyly at her friend, looking meaningfully at Arthur, who was tinkering with the engine. When Katy had thrown her bouquet into the air it had been Jessie who had caught it, which, according to custom, indicated that she might be the next bride.

Jessie blushed crimson. 'Shhh…' she admonished her stepsister. 'I've told you; he's just a friend,' she whispered as Arthur, having put down the bonnet, took his place at the wheel. But Maddy guessed that the two of them might possibly become rather more than friends.

She turned to her brother and his new wife. 'Have a lovely time,' she said, 'and give my regards to Mr and Mrs Jolly. And all the very best of luck and…and everything, to both of you.' She blinked away a tear as she saw her brother and Katy smile adoringly at one another.

Arthur started up the engine and the motor car slowly drove away in a cloud of smoke. Patrick and

Katy waved excitedly and the crowd of well-wishers waved back.

Grandad Isaac waved too. 'Aye, God bless 'em,' he said. 'I'm glad our Patrick's wed that lovely lass. I tell you what though, Will, lad.' He turned to his son, who was standing at his side. 'You wouldn't catch me in one o' them newfangled monsters.'

'No, Father; so you've said before,' smiled William.

'And I hope I never live to see the day when they take over from t' horses in our job,' Isaac continued. 'I've told you afore, lad. Over my dead body!'

'I should imagine that motor-driven hearses will be many years ahead,' replied William. But he knew that, possibly sooner rather than later, that day would come.

It was when they were back in the hall saying their goodbyes that Isaac clutched hold of his daughter-in-law's arm.

'Eeh, Faith lass,' he said, putting his other hand to his chest. 'I've gone all queer, like. I'll have to sit down a minute.'

'Here you are, Father,' she said, pulling a chair forward and easing him into it. 'It's been an exciting day, and I expect you've got overtired...' Then, 'William...!' she cried as her father-in-law clutched again at his chest and slumped forward. 'William...your father...he's ill. I think it's his heart.'

By the time William had dashed across the hall from where he was standing talking to Katy's parents, his father had fallen sideways in the chair, supported by Faith's arm. His face was ashen as he gave a rasping gasp of breath. Then his head lolled crookedly and his arms fell limply to his sides.

'Father!' cried William. Gently, he eased Faith away and put his fingers to the pulse point on Isaac's neck. 'It's too late,' he said, shaking his head. 'I'm afraid he's gone.' Tenderly, he took off his father's spectacles and closed the lids on the pale blue faded eyes.

Chapter Twenty-Three

But he can't be dead!' cried Jessie. 'Grandad Isaac? He waved to us, only half an hour ago, and he was so happy...' She burst into tears and Arthur Newsome put a comforting arm around her. She leant against him, her ginger head resting against his shoulder. He was a head or so taller than Jessie, a serious-looking bespectacled young man. Maddy, watching them, felt a moment's gladness, despite her sorrow. She had guessed that there was rather more than a friendship developing there.

Jessie had been very fond of Isaac Moon. He had become an honorary grandfather to her, far closer than her real grandparents, whom she saw only occasionally. Maddy felt sure that Jessie's grief would be just as acute as her own.

'It was a heart attack,' said Maddy. 'At least, that's what we think. We're waiting for the doctor to come and then...well, my father will see to what has to be done.'

'Aye, we'll take him home, and I'll do what I can for him,' said William. 'When I say home I don't mean our South Bay place; I mean North Marine Road. That was his home until the last few years.'

It had been both his home and his workplace. Isaac had grown up there as a lad and had stayed there helping his father to build up the reputation of the undertaking business of Joshua Moon and Son; afterwards to become Isaac Moon and Son. And now that was to change again.

'What about Patrick?' asked Maddy. Her brother was already on the train with his bride heading towards Blackpool. 'Are you going to get in touch with him?'

'No...' William shook his head. 'We'll leave him be. Let the lad enjoy his honeymoon. Goodness knows, he's worked his socks off recently. He'll be back on Thursday, and that'll be soon enough for him to know.'

'I can't believe it. I still can't take it in,' said Jessie in bewilderment. 'To go so suddenly.'

'He hadn't been well for a while, you know,' said Faith, putting an arm around her daughter. 'He tried to hide it from us, but we've known for some time that he was slowing down.'

'It's only recently we managed to persuade him to see the doctor,' added William. 'He was told to take it easy, to remember that he wasn't a spring chicken anymore. That made him even more determined to carry on, but these last couple of weeks...well, we've seen a big change in him, haven't we, Faith?'

His wife nodded. 'That's true. And he wouldn't have wanted to get old and infirm. I think you are right, William, not to let Patrick know. It's what your father would have wanted, for Patrick and Katy to enjoy their holiday. Father was so happy today, wasn't he? So pleased to be welcoming Katy into the family.'

'I thought Grandad Isaac would go on for ever,' said Maddy. 'I know I've said so before, but I can't imagine him not always being there.'

'Nor can I,' added Jessie. 'I did love him so much...' She burst into tears again, letting go of Arthur's hand, to which she had been clinging tightly and turning to her mother for comfort.

It was a sad ending, indeed, to what had been a most joyful occasion. Most of the guests, after expressing their condolences, had thought it was best to depart. Tommy and Tilly, bewildered at what was happening and not quite understanding it all, had gone back home with Mrs Baker. She usually had some time off on Sunday, but she had offered to take care of the twins until such time as Faith and the rest of the family returned.

Isaac had been laid gently on a piece of carpeting in a corner of the room. The doctor had been called as soon as he had collapsed although it had been obvious at once that there was nothing that anyone could do for him. By the time Dr Armitage, the Moon family physician, arrived, there were only the immediate family members still there, plus Katy's parents and Arthur Newsome, who was loath to leave Jessie in her distressed state.

'It seems that he had a massive heart attack,' said

the doctor, when he had examined him. 'He wouldn't have suffered at all, apart from the initial pain. It may have been brought on by the excitement of the day, but it was inevitable.' He signed a death certificate and he and William discussed how best to transport Isaac's body to what had been his childhood home.

The doctor owned a large Daimler car, and he suggested that that would be the most dignified way for Isaac to travel on his penultimate journey. The final journey would be when he was taken from his resting place at his own premises to the cemetery on the outskirts of the town. Very carefully and reverently, he was carried out and placed on the back seats of the motor car – he was not a tall man – and then covered with the doctor's travelling rug.

'I shall stay with him…when I have done what is necessary,' William told his wife. 'You understand, don't you, my dear?'

'Perfectly,' replied Faith. 'The children and I will be all right on our own. You stay…with your father.'

Dr Armitage, who was a family friend as well as the doctor, helped to carry Isaac's body into what was now Patrick – and Katy's – living room. The premises had been somewhat altered over the years, but they had formerly been the home of William and Clara and, before that, of Isaac and Hannah, and of Isaac's forbears too.

The doctor left, and as William performed the

last service he would ever do for his father, he recalled how he had done the same thing for his wife, Clara, seven years ago. Tenderly, he washed his father's body, dressed him in a temporary shroud, then placed him in a makeshift plywood coffin. The coffin he intended to make for Isaac would be one of his very best, as had been the one for Clara: oak wood, polished to a high gloss, with handles of silver gilt and lined with ivory satin. He knew that his son, Patrick, would have felt privileged to take his part in the making of his grandad's coffin, but it was better this way, William decided. When Patrick returned he would take his place at the funeral as the son, and not the grandson, of the business.

It was the end of an era. Very soon he would need to change the sign over the door and the wording on the notepaper and bill headings to 'William Moon and Son', no longer 'Isaac Moon and Son'. But not yet, not yet…

For the moment, until he had been finally laid to rest, Isaac was the head of the firm and of the family. And William would remain there with him, sleeping in Patrick's bed until his son and Katy returned.

The chapel on Queen Street was half full for the funeral of Isaac Moon, as it had been for the wedding of Patrick and Katy only ten days before. Many of the same people filled the pews, but this time as mourners rather than well-wishers.

The young couple had been shocked on arriving back home after a gloriously happy few days in Blackpool to hear that Isaac had gone; and that Patrick was now the son and not the grandson of the family firm. All the preliminary work, in which Patrick would normally have played his part, had been undertaken by his father. Isaac lay at peace in his splendid oak coffin, one of the very best that Moon and Son could supply. He had been a small white-haired, white-whiskered elderly man; but death, as so often happened, had taken away the age and care lines from his forehead and around his eyes, and he now looked serene, free from all anxiety.

It was the custom for the undertaker to walk at the head of the procession and William had asked Patrick if he would do the honours on that day. Prior to that, the coffin was carried from the old home that Isaac had loved so much, by William, Patrick, Samuel, and Joe Black, the assistant of the Moon family firm. A large wreath of white lilies, the family tribute, was laid on top of the coffin, covering almost the full length, and at the sides was a host of wreaths and sprays: roses, carnations, sweet peas, gladioli, in bright summer colours of red, pink, yellow and mauve; a vivid splash of colour seen through the glass sides of the hearse on what was a grey cloudy morning with, as yet, no promise of sunshine.

Patrick, wearing his customary black suit, black

gloves, black top hat, and with a black-bordered handkerchief in his breast pocket, led the procession the short distance from their premises to the chapel. Immediately behind him was the hearse, pulled by the two black horses, Velvet and Star. William, Samuel, Joe Black and several of the men who had been friends of Isaac for many years, walked behind the hearse, followed by Faith, Maddy, Jessie and Hetty in the family carriage, a horse-drawn brougham, such as William hired whenever one was required.

Throughout the service Maddy's eyes kept straying to the coffin, resting on a bier near to the chancel steps. It was almost impossible to believe that there lay the body of her beloved grandfather and that she would never see him again. He had been a vital part of her life for as long as she could remember.

They sang one of his favourite hymns, 'And Can it Be', by Charles Wesley, and she could imagine Grandad Isaac's voice joining in heartily, as he had done so many times.

'...Bold I approach the eternal throne
And claim the crown, through Christ my own.'

If ever anyone deserved to go to heaven it was her grandfather; and despite the doubts that sometimes assailed her with regard to such matters, she felt sure that he was there now. And maybe he was reunited with his beloved wife, Hannah, the grandmother whom she vaguely remembered.

The minister spoke of Isaac's life and his work; his commitment to his chosen profession, to his family, and to his church. His many friends and his family would miss him sorely and mourn him for a time, but a character such as Isaac Moon would not be forgotten.

Maddy managed to keep her tears in check until the final hymn, 'O Love that wilt not let me go', another of her grandfather's favourites, which spoke of the promise of eternal life.

> '...I trace the rainbow through the rain,
> And feel the promise is not vain;
> That morn shall tearless be.'

Her tears overflowed and ran down her cheeks. She remembered talking to Susannah about the promise in the rainbow, and here it was again. Despite her tears the thought came to her that the future was not entirely dark and cheerless. There would come a time when they would remember Grandad Isaac with joy rather than sadness. Their memories of him would be happy ones; she had found that this had happened after the death of her mother; her grief had gradually changed to a glad remembrance.

And in another part of her life, too, Maddy was finding contentment. She had realised that she could not go on pining for a lost love for ever. She was now able to look back on her time with Daniel with fondness and scarcely a regret, rather than banishing thoughts of him from her mind because they were too painful. Freddie had proved to be a very good friend to her. She had the feeling that he was only waiting for a signal from her before moving their friendship a step nearer to romance. Perhaps, one of these days...

She found herself smiling. Whatever was she thinking about, allowing her thoughts to wander at such a time? She composed her face again, wiping away the few tears that remained, but she could not still the feeling of joy and hopefulness that had stirred deep within her. She would regard it as a special gift from Grandad Isaac. He would have wanted her to be happy and to look forward.

The cemetery was on the outskirts of the town, and only the family and close friends gathered there. The committal at the graveside was heart-rending, as Isaac's coffin was lowered on top of that of his wife, Hannah. Handfuls of soil were scattered on the top by William and Patrick. And then it was all over.

Mrs Baker, after attending the service at the chapel, had returned to the house on Victoria Avenue, with two more of the chapel ladies, to put the finishing touches to the funeral repast, which she had prepared beforehand. The curtains, kept closed since Isaac's death, had been opened to let in the daylight. Fires had been lit in the dining room and the lounge, adding a cheerful aspect to the greyness of the day. After the glorious sunshine on the wedding day the weather had been changeable, not at all what the holidaymakers in the town had hoped for.

Maddy, of course, had been given permission to miss the morning and afternoon Pierrot shows, but she had agreed that she would take part in the evening performance. She knew that that was what her grandfather would have wanted, and she intended to sing his favourite songs tonight.

The twenty or so guests who had returned to the South Bay house drifted between the two rooms, after helping themselves to the selection of savoury items and desserts, and a glass of sherry, or orange juice for those who were strictly teetotal.

Samuel, to Maddy's surprise, had agreed to attend the funeral, although he had not been there for the wedding. But she supposed he could not do otherwise; even Samuel would not be so lacking in manners or decency as to stay away. She had spoken to him politely, quite affably, in fact, but no more than was necessary. He had stayed at the family home overnight but intended returning to Leeds later that evening.

She noticed that he was sitting next to Hetty on the settee in the lounge. She wondered what they were saying to one another, but on no account would she eavesdrop. Despite Hetty's condition, which was still no more obvious than it had been a week ago, she hoped against hope that the two of them would not get back together again.

'Hello there, Hetty,' he began, sitting down beside her. 'It's good to see you again. In spite of the sad circumstances, of course. It's a shame, isn't it, about the old chap? I had a shock when I heard that he had popped his clogs. Still, he'd had a good innings, as they say.'

'Yes, quite,' replied Hetty, giving him a disapproving glance. 'We've all been very distressed about it, as you can imagine.'

'Yes, maybe I can,' said Samuel. 'But he wasn't actually my grandfather, you know. Let me see; he was yours, wasn't he? I tend to forget, with all our family complications.'

'Jessie regarded him as her grandfather,' said Hetty. 'In fact, she seemed to be more upset than anyone; your sister is a very sensitive girl. And Tommy and Tilly loved Isaac. They are very perplexed by it all.'

'Yes; where are they, the terrible twins?' asked Samuel. He hadn't seen them as he had arrived in Scarborough late the previous evening, and by the time he had risen in the morning they had gone out.

'They are at school,' said Hetty. 'Faith thought it was better that they should carry on in their normal routine. They've taken sandwiches for lunch; they do sometimes.'

'Oh yes, I see...' Samuel nodded. Then, 'I feel that you are displeased with me for some reason,

Hetty,' he went on. 'I'm sorry that our little – er – romance has come to an end, but I thought the decision to part was mutual. You did write to say, didn't you, that you didn't want to see me again?'

'And I meant it, Samuel,' said Hetty, smiling brightly at him. 'I am sure you have other – what shall I say? – fish to fry, in Leeds, haven't you?' She would not tell him what she knew. He would no doubt guess that it was Maddy who had told her; he knew the company had been performing in Leeds and that he might well have been seen. She did not want to cause trouble for her sister; she guessed there was not much love lost now between Maddy and Samuel.

'I suppose you might say so,' he replied with a sly grin. 'Maybe more than one fish. You see…I'm not ready to settle down, Hetty. I thought for a time that I might be, but now I know that I'm not. Besides, you're a lovely young woman and you deserve someone much nicer than me. No hard feelings, I hope?'

'No…none at all, Samuel,' she replied.

'Maybe there is someone already?' he asked, eyeing her quizzically.

'Yes, maybe there is,' she replied. Their eyes met and held for several seconds as each contemplated the other in silence.

'If you will excuse me,' said Samuel after a few moments had passed. 'I must go and mingle a little.' He rose to his feet. 'I'm not often in Scarborough, so I had better go and socialise with the few people that I know. May I wish you all the very best, Hetty? I expect our paths will cross from time to time.'

'Yes, I'm sure they will,' replied Hetty.

She wondered, as she watched him walk across the room to talk to Patrick and Katy, how she could have imagined that she was in love with him. Beneath the surface charm and friendliness he was supercilious and calculating. Nevertheless, he was the father of the child she was expecting and there was no gainsaying that. Now that she was three months into her pregnancy she was experiencing a strange sort of calm and inevitability with regard to the situation. She was no longer feeling quite so queasy in the morning and evening as she had at first, a condition that had been easy to hide as she lived on her own.

What would Samuel's reaction have been had she told him? She honestly could not imagine how he would have reacted; with shock or denial or with a 'couldn't care less' attitude? She didn't know and didn't intend to worry about it; that was one problem that she would not think about until it became inescapable.

There were problems, indeed, in spite of the serenity that had settled upon her. Samuel's remark about the possibility of there being someone else in her life had started her thinking about Bertram Lucas. She and the photographer had enjoyed one another's company at the wedding reception. She had met him a couple of times before and had found him polite but somewhat uncommunicative.

He had soon overcome his initial reserve and diffidence of manner, however, when they met on what was a more social occasion. He had told her that his photography business, which was starting to flourish since he had opened his own premises, was forcing him to overcome his innate shyness. As an only child of elderly parents, he had never found it easy to mix; but the wedding of Patrick and Katy was the third one he had been asked to photograph, and it was impossible to be shy in such convivial surroundings.

He had told Hetty, but not in any flirtatious manner, that she was a beautiful young woman with classic features and a well-defined bone structure to her face. Would she be willing to pose for him as a model? he had asked. She had laughed and said that she would think about it. With many young men that would be seen as a provocative suggestion, but she knew that Bertram was totally sincere.

'But I will see you again, won't I?' he had persisted. 'Perhaps we could go to a concert together, at the Spa?'

'Yes, maybe we could,' she replied. 'That would be very nice. Or we could go and watch Maddy perform in her Pierrot show?'

On hearing her name Maddy's ears had pricked

up. 'Yes… Have you not seen one of our shows yet, Bertram?' she asked.

'No, I'm afraid not,' he replied.

'You don't know what you've been missing!' Maddy laughed.

'It is very remiss of me,' said Bertram seriously. 'It is something I must remedy very soon. We will sort out a convenient time for both of us, Hetty.'

But they had not yet done so. The sudden death of Isaac had banished thoughts of enjoyment and frivolity from everyone's mind. Bertram had attended the funeral service at the chapel but then had gone back to his shop and home premises.

Hetty felt, though, that he was a man of his word and that he would soon be asking her to go to a show with him, as they had tentatively suggested. It would look churlish if she were to refuse, but Hetty knew that to embark upon a friendship with Bertram Lucas might only lead to further complications.

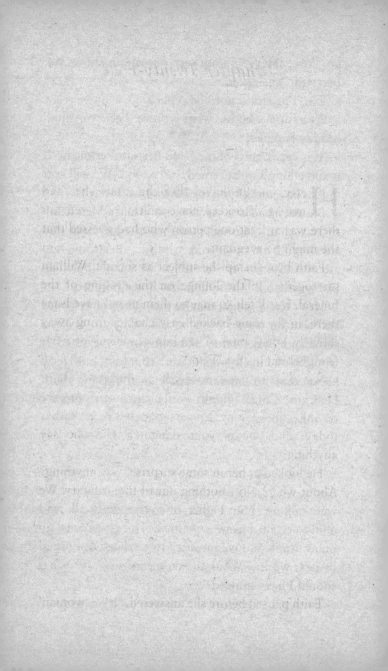

Chapter Twenty-Four

Hetty might have thought that she had managed to keep her condition a secret, but there was at least one person who had guessed that she might be pregnant.

Faith brought up the subject as she and William sat together in the lounge on the evening of the funeral. It still felt strange to them not to have Isaac there, in the wing-backed easy chair, puffing away serenely at his pipe or reading out items of news from behind his newspaper.

'Have you noticed anything different about Hetty recently, William?' she asked. 'I saw you were having quite a long conversation with her earlier today...and she is your daughter. Did she say anything?'

He looked at her in some surprise. 'Say anything? About what? No...nothing out of the ordinary. We were talking about Father, of course, that's all. And about certain business matters. Things have to go on as usual, and we must try to get back to normal by next week... What do you mean, anyway? What should I have noticed?'

Faith paused before she answered. 'It's a 'woman'

thing, I suppose. No, maybe it would not have occurred to you. But... I think she's pregnant, William.'

His mouth dropped open. 'What? But...she can't be!'

Faith sighed, shaking her head sadly. 'Please don't say she can't be, William. Because you know as well as I do that it is possible. I can't say I'm happy about it, because if it is so – and I'm pretty sure that I'm right – then I know who must be responsible.'

He stared at her in shocked amazement, then his face grew dark with anger as the truth began to dawn on him. 'You mean... Samuel? Yes, by God, Samuel, the stupid young fool! Just wait till I...' He stopped suddenly, and Faith could see that another thought was now occurring to him. William, too, gave a long drawn out sigh.

'But I've no room to talk, have I? Dear God! It's history repeating itself...and I don't have a leg to stand on. Forgive me, my dear, for being so hasty and insensitive. I wasn't thinking. Samuel is your son, of course...not mine.'

'But Hetty is your daughter, my dear, and you have every right to feel angry,' replied Faith calmly. 'And don't imagine that I am not just as angry with Samuel, because I am. I know that it takes two, as they say, but for him to behave so irresponsibly... I could see that Hetty was falling for him, but there was nothing I could do about it. I know Samuel can be very charming, but despite what you may think, William, I am not blind to his faults.'

'But who am I to take a moral stand?' said William. 'I was just as bad.'

'I don't think so,' said Faith stoutly. 'How old were you? Eighteen? Nobbut a young lad, as your father might have said. And what is more, I can guess who took the lead in...what happened. Bella was no sweet and innocent young miss, was she? And I know very well that Samuel is not a callow youth, wet behind the ears. He is twenty-two now, and he knew perfectly well what he was doing; I'm sure of that.'

'But how can you be sure?' asked William. 'I mean...sure that Hetty is pregnant. She looks a little fuller in the face... Yes, I've noticed that. But she appears to be her normal self, not agitated or upset, and she would be, surely, if what you say is true.'

Faith smiled. 'I might be wrong, but I don't think so. I've told you, women know about these things. I have had four children, William – well, three pregnancies, because of the twins – and I know that after the first few weeks expectant mothers have a certain look about them: a bloom, a sort of inner radiance, and other people notice it.' She nodded. 'I'm right; you'll see.'

'But Hetty and Samuel...they're not friendly now, are they?' remarked William. 'I mean, not as friendly as they have been?'

'No, that's the impression I've got,' said Faith. 'I noticed them earlier today. They were chatting together for a while, but there was no...what you might call...intimacy between them.'

'Well, I must say I'm relieved about that, in spite of what you think might have happened. That puts a different complexion on things, I must admit. But I was never happy about the two of them getting together. Hetty's a grand lass. She deserves somebody much better than...' William stopped, banging his fist against his head. 'Here I go again! Dear God, what am I saying? Do forgive me, my dear. I am the last person, the very last who ought to be condemning Samuel.'

'But I agree with you, William,' Faith smiled. 'Hetty deserves a good man; someone who would be a good husband and father to her child. Somehow I can't see Samuel fitting the bill. And I shouldn't imagine she's told him about it.'

'We'll just have to wait and see what happens,' said William. 'I'm blessed if I know what we can do about it, though. We can't play the heavy-handed parents and insist that they get married. They are old enough to make up their own minds.'

'And I don't think for one moment that it's something either of them would want,' agreed Faith. 'As you say, my dear; we will just have to wait and see.'

But Faith did not intend to wait much longer. She invited Hetty to come for tea on the following

Sunday and made sure they were left alone together. There were only she and William, with Hetty and the twins, at teatime. Jessie had gone for a bicycle ride with her cycling club and Maddy had been invited to go along as well. They had taken a picnic tea and would not be back until later in the evening.

William made himself scarce after tea, whilst Tommy and Tilly amused themselves with board games in Tommy's bedroom. Sunday was a day on which the twins usually played amicably together. On the other days of the week they preferred the company of schoolmates, boys and girls to whose homes they were sometimes invited, or who came to their house to have tea and then play in the garden. But Sunday was different. It was still regarded as a special day in the Moon household, as it was in many Edwardian families. Attendance at church and the wearing of one's best clothes was the order of the day, so there could be no running wild in the garden or any other sort of boisterous activity. Neither did Faith sew at her embroidery or do her knitting, although her fingers sometimes itched to get at the needles. She knew the restrictions stemmed from God's commandment that no work should be done on the Sabbath day; a commandment that was broken in the majority of households with the cooking of a huge Sunday dinner. But that, for some strange reason, seemed to be overlooked.

Together, Hetty and Faith washed and dried the

tea things, as it was Mrs Baker's half day off, and then they sat together in the lounge, each nursing another cup and saucer. Faith believed it was easier to chat over a cup of tea.

'You are looking well, Hetty,' she began. 'You have quite a radiance about you just lately. I can't help but notice it.'

Hetty smiled as Faith looked at her quizzically. 'Are you trying to ask me something?' she enquired.

'Yes...' Faith nodded. 'As a matter of fact, I am... You do have something to tell me, don't you, Hetty dear. Something that you may not be able to keep to yourself for very much longer?'

'Yes...' replied Hetty. 'I am expecting a baby. But I don't know how you have guessed. I didn't think I was showing at all yet.'

'No, you are not, apart from being a little fuller in the face. But there's just something about the way you look. I am a mother myself and one learns to recognise the signs.'

'Yes...I see. I've been to see a doctor and it's due at Christmas time... It is Samuel's baby, as you have probably guessed.' Hetty was staring down at her feet and not looking at Faith. 'He doesn't know. I haven't told him and I don't intend to, not yet anyway. We are not seeing one another now. It was a mutual decision for us to part. And I don't expect anything from him.' She looked up then at Faith.

'I am sorry, Faith,' she continued. 'I realise that this must be an embarrassment to you and William.

And you must not blame Samuel, not entirely. I know I have behaved foolishly and recklessly. And now...I must suffer the consequences.'

'You seem quite calm about it all, my dear,' said Faith. 'But then I suppose you have had time, haven't you, to come to terms with the idea? And I know that you are a very sensible young woman, in spite of what has happened. What do you intend to do? Have you decided?'

'I shall have the baby, and keep him...or her,' replied Hetty. 'There is no question about that. I am twenty-seven years old and well able to take care of myself, and a child. Tongues may wag, but I think I am strong enough to withstand that. I know that you and William may be disappointed with me, but I know you won't disown me, will you?' There was a slight twinkle in her eye as she smiled at Faith.

'No, indeed we won't,' said Faith. 'William knows, by the way. I confided in him about what I believed had happened. He went off the deep end as you can imagine, calling Samuel all the names under the sun, until he realised that it was actually a case of the pot calling the kettle black!'

Hetty gave a wry smile. 'Yes, I've thought of that too. Poor William! But the circumstances are different. I have a home and a job, for the moment, and I am not penniless. My mother – Bella, I mean – had no choice but to let me be adopted, but that is the last thing I would want to do. And now that I've got used to the idea, I don't mind at all...

Maddy knows, by the way,' she added. 'I was quite upset at first and I had to tell someone. Maddy happened to be there, and she was a great support to me.'

'Yes, Maddy's a grand girl,' agreed Faith. 'I have been very blessed with my family, and with William's children, including you, my dear. But I am concerned about Samuel. He has behaved foolishly and selfishly, in spite of you saying that he is not entirely to blame. He will have to know about it, won't he? He is responsible for what has happened and he should be there for you, financially, if not in any other way.'

'I wouldn't want to marry him, even if he were to offer,' said Hetty. 'I know now that we are not right for one another. But I fell for his charm. He is a very personable young man,' she smiled.

'But he is not reliable,' said Faith. 'No, I would not want to see you married to Samuel, but he is not going to escape scot-free. William and I will see to that.'

'Leave it a while, please,' said Hetty. 'We don't see him very often, do we? Maybe the next time he visits Scarborough we could break the news to him. Do you know…it has probably never even entered his head that I might be expecting his child.'

A few day's later Bertram Lucas came into the office where Hetty was working, to invite her, as he had promised, to accompany him to one of the evening Pierrot shows. She had been expecting him and she knew that she must agree to go with him. And then…well, she supposed she would be obliged to tell him that she could not go out with him again, always supposing that he wanted to do so, of course. But she guessed that he might want to continue their friendship. They had made friends so readily at Patrick and Katy's wedding.

'How about tonight?' he asked. 'No time like the present, unless you are doing something else?'

'No, I have no other plans,' Hetty told him. 'It will be good to go out for a change. I haven't been out anywhere for a while.'

'No, of course not. I waited a while as it didn't seem right to ask you so soon after Mr Moon's death. You don't think that it's still…too soon?' He looked at her a trifle anxiously.

'No, not at all,' she smiled. 'Grandad Isaac would have said, "Off you go, lass, and enjoy yerself…" I can almost hear him saying it now. It was a shock to us all with it happening so suddenly, but in another way we are all quite used to it, being surrounded by…all this sort of thing every day.' She gestured towards the vases and urns on display on the shelves, the purple drapes at the windows, and an eye-catching arrangement of flowers: lilies, irises, early chrysanthemums and carnations in funereal colours of white, purple and mauve.

Bertram nodded. 'Yes, it's a real family business, isn't it? Patrick was telling me that Katy has started to work here as well.'

'Yes, Katy does a little of everything as well as looking after their home. She helps me in the office two afternoons a week, she serves in the shop sometimes, and she has even offered to go out on jobs with Patrick and William.'

'Laying-out jobs, you mean?'

'Yes, that's right. It is something that Faith has never done – and I can't say I blame her – although William's first wife used to help him. Katy's a very down-to-earth sort of girl. She will be a great asset to the firm.'

'Patrick has told me a little of your family history,' said Bertram. 'I hadn't realised that Faith was not his mother. And he explained to me that you are his half-sister, and Maddy's, of course.'

'Yes, we're an odd bunch,' Hetty laughed, 'and we don't harbour any secrets about what has happened in the past. It's all a long time ago.' And destined to become even odder, she mused. Her forthcoming child, by some quirk of Fate, would be a grandchild to both William and Faith, but not in the usual way. And it would not be possible to keep it a secret for very much longer.

'The show starts at half past six,' said Bertram, 'so I will call for you at six o'clock, shall I? We want to get a seat near to the front.'

'Yes, so we do,' agreed Hetty. 'But that should be no problem; I'm sure Maddy will be only too pleased to reserve seats for us.'

She told him that she would remain on the

premises as it was too far for her to go home to South Bay and back again. She had a flat in an avenue off the Esplanade, near to where William and his family lived. It was a good distance from her place of work; she sometimes shared a cab with William and Faith, or else she cycled. It occurred to her that she might not be able to ride her bicycle for very much longer.

Hetty treated herself to a fish and chip lunch and ate the sandwiches she had brought with her for her tea. She would have to wear her working clothes to go out in the evening, but it would not matter. Her grey dress with the white collar and cuffs was smart enough to wear at any time. She always dressed smartly, but soberly, as the nature of her job required. Besides, she was in mourning at the moment. The bright colours that she loved, the dresses of red, royal blue and emerald green that hung in her wardrobe would have to stay there for a while. This was a trait handed down to her from her real mother, she supposed. Bella had loved bold colours, the gaudier the better.

The cult of mourning, at its height during the reign of Queen Victoria and particularly after the death of Albert, the Prince Consort, had eased off a little now. Hetty supposed she must wear her more sombre clothing for at least three months, and after that time, she realised with a jolt, they would no longer fit her.

Maddy, slipping out to her father's workshop at

lunchtime, had been told that Hetty and Bertram would be in the audience that evening. She had reserved them seats on the front row and they settled down to study the programme. It was a slightly larger programme this year with a touch of red as well as the usual black and white printing, and with a photograph of some of the Pierrots on the cover. It cost threepence instead of the penny of previous years.

'Their costs are continually rising, according to Maddy,' Hetty told Bertram. 'But I think they are having a pretty good season.'

'I could take some photographs for them at a reasonable rate,' said Bertram, studying the one on the cover. 'I see Maddy is in this one, but I don't know any of the others.'

'They have several new members now,' said Hetty, 'but I don't think they have renewed their photographs recently. The original ones were taken by Bamforth's in Huddersfield, but several of the old troupe from that time have left now.'

'Yes...' Bertram was thoughtful. 'I might be able to do them a good turn, as well as myself. It would be quite an innovation, wouldn't it, to have pictures of Uncle Percy's Pierrots in my window? A good advertisement for them and for me as well... And I haven't forgotten that I asked you if you would agree to model for me.' He turned to look at Hetty with a question in his eyes. 'I still haven't had an answer.'

'Oh, I don't know; I'll think about it,' she said evasively, which was what she had said before. There was no more time to talk about it as Letty, the pianist, struck up with the opening chords of 'Here we are again', and the Pierrots all ran onto the stage.

It was a delightful show, they both agreed, colourful and amusing, with a wide variety of acts; entertainment at its best, the sort that all ages and all strata of society could enjoy.

'I haven't heard Maddy sing before,' said Bertram at the interval. 'I was almost moved to tears by "Scarborough Fair".'

'Oh, that's her *pièce de résistance*,' Hetty told him. 'I expect she sang it specially because we are here. It always goes down well with the audience. I believe it was the very first song she sang for the Pierrots.'

'I'm not surprised that William is so proud of her,' observed Bertram. 'Does she have a boyfriend? Anyone special, I mean? I should imagine she has a lot of admirers.'

'Well, there was someone,' said Hetty, 'but it all came to an end a while ago. She was badly let down and I know she was quite broken-hearted for a while. She tried not to show it, being on the stage and having to perform every day, but it was hard for her. It's quite a long story…'

'She's only young though, surely?'

'Yes, she's eighteen. But not too young to have

457

thought she was very much in love. Anyway, she appears to be getting over it quite well now. I have an inkling, and so has Jessie, that she might be getting friendly with Freddie Nicholls, the conjurer we just saw performing. To my mind, he would be far more suitable for her than...the other one would have been. But, as you say, she's still very young.'

After the show Bertram invited her, though a little diffidently, as if he were afraid she might say no, to his flat above the shop premises. Once again, she felt it would be ill-mannered of her to refuse. There was no suggestion in his behaviour that he was offering her anything other than friendship. This young man was as different from Samuel as it was possible to be.

She enjoyed his hospitality; the freshly brewed coffee and shortbread biscuits, shop bought, but Huntley and Palmer's best. It was clear from his tidy living quarters and the immaculate state of his kitchen that he was well able to look after himself. She liked him a lot. He was serious minded without being stuffy. She listened intently, without any feeling of boredom, as he told her how his interest in photography had developed from owning a simple Kodak fixed-focus camera as a lad, to the time when he decided to take a college course and make a career of what had been his hobby.

Almost without realising she was doing so Hetty agreed to pose as a model for him, on the following Wednesday afternoon, when it was half-day closing at the Moon family shop and office.

'So nobody is allowed to die, I take it, on Wednesday afternoon?' said Bertram, quite seriously. He had a dry sense of humour. He did not laugh easily but could find droll amusement in some of the most serious circumstances.

Hetty smiled. 'There is a telephone in William's workshop, and there is always one of the men there to take the messages. Wednesday afternoon then. What do you want me to wear?'

'Have you a white dress? Or one that is pale-coloured? That would show up well and be a contrast to your dark hair. And holding a book in your hands…or a bunch of flowers…' He looked at her contemplatively. 'I haven't quite decided yet.'

'I shall leave it in your expert hands,' said Hetty. 'And now it's time I was getting back home.'

He went down to the street with her and hailed a passing cab. He shook hands with her formally, thanking her for a most enjoyable evening. She smiled to herself, reflecting again that he and Samuel were poles apart.

As Wednesday afternoon approached she made up her mind that she would tell him the truth. She would tell him that she hoped they would be able to continue as friendly acquaintances, but that it would not be wise for them to spend any time alone together.

She decided to wear her pale lilac dress of silk-chiffon. It had caught her eye several weeks ago, displayed on a model in Moon's Modes and she had made up her mind at once that she wanted to buy it. She was not usually given to such impulsive behaviour or to spending so much money on herself, but when Faith and Muriel Phipps both said that it suited her and fitted as though it had been made for her, she knew that she could not resist.

Fortunately the colour was one that was suitable for mourning wear; but it was definitely a 'best dress', one that could only be worn on special occasions. She had worn it at the party which had been held to celebrate the eighteenth birthdays of both Maddy and Jessie. This had been a grand occasion on a Sunday evening – Maddy's only free day – when William had booked a private room at the Crown Hotel, where they had enjoyed an evening dinner, for the family and a few special friends.

Hetty could not foresee that there would be many more such special occasions in the coming months; besides, it was doubtful that the dress would fit her for very much longer. The silk cummerbund was already feeling a little tight.

She posed, at Bertram's request, with her hands holding a leather-bound book, which she hoped would disguise any sign of a bulge at her midriff. It was a copy of *The Woman in White* by Wilkie Collins which, Bertram told her, was one of his favourite books; an intriguing mystery that Hetty, too, had enjoyed. She was glad he had not chosen *a&b*

to photograph her with a Bible in her hands, which was a popular pose with photographers. That would have seemed too pious.

He took several shots, full-face views, profiles and half-profiles, dodging in and out of the black curtain to his camera resting on the tripod. He then exchanged the book for a small bouquet of flowers: roses and sweet peas, several of which exactly matched the colour of her dress, which would make no difference, of course, because the photographs would be reproduced in sepia tones.

'Thank you for being so patient,' he said when, after more than half an hour, he had completed the sitting to his satisfaction. 'Now, I think we deserve a cup of tea.'

He led her from the studio to the living room, where he had entertained her the previous week. Whilst he made the tea, which he insisted on doing by himself, she looked around the living quarters, which Bertram had clearly made his own. She had noticed before that the room was tidy, but it was homely and comfortable too.

There was not an abundance of furniture, only such as was required for a young man living on his own. A small oak table and two dining chairs; two armchairs covered in beige moquette, enlivened with cushions in a bold William Morris design of green and blue leaves; matching curtains hung at the windows and the tiles on the fireplace were of a similar design. There was a well-filled bookcase and

Hetty, stooping to read the titles, noticed the works of Conan Doyle, Oscar Wilde and Sir Walter Scott, as well as the most popular books by Charles Dickens and the Brontë sisters. His taste in literature appeared to be the same as hers, she realised.

On a low table, and seeming to dominate the room, was a gramophone with a nickel-plated horn resembling the bell-like morning glory flower. The records were in a cabinet at the side, stacked on their ends, but she decided it would be too nosey to thumb through them. She remarked on the gramophone, though, as they drank their tea and nibbled at chocolate biscuits.

'Yes, that's one of my latest acquisitions,' Bertram told her. 'And I'm gradually building up my stock of records. We'll listen to one now, if you would like to?'

'Yes, I would,' she agreed.

'So what would you like to hear? I have quite a variety of music.'

'Oh, you choose the record,' she said. 'I'm afraid I don't know a great deal about music. William and Faith have a gramophone similar to yours but with a brass horn. William likes to listen to brass band music, and they like Gilbert and Sullivan, and music hall songs, and some of the more classical songs from operas. But I know there must be all kinds of music that I've never heard.'

'Nor had any of us until these came on the scene,'

said Bertram. 'The gramophone is a wonderful invention, on a par with the camera. And I guess we'll see more and more amazing inventions as this century goes on.'

Hetty nodded. 'I've heard of some of the composers of long ago. Beethoven and Mozart – wasn't he supposed to be a boy genius? – and Chopin and Schubert, but I've heard hardly any of their music. I've been to a few concerts here, at the Spa Pavilion, and when I lived up in the Newcastle area, but apart from that I'm not very knowledgeable.'

'Then we'll listen to some Chopin,' said Bertram. He took out the record from its paper cover with a hole in the centre. The label depicted a fox terrier listening to a horn gramophone, with the words 'His Master's Voice' written below, the name of the record company. He wound up the gramophone with the handle at the side and carefully placed the needle at the outside edge of the record. They listened in a companionable silence to a Chopin polonaise, followed by a more gentle waltz and a short étude.

'That was lovely,' exclaimed Hetty. 'It's so soothing, isn't it, to sit and listen to music?'

'Yes, it's what I enjoy doing at the end of a busy day,' agreed Bertram. 'And, speaking of the Spa...' He hesitated and Hetty looked enquiringly at him. 'You mentioned you had been to concerts there. Well, I've got two tickets for a concert there on

463

Saturday night, a light orchestra, and I wondered if you would like to come with me?'

He paused, whilst she continued to look at him, unsurely and a trifle anxiously. She had intended to tell him today about her condition, but there had not been an opportunity yet, and now…it would be so hurtful to refuse.

'Please say you will go with me, Hetty,' he said, and she could not resist the look of hopefulness in his eyes.

'Yes, of course I will, Bertram,' she answered. 'It is very kind of you to ask me.'

Hetty knew that she wanted to go with him. It was just the sort of entertainment that she enjoyed and she had not been to a concert for ages. And she could tell that he enjoyed her company, but she realised it would not be fair to him to keep on seeing him and allowing him to become more fond of her. She guessed that this was happening; she had known enough young men to recognise the signs. As for herself, she liked Bertram a lot, but she could not allow herself to think of what might have been. She had ruined her chances of such a friendship, for the time being at least, and she had to face up to reality. But it could do no harm to go with him just this once, she persuaded herself. Anyway, he might not have bought the tickets; they might be complimentary ones from a grateful client; she knew that such favours were handed out for all kinds of dramatic and musical performances.

The Spa Pavilion was not far from where she lived, on the Prince of Wales Terrace which led off the Esplanade, and so she had arranged to meet Bertram at the entrance to the Spa. He took hold of her hands as he greeted her and she could see from the delight in his eyes that he was very pleased to see her.

It was a local orchestra that was performing, with a solo pianist, cellist and two singers, a soprano and a tenor. The programme of light classical music was a delight to listen to. Overtures from *The Yeoman of the Guard* and *William Tell*; Strauss waltzes and Mozart's 'Eine Kleine Nachtmusik'; a Chopin prelude played brilliantly on the piano, and Bach's haunting cello composition, 'Air on a G-String'. The singers performed solo items, and then together they ended with the love duet from *La Bohème*.

Hetty knew that the melodies would linger in her mind for a long time to come, and she was sorry, indeed, for the news that she knew she must soon impart to Bertram. It had been a pleasure to be with him that evening and she knew that he felt the same. As her home was only five minutes' walk away she invited him back, ostensibly for a cup of tea.

'You are very quiet,' he remarked, when they had walked up the steep slope and the steps that led from the Spa to the higher promenade.

'I'm getting my breath back after the stiff climb,'

she told him, which was partly true. It was her condition, she supposed, that had made her notice the steepness of the incline more that evening but, also, her mind was on the forthcoming revelation she had to make to him.

She decided not to delay it any longer. When they were seated in her living room she told him that she would make some tea in a little while, but first of all there was something that she must say to him.

'It sounds ominous,' said Bertram. He was smiling at her unsurely, no doubt aware of her serious expression.

'Yes, I'm afraid it is, rather,' she replied. 'That is why I have been quiet tonight... I really have enjoyed the concert,' she went on, 'and I'm so pleased you asked me to go with you. But that must be the last time. I'm afraid that I won't be able to go on seeing you.'

He shook his head ruefully. 'I thought it was too good to be true, you agreeing to go out with me. I couldn't believe my luck at first, but now I was beginning to think that we might...well, that we might go on seeing one another, that we might even have a future together. But it isn't to be; I can see that. What is it, Hetty? Is there someone else, or is it that...you don't like me enough?'

Hetty shook her head vigorously. 'No...no!' she cried, with sorrow and regret in her voice. 'There is nobody else, at least, not in the way you mean it. And I do like you very much, Bertram. But the truth is – and I'm sorry I didn't tell you before – the truth is… I have behaved very foolishly; I'm afraid I'm expecting a child.'

He stared at her. He looked dumbfounded, as well he might, but not shocked or horrified. 'You said…there was no one else,' he faltered. 'You mean…you are not going to marry him?'

'No, that is not a possibility. He doesn't know yet, and even if he did it would make no difference. It is all over between us. I told you, I behaved foolishly and now I have to face the consequences. I'm sorry if I have shocked you, or perhaps hurt or disappointed you a little, Bertram. But you haven't known me for very long, have you?' She smiled sadly at him.

He did not answer straight away; he just continued to look at her, his eyes full of concern. Eventually he said, 'I have known you long enough, Hetty, to realise that I am forming a deep attachment to you. I admire you greatly and – no – of course I am not shocked by what you have told me…'

He paused, before going on a little hesitantly, 'As you no doubt realise, I am a little unsure of myself where women are concerned. I don't find it easy to form friendships with them. There was a young lady once; I even asked her to marry me…but I think I was not dashing or exciting enough for her. She very soon found somebody else. But with you…I thought we might have something worthwhile. I still think so, Hetty.' He looked at her in silence for several seconds, then, 'I would very much like to go on seeing you,' he said.

'In spite of...everything?' she asked. 'I find that hard to understand. Everyone will soon know...about me, and people will talk.'

'I shouldn't imagine you are the sort of person to worry much about what people think, are you?' he smiled. 'And I am not... Will you go on seeing me, Hetty? Just as friends, maybe, for the moment, if that is what you want?'

'Yes, thank you,' she replied humbly. 'I am certainly in need of a good friend like you. Come and sit next to me, Bertram.' She patted the seat next to her on the settee. 'You seem so far away.'

He sat down next to her; she took hold of his hand then leant across and kissed his cheek. 'You don't know how much that means to me, Bertram, to know that I still have your friendship; and that is all I expect from you. I will tell you another time about my circumstances. It is only fair that you should know.'

He turned towards her and, holding her shoulders, he kissed her gently on the lips, just once, then drew away.

'We will take things steadily, Hetty,' he said. 'I am that sort of a person. But I would be very pleased to think that you might become a part of my life. I knew when I met you that I might have found the part that was missing. Now...what about that cup of tea you promised me?'

Chapter Twenty-Five

Ahappy occasion in mid-August was the marriage of Susannah Brown and Frank Morrison; they had been waiting a while for the divorce decree to be made absolute. It was, of necessity, a register office wedding, and it took place at the Scarborough office on a Saturday, when the Pierrots had no afternoon performance. Percy and Letty Morgan acted as witnesses, and apart from Pete and Nancy Pritchard, who had been friends of the couple for many years, there were no others there to watch the simple ceremony.

The real celebration took place on the Sunday evening at the lodgings of Susannah and Frank and, indeed, several more of the troupe, in Castle Road. Mrs Ada Armstrong had put on a sumptuous spread and all the Pierrots, plus other friends and relations, were there to share it. Susannah's sister and brother-in-law and their children from Halifax were there, as were Frank's brother and his wife and his grown-up son and daughter from York.

One guest who was thrilled to be there was Emily Stringer, the one-time admirer of Benjy. She had met Maddy a few times through Louisa Montague who had long been a friend of the Moon family; and now she was delighted to meet all the other members of the Pierrot troupe whom she had so far known only in their stage personae. When Susannah introduced her as the lady who helped to make their costumes they all made a great fuss of her.

'I had quite a big hand in the making of yours,' she told Jeremy and Dora. 'And I do so enjoy your acts. Your lovely singing, my dear and those...characters of yours.' She turned to Jeremy. 'I don't like to call them dummies because you make them seem so much like real people; that Tommy the Toff and Belinda. They have me in fits of laughter no matter how many times I see them.'

'I'm so pleased you like them,' said Jeremy, putting his arm round his girlfriend, Dora. 'We lap up praise, don't we, darling? It's what makes it all worthwhile.'

'But we're constantly trying to improve and add a bit of variety to our acts, aren't we, Jeremy love?' said Dora. 'For our own sake as well as for the audiences. They would soon notice if we started to get stale.'

Emily smiled at them. 'So you two...you're...er... sweethearts, are you?' They looked at one another, laughing at the old-fashioned turn of phrase. 'Oh...pardon me; I'm sorry,' said Emily. 'I shouldn't have been so forward. But you look so...nice and right together.'

'Yes,' replied Jeremy. He planted a kiss on Dora's cheek. 'Dora's my girlfriend. We met when we came for our auditions and we decided that we liked one another.'

'But Percy took Jeremy on and not me at first,' said Dora. 'Then when Barney and Benjy split up for a while Percy asked me if I'd be Benjy's partner. That's how I got into the Pierrots, but Barney's back now, of course.'

'Yes...yes, I see,' replied Emily, feeling a little flustered and hoping that her cheeks were not turning pink. She really had got over all that silly nonsense now. 'Ah... Maddy!' she cried with some relief when that young lady came and joined the little group. 'I'm just getting to know some of your friends. And this is Freddie, the clever young conjuror, isn't it?' she trilled, nodding towards the young man at Maddy's side.'

Emily noticed that Freddie was holding Maddy's elbow, indicating subtly that the two of them were together. But she decided not to comment on the fact, as she had just done with Dora and Jeremy. They hadn't seemed to mind, but they had laughed as though she had said something amusing. Moreover, Emily knew that poor little Maddy had recently been 'let down in love', as Louisa Montague had termed it. Louisa was not exactly a gossip, but she did like to know what was going on, as did Emily. And Louisa was always interested in the goings-on in the Moon family and was very fond of Maddy. It certainly looked, to Emily, as though the lass might be well on the way to falling in love again, judging by the looks that she and Freddie were exchanging.

'Yes, this is Freddie,' replied Maddy. 'Freddie, this is Emily. She works for Miss Montague. Tell him how much you enjoy his conjuring tricks, Emily. You've told me often enough, haven't you?'

'Oh yes, I do!' enthused Emily. 'That rabbit popping out of the hat!' She clasped her hands together in excitement, like a small girl. 'That is so clever. And all those tiny little boxes that we think are empty. Well, they are; you can see right through them; and then you bring out all those yards and yards of coloured silks. I know it's all an illusion, isn't it?' She nodded sagely. 'The hand deceiving the eye, but I'm blessed if I know how you do it.'

'Aha! That would be telling, wouldn't it?' laughed Freddie. 'As you say, an optical illusion. I keep trying to persuade Maddy to do the trick with the lady in the box; you know, where the conjuror plunges a sword into it and then the lady steps out unharmed. But I don't think she trusts me enough, not yet!' He smiled at Maddy, giving her a gentle hug.

'Ooh no! I should think not,' exclaimed Emily. 'I saw that done once in a theatre in York and I was too scared to look. Don't you do it, Maddy love!'

'Actually, I think he's teasing,' said Maddy. 'Anyway, I'm not a contortionist. Those girls must be made of india-rubber. That's how they do it, you know, by squeezing themselves into a tiny space. By the way, Freddie, Emily is the lady who made your Pierrot costume.'

'Well then, I'm even more delighted to meet you,' said Freddie. 'This is my first season as a Pierrot, as you know, and the costume makes me feel that I really belong.' He smiled at Emily and then again at Maddy.

What a lovely young couple, mused Emily. She had never known the joy of young love and now…well, she was far too old for anything like that, but she was happier than she had ever been in her life. Her midlife silliness, as she termed it to herself, was over. There was deep satisfaction to be found in a job well done, interesting people to meet every day, good friends such as Louisa and Faith, and the warmth and peace of her own home at the end of each day.

'She's a nice old lady,' Freddie remarked to Maddy when they had wandered away from the little group. Emily was now talking animatedly to Pete and Nancy and her high colour showed how much she was enjoying the evening.

'Not so much of the old,' laughed Maddy. 'I don't think Emily would be very pleased to hear you say that. I doubt if she's much older than Faith, but I agree that she seems so. She's a friend of Susannah. I know that seems odd, too, but she befriended her when she was upset about something and feeling lonely. She's like that, of course, is Susannah; a real friend in times of need.' Susannah had confided in Maddy about Emily's secret little passion, but Maddy had no intention of telling anyone else, not even Freddie.

'It's getting very warm in here,' said Freddie. 'Shall we go out for a stroll before it gets dark? I don't suppose anyone will miss us.'

'Yes, I'll just get my coat,' agreed Maddy.

They strolled up Castle Road, past St Mary's church and on to the path that led round the castle ruins. Dusk was starting to fall after a day of glorious sunshine. Through the trees they glimpsed, far below, the twinkling lights around the harbour, the sweep of the South Bay and the four-square bulk of the Grand Hotel. Freddie had been holding Maddy's arm; and now he put both arms around her and held her close to him. He lowered his face to hers and gently kissed her lips.

As they drew apart he whispered, 'Maddy, I think it's time now that I asked you something... Will you start going out with me; properly, I mean, as my girlfriend? It's not still...too soon, is it?'

'No, Freddie,' she answered with certainty. 'It's not too soon...and of course I will.'

He kissed her again, more firmly, and this time she responded eagerly, savouring the rapture of this first true lover's kiss.

Over the last few weeks they had gone out together more frequently, for supper or for walks, as they were doing now. He had kissed her, but only in a friendly fashion, as though he were loath to spoil the fragile nature of their friendship. Many in the company believed them to be 'going out together', but Maddy had known that he was still waiting; waiting until such time as he was sure – or almost sure – that she had quite got over Daniel. Maddy knew now that she had and that it was time for her to move on.

'Come along; let's get back before it goes dark,' she said. 'We must be there for the last hour of the wedding party.'

'Last hour?' queried Freddie. 'It looked to me as though they would keep on going till the early hours!'

Susannah, who had noticed them going out, was aware, too, of their reappearance. She looked at Maddy questioningly and made a thumbs-up sign. Her young friend smiled back and gave a little nod. About time, thought Susannah. Freddie still confided in her about his feelings, and she had guessed that he had made up his mind to speak to Maddy. Not to ask her to marry him or even to get engaged; she was still far too young to be thinking of that. But Susannah knew that Freddie needed to know that Maddy was his girlfriend, and his alone.

Freddie had visited Maddy's family home several times whilst they had been performing in Scarborough. William and Faith liked the young man very much, considering him to be far more suitable for Maddy than her previous boyfriend. They hoped, though, that there would be no serious courtship on the near horizon; Maddy was too young to be thinking of marriage.

As the summer progressed, through August and into early September, they noticed a subtle difference in Maddy's and Freddie's relationship. They seemed more 'together' in every sense. The looks they exchanged were more affectionate, and they sometimes spent the whole of Sunday together, enjoying a family dinner at the Moons' home and then setting off with a picnic tea for a long cycle ride; William had a spare bicycle for Freddie to borrow.

'I reckon those two are doing a bit o' courting,' William remarked to his wife.

'Aye, I reckon you're right, Will,' replied Faith, gently imitating his native accent and turn of phrase. 'But it's only to be expected, surely? They spend a lot of time together with the troupe, and they'll have got to know one another quite well by now.'

'Aye, and that's what worries me,' said William. 'They'll be off on their travels again soon, come the end of September, and we'll not have the foggiest idea what they're getting up to.'

'But we have to trust them, William. Freddie's a sensible young man, and Maddy's been brought up to know right from wrong.'

'Aye...and so was Hetty; so was Samuel; and

look what happened there. And that's another problem that'll have to be sorted out afore long,' William sighed.

'I don't think you can compare Freddie with Samuel,' remarked Faith. 'Samuel is my own son, but I believe that Freddie is far more reliable.'

'Yes, I agree with you, my dear...but I think I shall have a word, on the quiet, like, the next time I see him – Freddie, I mean.'

'Now, you mustn't go embarrassing them, Will, or putting ideas into their heads.'

William chuckled. 'I doubt that I'll be telling them anything they've not thought of already! Don't worry, Faith. I'll have a chat to Freddie on his own.'

He spoke with him the following Sunday when Freddie was returning his borrowed bicycle to the garden shed.

'I can't help noticing,' William began, 'that you and my lass have got more friendly just lately.'

'So we have, Mr Moon,' replied Freddie. He still addressed him formally, despite having been invited to call him William, which was to the lad's credit, William supposed. 'I am very fond of Maddy,' he went on. 'I waited a while before asking her to go out with me – as a girlfriend, that is – because I knew she was still quite upset about her previous friendship.'

'Aye, that was a rum do and no mistake,' observed William. 'Not that there was owt wrong with the lad. But it would never have done, him being a Catholic an' all. Still, that's all water under the bridge, now...'

Freddie nodded. 'I know you must feel concerned, especially when your daughter is away from home. But I want you to know, sir, that I will take the greatest care of Maddy. I love her and I respect her...and she will come to no harm with me. I give you my word on that.'

William grasped hold of his arm. 'It means a great deal to me to hear you say that, my lad. She's still very young, you know, but I feel I can trust her to your care. Thanks, Freddie lad...' He put his hand to his head as a thought suddenly struck him. 'I tell you what; why don't you take this old bicycle of mine and use it whilst you're here? I can't imagine why I didn't think of it before. It's a fair step back to your digs, and I doubt if I shall be using it much more...

'To be quite honest, Freddie,' he continued as they made their way up the garden path and back to the house, 'I'm thinking of buying a motor car.'

'Gosh! Are you really, Mr Moon?'

'Aye; just for our own use; the family, I mean, not the firm. I reckon it'll be a few years yet before we have motor-driven hearses.' He gave a sad little laugh. 'My father – God rest his soul – the very idea of them was like a red rag to a bull. But he might not have minded a family motor quite as much...'

* * *

A letter from Samuel that arrived a few days later announced to William and Faith that he would be coming to stay with them the following weekend, arriving on Friday and returning to Leeds on Sunday. It would be his last free weekend before the commencement of the autumn term at university. He had been busy all through the summer vacation on field trips – climbing and potholing and excavating in the Welsh mountains – and he had been over to France for a few days with a couple more of the young lecturers.

'Hmm…tricky,' observed William as they sat at the breakfast table, just the two of them left there, lingering over their tea and coffee. 'But we knew this would happen eventually, and Hetty can't go on hiding her condition for ever.'

'I don't think she wants to hide it,' replied Faith. 'But she's still adamant that it's a closed book as far as she and Samuel are concerned. But as you say, my dear, he will have to know, and it had better be this weekend, hadn't it?'

'Yes…' William shook his head thoughtfully. 'D'you know, I can't imagine what his reaction will be. And now, of course, that young photographer has come on the scene. He certainly seems very fond of Hetty.'

'Yes, so he is. She told me how considerate he has been towards her, and he insisted that he wanted to go on seeing her and taking her out. I couldn't say whether or not they have an…understanding;

whether they intend to get married.'

'It's not his child though, is it?' said William. 'He must be a remarkable young man to even think of taking on a responsibility like that.'

'That's not the issue, though, at the moment, is it?' said Faith. 'We must make sure that Hetty is here on Friday, and that we leave them alone together for a while.'

'Yes, I suppose we'll have to,' agreed William. 'I'll give Hetty the afternoon off; Katy can stand in for her for a few hours. Samuel doesn't say what time his train gets in, does he?'

'No, except that he'll be here in the afternoon. It's always "expect me when you see me" with Samuel. I feel quite anxious when I think about it all,' said Faith. 'But really, it's their business, isn't it, not ours, and they're quite old enough to sort it out for themselves.'

When Samuel arrived, however, it was not by train. He made his appearance on the roadside of Victoria Avenue in a Fort T two-seater motor car. Faith had heard the sound of the engine and had dashed to the door ahead of Mrs Baker. Trust that son of mine to steal a march on William, she thought. Her husband was full of excited plans at the moment about purchasing their first motor car, and although she was not quite as enthusiastic as he was, she had shown keen interest in what he was telling her. And now Samuel had gone and spoilt it all.

'Hello, Mother,' he said affably, meeting her

halfway up the garden path. He put his leather-gauntleted hands on her shoulders, kissing her on both cheeks. 'How d'you like her?' he grinned, gesturing with his thumb. 'She's a grand little mover. I'll take you for a spin later, if you like.'

'Well, we'll see about that, dear,' she replied. She frowned a little. 'How have you managed to afford that?' She was sure that the starting salary of a very junior university lecturer could not be all that high.

'Oh, ways and means, you know,' he answered, tapping his nose. 'Actually…I might as well tell you; Father helped me out. It was his idea really. They have a Renault, a much bigger model than mine, of course. He persuaded me that I must be able to drive in today's world.'

'Yes…I see,' replied Faith. She was not much interested in her former husband's doings, although she knew that Samuel saw him quite regularly. She did not say, as she might have done, that William, also, would soon be getting a motor car. That might seem too much like a retaliatory comment.

She took a deep breath. 'Hetty is here,' she said. 'She's got the afternoon off work and she's staying for a meal with us. William is at work, of course, but we'll all be here later, all except Maddy, that is. It's her last week with the Pierrots.' She realised she was gabbling rather, so she smiled and opened the door to the lounge.

'Here is Hetty, see. You go and have a chat to her whilst I make a pot of tea.'

'Mother! We're not...I mean, I don't see her anymore,' whispered Samuel, a little agitatedly.

'No, I realise that, dear. But it doesn't mean you can't talk to her, does it?' She disappeared quickly in the direction of the kitchen.

Hetty stood up as he entered the room. He stepped forward, about to kiss her on the cheek in a friendly manner. Then he drew back. Her high-waisted dress of lilac and white striped cotton could not disguise – nor did it attempt to – the fact that she was pregnant; several months so, it appeared. Samuel gasped. 'Hetty...!' He looked her up and down, but, she had to admit to herself, not disgustedly or with any annoyance. He just looked stunned, and then a little dismayed. 'Is it...?' he asked.

Hetty nodded her head. 'Yes...it's your baby, Samuel. It is due at Christmas.' She sat down again on the nearest chair and Samuel sat opposite her, gripping hold of the chair arms.

'But...that's only just over three months away. Why didn't you tell me?'

'Would it have made any difference, Samuel? We agreed, didn't we, that it would be best if we stopped seeing one another? And...it was the right decision.'

'But you knew...then? When we decided to part company?'

'Yes, I knew. But I had already made up my mind that we were not right for one another. And so had you. I couldn't see that me being pregnant could alter the fact.'

'But...what will you do?'

Hetty smiled. 'I shall have the baby, of course, and then I shall look after him, or her.'

'And...everybody knows, do they?' He gestured around him; the family, she supposed he meant.

'Yes, they know, Samuel. It's inevitable, isn't it? I can't hide it and nor do I want to. I'm not sure what Tommy and Tilly know about it all, but as for everyone else, they are quite used to the idea.'

'So everyone knew but me?'

'Yes...I'm sorry, Samuel, but you haven't been back here for ages and I didn't want to write and tell you. I don't expect you to do anything about it, you see... As a matter of fact, I am seeing a young man. He has been a very good friend to me. Well, actually, he is far more than that. And he wants to marry me.'

Hetty thought she saw – or she might have imagined – a spasm of relief flit across Samuel's face. He closed his eyes for a brief moment, then he said, 'Who is he? Do I know him?'

'He's called Bertram Lucas. He took the photographs at Patrick and Katy's wedding...but you weren't there, were you? And he was at Grandad Isaac's funeral. He has a studio near to William's place of work, and mine, too, of course. That was how I got to know him.'

'Yes, I have heard about him.' Samuel nodded. 'A

very able photographer, I have been told. But…this child is my responsibility. Financially, I mean. I can't expect…'

She was not sure what it was he could not expect, but she guessed his words might be idle ones, spoken on the spur of the moment. She interrupted him. 'As I have said, Samuel, I don't expect anything of you. I want to make that quite clear. It is all over between you and me, just as it was before you knew about…this.'

Hetty was aware of Faith hovering outside the door with a tea tray. 'Come on in, Faith,' she called. 'Samuel and I have had our little chat.'

Samuel had the grace to look a little shamefaced as he took the tray from his mother and placed it on a small table. 'I'm really sorry about all this, Mother,' he said. 'I had no idea. I've just said to Hetty that she should have told me. But she does seem to have everything under control.'

'Yes, so she has,' replied Faith briskly. 'But that is no thanks to you, Samuel. However, we will say no more about it at the moment. Now Hetty…are you going to pour?' She smiled. 'I suppose I should say, "Are you going to be Mother?"'

Chapter Twenty-Six

When Maddy started her autumn tour with the Melody Makers, Daniel, unbeknown to her, was settling into the seminary that would be his home for the next few years. It was in Northumberland and had been built in the mid-nineteenth century, near to the ruins of an Augustinian priory.

There had been some talk of him going to Rome where his tutor, Father Fitzgerald, had studied; but after a great deal of thought, Daniel had opted for Rothburn Priory College. It was situated way up in the Cheviot Hills in a clearing on the banks of the River Coquet, near to where the Romans had once built a camp. Daniel's main reason for spurning the 'Eternal City' was because his mother, after encouraging him throughout his childhood and young adulthood to enter the priesthood, as the time drew nearer, had started to bemoan the fact that Rome was a very long way away. She would miss him. Whenever would she see him? He had told her that the summer months, when the heat in Rome became unbearable, were spent on retreat at a lake resort in the Appian Hills. It seemed as though he might not be able to get home from one year's end to the next.

Rothburn Priory College was nearer, at least it was in the same country, but neither road nor rail transport was all that easily accessible. Daniel realised that this was intentional. Trainee priests were given leave to go home only rarely, and they had to accept this, as should their families, respecting that their loved ones had been called to make and to adhere to this sacrifice. He made up his mind that he would try to settle into his new life as quickly as possible; and as for his mother, he hoped she would gradually get used to his absence, although he had not expected her to be quite so tearful at his departure. Was it not what she had wanted all his life?

As for himself, he had not expected to feel quite so homesick. He had known that the seminary would be spartan – that was the first of the three vows they made, for poverty, chastity and obedience – but he had not imagined quite such stark surroundings. His bedroom – which, fortunately, he had to himself – was more like a cell with stone walls, and there was only an enamel bowl in which to wash. He would be allowed one bath each week, he was informed. No one was allowed to visit him in his room except in the case of illness, and then never alone. The clothes in which he arrived had been taken away from him and in exchange he was given a bundle containing two cassocks, one of a much coarser woollen weave than the other, which he gathered was for winter wear; also two calico shirts and two sets of underwear.

The morning bell rang at five-thirty and the early Mass followed at six o'clock, after which they all gathered in the dining hall for breakfast. He could not complain of the quantity of the food at any of the meals; the vast piles of bread and potatoes, and pasta, such as was eaten by their Italian brethren. There were huge carafes of wine, too, which was a surprise, but the fare, on the whole, was plain and monotonous.

They dined beneath frescoes of the Virgin Mary and innumerable saints. Wherever they looked, indeed, there were reminders of why they were there and of the path they had chosen. In the main chapel Daniel's eyes were constantly drawn to a painting, in allegorical style, of Christ conquering the heathen world. The blood that flowed from his side, hands and feet appeared to be engulfing the whole world and setting fire to England.

He was disturbed by this. Although he was a Roman Catholic, he was English, too. Well, partly Irish, but he had been born in England and he felt that he had a certain loyalty to his native land. He had no desire, personally, to reclaim England for what their tutors called the 'true faith' or Holy Mother Church.

'Don't forget,' Father Crispin told them, 'that many were lured away from the true faith in the dark days of the Reformation. I appreciate that there is more religious tolerance nowadays... nevertheless, we must hold fast to what we believe. There is still a good deal of missionary work to be done...'

Religious tolerance, mused Daniel, when he was alone in his cell bedroom. He had not experienced much of that in his own family; or rather, to be fair, in his mother. A memory of that grand old man, Isaac Moon, flitted across his mind. A staunch Methodist, as he had been since childhood. How he had loved those grand old hymns by one of the most notable dissenters of all time, Charles Wesley. How could one think of Isaac Moon as a heretic, which was how he would be regarded in this place? He had made Daniel most welcome in his home, as had William. A united family, as firm in their beliefs as was Daniel in his.

His thoughts led inevitably to Madeleine, the lovely girl who had brought such joy into his life for such a brief time. But thoughts of her were futile. He had learnt to dismiss them as soon as they appeared; but here in his solitude he found that they would not go away quite so readily.

Daniel missed his family life; his wise and understanding father, his lovable, somewhat childlike brother, and his mother. She had been stubborn and determined to have her own way, but she had loved him; she had always been there, a constant in his life.

He did not particularly like this communal life, nor the regimentation. He was relieved, though, to discover that some of his fellow postulants were of the same mind. They were encouraged to walk everywhere. The gentle countryside of rounded hills and dales was ideal walking country, but they were not allowed outside the college grounds by themselves. On the other hand, neither were they encouraged to form a close friendship with just one other postulant. So they usually walked in threes. Daniel was part of a trio with Father Michael and Father Bernard, which was how they were expected to address one another. All three of them were northerners, Michael O' Riordan from Bradford in Yorkshire, and Bernard Flynn from Darlington, which was not very far away.

On a free afternoon, when they had been at the college for about a month, they went for a walk along the banks of the river. And there, away from listening ears and prying eyes, they allowed themselves the luxury of a gentle moan. They all agreed that they missed their homes and their families.

'Sure, we're told, though, that this is our family now,' said Michael. 'And we're getting more used to them all...aren't we?'

'I just want to be ordinary,' said Bernard. 'You know; do ordinary things; play a game of football and wear normal clothes.'

'Priests aren't ordinary though, are they?' said

Daniel. 'That's what we're always being told. If we want to be ordinary we shouldn't be here. But there's nothing to say we can't play football or cricket. And we only have to wear these silly clothes whilst we're here. When we go home we can wear our normal things, apart from the dog collar... But what I don't like is the solitude. It gets to me when I'm in my room at night, and I sometimes wonder how I could bear to live by myself in one of those gloomy presbyteries.'

They did not talk about the vow of chastity, which would deny them the company of women, except in a very asexual sort of friendship. Nor did they talk about what had led them to take the step that had brought them eventually to Rothburn Priory College. Michael and Bernard were both young men, similar in age to Daniel, both reasonably good-looking and personable. And despite their grumblings they must, at one time, have felt God calling them to His service.

Gradually, Daniel settled down to his new life. Airing his grievances had done him good. He knew now that others felt the same way and this was a great consolation to him.

They were granted a few days' leave at Christmas time, to which Daniel had been looking forward all through the term. The first agony of homesickness had eased quite a lot, however, and he had begun to enjoy the lectures and discussions, the regular attendances at Mass, the music and the mysticism of it all, which had attracted him since boyhood in his own parish churches. But the atmosphere of sanctity and wonder was so much more potent here.

It was good to be home. There was only the immediate family there on Christmas Day, plus Myrtle, Joe's girlfriend; that friendship was clearly progressing very nicely. They attended Mass, of course, where Anna visibly preened herself in front of the other women at having her elder son, the priest in training, at her side. She had burst into tears at first seeing him, tears of happiness, and her joy at having him back in the fold was transparent.

As the time drew near for him to return to college Anna's joy turned to sorrow, as she continually lamented, 'Oh, Daniel...I do wish you hadn't to go back.'

He was perplexed, also somewhat annoyed. 'But, Mammy, you know I have to go back,' he told her. 'And isn't this what you have wanted, all my life?'

'Yes...yes, of course it is,' she replied tearfully. 'I'm just being silly. But I do miss you so much.'

'Take no notice,' said his father. 'She'll get over it. She was terrible when you first went away. I thought she'd have hysterics at one time, going on about how she wanted you back. But there was no point in telling you and upsetting you, son. She calmed down after a while. She'll be all right. I'll take care of her.'

Her parting from him, once again, was tearful,

and she did not go to the station with him as did his father and Joe. 'I'll see you in a few months' time, hopefully,' said Daniel. 'I'm not sure when. Look after Mammy. I'll write as often as I can.'

His mother had brought all this on herself, he pondered, waving goodbye as the train pulled away. There was a grim satisfaction in the thought. She would just have to get used to it. And, strangely, he did not feel half so bad as he had anticipated at the thought of returning to Northumberland.

He was surprised, one morning in mid-January, to be summoned to the study of the college principal, Father Vincent. What have I done wrong? was his immediate thought. A summons usually followed a misdemeanour of some sort. Father Vincent, however, smiled at him and invited him to sit down.

'I am afraid I have some bad news for you, Father Daniel,' he began. 'There is a telegram for you from your home…' Mammy, thought Daniel. He had been worried about her state of health, or, more particularly, her state of mind. But he was wrong.

'It's your father,' said the priest. 'He has had an accident and it sounds as though he is seriously injured. You must go home at once.' He handed Daniel the telegram to read. Daniel understood that the college principal would have had to read it first, when it arrived.

'Please come home,' it read. 'Daddy badly hurt

following accident at work. Love, Mammy.'

'My father is a builder,' he said dazedly. 'I expect he had a fall; he's usually so careful. Will it be all right then...for me to go?'

'Yes, you may go at once. As soon as you can get ready,' said Father Vincent. 'And stay for as long as they need you there.'

He was driven by pony and trap, which was their usual means of transport, to the nearest railway station, which was at Alnwick. Then he started on his long journey back to Blackpool.

It was late evening when he arrived. His mother met him at the door in a paroxysm of grief. 'He's gone, Daniel,' she cried. 'It's too late. Your daddy's...dead, God rest his soul.'

Daniel crossed himself, repeating the words silently: God bless him and keep him... This was dreadful! He felt his tears begin to flow as he put his arms around his mother and drew her close to him, feeling the sobs racking her body.

His brother appeared at his side, his face, also, ravaged with pain. 'Aye, it's a bad do, Dan,' said Joe. 'She's been nearly out of her mind, waiting for you to come home.'

'Come and sit down, Mammy,' said Daniel, leading her into the living room and making her sit down in an easy chair. 'Now, tell me what happened. I must know. And...where is Daddy?'

'He's in hospital,' she managed to say, between the sobs that were still shaking her body. 'They're seeing to…everything. He never came round…after the fall.'

Gradually he learnt that his father had insisted on going to the building site where new houses were being erected, to supervise a rather tricky procedure. The ground was icy after a light fall of snow, but it was vital, or so they said, that the work should be completed that day. Thomas had lost his footing on a high piece of scaffolding and had fallen from the first floor storey level to the ground. His back was broken and, as Anna had said, he never regained consciousness.

She and Joe had stayed with him in the hospital after she had sent the telegram to Daniel, but there had been nothing they could do for him. The doctors had tried, but to no avail. He had died in the late afternoon.

It was a tragic few days, but Anna overcame the worst of her grief with her beloved elder son there at her side. Daniel made a long-distance call to the college and it was confirmed that he could stay as long as it was necessary.

The church was half full to say farewell to Thomas Murphy, who had been a steadfast member of the church and a good friend and workmate to many. His family and colleagues gathered afterwards at the graveside in Layton Cemetery. It was noticed that Anna, with a son on either side of her, was bearing up very well. It had seemed at first as though her grief would consume her, but she was dry-eyed and stoical of face as she scattered the clods of earth on top of the coffin.

Anna and some helpful neighbours had prepared a funeral meal beforehand at the Murphys' home; and the same neighbours were there to welcome them to a warm house with the curtains drawn back, the inevitable cup of tea and a goodly spread of sandwiches, savouries and cakes.

It could not be said that Anna was cheerful, but she was well in control of herself and able to speak of Thomas without dissolving into tears. It was commented upon, afterwards, by her neighbours and friends, that she made constant reference to her son – her elder son, Daniel, who was training to be a priest; they were never allowed to forget that – and what a tower of strength he had been to her over the last few days. They felt sorry for Joe, the younger son, whom they all agreed was a grand lad. He worked jolly hard in the boarding house, and had always done so, whilst the other one had had his head stuck in his books and worked in a fancy gents' outfitters before going off to college. Sure enough, Anna had been distraught that time when Joe had had his accident, but she seemed to be giving him scant attention now, poor lad.

Daniel wondered how long it might be considered reasonable for him to remain at home. Father Vincent had said as long as was necessary, but he was not sure how long that meant. Another week? Another two weeks? He noticed that his mother did not mention his returning. It was almost as though she was regarding him as a permanent member of the family again. As for her state of mind, she seemed quite composed. He knew she was a strong woman and, financially, she was not too badly fixed. The boarding house was proving to be quite a profitable business, although she would, of course, no longer have his father's wage.

It was a full week after the funeral when the two of them sat together in the family living room; Joe had gone out with his girlfriend as he did on several evenings.

'I've been thinking...' began Anna. 'In fact, I've been doing a good deal of thinking lately, Daniel. And I've realised that I haven't been fair to you.'

'What do you mean, Mammy?' he asked, feeling the first stirrings of unease.

'Well, you never really wanted to be a priest, did you? I forced you into it. You told me so at the time, but I wouldn't listen. And now... Well, I think that it might not really be right for you. You are not truly committed to it...are you?' She was smiling at him in a pensive way, as though pleading with him to agree with her. But he knew her of old, and her determination to have her own way. If she had now changed her mind about his calling it didn't mean that he had to do the same.

'Now, wait a minute, Mammy,' he said. 'It was what you wanted. You've just admitted it. Right from the time I was a little boy you tried to convince me that it was what I must do. And – no – I wasn't keen on the idea at first. And – yes – I changed my mind and decided that it was not for me. But all hell was let loose, wasn't it, when I told you about... Madeleine?'

Anna hung her head. 'Yes...I know,' she agreed in a surprisingly humble voice. 'I'm really sorry about that now, Daniel.'

'I don't know what is going through your mind, Mammy,' he continued, 'but whatever it is, you must understand that I have made my choice now and there can be no turning back.' He made a sudden decision. 'I will be going back to college next week.'

'But I miss you so much...' He could see tears in her eyes now. 'And I'm willing to admit that I was wrong, so very wrong. And now that your father's gone, however am I going to manage?'

'The same as you always do, Mammy. You are a strong person. You've run this boarding house without any help from Daddy and you will go on doing so. A lot of the boarding houses in Blackpool are run by widows. Besides, you've got Joe...and Myrtle too.'

'Yes, I know I've got Joe.' She gave a faint smile. 'But he's not like you. He's not intelligent and interesting to talk to, like you are. I can't have a proper conversation with him. I miss our little chats, Daniel.'

He was beginning to feel angry. 'He is your

son...Mother, just as I am. And you love him; you know that you do. Remember when we nearly lost him? You were frantic with worry. And God was good to you. He made Joe well again. And he'll get married, maybe sooner than you think; most likely he will marry Myrtle. Then you will have grandchildren to look forward to. Don't start feeling sorry for yourself, Mother.'

'I'm not...I'm not! I'm just telling you that I know now that I was wrong, and I want to put things right.'

'You mean you have changed your mind and you want me to do the same. No, I'm afraid I can't. I was homesick at first when I went to Rothburn, but I got over it, just as you will get used to me not being here. And now...I'm looking forward to going back and following the path I have chosen. Yes, the path *I* have chosen, Mother, not you.'

She looked at him sorrowfully for a moment, then she said, 'I remember the time you met that girl...Madeleine. I was wrong about her. I'm sure you were very fond of her...' Goodness, she was crafty! She knew just where to find his Achilles heel. He tried never to think of Madeleine, but he was forced to do so now. Yes, he had been very fond of her. He had loved her, and he believed, if they had been allowed to stay together, that he would eventually have married her. But what was the use of thinking of her now?

'That's all in the past, Mother,' he said. 'I was

forced to part from Madeleine and I have no doubt that I hurt her very much. I hope she's happy now. She deserves to be. She is a lovely girl, but I know that I mustn't think of her anymore. It has been...quite a long time now.'

Anna smiled. 'She's here in Blackpool,' she said. Her words hit him like a thunderbolt.

'What do you mean? Madeleine is...here?'

'The Melody Makers are performing for two weeks at the North Pier Pavilion,' said Anna, 'where they were before. But that was in April as I recall. They're here for the first two weeks in February. I've seen the posters.' She smiled slyly as he went on staring fixedly at her. 'She's still billed as "Yorkshire's own songbird". Why don't you go and see her?'

He observed her shrewdly for a few moments. He could scarcely believe what he was hearing, nor the lengths she would go to, to get her own way. She had decided that she wanted him at home and so, once more, he was expected to give way to her selfish desires. In a sudden movement he stood up. 'I can't, Mother,' he said, as he walked out of the room.

The temptation, however, proved too great. He decided he would go to the Saturday afternoon performance. There could be no harm, surely, in seeing her just once? He decided, at first, that he would watch her performance and leave it at that. Then he could carry in his mind for all time the memory of her beauty and her glorious voice. Perhaps he had been wrong to try to banish all thoughts of her? Memory was a precious thing, and he was strong now in the path he had chosen. It could do no harm to remember her.

He chose a seat about halfway back in the auditorium, from where he could not easily be seen, should she happen to glance in his direction. The show was very good, much more polished than the one he had seen two years ago, and there were some new acts. Freddie, the conjuror; he was a very talented young chap; Daniel remembered meeting him when he had visited Madeleine in... Halifax, was it? The ventriloquist, and the new soprano, Dora; Barney and Benjy, as dashing and sprightly as ever; Nancy's clever little dogs, possibly not quite as agile as before; they were all superb. But there was only one act that he really wanted to see.

Madeleine stood in the spotlight, as lovely as ever. The light shining down on her flowing golden hair and her shimmering silver-white dress gave her an ethereal appearance. And her voice was truly the voice of an angel. The number she sang unaccompanied was one that he remembered.

'Dear thoughts are in my mind,
And my soul soars enchanted
As I hear the sweet lark sing
In the clear air of the day.'

He felt tears misting his eyes. Her final song, though, in the first half of the show made him smile as she sang, 'I wouldn't leave my little wooden hut for you!'

He could hardly wait for her appearance in the second half. Her last song, 'Silver Threads among the Gold', was particularly poignant.

'But my darling you will be
Always young and fair to me...' she sang.

He felt a spasm of sadness and pain that was almost too much to bear. The words were so true; Madeleine would always be young and fair to him because he would never see her again after that day. They would not be able to grow old together; he would never see the silver threads in her golden hair...

He knew then that he had to speak to her, just once more. Surely he owed her that? He would wait for her after the performance. He would tell her how sorry he was about the way they had parted; that it had been cowardly to write to her instead of telling her face to face that he could not see her again. It would be good to know that she still regarded him as a friend.

He stood at the pier entrance, knowing that she must come out that way, through the pier turnstile. He waited for what seemed ages. All the members of the audience had gone, and then he saw some of the artistes: Nancy with her two little dogs, and her husband, Pete; Susannah, with Frank, the 'Music Man'. He averted his face, looking out towards the sea; Susannah was one who might recognise him.

And then she was there, Madeleine, dressed in a russet-brown coat with a fur collar and a little fur hat that partially covered her golden hair. She was laughing as she came along the pier, and then he noticed that she was laughing up into the face of Freddie Nicholls, the young conjuror...and they were holding hands. They drew apart to go singly through the turnstile, and that was when Daniel turned away. He felt a sharp stab of anguish. It had been a mistake to come. He had seen her; he could tell that she was happy and that was what he had told himself he wanted. He had not realised, though, how much it would hurt. Now it was time for him to go, but she must not see him.

He took a few steps away, then he heard her voice, 'Dan...Daniel...!' He turned back, knowing that he must speak with her. 'Dan...I thought I was seeing things.' Her smile was as radiant as ever. 'Have you been to see the show? You weren't going to go without saying hello to me, were you?'

'I...I thought we might have a little chat,' he stumbled. 'But...I can see that you're busy.' She and Freddie were holding hands again.

She turned to Freddie. 'You remember Daniel, don't you, Freddie?'

'Yes, I remember him,' said Freddie. The two

men nodded at one another and murmured, 'How do you do?' Freddie actually held out his hand for Daniel to shake, which Dan thought was very noble of him. Then he said to Madeleine, 'Off you go, love, and have a chat with Daniel; and I'll see you later, back at the digs.'

'Are you sure?' she asked.

'Of course I'm sure,' he smiled, giving her a friendly little push. Then he walked away, leaving them together.

She and Dan stood and stared at one another for a few moments, then he said, 'Freddie's your boyfriend, is he?'

She nodded. 'Yes, he is. But apart from that he's a very good pal, and he takes care of me whilst we're travelling around.'

'That's good,' said Dan. 'I'm glad you're happy. I can see that you are. I am sorry about...what happened between us. That is what I've come to tell you. I know I must have hurt you...and I hope you have forgiven me?'

'Of course,' she replied. 'A long time ago... Come along, Dan. I don't know why we're standing here getting cold. Let's go and have a cup of tea.'

They crossed the tramtrack into the town and found a little café on Bank Hey Street, behind the Tower. Maddy was aware that her heart was beating twenty to the dozen. It had been ages since she had set eyes on Dan. She had wondered why he was there. Did he have an idea that they might be able to get together again? And then he had seen Freddie? For a moment her heart had leapt on seeing him again, then she realised that he had, in fact, come to make his peace with her.

'What are you doing here?' she asked, when the waitress had brought them a pot of tea and some toasted teacakes. That would be all that Maddy would need before the evening performance. They usually had a late meal on Saturday, following the show. 'I presume you are at college now, aren't you?'

'Yes, I've been there – up in Northumberland – since September.' Dan went on to explain that his father had been killed in an accident and that he had been given extended leave from the seminary. 'I shall be going back sometime next week,' he said.

'Oh…I'm so sorry to hear about your father,' said Maddy. 'It must have been a great shock to you all. Your mother…how is she?'

'She's bearing up quite well,' said Dan. 'My father's death has affected her quite badly, of course. But she's a strong woman and I know she will be able to cope with the boarding house and everything. And my brother – you remember Joe? – he works like a Trojan for my mother, he and his girlfriend, Myrtle. Yes, our little Joe has a lady friend now; she's what you might call a "maid of all work" at the boarding house. I'm not sure that my mother has always appreciated all the work they do, but no doubt she will come to realise it now.'

'I'm sure she misses you…' observed Maddy.

'Yes…so she does,' he replied. 'But it was what she wanted, wasn't it?' How easy it would have been for him, at that moment, to admit that his mother, in fact, had changed her mind about his calling. And to admit that he, too, had felt such a pang of regret on seeing Madeleine again that, for a short time, he had been tempted to stay, even to ask if they might resume their friendship. And then he had seen her with Freddie and he had known that she had moved on. And so must he.

'My mother and I have reached an understanding now,' he said. At least he trusted that they would have done so before the day ended. 'She was wrong to pressurise me into becoming a priest, and I'm sure she knows that now. But in the end…I know I have made the right decision.'

'I am pleased that you're happy about it now, Dan,' she said. 'About being a priest, I mean.' She would never know how regretful that made him feel as he looked at her sitting across the table from him, so lovely and desirable. But he knew he could not tell her how he felt. 'I realise you're not happy at the moment,' she went on, 'losing your father so suddenly. But in time you won't feel quite so sad about it.' She smiled wryly. 'Who am I to be preaching to you? I do remember, though, how sad I was when my mother died. And we had a bereavement in the family not long ago; well, last summer. My Grandfather Isaac died.'

'Oh, I'm sorry,' said Dan. 'I was thinking of him a little while ago.' He would not tell her it was when one of the more zealous lecturers was haranguing them about dissenters and heretics. 'He was a grand old man…a very wise man. So the Moon and Son are now your father and your brother, I presume?'

'Yes, that's right. Patrick is married now, and so is my half-sister, Hetty. Her husband is a photographer, and they have a baby girl, born on Christmas Day; she's called Angela.'

'Very appropriate,' said Dan. '"Hark the Herald Angels Sing…" And what about Jessie? I remember how you and she were very good friends.'

'Oh, we still are…Jessie has a young man at her cycling club. I don't see any of them as much as I would like to. I won't be back in Scarborough until the middle of May.'

'But you are happy…and you have Freddie?'

'So I have,' she smiled. They stayed in the café rather longer than they ought to have done, and Maddy realised there was not enough time for her to go back to her digs before the evening performance. It would be too much of a rush, so she decided to wait in the dressing room for the rest of the troupe to arrive.

Daniel walked back to the pier entrance with her. He took hold of her hand, then gently kissed her cheek. 'Be happy, Madeleine,' he said, then he walked away.

When he arrived home his mother was in the kitchen preparing an evening meal. She looked at him enquiringly but did not ask where he had been all afternoon. They had not spoken together very much since their conversation a couple of days ago, when she had tried to persuade him not to go back. They were polite to one another, but there was a coolness between them which, fortunately, Joe did not seem to have noticed.

'I have been to see the show at the pier pavilion,' said Daniel. 'You did tell me to go, didn't you, Mammy...and to see Madeleine?'

'Yes, so I did...' She was looking at him anxiously, almost fearfully. What did she want? he wondered. Did she really expect him to say that Madeleine was back in his life again? Or did she know, in her heart, that it was not possible? 'And...did you speak to her?' she asked.

'Yes...I met her afterwards. She is well and happy, Mammy, which is what I wanted to find out. There is no chance whatsoever of us getting back together...I think you knew that all along, didn't you?'

Anna nodded, slowly and resignedly. 'Yes...I knew,' she agreed. 'I guessed that you wouldn't turn back, not now. But I wasn't prepared for how much I would miss you. I've been thinking about what you said, though, Daniel. I must look forward now – to Joe getting married and the possibility of being a grandmother... Joe's a grand lad, sure enough. I do know that. And I shall look forward to my elder son entering the priesthood... God bless you, Daniel.'

They embraced fondly and, Dan felt, with a new understanding. 'You were wrong, though, Mammy,' he told her, 'to try and force me into a way I was not sure about.'

'Yes...I realise that now,' she replied humbly.

'Because, in the long run, you see, it is what I would have decided for myself.' He smiled at her. 'I've had to go through a lot of trials and temptations, and it may be that they're not over yet... But in the end it was my decision. Mine...and God's,' he added.

Maddy wondered what Freddie would be thinking. She had said she was going back to the digs and he would be waiting there for her. She had spent too long talking to Dan; he had seemed so interested in her family and in what was happening to the Melody Makers. It had been good to see him again. At first she had felt the familiar heart stirrings at the sight of him, then she had realised that he had chosen his way in life, as she had chosen hers. And it was the right way, for both of them.

She felt a glow of warmth as she thought of Freddie's cheerful face; the way he had of raising one eyebrow in a quirky smile, his ready wit and his ability to lift her spirits when she was feeling low, his kindness and the love she knew he felt for her. Yes, she had loved Daniel, but there had always been a dreamlike quality about their friendship. Her relationship with Freddie was solid and down to earth. It had taken a while for her to realise that she loved him, but she did, unreservedly, and she hoped it might be for all time.

The door opened suddenly, and there he was, a bright smile lighting up his face. 'So there you are,' he said. 'I thought I would find you here.'

'Freddie, I'm so sorry...I hope you weren't worried, about me being with Dan, I mean. We got talking, so we went and had some tea in town. His father has died; that's why he's in Blackpool; but he's going back next week to his college in Northumberland. I hope you didn't mind me spending some time with him. He seemed to want to talk and...'

'Shh... Steady on there. There's no need to apologise.' He put his arms around her and kissed the tip of her nose. 'Now, why on earth should I worry because you were with Dan? He's an old friend. And there is nothing to worry about...is there?'

'No, Freddie...nothing at all,' Maddy replied.

He kissed her then, tenderly but with all the eagerness and longing that they always felt. Her feet were firmly on the ground, but she felt, too, that heaven was not far away.